SO-AHS-342

Praise for

STEPHEN KING

and the #1 *New York Times* bestseller

FINDERS KEEPERS

"Superb. . . . King's restless imagination is a power that cannot be contained."

—Laura Lippmann, *The New York Times Book Review*

"Wonderful, scary, moving."

—Elizabeth Hand, *The Washington Post*

"[A] taut thriller about the thin line separating fandom from fanaticism . . . [Morris] Bellamy is one of King's creepiest creations—a literate and intelligent character whom any passionate reader will both identify with and be repelled by. . . . nail-biting suspense that's the hallmark of King's best work."

—*Publishers Weekly*

"[*Finders Keepers*] delivers on what it promises: a gripping setup, a group of resourceful good guys, an antagonist capable of terrible violence. It also speaks to the powerful allure of fiction, of how a great story can capture someone's imagination and make him or her see the world in a completely different way."

—*The Portland Press Herald*

"A thrilling, taut read."

—*Miami Herald*

"Expertly plotted, a series of pieces falling into place with almost audible satisfaction as [King] burns towards his suitably
horrific climax. . . . once you're hooked, you're hooked. [And]
Finders Keepers is just as fascinating for its fresh take on a topic
that perennially fascinates King: the relationship between a
writer and their fans."

—*The Guardian* (UK)

"A nail-biting suspense-horror-mystery tale. . . . a breath-
takingly fast-paced read."

—*The Plain Dealer* (Cleveland)

"Stephen King never seems to run short of intriguing plots,
compelling characters, and just enough gore and guts to bring
in a vast audience of readers."

—*St. Louis Post-Dispatch*

"A cool thriller packed with literary allusions and the theme
that reading literature can change a reader's heart—for good
or bad."

—*Minneapolis Star Tribune*

"King is, above all, a master storyteller, building the story's
tension—a slow burn throughout—to a near unbearable level
by the end."

—*Milwaukee Journal Sentinel*

"The narrative hums and roars along like a high-performance
vehicle . . . a rip-snorting entertainment; one that also works
as a sneaky-smart satire of literary criticism and how even the
most attentive readers can often miss the whole point."

—*Kirkus Reviews* (starred review)

AUTHOR'S NOTE

You write a book in a room by yourself, that's just how it's done. I wrote the first draft of this one in Florida, looking out at palm trees. I rewrote it in Maine, looking out at pine trees sloping down to a beautiful lake where the loons converse at sunset. But I wasn't entirely alone in either place; few writers are. When I needed help, help was there.

NAN GRAHAM edited the book. SUSAN MOLDOW and ROZ LIPPEL also work for Scribner, and I couldn't get along without them. Those women are invaluable.

CHUCK VERRILL agented the book. He's been my go-to guy for thirty years, smart, funny, and fearless. No yes-man he; when my shit's not right, he never hesitates to tell me.

RUSS DORR does research, and he's gotten better and better at the job as the years pass. Like a good first assist PA in the OR, he's ready with the next instrument I need before I even call for it. His contributions to this book are on almost every page. Literally: Russ gave me the title when I was stumped for one.

OWEN KING and KELLY BRAFFET, both excellent novelists, read the first draft and sharpened it considerably. Their contributions are also on just about every page.

MARSHA DeFILIPPO and JULIE EUGLEY run my office in Maine, and keep me tethered to the real world. BARBARA

MacINTYRE runs the office in Florida and does the same. SHIRLEY SONDEREGGER is emeritus.

TABITHA KING is my best critic and one true love.

And you, CONSTANT READER. Thank God you're still there after all these years. If you're having fun, I am, too.

"A master storyteller."

—*Los Angeles Times*

"The most wonderfully gruesome man on the planet."

—*USA Today*

"Stephen King knows exactly what scares you most…"

—*Esquire*

"King probably knows more about scary goings-on in confined, isolated places than anybody since Edgar Allan Poe."

—*Entertainment Weekly*

"America's greatest living novelist."

—Lee Child

STEPHEN KING

A NOVEL

G

GALLERY BOOKS

New York   London   Toronto   Sydney   New Delhi

G

Gallery Books
An Imprint of Simon & Schuster, Inc.
1230 Avenue of the Americas
New York, NY 10020

This book is a work of fiction. Any references to historical events, real people, or real places are used fictitiously. Other names, characters, places, and events are products of the author's imagination, and any resemblance to actual events or places or persons, living or dead, is entirely coincidental.

Copyright © 2015 by Stephen King

All rights reserved, including the right to reproduce this book or portions thereof in any form whatsoever. For information, address Scribner Subsidiary Rights Department, 1230 Avenue of the Americas, New York, NY 10020.

This Gallery Books trade paperback edition September 2018

GALLERY BOOKS and colophon are registered trademarks of Simon & Schuster, Inc.

For information about special discounts for bulk purchases, please contact Simon & Schuster Special Sales at 1-866-506-1949 or business@simonandschuster.com.

The Simon & Schuster Speakers Bureau can bring authors to your live event. For more information or to book an event, contact the Simon & Schuster Speakers Bureau at 1-866-248-3049 or visit our website at www.simonspeakers.com.

Manufactured in the United States of America

10   9

ISBN 978-1-5011-0007-9
ISBN 978-1-5011-9036-0 (pbk)
ISBN 978-1-5011-0013-0 (ebook)

Thinking of John D. MacDonald

"It is by going down into the abyss that
we recover the treasures of life."
Joseph Campbell

"Shit don't mean shit."
Jimmy Gold

PART 1: BURIED TREASURE

1978

"Wake up, genius."

Rothstein didn't want to wake up. The dream was too good. It featured his first wife months before she became his first wife, seventeen and perfect from head to toe. Naked and shimmering. Both of them naked. He was nineteen, with grease under his fingernails, but she hadn't minded that, at least not then, because his head was full of dreams and that was what she cared about. She believed in the dreams even more than he did, and she was right to believe. In this dream she was laughing and reaching for the part of him that was easiest to grab. He tried to go deeper, but then a hand began shaking his shoulder, and the dream popped like a soap bubble.

He was no longer nineteen and living in a two-room New Jersey apartment, he was six months shy of his eightieth birthday and living on a farm in New Hampshire, where his will specified he should be buried. There were men in his bedroom. They were wearing ski masks, one red, one blue, and one canary-yellow. He saw this and tried to believe it was just another dream—the sweet one had slid into a nightmare, as they sometimes did—but then the hand let go of his arm, grabbed his shoulder, and tumbled him onto the floor. He struck his head and cried out.

"Quit that," said the one in the yellow mask. "You want to knock him unconscious?"

"Check it out." The one in the red mask pointed. "Old fella's got a woody. Must have been having one hell of a dream."

Blue Mask, the one who had done the shaking, said, "Just a piss hard-on. When they're that age, nothing else gets em up. My grandfather—"

"Be quiet," Yellow Mask said. "Nobody cares about your grandfather."

Although dazed and still wrapped in a fraying curtain of sleep, Rothstein knew he was in trouble here. Two words surfaced in his mind: *home invasion*. He looked up at the trio that had materialized in his bedroom, his old head aching (there was going to be a huge bruise on the right side, thanks to the blood thinners he took), his heart with its perilously thin walls banging against the left side of his ribcage. They loomed over him, three men with gloves on their hands, wearing plaid fall jackets below those terrifying balaclavas. Home invaders, and here he was, five miles from town.

Rothstein gathered his thoughts as best he could, banishing sleep and telling himself there was one good thing about this situation: if they didn't want him to see their faces, they intended to leave him alive.

Maybe.

"Gentlemen," he said.

Mr. Yellow laughed and gave him a thumbs-up. "Good start, genius."

Rothstein nodded, as if at a compliment. He glanced at the bedside clock, saw it was quarter past two in the morning, then looked back at Mr. Yellow, who might be the leader. "I have only a little money, but you're welcome to it. If you'll only leave without hurting me."

The wind gusted, rattling autumn leaves against the west side of the house. Rothstein was aware that the furnace was running for the first time this year. Hadn't it just been summer?

"According to our info, you got a lot more than a little." This was Mr. Red.

"Hush." Mr. Yellow extended a hand to Rothstein. "Get off the floor, genius."

Rothstein took the offered hand, got shakily to his feet, then sat on the bed. He was breathing hard, but all too aware (self-awareness had been both a curse and a blessing all his life) of the picture he must make: an old man in flappy blue pajamas, nothing left of his hair but white popcorn puffs above the ears. This was what had become of the writer who, in the year JFK became president, had been on the cover of *Time* magazine: JOHN ROTHSTEIN, AMERICA'S RECLUSIVE GENIUS.

Wake up, genius.

"Get your breath," Mr. Yellow said. He sounded solicitous, but Rothstein did not trust this. "Then we'll go into the living room, where normal people have their discussions. Take your time. Get serene."

Rothstein breathed slowly and deeply, and his heart quieted a little. He tried to think of Peggy, with her teacup-sized breasts (small but perfect) and her long, smooth legs, but the dream was as gone as Peggy herself, now an old crone living in Paris. On his money. At least Yolande, his second effort at marital bliss, was dead, thus putting an end to the alimony.

Red Mask left the room, and now Rothstein heard rummaging in his study. Something fell over. Drawers were opened and closed.

"Doing better?" Mr. Yellow asked, and when Rothstein nodded: "Come on, then."

Rothstein allowed himself to be led into the small living room, escorted by Mr. Blue on his left and Mr. Yellow on his right. In his study the rummaging went on. Soon Mr. Red would open the closet and push back his two jackets and three sweaters, exposing the safe. It was inevitable.

All right. As long as they leave the notebooks, and why would they take them? Thugs like these are only interested in money. They probably can't even read anything more challenging than the letters in Penthouse.

Only he wasn't sure about the man in the yellow mask. That one sounded educated.

All the lamps were on in the living room, and the shades weren't drawn. Wakeful neighbors might have wondered what was going on in the old writer's house . . . if he had neighbors. The closest ones were two miles away, on the main highway. He had no friends, no visitors. The occasional salesman was sent packing. Rothstein was just that peculiar old fella. The retired writer. The hermit. He paid his taxes and was left alone.

Blue and Yellow led him to the easy chair facing the seldom-watched TV, and when he didn't immediately sit, Mr. Blue pushed him into it.

"Easy!" Yellow said sharply, and Blue stepped back a bit, muttering. Mr. Yellow was the one in charge, all right. Mr. Yellow was the wheeldog.

He bent over Rothstein, hands on the knees of his corduroys. "Do you want a little splash of something to settle you?"

"If you mean alcohol, I quit twenty years ago. Doctor's orders."

"Good for you. Go to meetings?"

"I wasn't an *alcoholic*," Rothstein said, nettled. Crazy to be nettled in such a situation . . . or was it? Who knew how one was supposed to react after being yanked out of bed in the middle of the night by men in colorful ski masks? He wondered how he might write such a scene and had no idea; he did not write about situations like this. "People assume any twentieth-century white male writer must be an *alcoholic*."

"All right, all right," Mr. Yellow said. It was as if he were placating a grumpy child. "Water?"

"No, thank you. What I want is for you three to leave, so I'm going to be honest with you." He wondered if Mr. Yellow understood the most basic rule of human discourse: when someone says they're going to be honest with you, they are in most cases preparing to lie faster than a horse can trot. "My wallet is on the dresser in the bedroom. There's a little over eighty dollars in it. There's a ceramic teapot on the mantel . . ."

He pointed. Mr. Blue turned to look, but Mr. Yellow did not. Mr. Yellow continued to study Rothstein, the eyes behind the mask almost amused. *It's not working,* Rothstein thought, but he persevered. Now that he was awake, he was pissed off as well as scared, although he knew he'd do well not to show that.

"It's where I keep the housekeeping money. Fifty or sixty dollars. That's all there is in the house. Take it and go."

"Fucking liar," Mr. Blue said. "You got a lot more than that, guy. We know. Believe me."

As if this were a stage play and that line his cue, Mr. Red yelled from the study. "Bingo! Found a safe! Big one!"

Rothstein had known the man in the red mask would find it, but his heart sank anyway. Stupid to keep cash, there was no reason for it other than his dislike of credit cards and checks and stocks and instruments of transfer, all the tempting chains that tied people to America's overwhelming and ultimately destructive debt-and-spend machine. But the cash might be his salvation. Cash could be replaced. The notebooks, over a hundred and fifty of them, could not.

"Now the combo," said Mr. Blue. He snapped his gloved fingers. "Give it up."

Rothstein was almost angry enough to refuse, according to Yolande anger had been his lifelong default position ("Probably even in your goddam cradle," she had said), but he was also tired and frightened. If he balked, they'd beat it out of him. He might even have another heart attack, and one more would almost certainly finish him.

"If I give you the combination to the safe, will you take the money inside and go?"

"Mr. Rothstein," Mr. Yellow said with a kindliness that seemed genuine (and thus grotesque), "you're in no position to bargain. Freddy, go get the bags."

Rothstein felt a huff of chilly air as Mr. Blue, also known as Freddy, went out through the kitchen door. Mr. Yellow, meanwhile, was smiling again. Rothstein already detested that smile. Those red lips.

"Come on, genius—give. Soonest begun, soonest done."

Rothstein sighed and recited the combination of the Gardall in his study closet. "Three left two turns, thirty-one right two turns, eighteen left one turn, ninety-nine right one turn, then back to zero."

Behind the mask, the red lips spread wider, now showing teeth. "I could have guessed that. It's your birth date."

As Yellow called the combination to the man in his closet, Rothstein made certain unpleasant deductions. Mr. Blue and Mr. Red had come for money, and Mr. Yellow might take his share, but he didn't believe money was the primary objective of the man who kept calling him *genius*. As if to underline this, Mr. Blue reappeared, accompanied by another puff of cool outside air. He had four empty duffel bags, two slung over each shoulder.

"Look," Rothstein said to Mr. Yellow, catching the man's eyes and holding them. "Don't. There's nothing in that safe worth taking except for the money. The rest is just a bunch of random scribbling, but it's important to me."

From the study Mr. Red cried: "Holy hopping Jesus, Morrie! We hit the jackpot! Eee-doggies, there's a *ton* of cash! Still in the bank envelopes! Dozens of them!"

At least sixty, Rothstein could have said, maybe as many as eighty. With four hundred dollars in each one. From Arnold Abel, my accountant in New York. Jeannie cashes the expense checks and brings back the cash envelopes and I put them in the safe. Only I have few expenses, because Arnold also pays the major bills from New York. I tip Jeannie once in awhile, and the postman at Christmas, but otherwise, I rarely spend the cash. For years this has gone on, and why? Arnold never asks what I use the money for. Maybe he thinks I have an arrangement with a call girl or two. Maybe he thinks I play the ponies at Rockingham.

But here is the funny thing, he could have said to Mr. Yellow (also known as Morrie). I have never asked *myself*. Any more than I've asked myself why I keep filling notebook after notebook. Some things just *are*.

He *could* have said these things, but kept silent. Not because Mr. Yellow wouldn't understand, but because that knowing red-lipped smile said he just might.

And wouldn't care.

"What else is in there?" Mr. Yellow called. His eyes were still locked on Rothstein's. "Boxes? Manuscript boxes? The size I told you?"

"Not boxes, notebooks," Mr. Red reported back. "Fuckin safe's filled with em."

Mr. Yellow smiled, still looking into Rothstein's eyes. "Handwritten? That how you do it, genius?"

"Please," Rothstein said. "Just leave them. That material isn't meant to be seen. None of it's ready."

"And never will be, that's what I think. Why, you're just a great big hoarder." The twinkle in those eyes—what Rothstein thought of as an Irish twinkle—was gone now. "And hey, it isn't as if you *need* to publish anything else, right? Not like there's any *financial imperative*. You've got royalties from *The Runner*. And *The Runner Sees Action*. And *The Runner Slows*

Down. The famous Jimmy Gold trilogy. Never out of print. Taught in college classes all over this great nation of ours. Thanks to a cabal of lit teachers who think you and Saul Bellow hung the moon, you've got a captive audience of book-buying undergrads. You're all set, right? Why take a chance on publishing something that might put a dent in your solid gold reputation? You can hide out here and pretend the rest of the world doesn't exist." Mr. Yellow shook his head. "My friend, you give a whole new meaning to anal retentive."

Mr. Blue was still lingering in the doorway. "What do you want me to do, Morrie?"

"Get in there with Curtis. Pack everything up. If there isn't room for all the notebooks in the duffels, look around. Even a cabin rat like him must have at least one suitcase. Don't waste time counting the money, either. I want to get out of here ASAP."

"Okay." Mr. Blue—Freddy—left.

"Don't do this," Rothstein said, and was appalled at the tremble in his voice. Sometimes he forgot how old he was, but not tonight.

The one whose name was Morrie leaned toward him, greenish-gray eyes peering through the holes in the yellow mask. "I want to know something. If you're honest, maybe we'll leave the notebooks. Will you be honest with me, genius?"

"I'll try," Rothstein said. "And I never called myself that, you know. It was *Time* magazine that called me a genius."

"But I bet you never wrote a letter of protest."

Rothstein said nothing. *Sonofabitch*, he was thinking. *Smartass sonofabitch. You won't leave anything, will you? It doesn't matter what I say.*

"Here's what I want to know—why in God's name couldn't you leave Jimmy Gold alone? Why did you have to push his face down in the dirt like you did?"

The question was so unexpected that at first Rothstein had

no idea what Morrie was talking about, even though Jimmy Gold was his most famous character, the one he would be remembered for (assuming he was remembered for anything). The same *Time* cover story that had referred to Rothstein as a genius had called Jimmy Gold "an American icon of despair in a land of plenty." Pretty much horseshit, but it had sold books.

"If you mean I should have stopped with *The Runner*, you're not alone." But almost, he could have added. *The Runner Sees Action* had solidified his reputation as an important American writer, and *The Runner Slows Down* had been the capstone of his career: critical bouquets up the wazoo, on the *New York Times* bestseller list for sixty-two weeks. National Book Award, too—not that he had appeared in person to accept it. "The *Iliad* of postwar America," the citation had called it, meaning not just the last one but the trilogy as a whole.

"I'm not saying you should have stopped with *The Runner*," Morrie said. "*The Runner Sees Action* was just as good, maybe even better. They were *true*. It was the last one. Man, what a crap carnival. Advertising? I mean, *advertising*?"

Mr. Yellow then did something that tightened Rothstein's throat and turned his belly to lead. Slowly, almost reflectively, he stripped off his yellow balaclava, revealing a young man of classic Boston Irish countenance: red hair, greenish eyes, pasty-white skin that would always burn and never tan. Plus those weird red lips.

"House in the *suburbs*? Ford sedan in the *driveway*? Wife and two little *kiddies*? Everybody sells out, is that what you were trying to say? Everybody eats the poison?"

"In the notebooks . . ."

There were two more Jimmy Gold novels in the notebooks, that was what he wanted to say, ones that completed the circle. In the first of them, Jimmy comes to see the hollowness of his suburban life and leaves his family, his job, and his comfy Connecticut home. He leaves on foot, with nothing but a knapsack and the clothes on his back. He becomes an older version of the kid who dropped out of school, rejected his materialistic family, and decided to join the army after a booze-filled weekend spent wandering in New York City.

"In the notebooks what?" Morrie asked. "Come on, genius, speak. Tell me why you had to knock him down and step on the back of his head."

In The Runner Goes West *he becomes himself again,* Rothstein wanted to say. *His essential self.* Only now Mr. Yellow had shown his face, and he was removing a pistol from the right front pocket of his plaid jacket. He looked sorrowful.

"You created one of the greatest characters in American literature, then shit on him," Morrie said. "A man who could do that doesn't deserve to live."

The anger roared back like a sweet surprise. "If you think that," John Rothstein said, "you never understood a word I wrote."

Morrie pointed the pistol. The muzzle was a black eye.

Rothstein pointed an arthritis-gnarled finger back, as if it were his own gun, and felt satisfaction when he saw Morrie blink and flinch a little. "Don't give me your dumbass literary criticism. I got a bellyful of that long before you were born. What are you, anyway, twenty-two? Twenty-three? What do you know about life, let alone literature?"

"Enough to know not everyone sells out." Rothstein was astounded to see tears swimming in those Irish eyes. "Don't lecture me about life, not after spending the last twenty years hiding away from the world like a rat in a hole."

This old criticism—how *dare* you leave the Fame Table?—sparked Rothstein's anger into full-blown rage—the sort of glass-throwing, furniture-smashing rage both Peggy and Yolande would have recognized—and he was glad. Better to die raging than to do so cringing and begging.

"How will you turn my work into cash? Have you thought

of that? I assume you have. I assume you know that you might as well try to sell a stolen Hemingway notebook, or a Picasso painting. But your friends aren't as educated as you are, are they? I can tell by the way they speak. Do they know what you know? I'm sure they don't. But you sold them a bill of goods. You showed them a large pie in the sky and told them they could each have a slice. I think you're capable of that. I think you have a lake of words at your disposal. But I believe it's a shallow lake."

"Shut up. You sound like my mother."

"You're a common thief, my friend. And how stupid to steal what you can never sell."

"Shut up, genius, I'm warning you."

Rothstein thought, And if he pulls the trigger? No more pills. No more regrets about the past, and the litter of broken relationships along the way like so many cracked-up cars. No more obsessive writing, either, accumulating notebook after notebook like little piles of rabbit turds scattered along a woodland trail. A bullet in the head would not be so bad, maybe. Better than cancer or Alzheimer's, that prime horror of anyone who has spent his life making a living by his wits. Of course there would be headlines, and I'd gotten plenty of those even before that damned *Time* story . . . but if he pulls the trigger, I won't have to read them.

"You're *stupid*," Rothstein said. All at once he was in a kind of ecstasy. "You think you're smarter than those other two, but you're not. At least they understand that cash can be spent." He leaned forward, staring at that pale, freckle-spattered face. "You know what, kid? It's guys like you who give reading a bad name."

"Last warning," Morrie said.

"Fuck your warning. And fuck your mother. Either shoot me or get out of my house."

Morris Bellamy shot him.

2009

The first argument about money in the Saubers household—the first one the kids overheard, at least—happened on an evening in April. It wasn't a big argument, but even the greatest storms begin as gentle breezes. Peter and Tina Saubers were in the living room, Pete doing homework and Tina watching a *SpongeBob* DVD. It was one she'd seen before, many times, but she never seemed to tire of it. This was fortunate, because these days there was no access to the Cartoon Network in the Saubers household. Tom Saubers had canceled the cable service two months ago.

Tom and Linda Saubers were in the kitchen, where Tom was cinching his old pack shut after loading it up with PowerBars, a Tupperware filled with cut veggies, two bottles of water, and a can of Coke.

"You're nuts," Linda said. "I mean, I've always known you were a Type A personality, but this takes it to a whole new level. If you want to set the alarm for five, fine. You can pick up Todd, be at City Center by six, and you'll still be first in line."

"I wish," Tom said. "Todd says there was one of these job fairs in Brook Park last month, and people started lining up the day before. *The day before*, Lin!"

"Todd says a lot of things. And you listen. Remember when

Todd said Pete and Tina would just *love* that Monster Truck Jam thingie—"

"This isn't a Monster Truck Jam, or a concert in the park, or a fireworks show. This is our *lives*."

Pete looked up from his homework and briefly met his little sister's eyes. Tina's shrug was eloquent: *Just the parents*. He went back to his algebra. Four more problems and he could go down to Howie's house. See if Howie had any new comic books. Pete certainly had none to trade; his allowance had gone the way of the cable TV.

In the kitchen, Tom had begun to pace. Linda caught up with him and took his arm gently. "I know it's our lives," she said.

Speaking low, partly so the kids wouldn't hear and be nervous (she knew Pete already was), mostly to lower the temperature. She knew how Tom felt, and her heart went out to him. Being afraid was bad; being humiliated because he could no longer fulfill what he saw as his primary responsibility to support his family was worse. And humiliation really wasn't the right word. What he felt was shame. For the ten years he'd been at Lakefront Realty, he'd consistently been one of their top salesmen, often with his smiling photo at the front of the shop. The money she brought in teaching third grade was just icing on the cake. Then, in the fall of 2008, the bottom fell out of the economy, and the Sauberses became a single-income family.

It wasn't as if Tom had been let go and might be called back when things improved; Lakefront Realty was now an empty building with graffiti on the walls and a FOR SALE OR LEASE sign out front. The Reardon brothers, who had inherited the business from their father (and their father from his), had been deeply invested in stocks, and lost nearly everything when the market tanked. It was little comfort to Linda that Tom's best friend, Todd Paine, was in the same boat. She thought Todd was a dingbat.

"Have you seen the weather forecast? I have. It's going to be cold. Fog off the lake by morning, maybe even freezing drizzle. *Freezing drizzle,* Tom."

"Good. I hope it happens. It'll keep the numbers down and improve the odds." He took her by the forearms, but gently. There was no shaking, no shouting. That came later. "I've *got* to get something, Lin, and the job fair is my best shot this spring. I've been pounding the pavement—"

"I know—"

"And there's *nothing.* I mean *zilch.* Oh, a few jobs down at the docks, and a little construction at the shopping center out by the airport, but can you see me doing that kind of work? I'm thirty pounds overweight and twenty years out of shape. I might find something downtown this summer—clerking, maybe—*if* things ease up a little . . . but that kind of job would be low-paying and probably temporary. So Todd and me're going at midnight, and we're going to stand in line until the doors open tomorrow morning, and I promise you I'm going to come back with a job that pays actual money."

"And probably with some bug we can all catch. Then we can scrimp on groceries to pay the doctor's bills."

That was when he grew really angry with her. "I would like a little support here."

"Tom, for God's sake, I'm *try*—"

"Maybe even an attaboy. 'Way to show some initiative, Tom. We're glad you're going the extra mile for the family, Tom.' That sort of thing. If it's not too much to ask."

"All I'm saying—"

But the kitchen door opened and closed before she could finish. He'd gone out back to smoke a cigarette. When Pete looked up this time, he saw distress and worry on Tina's face. She was only eight, after all. Pete smiled and dropped her a wink. Tina gave him a doubtful smile in return, then went back to the doings in the deepwater kingdom called Bikini

Bottom, where dads did not lose their jobs or raise their voices, and kids did not lose their allowances. Unless they were bad, that was.

Before leaving that night, Tom carried his daughter up to bed and kissed her goodnight. He added one for Mrs. Beasley, Tina's favorite doll—for good luck, he said.

"Daddy? Is everything going to be okay?"

"You bet, sugar," he said. She remembered that. The confidence in his voice. "Everything's going to be just fine. Now go to sleep." He left, walking normally. She remembered that, too, because she never saw him walk that way again.

At the top of the steep drive leading from Marlborough Street to the City Center parking lot, Tom said, "Whoa, hold it, stop!"

"Man, there's cars behind me," Todd said.

"This'll just take a second." Tom raised his phone and snapped a picture of the people standing in line. There had to be a hundred already. At least that many. Running above the auditorium doors was a banner reading **1000 JOBS GUARAN-TEED!** And *"We Stand With the People of Our City!"*—**MAYOR RALPH KINSLER**.

Behind Todd Paine's rusty '04 Subaru, someone laid on his horn.

"Tommy, I hate to be a party pooper while you're memorializing this wonderful occasion, but—"

"Go, go. I got it." And, as Todd drove into the parking lot, where the spaces nearest the building had already been filled: "I can't wait to show that picture to Linda. You know what she said? That if we got here by six, we'd be first in line."

"Told you, my man. The Toddster does not lie." The Toddster parked. The Subaru died with a fart and a wheeze. "By daybreak, there's gonna be, like, a couple-thousand people here. TV, too. All the stations. *City at Six*, *Morning Report*, *Metro-Scan*. We might get interviewed."

"I'll settle for a job."

Linda had been right about one thing, it was damp. You could smell the lake in the air: that faintly sewery aroma. And it was almost cold enough for him to see his breath. Posts with yellow DO NOT CROSS tape had been set up, folding the job-seekers back and forth like pleats in a human accordion. Tom and Todd took their places between the final posts. Others fell in behind them at once, mostly men, some in heavy fleece workmen's jackets, some in Mr. Businessman topcoats and Mr. Businessman haircuts that were beginning to lose their finely barbered edge. Tom guessed that the line would stretch all the way to the end of the parking lot by dawn, and that would still be at least four hours before the doors opened.

His eye was caught by a woman with a baby hanging off the front of her. They were a couple of zigzags over. Tom wondered how desperate you had to be to come out in the middle of a cold, damp night like this one with an infant. The kiddo was in one of those papoose carriers. The woman was talking to a burly man with a sleeping bag slung over his shoulder, and the baby was peering from one to the other, like the world's smallest tennis fan. Sort of comical.

"Want a little warm-up, Tommy?" Todd had taken a pint of Bell's from his pack and was holding it out.

Tom almost said no, remembering Linda's parting shot— *Don't you come home with booze on your breath, mister*—and then took the bottle. It was cold out here, and a short one wouldn't hurt. He felt the whiskey go down, heating his throat and belly.

Rinse your mouth before you hit any of the job booths, he reminded himself. Guys who smell of whiskey don't get hired for anything.

When Todd offered him another nip—this was around two

o'clock—Tom refused. But when he offered again at three, Tom took the bottle. Checking the level, he guessed the Toddster had been fortifying himself against the cold quite liberally.

Well, what the hell, Tom thought, and bit off quite a bit more than a nip; this one was a solid mouthful.

"Atta-baby," Todd said, sounding the teensiest bit slurry. "Go with your bad self."

Job hunters continued to arrive, their cars nosing up from Marlborough Street through the thickening fog. The line was well past the posts now, and no longer zigzagging. Tom had believed he understood the economic difficulties currently besetting the country—hadn't he lost a job himself, a very good job?—but as the cars kept coming and the line kept growing (he could no longer see where it ended), he began to get a new and frightening perspective. Maybe *difficulties* wasn't the right word. Maybe the right word was *calamity*.

To his right, in the maze of posts and tape leading to the doors of the darkened auditorium, the baby began to cry. Tom looked around and saw the man with the sleeping bag holding the sides of the papoose carrier so the woman (God, Tom thought, she doesn't look like she's out of her teens yet) could pull the kid out.

"What the fuck's zat?" Todd asked, sounding slurrier than ever.

"A kid," Tom said. "Woman with a kid. *Girl* with a kid."

Todd peered. "Christ on a pony," he said. "I call that pretty irra . . . irry . . . you know, not responsible."

"Are you drunk?" Linda disliked Todd, she didn't see his good side, and right now Tom wasn't sure he saw it, either.

"L'il bit. I'll be fine by the time the doors open. Got some breath mints, too."

Tom thought of asking the Toddster if he'd also brought some Visine—his eyes were looking mighty red—and decided he didn't want to have that discussion just now. He turned his attention back to where the woman with the crying baby had been. At first he thought they were gone. Then he looked lower and saw her sliding into the burly man's sleeping bag with the baby on her chest. The burly man was holding the mouth of the bag open for her. The infant was still bawling his or her head off.

"Can't you shut that kid up?" a man called.

"Someone ought to call Social Services," a woman added.

Tom thought of Tina at that age, imagined her out on this cold and foggy predawn morning, and restrained an urge to tell the man and woman to shut up . . . or better yet, lend a hand somehow. After all, they were in this together, weren't they? The whole screwed-up, bad-luck bunch of them.

The crying softened, stopped.

"She's probably feeding im," Todd said. He squeezed his chest to demonstrate.

"Yeah."

"Tommy?"

"What?"

"You know Ellen lost her job, right?"

"Jesus, no. I *didn't* know that." Pretending he didn't see the fear in Todd's face. Or the glimmering of moisture in his eyes. Possibly from the booze or the cold. Possibly not.

"They said they'd call her back when things get better, but they said the same thing to me, and I've been out of work going on half a year now. I cashed my insurance. That's gone. And you know what we got left in the bank? Five hundred dollars. You know how long five hundred dollars lasts when a loaf of bread at Kroger's costs a buck?"

"Not long."

"You're fucking A it doesn't. I *have* to get something here. *Have* to."

"You will. We both will."

Todd lifted his chin at the burly man, who now appeared to

be standing guard over the sleeping bag, so no one would accidentally step on the woman and baby inside. "Think they're married?"

Tom hadn't considered it. Now he did. "Probably."

"Then they both must be out of work. Otherwise, one of em would have stayed home with the kid."

"Maybe," Tom said, "they think showing up with the baby will improve their chances."

Todd brightened. "The pity card! Not a bad idea!" He held out the pint. "Want a nip?"

He took a small one, thinking, If I don't drink it, Todd will.

Tom was awakened from a whiskey-assisted doze by an exuberant shout: "Life is discovered on other planets!" This sally was followed by laughter and applause.

He looked around and saw daylight. Thin and fog-draped, but daylight, just the same. Beyond the bank of auditorium doors, a fellow in gray fatigues—a man with a job, lucky fellow—was pushing a mop-bucket across the lobby.

"Whuddup?" Todd asked.

"Nothing," Tom said. "Just a janitor."

Todd peered in the direction of Marlborough Street. "Jesus, and still they come."

"Yeah," Tom said. Thinking, And if I'd listened to Linda, we'd be at the end of a line that stretches halfway to Cleveland. That was a good thought, a little vindication was always good, but he wished he'd said no to Todd's pint. His mouth tasted like kitty litter. Not that he'd ever actually *eaten* any, but—

Someone a couple of zigzags over—not far from the sleeping bag—asked, "Is that a Benz? It looks like a Benz."

Tom saw a long shape at the head of the entrance drive leading up from Marlborough, its yellow fog-lamps blazing. It wasn't moving; it just sat there.

"What's he think he's doing?" Todd asked.

The driver of the car immediately behind must have wondered the same thing, because he laid on his horn—a long, pissed-off blat that made people stir and snort and look around. For a moment the car with the yellow fog-lamps stayed where it was. Then it shot forward. Not to the left, toward the now full-to-overflowing parking lot, but directly at the people penned within the maze of tapes and posts.

"Hey!" someone shouted.

The crowd swayed backward in a tidal motion. Tom was shoved against Todd, who went down on his ass. Tom fought for balance, almost found it, and then the man in front of him—yelling, no, *screaming*—drove his butt into Tom's crotch and one flailing elbow into his chest. Tom fell on top of his buddy, heard the bottle of Bell's shatter somewhere between them, and smelled the sharp reek of the remaining whiskey as it ran across the pavement.

Great, now I'll smell like a barroom on Saturday night.

He struggled to his feet in time to see the car—it was a Mercedes, all right, a big sedan as gray as this foggy morning—plowing into the crowd, spinning bodies out of its way as it came, describing a drunken arc. Blood dripped from the grille. A woman went skidding and rolling across the hood with her hands out and her shoes gone. She slapped at the glass, grabbed at one of the windshield wipers, missed, and tumbled off to one side. Yellow DO NOT CROSS tapes snapped. A post clanged against the side of the big sedan, which did not slow its roll in the slightest. Tom saw the front wheels pass over the sleeping bag and the burly man, who had been crouched protectively over it with one hand raised.

Now it was coming right at him.

"Todd!" he shouted. "Todd, *get up*!"

He grabbed at Todd's hands, got one of them, and pulled. Someone slammed into him and he was driven back to his knees. He could hear the rogue car's motor, revving full-out. Very close now. He tried to crawl, and a foot clobbered him in the temple. He saw stars.

"Tom?" Todd was behind him now. How had that happened? "Tom, what the *fuck*?"

A body landed on top of him, and then something else was on top of him, a huge weight that pressed down, threatening to turn him to jelly. His hips snapped. They sounded like dry turkey bones. Then the weight was gone. Pain with its own kind of weight rushed in to replace it.

Tom tried to raise his head and managed to get it off the pavement just long enough to see taillights dwindling into the fog. He saw glittering shards of glass from the busted pint. He saw Todd sprawled on his back with blood coming out of his head and pooling on the pavement. Crimson tire-tracks ran away into the foggy half-light.

He thought, Linda was right. I should have stayed home.

He thought, I'm going to die, and maybe that's for the best. Because, unlike Todd Paine, I never got around to cashing in my insurance.

He thought, Although I probably would have, in time.

Then, blackness.

When Tom Saubers woke up in the hospital forty-eight hours later, Linda was sitting beside him. She was holding his hand. He asked her if he was going to live. She smiled, squeezed his hand, and said you bet your patootie.

"Am I paralyzed? Tell me the truth."

"No, honey, but you've got a lot of broken bones."

"What about Todd?"

She looked away, biting her lips. "He's in a coma, but they think he's going to come out of it eventually. They can tell by his brainwaves, or something."

"There was a car. I couldn't get out of the way."

"I know. You weren't the only one. It was some madman. He got away with it, at least so far."

Tom could have cared less about the man driving the Mercedes-Benz. Not paralyzed was good, but—

"How bad did I get it? No bullshit—be honest."

She met his eyes but couldn't hold them. Once more looking at the get-well cards on his bureau, she said, "You . . . well. It's going to be awhile before you can walk again."

"How long?"

She raised his hand, which was badly scraped, and kissed it. "They don't know."

Tom Saubers closed his eyes and began to cry. Linda listened to that awhile, and when she couldn't stand it anymore, she leaned forward and began to punch the button on the morphine pump. She kept doing it until the machine stopped giving. By then he was asleep.

1978

Morris grabbed a blanket from the top shelf of the bedroom closet and used it to cover Rothstein, who now sprawled askew in the easy chair with the top of his head gone. The brains that had conceived Jimmy Gold, Jimmy's sister Emma, and Jimmy's self-involved, semi-alcoholic parents—so much like Morris's own—were now drying on the wallpaper. Morris wasn't shocked, exactly, but he was certainly amazed. He had expected some blood, and a hole between the eyes, but not this gaudy expectoration of gristle and bone. It was a failure of imagination, he supposed, the reason why he could *read* the giants of modern American literature—read them and appreciate them—but never *be* one.

Freddy Dow came out of the study with a loaded duffel bag over each shoulder. Curtis followed, head down and carrying nothing at all. All at once he sped up, hooked around Freddy, and bolted into the kitchen. The door to the backyard banged against the side of the house as the wind took it. Then came the sound of retching.

"He's feelin kinda sick," Freddy said. He had a talent for stating the obvious.

"You all right?" Morris asked.

"Yuh." Freddy went out through the front door without looking back, pausing to pick up the crowbar leaning against the porch glider. They had come prepared to break in, but the front door had been unlocked. The kitchen door, as well. Rothstein had put all his confidence in the Gardall safe, it seemed. Talk about failures of the imagination.

Morris went into the study, looked at Rothstein's neat desk and covered typewriter. Looked at the pictures on the wall. Both ex-wives hung there, laughing and young and beautiful in their fifties clothes and hairdos. It was sort of interesting that Rothstein would keep those discarded women where they could look at him while he was writing, but Morris had no time to consider this, or to investigate the contents of the writer's desk, which he would dearly have loved to do. But was such investigation even necessary? He had the notebooks, after all. He had the contents of the writer's *mind*. Everything he'd written since he stopped publishing eighteen years ago.

Freddy had taken the stacks of cash envelopes in the first load (of course; cash was what Freddy and Curtis understood), but there were still plenty of notebooks on the shelves of the safe. They were Moleskines, the kind Hemingway had used, the kind Morris had dreamed of while in the reformatory, where he had also dreamed of becoming a writer himself. But in Riverview Youth Detention he had been rationed to five sheets of pulpy Blue Horse paper each week, hardly enough to begin writing the Great American Novel. Begging for more did no good. The one time he'd offered Elkins, the commissary trustee, a blowjob for a dozen extra sheets, Elkins had punched him in the face. Sort of funny, when you considered all the non-consensual sex he had been forced to participate in during his nine-month stretch, usually on his knees and on more than one occasion with his own dirty undershorts stuffed in his mouth.

He didn't hold his mother *entirely* responsible for those rapes, but she deserved her share of the blame. Anita Bellamy, the famous history professor whose book on Henry Clay Frick had been nominated for a Pulitzer. So famous that she presumed to know all about modern American literature, as well. It was an argument about the Gold trilogy that had sent him out one night, furious and determined to get drunk. Which he did, although he was underage and looked it.

Drinking did not agree with Morris. He did things when he was drinking that he couldn't remember later, and they were never good things. That night it had been breaking and entering, vandalism, and fighting with a neighborhood rent-a-cop who tried to hold him until the regular cops got there.

That was almost six years ago, but the memory was still fresh. It had all been so stupid. Stealing a car, joyriding across town, then abandoning it (perhaps after pissing all over the dashboard) was one thing. Not smart, but with a little luck, you could walk away from that sort of deal. But breaking into a place in Sugar Heights? Double stupid. He had wanted *nothing* in that house (at least nothing he could remember later). And when he *did* want something? When he offered up his mouth for a few lousy sheets of Blue Horse paper? Punched in the face. So he'd laughed, because that was what Jimmy Gold would have done (at least before Jimmy grew up and sold out for what he called the Golden Buck), and what happened next? Punched in the face again, even harder. It was the muffled crack of his nose breaking that had started him crying.

Jimmy never would have cried.

He was still looking greedily at the Moleskines when Freddy Dow returned with the other two duffel bags. He also had a scuffed leather carryall. "This was in the pantry. Along with like a billion cans of beans and tuna fish. Go figure, huh? Weird guy. Maybe he was waiting for the Acropolipse. Come on, Morrie, put it in gear. Someone might have heard that shot."

"There aren't any neighbors. Nearest farm is two miles away. Relax."

"Jails're full of guys who were relaxed. We need to get out of here."

Morris began gathering up handfuls of notebooks, but couldn't resist looking in one, just to make sure. Rothstein *had* been a weird guy, and it wasn't out of the realm of possibility that he had stacked his safe with blank books, thinking he might write something in them eventually.

But no.

This one, at least, was loaded with Rothstein's small, neat handwriting, every page filled, top to bottom and side to side, the margins as thin as threads.

—wasn't sure why it mattered to him and why he couldn't sleep as the empty boxcar of this late freight bore him on through rural oblivion toward Kansas City and the sleeping country beyond, the full belly of America resting beneath its customary comforter of night, yet Jimmy's thoughts persisted in turning back to—

Freddy thumped him on the shoulder, and not gently. "Get your nose out of that thing and pack up. We already got one puking his guts out and pretty much useless."

Morris dropped the notebook into one of the duffels and grabbed another double handful without a word, his thoughts brilliant with possibility. He forgot about the mess under the blanket in the living room, forgot about Curtis Rogers puking his guts in the roses or zinnias or petunias or whatever was growing out back. Jimmy Gold! Headed west, in a boxcar! Rothstein hadn't been done with him, after all!

"These're full," he told Freddy. "Take them out. I'll put the rest in the valise."

"That what you call that kind of bag?"

"I think so, yeah." He knew so. "Go on. Almost done here."

Freddy shouldered the duffels by their straps, but lingered a moment longer. "Are you sure about these things? Because Rothstein said—"

"He was a hoarder trying to save his hoard. He would have said anything. Go on."

Freddy went. Morris loaded the last batch of Moleskines into the valise and backed out of the closet. Curtis was standing by Rothstein's desk. He had taken off his balaclava; they all had. His face was paper-pale and there were dark shock circles around his eyes.

"You didn't have to kill him. You weren't *supposed* to. It wasn't in the plan. Why'd you do that?"

Because he made me feel stupid. Because he cursed my mother and that's my job. Because he called me a kid. Because he needed to be punished for turning Jimmy Gold into one of *them*. Mostly because nobody with his kind of talent has a right to hide it from the world. Only Curtis wouldn't understand that.

"Because it'll make the notebooks worth more when we sell them." Which wouldn't be until he'd read every word in them, but Curtis wouldn't understand the need to do that, and didn't need to know. Nor did Freddy. He tried to sound patient and reasonable. "We now have all the John Rothstein output there's ever going to be. That makes the unpublished stuff even more valuable. You see that, don't you?"

Curtis scratched one pale cheek. "Well . . . I guess . . . yeah."

"Also, he can never claim they're forgeries when they turn up. Which he would have done, just out of spite. I've read a lot about him, Curtis, just about everything, and he was one spiteful motherfucker."

"Well . . ."

Morrie restrained himself from saying That's an extremely deep subject for a mind as shallow as yours. He held out the valise instead. "Take it. And keep your gloves on until we're in the car."

"You should have talked it over with us, Morrie. We're your *partners*."

Curtis started out, then turned back. "I got a question."

"What is it?"

"Do you know if New Hampshire has the death penalty?"

They took secondary roads across the narrow chimney of New Hampshire and into Vermont. Freddy drove the Chevy Biscayne, which was old and unremarkable. Morris rode shotgun with a Rand McNally open on his lap, thumbing on the dome light from time to time to make sure they didn't wander off their pre-planned route. He didn't need to remind Freddy to keep to the speed limit. This wasn't Freddy Dow's first rodeo.

Curtis lay in the backseat, and soon they heard the sound of his snores. Morris considered him lucky; he seemed to have puked out his horror. Morris thought it might be awhile before he himself got another good night's sleep. He kept seeing the brains dribbling down the wallpaper. It wasn't the killing that stayed on his mind, it was the spilled talent. A lifetime of honing and shaping torn apart in less than a second. All those stories, all those images, and what came out looked like so much oatmeal. What was the point?

"So you really think we'll be able to sell those little books of his?" Freddy asked. He was back to that. "For real money, I mean?"

"Yes."

"And get away with it?"

"Yes, Freddy, I'm sure."

Freddy Dow was quiet for so long that Morris thought the issue was settled. Then he spoke to the subject again. Two words. Dry and toneless. "I'm doubtful."

Later on, once more incarcerated—not in Youth Detention

this time, either—Morris would think, That's when I decided to kill them.

But sometimes at night, when he couldn't sleep, his asshole slick and burning from one of a dozen soap-assisted shower-room buggeries, he would admit that wasn't the truth. He'd known all along. They were dumb, and career criminals. Sooner or later (probably sooner) one of them would be caught for something else, and there would be the temptation to trade what they knew about this night for a lighter sentence or no sentence at all.

I just knew they had to go, he would think on those cellblock nights when the full belly of America rested beneath its customary comforter of night. It was inevitable.

In upstate New York, with dawn not yet come but beginning to show the horizon's dark outline behind them, they turned west on Route 92, a highway that roughly paralleled I-90 as far as Illinois, where it turned south and petered out in the industrial city of Rockford. The road was still mostly deserted at this hour, although they could hear (and sometimes see) heavy truck traffic on the interstate to their left.

They passed a sign reading REST AREA 2 MI., and Morris thought of *Macbeth*. If it were to be done, then 'twere well it were done quickly. Not an exact quote, maybe, but close enough for government work.

"Pull in there," he told Freddy. "I need to drain the dragon."

"They probably got vending machines, too," said the puker in the backseat. Curtis was sitting up now, his hair crazy around his head. "I could get behind some of those peanut butter crackers."

Morris knew he'd have to let it go if there were other cars in the rest area. I-90 had sucked away most of the through traffic that used to travel on this road, but once daybreak arrived, there would be lots of local traffic, pooting along from one Hicksville to the next.

For now the rest area was deserted, at least in part because of the sign reading OVERNIGHT RVS PROHIBITED. They parked and got out. Birds chirruped in the trees, discussing the night just past and plans for the day. A few leaves—in this part of the world they were just beginning to turn—drifted down and scuttered across the lot.

Curtis went to inspect the vending machines while Morris and Freddy walked side by side to the men's half of the restroom facility. Morris didn't feel particularly nervous. Maybe what they said was true, after the first one it got easier.

He held the door for Freddy with one hand and took the pistol from his jacket pocket with the other. Freddy said thanks without looking around. Morris let the door swing shut before raising the gun. He placed the muzzle less than an inch from the back of Freddy Dow's head and pulled the trigger. The gunshot was a flat loud bang in the tiled room, but anyone who heard it from a distance would think it was a motorcycle backfiring on I-90. What he worried about was Curtis.

He needn't have. Curtis was still standing in the snack alcove, beneath a wooden eave and a rustic sign reading ROADSIDE OASIS. In one hand he had a package of peanut butter crackers.

"Did you hear that?" he asked Morris. Then, seeing the gun, sounding honestly puzzled: "What's that for?"

"You," Morris said, and shot him in the chest.

Curtis went down, but—this was a shock—did not die. He didn't seem even *close* to dying. He squirmed on the pavement. A fallen leaf cartwheeled in front of his nose. Blood began to seep out from beneath him. He was still clutching his crackers. He looked up, his oily black hair hanging in his eyes. Beyond the screening trees, a truck went past on Route 92, droning east.

Morris didn't want to shoot Curtis again, out here a gunshot didn't have that hollow backfire sound, and besides, someone might pull in at any second. "If it were to be done, then 'twere well it were done quickly," he said, and dropped to one knee.

"You shot me," Curtis said, sounding breathless and amazed. "You fucking *shot* me, Morrie!"

Thinking how much he hated that nickname—he'd hated it all his life, and even teachers, who should have known better, used it—he reversed the gun and began to hammer Curtis's skull with the butt. Three hard blows accomplished very little. It was only a .38, after all, and not heavy enough to do more than minor damage. Blood began to seep through Curtis's hair and run down his stubbly cheeks. He was groaning, staring up at Morris with desperate blue eyes. He waved one hand weakly.

"Stop it, Morrie! Stop it, that *hurts*!"

Shit. Shit, shit, *shit*.

Morris slid the gun back into his pocket. The butt was now slimy with blood and hair. He went to the Biscayne, wiping his hand on his jacket. He opened the driver's door, saw the empty ignition, and said *fuck* under his breath. Whispering it like a prayer.

On 92, a couple of cars went by, then a brown UPS truck.

He trotted back to the men's room, opened the door, knelt down, and began to go through Freddy's pockets. He found the car keys in the left front. He got to his feet and hurried back to the snack alcoves, sure a car or truck would have pulled in by now, the traffic was getting heavier all the time, *somebody* would have to piss out his or her morning coffee, and he would have to kill *that* one, too, and possibly the one after that. An image of linked paper dolls came to mind.

No one yet, though.

He got into the Biscayne, legally purchased but now bearing stolen Maine license plates. Curtis Rogers was slithering a slow course down the cement walkway toward the toilets, pulling with his hands and pushing feebly with his feet and leaving a snail-trail of blood behind. It was impossible to know for sure, but Morris thought he might be trying to reach the pay telephone on the wall between the mens' and the ladies'.

This wasn't the way it was supposed to go, he thought, starting the car. It was spur-of-the-moment stupid, and he was probably going to be caught. It made him think of what Rothstein had said at the end. *What are you, anyway, twenty-two? Twenty-three? What do you know about life, let alone literature?*

"I know I'm no sellout," he said. "I know that much."

He put the Biscayne in drive and rolled slowly forward toward the man eeling his way up the cement walkway. He wanted to get out of here, his brain was *yammering* at him to get out of here, but this had to be done carefully and with no more mess than was absolutely necessary.

Curtis looked around, his eyes wide and horrified behind the jungle foliage of his dirty hair. He raised one hand in a feeble *stop* gesture, then Morris couldn't see him anymore because the hood was in the way. He steered carefully and continued creeping forward. The front of the car bumped up over the curbing. The pine tree air freshener on the rearview mirror swung and bobbed.

There was nothing . . . and nothing . . . and then the car bumped up again. There was a muffled *pop*, the sound of a small pumpkin exploding in a microwave oven.

Morris cut the wheel to the left and there was another bump as the Biscayne went back into the parking area. He looked in the mirror and saw that Curtis's head was gone.

Well, no. Not exactly. It was there, but all spread out. Mooshed. No loss of talent in *that* mess, Morrie thought.

He drove toward the exit, and when he was sure the road was empty, he sped up. He would need to stop and examine the front of the car, especially the tire that had run over Curtis's head, but he wanted to get twenty miles farther down the road first. Twenty at least.

"I see a car wash in my future," he said. This struck him funny (*inordinately* funny, and there was a word neither Freddy nor Curtis would have understood), and he laughed long and loud. He kept exactly to the speed limit. He watched the odometer turn the miles, and even at fifty-five, each revolution seemed to take five minutes. He was sure the tire had left a blood-trail going out of the exit, but that would be gone now. Long gone. Still, it was time to turn off onto the secondary roads again, maybe even the tertiary ones. The smart thing would be to stop and throw all the notebooks—the cash, too—into the woods. But he would not do that. Never would he do that.

Fifty-fifty odds, he told himself. Maybe better. After all, no one saw the car. Not in New Hampshire and not at that rest area.

He came to an abandoned restaurant, pulled into the side lot, and examined the Biscayne's front end and right front tire. He thought things looked pretty good, all in all, but there was some blood on the front bumper. He pulled a handful of weeds and wiped it off. He got back in and drove on west. He was prepared for roadblocks, but there were none.

Over the Pennsylvania state line, in Gowanda, he found a coin-op car wash. The brushes brushed, the jets rinsed, and the car came out spanking clean—underside as well as topside.

Morris drove west, headed for the filthy little city residents called the Gem of the Great Lakes. He had to sit tight for awhile, and he had to see an old friend. Also, home was the place where, when you go there, they have to take you in—the gospel according to Robert Frost—and that was especially true when there was no one to bitch about the return of the prodigal son. With dear old Dad in the wind for years now and dear old Mom spending the fall semester at Princeton guest-lecturing on the robber barons, the house on Sycamore Street would be empty. Not much of a house for a fancy-schmancy teacher—

not to mention a writer once nominated for the Pulitzer—but blame dear old Dad for that. Besides, Morris had never minded living there; that had been Mother's resentment, not his.

Morris listened to the news, but there was nothing about the murder of the novelist who, according to that *Time* cover story, had been "a voice shouting at the children of the silent fifties to wake up and raise their own voices." This radio silence was good news, but not unexpected; according to Morris's source in the reformatory, Rothstein's housekeeper only came in once a week. There was also a handyman, but he only came when called. Morris and his late partners had picked their time accordingly, which meant he could reasonably hope the body might not be discovered for another six days.

That afternoon, in rural Ohio, he passed an antiques barn and made a U-turn. After a bit of browsing, he bought a used trunk for twenty dollars. It was old, but looked sturdy. Morris considered it a steal.

2010

Pete Saubers's parents had lots of arguments now. Tina called them the arkie-barkies. Pete thought she had something there, because that was what they sounded like when they got going: ark-ark-ark, bark-bark-bark. Sometimes Pete wanted to go to the head of the stairs and scream down at them to quit it, just quit it. *You're scaring the kids,* he wanted to yell. *There are kids in this house,* kids, *did you two stupes forget that?*

Pete was home because Honor Roll students with nothing but afternoon study hall and activity period after lunch were allowed to cut out early. His door was open and he heard his father go thumping rapidly across the kitchen on his crutches as soon as his mother's car pulled into the driveway. Pete was pretty sure today's festivities would start with his dad saying Gosh, she was home early. Mom would say he could never seem to remember that Wednesdays were now her early days. Dad would reply that he still wasn't used to living in this part of the city, saying it like they'd been forced to relocate into deepest darkest Lowtown instead of just the Tree Streets section of Northfield. Once the preliminaries were taken care of, they could get down to the real arking and barking.

Pete wasn't crazy about the North Side himself, but it wasn't *terrible,* and even at thirteen he seemed to understand the economic realities of their situation better than his father.

Maybe because he wasn't swallowing OxyContin pills four times a day like his father.

They were here because Grace Johnson Middle School, where her mother used to teach, had been closed as part of the city council's cost-cutting initiative. Many of the GJ teachers were now unemployed. Linda, at least, had been hired as a combination librarian and study hall monitor at Northfield Elementary. She got out early on Wednesdays because the library closed at noon that day. All the school libraries did. It was another cost-cutting initiative. Pete's dad railed at this, pointing out that the council members hadn't cut their *salaries*, and calling them a bunch of goddam Tea Party hypocrites.

Pete didn't know about that. What he knew was that these days Tom Saubers railed at everything.

The Ford Focus, their only car now, pulled up in the driveway and Mom slid out, dragging her old scuffed briefcase. She skirted the patch of ice that always formed in the shady spot under the front porch downspout. It had been Tina's turn to salt that down, but she had forgotten, as usual. Mom climbed the steps slowly, her shoulders low. Pete hated to see her walk that way, as if she had a sack of bricks on her back. Dad's crutches, meanwhile, thumped a double-time rhythm into the living room.

The front door opened. Pete waited. Hoped for something nice like *Hiya, honey, how was your morning?*

As if.

He didn't exactly *want* to eavesdrop on the arkie-barkies, but the house was small and it was practically impossible not to overhear . . . unless he left, that is, a strategic retreat he made more and more frequently this winter. And he sometimes felt that, as the older kid, he had a *responsibility* to listen. Mr. Jacoby liked to say in history class that knowledge was power, and Pete supposed that was why he felt compelled to monitor his parents' escalating war of words. Because each arkie-barkie stretched the fabric of the marriage thinner, and one of these days it would tear wide open. Best to be prepared.

Only prepared for what? Divorce? That seemed the most likely outcome. In some ways things might be better if they did split up—Pete felt this more and more strongly, although he had not yet articulated it as a conscious thought—but what exactly would a divorce mean in (another of Mr. Jacoby's faves) *real world terms*? Who would stay and who would go? If his dad went, how would he get along without a car when he could hardly walk? For that matter, how could either of them *afford* to go? They were broke already.

At least Tina wasn't here for today's spirited exchange of parental views; she was still in school, and probably wouldn't be home directly after. Maybe not until dinner. She had finally made a friend, a bucktoothed girl named Ellen Briggs, who lived on the corner of Sycamore and Elm. Pete thought Ellen had the brains of a hamster, but at least Tina wasn't always moping around the house, missing her friends in the old neighborhood, and sometimes crying. Pete hated it when Tina cried.

Meanwhile, silence your cell phones and turn off your pagers, folks. The lights are going down and this afternoon's installment of *We're in Deep Shit* is about to begin.

TOM: "Hey, you're home early."

LINDA (wearily): "Tom, it's—"

TOM: "Wednesday, right. Early day at the library."

LINDA: "You've been smoking in the house again. I can smell it."

TOM (getting his sulk on): "Just one. In the kitchen. With the window open. There's ice on the back steps, and I didn't want to risk a tumble. Pete forgot to salt them again."

PETE (aside to the audience): "As he should know, since he made the schedule of chores, it's actually Tina's week to salt. Those OxyContins he takes aren't just pain pills, they're stupid pills."

LINDA: "I can still smell it, and you know the lease specifically prohibits—"

TOM: "All right, okay, I get it. Next time I'll go outside and risk falling off my crutches."

LINDA: "It's not *just* the lease, Tommy. The secondary smoke is bad for the kids. We've discussed that."

TOM: "And discussed it, and discussed it . . ."

LINDA (now wading into even deeper water): "Also, how much does a pack of cigarettes cost these days? Four-fifty? Five dollars?"

TOM: "I smoke a pack a *week*, for Christ's sake!"

LINDA (overrunning his defenses with an arithmetic Panzer assault): "At five a pack, that's over twenty dollars a month. And it all comes out of my salary, because it's the only one—"

TOM: "Oh, here we go—"

LINDA: "—we've got now."

TOM: "You never get tired of rubbing that in, do you? Probably think I got run over on purpose. So I could laze around the house."

LINDA (after a long pause): "Is there any wine left? Because I could use half a glass."

PETE (aside): "Say there is, Dad. Say there is."

TOM: "It's gone. Maybe you'd like me to crutch my way down to the Zoney's and get another bottle. Of course you'd have to give me an advance on my *allowance*."

LINDA (not crying, but sounding on the verge): "You act as though what happened to you is my fault."

TOM (shouting): "It's *nobody's* fault, and that's what drives me crazy! Don't you get that? They never even caught the guy who did it!"

At this point Pete decided he'd had enough. It was a stupid play. Maybe they didn't see that, but he did. He closed his lit book. He would read the assigned story—something by a guy named John Rothstein—that night. Right now he had to get out and breathe some uncontentious air.

LINDA (quiet): "At least you didn't die."

TOM (going totally soap opera now): "Sometimes I think it would be better if I had. Look at me—hooked through the bag on Oxy, and still in pain because it doesn't work for shit anymore unless I take enough to half-kill me. Living on my wife's salary—which is a thousand less than it used to be, thanks to the fucking Tea-Partiers—"

LINDA: "Watch your lang—"

TOM: "House? Gone. Motorized wheelchair? Gone. Savings? Almost used up. And now I can't even have a fucking cigarette!"

LINDA: "If you think whining will solve anything, be my guest, but—"

TOM (roaring): "Is whining what you call it? I call it reality. You want me to drop my pants so you can get a good look at what's left of my legs?"

Pete floated downstairs in his stocking feet. The living room was right there at the bottom, but they didn't see him; they were face-to-face and busy acting in a dipshit play no one would ever pay to see. His father hulking on his crutches, his eyes red and his cheeks scruffy with beard, his mother holding her purse in front of her breasts like a shield and biting her lips. It was awful, and the worst part? He loved them.

His father had neglected to mention the Emergency Fund, started a month after the City Center Massacre by the town's one remaining newspaper, in cooperation with the three local TV stations. Brian Williams had even done a story about it on *NBC Nightly News*—how this tough little city took care of its own when disaster struck, all those caring hearts, all those helping hands, all that blah-blah-blah, and now a word from our sponsor. The Emergency Fund made everybody feel good for like six days. What the media didn't talk about was how little the fund had actually raised, even with the charity walks, and the charity bike rides, and a concert by an *American Idol* runner-up. The Emergency Fund was thin because times were hard for everyone. And, of course, what *was* raised had to be divided among so many. The Saubers family got a check for twelve hundred dollars, then one for five hundred, then one for two. Last month's check, marked FINAL INSTALLMENT, came to fifty dollars.

Big whoop.

Pete slipped into the kitchen, grabbed his boots and jacket, and went out. The first thing he noticed was that there wasn't any ice on the back stoop; his father had been totally lying about that. The day was too warm for ice, at least in the sun. Spring was still six weeks away, but the current thaw had gone on for almost a week, and the only snow left in the backyard was a few crusty patches under the trees. Pete crossed to the fence and let himself out through the gate.

One advantage to living in the Tree Streets of the North Side was the undeveloped land behind Sycamore. It was easily as big as a city block, five tangled acres of undergrowth and scrubby trees running downhill to a frozen stream. Pete's dad said the land had been that way for a long time and was apt to stay that way even longer, due to some endless legal wrangle over who owned it and what could be built on it. "In the end, no one wins these things but the lawyers," he told Pete. "Remember that."

In Pete's opinion, kids who wanted a little mental health vacation from their parents also won.

A path ran through the winter-barren trees on a meandering diagonal, eventually coming out at the Birch Street Rec, a longtime Northfield youth center whose days were now numbered. Big kids hung out on and around the path in warm weather—smoking cigarettes, smoking dope, drinking beer, probably laying their girlfriends—but not at this time of year. No big kids equaled no hassle.

Sometimes Pete took his sister along the path if his mother and father were seriously into it, as was more and more often the case. When they arrived at the Rec, they'd shoot baskets or watch videos or play checkers. He didn't know where he could take her once the Rec closed. There was no place else except for Zoney's, the convenience store. On his own, he mostly just went as far as the creek, splooshing stones into it if it was flowing, bouncing them off the ice when it was frozen. Seeing if he could make a hole and enjoying the quiet.

The arkie-barkies were bad enough, but his worst fear was that his dad—now always a little high on the Oxy pills—might someday actually take a swing at his mother. That would almost certainly tear the thin-stretched cloth of the marriage. And if it didn't? If she put up with being hit? That would be even worse.

Never happen, Pete told himself. Dad never would.

But if he did?

Ice still covered the stream this afternoon, but it looked rotten, and there were big yellow patches in it, as if some giant had stopped to take a leak. Pete wouldn't dare walk on it. He wouldn't drown or anything if the ice gave way, the water was only ankle deep, but he had no wish to get home and have to explain why his pants and socks were wet. He sat on a fallen log, tossed a few stones (the small ones bounced and rolled, the big ones went through the yellow patches), then just looked at the sky for awhile. Big fluffy clouds floated along up there, the kind that looked more like spring than winter, moving from west to east. There was one that looked like an old woman with a hump on her back (or maybe it was a packsack); there was a rabbit; there was a dragon; there was one that looked like a—

A soft, crumbling thump on his left distracted him. He turned and saw an overhanging piece of the embankment, loosened by a week's worth of melting snow, had given way, exposing the roots of a tree that was already leaning precariously. The space created by the fall looked like a cave, and unless he was mistaken—he supposed it might be just a shadow—there was something in there.

Pete walked to the tree, grabbed one of its leafless branches, and bent for a better look. There was something there, all right, and it looked pretty big. The end of a box, maybe?

He worked his way down the bank, creating makeshift steps by digging the heels of his boots into the muddy earth. Once he was below the site of the little landspill, he squatted. He saw cracked black leather and metal strips with rivets in them. There was a handle the size of a saddle-stirrup on the end. It was a trunk. Someone had buried a trunk here.

Excited now as well as curious, Pete grabbed the handle and yanked. The trunk didn't budge. It was socked in good and tight. Pete gave another tug, but just for form's sake. He wasn't going to get it out. Not without tools.

He hunkered with his hands dangling between his thighs, as his father often used to do before his hunkering days came to an end. Just staring at the trunk jutting out of the black, root-snarled earth. It was probably crazy to be thinking of *Treasure Island* (also "The Gold Bug," a story they'd read in English the year before), but he *was* thinking of it. And was it crazy? Was it really? As well as telling them that knowledge was power, Mr. Jacoby stressed the importance of logical thinking. Wasn't it logical to think that someone wouldn't bury a trunk in the woods unless there was something valuable inside?

It had been there for awhile, too. You could tell just looking at it. The leather was cracked, and gray in places instead of black. Pete had an idea that if he pulled on the handle with all his might and kept pulling, it might break. The metal binding-strips were dull and lacy with rust.

He came to a decision and pelted back up the path to the house. He let himself in through the gate, went to the kitchen door, listened. There were no voices and the TV was off. His father had probably gone into the bedroom (the one on the first floor, Mom and Dad had to sleep there even though it was small, because Dad couldn't climb stairs very well now) to take a nap. Mom might have gone in with him, they sometimes made up that way, but more likely she was in the laundry room that doubled as her study, working on her résumé and applying for jobs online. His dad might have given up (and Pete had to admit he had his reasons), but his mom hadn't. She wanted to go back to teaching full-time, and not just for the money.

There was a little detached garage, but his mom never put the Focus in it unless there was going to be a snowstorm. It was full of stuff from the old house that they had no room for in this smaller rented place. His dad's toolbox was in there (Tom had listed the tools on craigslist or something, but hadn't been able to get what he considered a fair price for them), and some of Tina's and his old toys, and the tub of salt with its scoop, and a few lawn-and-garden implements leaning against the back wall. Pete selected a spade and ran back down the path, holding it in front of him like a soldier with his rifle at high port.

He eased his way almost all the way down to the stream, using the steps he'd made, and went to work on the little landslide that had revealed the trunk. He shoveled as much of the fallen earth as he could back into the hole under the tree. He wasn't able to fill it all the way to the gnarled roots, but he was able to cover the end of the trunk, which was all he wanted.

For now.

• • •

There was some arking and barking at dinner, not too much, and Tina didn't seem to mind, but she came into Pete's room just as he was finishing his homework. She was wearing her footy pajamas and dragging Mrs. Beasley, her last and most important comfort-doll. It was as if she had returned to the age of five.

"Can I get in your bed for awhile, Petie? I had a bad dream."

He considered making her go back, then decided (thoughts of the buried trunk flickering in his mind) that to do so might be bad luck. It would also be mean, considering the dark hollows under her pretty eyes.

"Yeah, okay, for awhile. But we're not going to make a practice of it." One of their mom's favorite phrases.

Tina scooted across the bed until she was against the wall— her sleeping position of choice, as if she planned to spend the night. Pete closed his Earth Science book, sat down beside her, and winced.

"Doll warning, Teens. Mrs. Beasley's head is halfway up my butt."

"I'll scrunch her down by my feet. There. Is that better?"

"What if she smothers?"

"She doesn't breathe, stupid. She's just a doll and Ellen says pretty soon I'll get tired of her."

"Ellen's a doofus."

"She's my friend." Pete realized with some amusement that this wasn't exactly disagreeing. "But she's probably right. People grow up."

"Not you. You'll always be my little sister. And don't go to sleep. You're going back to your room in like five minutes."

"Ten."

"Six."

She considered. "Okay."

From downstairs came a muffled groan, followed by the thump of crutches. Pete tracked the sound into the kitchen, where Dad would sit down, light a cigarette, and blow the smoke out the back door. This would cause the furnace to run, and what the furnace burned, according to their mother, was not oil but dollar bills.

"Are they gonna get divorced, do you think?"

Pete was doubly shocked: first by the question, then by the adult matter-of-factness of it. He started to say No, course not, then thought how much he disliked movies where adults lied to children, which was like *all* movies.

"I don't know. Not tonight, anyway. The courts are closed."

She giggled. That was probably good. He waited for her to say something else. She didn't. Pete's thoughts turned to the trunk buried in the embankment, beneath that tree. He had managed to keep those thoughts at arm's length while he did his homework, but . . .

No, I didn't. Those thoughts were there all the time.

"Teens? You better not go to sleep."

"I'm not . . ." But damn close, from the sound.

"What would you do if you found a treasure? A buried treasure chest full of jewels and gold doubloons?"

"What are doubloons?"

"Coins from olden days."

"I'd give it to Daddy and Mommy. So they wouldn't fight anymore. Wouldn't you?"

"Yes," Pete said. "Now go back to your own bed, before I have to carry you."

Under his insurance plan, Tom Saubers only qualified for therapy twice a week now. A special van came for him every Monday and Friday at nine o'clock and brought him back at four in the afternoon, after hydrotherapy and a meeting where people with long-term injuries and chronic pain sat around in a circle and talked about their problems. All of which meant that the house was empty for seven hours on those days.

On Thursday night, Pete went to bed complaining of a sore throat. The next morning he woke up saying it was still sore, and now he thought he had a fever, too.

"You're hot, all right," Linda said after putting the inside of her wrist to his brow. Pete certainly hoped so, after holding his face two inches from his bedside lamp before going downstairs. "If you're not better tomorrow, you probably should see the doctor."

"Good idea!" Tom exclaimed from his side of the table, where he was pushing around some scrambled eggs. He looked like he hadn't slept at all. "A specialist, maybe! Just let me call Shorty the Chauffeur. Tina's got dibs on the Rolls for her tennis lesson at the country club, but I think the Town Car is available."

Tina giggled. Linda gave Tom a hard look, but before she could respond, Pete said he didn't feel all *that* bad, a day at home would probably fix him up. If that didn't, the weekend would.

"I suppose." She sighed. "Do you want something to eat?"

Pete did, but thought it unwise to say so, since he was supposed to have a sore throat. He cupped his hand in front of his mouth and created a cough. "Maybe just some juice. Then I guess I'll go upstairs and try to get some more sleep."

Tina left the house first, bopping down to the corner where she and Ellen would discuss whatever weirdo stuff nine-year-olds discussed while waiting for the schoolbus. Then Mom for her school, in the Focus. Last of all Dad, who made his way down the walk on his crutches to the waiting van. Pete watched him go from his bedroom window, thinking that his father seemed smaller now. The hair sticking out around his Groundhogs cap had started to turn gray.

When the van was gone, Pete threw on some clothes, grabbed one of the reusable grocery shopping bags Mom kept in the pantry, and went out to the garage. From his father's toolbox he selected a hammer and chisel, which he dumped into the bag. He grabbed the spade, started out, then came back and took the crowbar as well. He had never been a Boy Scout, but believed in being prepared.

The morning was cold enough for him to see his breath, but by the time Pete dug enough of the trunk free to feel he had a chance of pulling it out, the air had warmed up to well above freezing and he was sweating under his coat. He draped it over a low branch and peered around to make sure he was still alone here by the stream (he had done this several times). Reassured, he got some dirt and rubbed his palms with it, like a batter getting ready to hit. He grasped the handle at the end of the trunk, reminding himself to be ready if it broke. The last thing he wanted to do was tumble down the embankment ass over teapot. If he fell into the stream, he really might get sick.

Probably nothing in there but a bunch of moldy old clothes, anyway . . . except why would anyone bury a trunk filled with old clothes? Why not just burn them, or take them to the Goodwill?

Only one way to find out.

Pete took a deep breath, locked it down in his chest, and pulled. The trunk stayed put, and the old handle creaked warningly, but Pete was encouraged. He found he could now shift the trunk from side to side a little. This made him think of Dad tying a thread around one of Tina's baby teeth and giving a brisk yank when it wouldn't come out on its own.

He dropped to his knees (reminding himself he would do well to either wash these jeans later on or bury them deep in his closet) and peered into the hole. He saw a root had closed around the rear of the trunk like a grasping arm. He grabbed the spade, choked up on the handle, and chopped at it. The root was thick and he had to rest several times, but finally he cut all the way through. He laid the spade aside and grabbed the handle again. The trunk was looser now, almost ready to come out. He glanced at his watch. Quarter past ten. He thought of Mom calling home on her break to see how he was doing. Not a big problem, when he didn't answer she'd just think he was sleeping, but he reminded himself to check the answering machine when he got back. He grabbed the spade and began to dig around the trunk, loosening the dirt and cutting a few smaller roots. Then he took hold of the handle again.

"This time, you mother," he told it. "This time for sure."

He pulled. The trunk slid forward so suddenly and easily that he would have fallen over if his feet hadn't been braced far apart. Now it was leaning out of the hole, its top covered with sprays and clods of dirt. He could see the latches on the front, old-fashioned ones, like the latches on a workman's lunchbox. Also a big lock. He grabbed the handle again and this time it snapped. "Fuck a duck," Pete said, looking at his hands. They were red and throbbing.

Well, in for a penny, in for a pound (another of Mom's favorite sayings). He gripped the sides of the trunk in a clumsy bearhug and rocked back on his heels. This time it came all the way out of its hidey-hole and into the sunlight for the first time in what had to be years, a damp and dirty relic with rusty fittings. It looked to be two and a half feet long and at least a foot and a half deep. Maybe more. Pete hefted the end and guessed it might weigh as much as sixty pounds, half his own weight, but it was impossible to tell how much of that was the contents and how much the trunk itself. In any case, it wasn't doubloons; if the trunk had been filled with gold, he wouldn't have been able to pull it out at all, let alone lift it.

He snapped the latches up, creating little showers of dirt,

and then bent close to the lock, prepared to bust it off with the hammer and chisel. Then, if it still wouldn't open—and it probably wouldn't—he'd use the crowbar. But first . . . you never knew until you tried . . .

He grasped the lid and it came up in a squall of dirty hinges. Later he would surmise that someone had bought this trunk secondhand, probably getting a good deal because the key was lost, but for now he only stared. He was unaware of the blister on one palm, or the ache in his back and thighs, or the sweat trickling down his dirt-streaked face. He wasn't thinking of his mother, his father, or his sister. He wasn't thinking of the arkie-barkies, either, at least not then.

The trunk had been lined with clear plastic to protect against moisture. Beneath it he could see piles of what looked like notebooks. He used the side of his palm as a windshield wiper and cleared a crescent of fine droplets from the plastic. They were notebooks, all right, nice ones with what almost had to be real leather covers. It looked like a hundred at least. But that wasn't all. There were also envelopes like the ones his mom brought home when she cashed a check. Pete pulled away the plastic and stared into the half-filled trunk. The envelopes had GRANITE STATE BANK and *"Your Hometown Friend!"* printed on them. Later he would notice certain differences between these envelopes and the ones his mom got at Corn Bank and Trust—no email address, and nothing about using your ATM card for withdrawals—but for now he only stared. His heart was beating so hard he saw black dots pulsing in front of his eyes, and he wondered if he was going to faint.

Bullshit you are, only girls do that.

Maybe, but he felt decidedly woozy, and realized part of the problem was that since opening the trunk he had forgotten to breathe. He inhaled deeply, whooshed it out, and inhaled again. All the way down to his toes, it felt like. His head cleared, but his heart was whamming harder than ever and his hands were shaking.

Those bank envelopes will be empty. You know that, don't you? People find buried money in books and movies, but not in real life.

Only they didn't *look* empty. They looked *stuffed*.

Pete started to reach for one, then gasped when he heard rustling on the other side of the stream. He whirled around and saw two squirrels there, probably thinking the weeklong thaw meant spring had arrived, making merry in the dead leaves. They raced up a tree, tails twitching.

Pete turned back to the trunk and grabbed one of the bank envelopes. The flap wasn't sealed. He flipped it up with a finger that felt numb, even though the temperature now had to be riding right around forty. He squeezed the envelope open and looked inside.

Money.

Twenties and fifties.

"Holy Jesus God Christ in heaven," Pete Saubers whispered.

He pulled out the sheaf of bills and tried to count, but at first his hands were shaking too badly and he dropped some. They fluttered in the grass, and before he scrambled them up, his overheated brain assured him that Ulysses Grant had actually winked at him from one of the bills.

He counted. Four hundred dollars. Four hundred in this one envelope, and there were *dozens* of them.

He stuffed the bills back into the envelope—not an easy job, because now his hands were shaking worse than Grampa Fred's in the last year or two of his life. He flipped the envelope into the trunk and looked around, eyes wide and bulging. Traffic sounds that had always seemed faint and far and unimportant in this overgrown stretch of ground now sounded close and threatening. This was not Treasure Island; this was a city of over a million people, many now out of work, and they would love to have what was in this trunk.

Think, Pete Saubers told himself. *Think,* for God's sake. This is the most important thing that's ever happened to you, maybe the most important thing that ever *will* happen to you, so think hard and think right.

What came to mind first was Tina, snuggled up next to the wall in his bed. *What would you do if you found a treasure?* he had asked.

Give it to Daddy and Mommy, she had replied.

But suppose Mom wanted to give it back?

It was an important question. Dad never would—Pete knew that—but Mom was different. She had strong ideas about what was right and what wasn't. If he showed them this trunk and what was inside it, it might lead to the worst arkie-barkie about money ever.

"Besides, give it back to *who*?" Pete whispered. "The bank?"

That was ridiculous.

Or was it? Suppose the money really was pirate treasure, only from bank robbers instead of buccaneers? But then why was it in envelopes, like for withdrawals? And what about all those black notebooks?

He could consider such things later, but not now; what he had to do now was *act*. He looked at his watch and saw it was already quarter to eleven. He still had time, but he had to use it.

"Use it or lose it," he whispered, and began tossing the Granite State Bank cash envelopes into the cloth grocery bag that held the hammer and chisel. He placed the bag on top of the embankment and covered it with his jacket. He crammed the plastic wrap back into the trunk, closed the lid, and muscled the trunk back into the hole. He paused to wipe his forehead, which was greasy with dirt and sweat, then seized the spade and began to shovel like a maniac. He got the trunk covered—mostly—then seized the bag and his jacket and ran back along the path toward home. He would hide the bag in the back of his closet, that would do to start with, and see if there was a message from his mother on the answering machine. If everything was okay on the Mom front (and if Dad hadn't come home early from therapy—that would be horrible), he could whip back to the stream and do a better job of concealing the trunk. Later he might check out the notebooks, but as he made his way home on that sunny February morning, his only thought about them was that there might be more money envelopes mixed in with them. Or lying beneath them.

He thought, I'll have to take a shower. And clean the dirt out of the bathtub after, so she doesn't ask what I was doing outside when I was supposed to be sick. I have to be really careful, and I can't tell anyone. No one at all.

In the shower, he had an idea.

1978

Home is the place that when you go there, they have to take you in, but when Morris arrived at the house on Sycamore Street, there were no lights to brighten the evening gloom and no one to welcome him at the door. Why would there be? His mother was in New Jersey, lecturing about how a bunch of nineteenth-century businessmen had tried to steal America. Lecturing grad students who would probably go on to steal everything they could lay their hands on as they chased the Golden Buck. Some people would undoubtedly say that Morris had chased a few Golden Bucks of his own in New Hampshire, but that wasn't so. He hadn't gone there for money.

He wanted the Biscayne in the garage and out of sight. Hell, he wanted the Biscayne *gone*, but that would have to wait. His first priority was Pauline Muller. Most of the people on Sycamore Street were so wedded to their televisions once prime time started that they wouldn't have noticed a UFO if one landed on their lawn, but that wasn't true of Mrs. Muller; the Bellamys' next-door neighbor had raised snooping to a fine art. So he went there first.

"Why, look who it is!" she cried when she opened the door . . . just as if she hadn't been peering out her kitchen window when Morris pulled into the driveway. "Morrie Bellamy! Big as life and twice as handsome!"

Morris produced his best aw-shucks smile. "How you doin, Mrs. Muller?"

She gave him a hug which Morris could have done without but dutifully returned. Then she turned her head, setting her wattles in motion, and yelled, "Bert! *Bertie!* It's Morrie Bellamy!"

From the living room came a triple grunt that might have been *how ya doin*.

"Come in, Morrie! Come in! I'll put on coffee! And guess what?" She gave her unnaturally black eyebrows a horrifyingly flirtatious wiggle. "There's Sara Lee poundcake!"

"Sounds delicious, but I just got back from Boston. Drove straight through. I'm pretty beat. Just didn't want you to see lights next door and call the police."

She gave a monkey-shriek of laughter. "You're so *thoughtful*! But you always were. How's your mom, Morrie?"

"Fine."

He had no idea. Since his stint in reform school at seventeen and his failure to make a go of City College at twenty-one, relations between Morris and Anita Bellamy amounted to the occasional telephone call. These were frosty but civil. After one final argument the night of his arrest for breaking and entering and assorted other goodies, they had basically given up on each other.

"You've really put on some muscle," Mrs. Muller said. "The girls must love *that*. You used to be such a *scrawny* thing."

"Been building houses—"

"Building *houses*! *You!* Holy gosh! Bertie! *Morris has been building houses!*"

This produced a few more grunts from the living room.

"But then the work dried up, so I came back here. Mom said I was welcome to use the place unless she managed to rent it, but I probably won't stay long."

How right *that* turned out to be.

"Come in the living room, Morrie, and say hello to Bert."

"I better take a rain check." To forestall further importuning, he called, "*Yo, Bert!*"

Another grunt, unintelligible over the laugh track accompanying *Welcome Back, Kotter*.

"Tomorrow, then," Mrs. Muller said, her eyebrows once more waggling. She looked like she was doing a Groucho imitation. "I'll save the poundcake. I might even *whip* some *cream.*"

"Great," Morris said. It wasn't likely Mrs. Muller would die of a heart attack before tomorrow, but it was possible; as another great poet said, hope springs eternal in the human breast.

The keys to house and garage were where they'd always been, hanging under the eave to the right of the stoop. Morris garaged the Biscayne and set the trunk from the antiques barn on the concrete. He itched to get at that fourth Jimmy Gold novel right away, but the notebooks were all jumbled up, and besides, his eyes would cross before he read a single page of Rothstein's tiny handwriting; he really was bushed.

Tomorrow, he promised himself. *After I talk to Andy, get some idea of how he wants to handle this, I'll put them in order and start reading.*

He pushed the trunk under his father's old worktable and covered it with a swatch of plastic he found in the corner. Then he went inside and toured the old homestead. It looked pretty much the same, which was lousy. There was nothing in the fridge except a jar of pickles and a box of baking soda, but there were a few Hungry Man dinners in the freezer. He stuck one in the oven, turned the dial to 350, then climbed the stairs to his old bedroom.

I did it, he thought. *I made it. I'm sitting on eighteen years' worth of unpublished John Rothstein manuscripts.*

He was too tired to feel exultation, or even much pleasure. He almost fell asleep in the shower, and again over some really crappy meatloaf and instant potatoes. He shoveled it in, though, then trudged back up the stairs. He was asleep forty seconds after his head hit the pillow, and didn't wake up until nine twenty the following morning.

Well rested and with a bar of sunlight pouring across his childhood bed, Morris *did* feel exultation, and he couldn't wait to share it. Which meant Andy Halliday.

He found khakis and a nice madras shirt in his closet, slicked back his hair, and peeked briefly into the garage to make sure all was well there. He gave Mrs. Muller (once more looking out through the curtains) what he hoped was a jaunty wave as he headed down the street to the bus stop. He arrived downtown just before ten, walked a block, and peered down Ellis Avenue to the Happy Cup, where the outside tables sat under pink umbrellas. Sure enough, Andy was on his coffee break. Better yet, his back was turned, so Morris could approach undetected.

"*Booga-booga!*" he cried, grabbing the shoulder of Andy's old corduroy sportcoat.

His old friend—really his only friend in this benighted joke of a city—jumped and wheeled around. His coffee overturned and spilled. Morris stepped back. He had meant to startle Andy, but not *that* much.

"Hey, sor—"

"What did you *do?*" Andy asked in a low, grinding whisper. His eyes were blazing behind his glasses—hornrims Morris had always thought of as sort of an affectation. "What the fuck did you *do?*"

This was not the welcome Morris had anticipated. He sat down. "What we talked about." He studied Andy's face and saw none of the amused intellectual superiority his friend usually affected. Andy looked scared. Of Morris? Maybe. For himself? Almost certainly.

"I shouldn't be seen with y—"

Morris was carrying a brown paper bag he'd grabbed from the kitchen. From it he took one of Rothstein's notebooks and put it on the table, being careful to avoid the puddle of spilled coffee. "A sample. One of a great many. At least a hundred and fifty. I haven't had a chance to do a count yet, but it's the total jackpot."

"Put that away!" Andy was still whispering like a character in a bad spy movie. His eyes shifted from side to side, always returning to the notebook. "Rothstein's murder is on the front page of the *New York Times* and all over the TV, you idiot!"

This news came as a shock. It was supposed to be at least three days before anyone found the writer's body, maybe as long as six. Andy's reaction was even more of a shock. He looked like a cornered rat.

Morris flashed what he hoped was a fair approximation of Andy's I'm-so-smart-I-bore-myself smile. "Calm down. In this part of town there are kids carrying notebooks everywhere." He pointed across the street toward Government Square. "There goes one now."

"Not Moleskines, though! Jesus! The housekeeper knew the kind Rothstein used to write in, and the paper says the safe in his bedroom was open and empty! Put . . . it . . . *away*!"

Morrie pushed it toward Andy instead, still being careful to avoid the coffee stain. He was growing increasingly irritated with Andy—PO'd, as Jimmy Gold would have said—but he also felt a perverse sort of pleasure at watching the man cringe in his seat, as if the notebook were a vial filled with plague germs.

"Go on, have a look. This one's mostly poetry. I was paging through it on the bus—"

"On the *bus*? Are you *insane*?"

"—and it's not very good," Morris went on as if he hadn't heard, "but it's his, all right. A holograph manuscript. Extremely valuable. We talked about that. Several times. We talked about how—"

"Put it *away*!"

Morris didn't like to admit that Andy's paranoia was catching, but it sort of was. He returned the notebook to the bag and looked at his old friend (his *one* friend) sulkily. "It's not like I was suggesting we have a sidewalk sale, or anything."

"Where are the rest?" And before Morris could answer: "Never mind. I don't want to know. Don't you understand how hot those things are? How hot *you* are?"

"I'm not hot," Morris said, but he was, at least in the physical sense; all at once his cheeks and the nape of his neck were burning. Andy was acting as if he'd shit his pants instead of pulling off the crime of the century. "No one can connect me to Rothstein, and I *know* it'll be awhile before we can sell them to a private collector. I'm not stupid."

"Sell them to a col— Morrie, do you *hear* yourself?"

Morris crossed his arms and stared at his friend. The man who used to be his friend, at least. "You act as if we never talked about this. As if we never planned it."

"We didn't plan *anything*! It was a story we were telling ourselves, I thought you understood that!"

What Morris understood was Andy Halliday would tell the police exactly that if he, Morris, were caught. And Andy *expected* him to be caught. For the first time Morris realized consciously that Andy was no intellectual giant eager to join him in an existential act of outlawry but just another nebbish. A bookstore clerk only a few years older than Morris himself.

Don't give me your dumbass literary criticism, Rothstein had said to Morris in the last two minutes of his life. *You're a common thief, my friend.*

His temples began to throb.

"I should have known better. All your big talk about private collectors, movie stars and Saudi princes and I don't know who-all. Just a lot of big talk. You're nothing but a blowhard."

That was a hit, a palpable hit. Morris saw it and was glad, just as he had been when he had managed to stick it to his mother once or twice in their final argument.

Andy leaned forward, cheeks flushed, but before he could speak, a waitress appeared with a wad of napkins. "Let me get that spill," she said, and wiped it up. She was young, a natural ash-blonde, pretty in a pale way, maybe even beautiful. She smiled at Andy. He returned a pained grimace, at the same time drawing away from her as he had from the Moleskine notebook.

He's a homo, Morris thought wonderingly. He's a goddam homo. How come I didn't know that? How come I never saw? He might as well be wearing a sign.

Well, there were a lot of things about Andy he'd never seen, weren't there? Morris thought of something one of the guys on the housing job liked to say: *All pistol and no bullets.*

With the waitress gone, taking her toxic atmosphere of girl with her, Andy leaned forward again. "Those collectors are out there," he said. "They pile up paintings, sculpture, first editions . . . there's an oilman in Texas who's got a collection of early wax-cylinder recordings worth a million dollars, and another one who's got a complete run of every western, science fiction, and shudder-pulp magazine published between 1910 and 1955. Do you think all of that stuff was legitimately bought and sold? The fuck it was. Collectors are insane, the worst of them don't care if the things they covet were stolen or not, and they most assuredly do not want to share with the rest of the world."

Morris had heard this screed before, and his face must have shown it, because Andy leaned even farther forward. Now their noses were almost touching. Morris could smell English

Leather, and wondered if that was the preferred aftershave of homos. Like a secret sign, or something.

"But do you think any of those guys would listen to *me*?"

Morris Bellamy, who was now seeing Andy Halliday with new eyes, said he guessed not.

Andy pooched out his lower lip. "They will someday, though. Yeah. Once I get my own shop and build up a clientele. But that'll take *years*."

"We talked about waiting five."

"*Five?*" Andy barked a laugh and drew back to his side of the table again. "I might be able to open my *shop* in five years—I've got my eye on a little place in Lacemaker Lane, there's a fabric store there now but it doesn't do much business—but it takes longer than that to find big-money clients and establish trust."

Lots of buts, Morris thought, but there were no buts before.

"How long?"

"Why don't you try me on those notebooks around the turn of the twenty-first century, if you still have them? Even if I *did* have a call list of private collectors right now, today, not even the nuttiest of them would touch anything so hot."

Morris stared at him, at first unable to speak. At last he said, "You never said anything like *that* when we were planning—"

Andy clapped his hands to the sides of his head and clutched it. "We planned *nothing*! And don't you try to lay this off on me! Don't you ever! I know you, Morrie. You didn't steal them to sell them, at least not until you've read them. Then I suppose you might be willing to give some of them to the world, if the price was right. Basically, though, you're just batshit-crazy on the subject of John Rothstein."

"Don't call me that." His temples were throbbing worse than ever.

"I will if it's the truth, and it is. You're batshit-crazy on the subject of Jimmy Gold, too. He's why you went to jail."

"I went to jail because of my mother. She might as well have locked me up herself."

"Whatever. It's water under the bridge. This is now. Unless you're lucky, the police are going to be paying you a visit very soon, and they'll probably arrive with a search warrant. If you have those notebooks when they knock on your door, your goose will be cooked."

"Why would they come to me? Nobody saw us, and my partners . . ." He winked. "Let's just say that dead men tell no tales."

"You . . . what? *Killed* them? Killed them, *too*?" Andy's face was a picture of dawning horror.

Morris knew he shouldn't have said that, but—funny how that *but* kept coming around—Andy was just being such an asshole.

"What's the name of the town that Rothstein lived in?" Andy's eyes were shifting around again, as if he expected the cops to be closing in even now, guns drawn. "Talbot Corners, right?"

"Yes, but it's mostly farms. What they call the Corners is nothing but a diner, a grocery store, and a gas station where two state roads cross."

"How many times were you there?"

"Maybe five." It had actually been closer to a dozen, between 1976 and 1978. Alone at first, then with either Freddy or Curtis or both.

"Ever ask questions about the town's most famous resident while you were there?"

"Sure, once or twice. So what? Probably everybody who ever stops at that diner asks about—"

"No, that's where you're wrong. Most out-of-towners don't give a shit about John Rothstein. If they've got questions, it's about when deer season starts or what kind of fish they could catch in the local lake. You don't think the locals will remember you when the police ask if there have been any strangers curious about the guy who wrote *The Runner*? Curious strangers who made repeat visits? Plus you have a *record*, Morrie!"

"Juvenile. It's sealed."

"Something as big as this, the seal might not hold. And what about your partners? Did either of *them* have records?"

Morris said nothing.

"You don't know who saw you, and you don't know who your partners might have bragged to about the big robbery they were going to pull off. The police could nail you *today*, you idiot. If they do and you bring my name up, I'll deny we ever talked about this. But I'll give you some advice. Get rid of *that*." He was pointing to the brown paper bag. "That and all the rest of the notebooks. Hide them somewhere. Bury them! If you do that, maybe you can talk your way out of it, if push comes to shove. Always supposing you didn't leave fingerprints, or something."

We didn't, Morris thought. I wasn't stupid. And I'm not a cowardly big-talking homo, either.

"Maybe we can revisit this," Andy said, "but it will be much later on, and only if they don't grab you." He got up. "In the meantime, stay clear of me, or I'll call the police myself."

He walked away fast with his head down, not looking back.

Morris sat there. The pretty waitress returned to ask if she could get him anything. Morris shook his head. When she left, he picked up the bag with the notebook inside it and walked away himself. In the opposite direction.

He knew what the pathetic fallacy was, of course—nature echoing the feelings of human beings—and understood it to be the cheap, mood-creating trick of second-rate writers, but that day it seemed to be true. The morning's bright sunlight had both mirrored and amplified his feeling of exultation, but by noon the sun was only a dim circle behind a blear of clouds, and by three o'clock that afternoon, as his worries multiplied, the day grew dark and it began to drizzle.

He drove the Biscayne out to the mall near the airport, constantly watching for police cars. When one came roaring up behind him on Airline Boulevard with its blues flashing, his stomach froze and his heart seemed to climb all the way into his mouth. When it sped by without slowing, he felt no relief.

He found a news broadcast on BAM-100. The lead story was about a peace conference between Sadat and Begin at Camp David (Yeah, like *that'll* ever happen, Morris thought distractedly), but the second one concerned the murder of noted American writer John Rothstein. Police were saying it was the work of "a gang of thieves," and that a number of leads were being followed. That was probably just PR bullshit.

Or maybe not.

Morris didn't think he could be tracked down as a result of interviews with the half-deaf old codgers who hung out at the Yummy Diner in Talbot Corners, no matter what Andy thought, but there was something else that troubled him far more. He, Freddy, and Curtis had all worked for Donahue Construction, which was building homes in both Danvers and North Beverly. There were two different work crews, and for most of Morris's sixteen months, spent carrying boards and nailing studs, he had been in Danvers while Curtis and Freddy toiled at the other site, five miles away. Yet for awhile they *had* worked on the same crew, and even after they were split up, they usually managed to eat lunch together.

Plenty of people knew this.

He parked the Biscayne with about a thousand others at the JC Penney end of the mall, wiped down every surface he had touched, and left the keys in the ignition. He walked away fast, turning up his collar and yanking down his Indians cap. At the mall's main entrance, he waited on a bench until a Northfield bus came, and dropped his fifty cents into the box. The rain grew heavier and the ride back was slow, but he didn't mind. It gave him time to think.

Andy was cowardly and full of himself, but he had been right about one thing. Morris had to hide the notebooks, and he had to do so immediately, no matter how much he wanted to read them, starting with that undiscovered Jimmy Gold novel. If the cops *did* come and he didn't have the notebooks, they could do nothing . . . right? All they'd have would be suspicion.

Right?

There was no one peeking through the curtains next door, which saved him another conversation with Mrs. Muller, and perhaps having to explain that he had sold his car. The rain had become a downpour, and that was good. There would be no one rambling around in the undeveloped land between Sycamore and Birch. Especially after dark.

He pulled everything out of the secondhand trunk, resisting an almost overpowering urge to look into the notebooks. He couldn't do that, no matter how much he wanted to, because once he started, he wouldn't be able to stop. Later, he thought. *Must postpone your gratifications, Morrie.* Good advice, but spoken in his mother's voice, and that started his head throbbing again. At least he wouldn't have to postpone his gratifications for long; if three weeks went by with no visits from the police—a month at most—he would be able to relax and begin his researches.

He lined the trunk with plastic to make sure the contents would stay dry, and put the notebooks, including the one he'd taken to show Andy, back inside. He dumped the money envelopes on top. He closed the trunk, considered, and opened it again. He pawed the plastic aside and took a couple of hundred dollars from one of the bank envelopes. Surely no cop would think that an excessive amount, even if he were searched. He could tell them it was his severance pay, or something.

The sound of the rain on the garage roof was not soothing. To Morris it sounded like skeletal tapping fingers, and made his headache worse. He froze every time a car went by, waiting for headlights and pulsing blue strobes to splash up the driveway. Fuck Andy Halliday for putting all these pointless worries in my head, he thought. Fuck him and the homo horse he rode in on.

Only the worries might not be pointless. As afternoon wound down toward twilight, the idea that the cops could put Curtis and Freddy together with Morris Bellamy seemed more and more likely. That fucking rest area! Why hadn't he dragged the bodies into the woods, at least? Not that it would have slowed the cops down much once someone pulled in, saw all the blood, and called 911. The cops would have dogs . . .

"Besides," he told the trunk, "I was in a hurry. Wasn't I?"

His father's hand dolly was still standing in the corner, along with a rusty pick and two rusty shovels. Morris tipped the trunk endwise onto the dolly, secured the straps, and peered out of the garage window. Still too much light. Now that he was so close to getting rid of the notebooks and the money—Temporarily, he soothed himself, this is just a temporary measure—he became more and more sure that the cops would be here soon. Suppose Mrs. Muller had reported him as acting suspicious? It didn't seem likely, she was thicker than an oak plank, but who really knew?

He forced himself to stuff down another frozen dinner, thinking it might soothe his head. It made the headache worse, instead. He looked in his mother's medicine cabinet for aspirin or Advil, and found . . . nothing. Fuck you, Mom, he thought. Really. Sincerely. Fuck . . . *you*.

He saw her smile. Thin as a hook, that smile.

It was still light at seven o'clock—goddam daylight saving time, what genius thought *that* up?—but the windows next door were still dark. That was good, but Morris knew the Mullers might be back at any time. Besides, he was too nervous to wait any longer. He rooted around in the front hall closet until he found a poncho.

He used the garage's rear door and yanked the dolly across the back lawn. The grass was wet, the ground underneath spongy, and it was hard going. The path he had used so many times as a kid—usually going to the Birch Street Rec—was sheltered by overhanging trees, and he was able to make better progress. By the time he got to the little stream that flowed diagonally across this block-sized square of waste ground, full dark had arrived.

He had brought a flashlight and used it in brief winks to pick out a likely location on the embankment of the stream, a safe distance from the path. The dirt was soft, and it was easy digging until he got to the tangle of roots from an overhanging tree. He thought about trying a different spot, but the hole was almost big enough for the trunk already, and he was damned if he was going to start all over again, especially when this was just a temporary precaution. He laid the flashlight in the hole, propping it on a rock so the beam shone on the roots, and chopped through them with the pick.

He slid the trunk into the hole and shoveled the dirt back around it and over it quickly. He finished by tamping it down with the flat of the shovel. He thought it would be okay. The bank wasn't particularly grassy, so the bald spot wouldn't stand out. The important thing was that it was out of the house, right?

Right?

He felt no relief as he dragged the dolly back along the path. Nothing was working out the way it was supposed to, nothing.

It was as if malignant fate had come between him and the note-books, just as fate had come between Romeo and Juliet. That comparison seemed both ludicrous and perfectly apt. He *was* a lover. Goddam Rothstein had jilted him with *The Runner Slows Down*, but that didn't change the fact.

His love was true.

When he got back to the house, he went immediately to the shower, as a boy named Pete Saubers would do many years later in this very same bathroom, after visiting that very same embankment and overhanging tree. Morris stayed in until his fingers were pruney and the hot water was gone, then dried off and dressed in fresh clothes from his bedroom closet. They looked childish and out of fashion to him, but they still fit (more or less). He put his dirt-smeared jeans and sweatshirt in the washer, an act that would also be replicated by Pete Saubers years later.

Morris turned on the TV, sat in his father's old easy chair—his mother said she kept it as a reminder, should she ever be tempted into stupidity again—and saw the usual helping of ad-driven inanity. He thought that any of those ads (jumping laxative bottles, primping moms, singing hamburgers) could have been written by Jimmy Gold, and that made his head-ache worse than ever. He decided to go down to Zoney's and get some Anacin. Maybe even a beer or two. Beer wouldn't hurt. It was the hard stuff that caused trouble, and he'd learned his lesson on that score.

He did get the Anacin, but the idea of drinking beer in a house full of books he didn't want to read and TV he didn't want to watch made him feel worse than ever. Especially when the stuff he *did* want to read was so maddeningly close. Morris rarely drank in bars, but all at once he felt that if he didn't get out and find some company and hear some fast music, he would go completely insane. Somewhere out in this rainy night, he was sure there was a young lady who wanted to dance.

He paid for his aspirin and asked the young guy at the register, almost idly, if there was a bar with live music that he could get to on the bus.

The young guy said there was.

2010

When Linda Saubers got home that Friday afternoon at three thirty, Pete was sitting at the kitchen table drinking a cup of cocoa. His hair was still damp from the shower. She hung her coat on one of the hooks by the back door, and placed the inside of her wrist against his forehead again. "Cool as a cucumber," she pronounced. "Do you feel better?"

"Yeah," he said. "When Tina came home, I made her peanut butter crackers."

"You're a good brother. Where is she now?"

"Ellen's, where else?"

Linda rolled her eyes and Pete laughed.

"Mother of Mercy, is that the dryer I hear?"

"Yeah. There were a bunch of clothes in the basket, so I washed em. Don't worry, I followed the directions on the door, and they came out okay."

She bent down and kissed his temple. "Aren't you the little do-bee?"

"I try," Pete said. He closed his right hand to hide the blister on his palm.

The first envelope came on a snow-showery Thursday not quite a week later. The address—Mr. Thomas Saubers, 23 Sycamore Street—was typed. Stuck on the upper-right-hand corner was a forty-four-cent stamp featuring the Year of The Tiger. There was no return address on the upper left. Tom—the only member of Clan Saubers home at midday—tore it open in the hall, expecting either some sort of come-on or another past due notice. God knew there had been plenty of those lately. But it wasn't a come-on, and it wasn't a past due.

It was money.

The rest of the mail—catalogues for expensive stuff they couldn't afford and advertising circulars addressed to OCCUPANT—fell from his hand and fluttered around his feet, unnoticed. In a low voice, almost a growl, Tom Saubers said, "What the *fuck* is *this*?"

When Linda came home, the money was sitting in the middle of the kitchen table. Tom was seated before the neat little pile with his chin resting on his folded hands. He looked like a general considering a battle plan.

"What's that?" Linda asked.

"Five hundred dollars." He continued to look at the bills— eight fifties and five twenties. "It came in the mail."

"From who?"

"I don't know."

She dropped her briefcase, came to the table, and picked up the stack of currency. She counted it, then looked at him with wide eyes. "My God, Tommy! What did the letter say?"

"There was no letter. Just the money."

"But who would—"

"I don't know, Lin. But I know one thing."

"What?"

"We can sure use it."

"Holy shit," Pete said when they told him. He had stayed late at school for intramural volleyball, and didn't come in until almost dinnertime.

"Don't be vulgar," Linda said, sounding distracted. The money was still on the kitchen table.

"How much?" And when his father told him: "Who sent it?"

"That's a good question," Tom said. "Now for Double Jeopardy, where the scores can really change." It was the first joke Pete had heard him make in a very long time.

Tina came in. "Daddy's got a fairy godmother, that's what I think. Hey, Dad, Mom! Look at my fingernails! Ellen got sparkle polish, and she shared."

"Excellent look for you, my little punkin," Tom said.

First a joke, then a compliment. Those things were all it took to convince Pete that he had done the right thing. *Totally* the right thing. They couldn't exactly send it back, could they? Not without a return address, they couldn't. And by the way, when was the last time Dad had called Teens his little punkin?

Linda gave her son a piercing look. "*You* don't know anything about this, do you?"

"Uh-uh, but can I have some?"

"Dream on," she said, and turned to her husband, hands on hips. "Tom, someone's obviously made a mistake."

Tom considered this, and when he spoke, there was no arking and barking. His voice was calm. "That doesn't seem likely." He pushed the envelope toward her, tapping his name and address.

"Yes, but—"

"But me no buts, Lin. We owe the oil company, and before we pay them, we have to pay down your MasterCard. Or you're going to lose it."

"Yes, but—"

"Lose the credit card, lose your credit rating." Still not arking and barking. Calm and reasonable. Persuasive. To Pete it was as if his father had been suffering from a high fever that had just broken. He even smiled. Smiled and touched her hand. "It so happens that for now, your credit rating is the only one we've got, so we have to protect it. Besides, Tina could be right. Maybe I've got a fairy godmother."

No, Pete thought. A fairy god*son* is what you've got.

Tina said, "Oh, wait! I know where it *really* came from."

They turned to her. Pete felt suddenly warm all over. She couldn't know, could she? *How* could she? Only he'd said that stupid thing about buried treasure, and—

"Where, hon?" Linda asked.

"The Emergency Fund thingy. It must have got some more money, and now they're spreading it out."

Pete let out a soundless breath of air, only realizing as it passed his lips that he had been holding it.

Tom ruffled her hair. "They wouldn't send cash, punkin. They'd send a check. Also a bunch of forms to sign."

Pete went to the stove. "I'm making more cocoa. Does anyone want some?"

Turned out they all did.

The envelopes kept coming.

The price of postage went up, but the amount never changed. An extra six thousand dollars per annum, give or take. Not a huge sum, but tax-free and just enough to keep the Saubers family from drowning in debt.

The children were forbidden to tell anyone.

"Tina will never be able to keep it to herself," Linda told Tom one night. "You know that, don't you? She'll tell her idiot friend, and Ellen Briggs will broadcast it to everyone she knows."

But Tina kept the secret, partly because her brother, whom she idolized, told her she would never be allowed in his room again if she spilled the beans, and mostly because she remembered the arkie-barkies.

Pete stowed the cash envelopes in the cobweb-festooned hollow behind a loose baseboard in his closet. Once every four weeks or so, he took out five hundred dollars and put it in his backpack along with an addressed envelope, one of several dozen he had prepared at school on a computer in the school's Business Ed room. He did the envelopes after intramurals one late afternoon when the room was empty.

He used a variety of city mailboxes to send them on their way to Mr. Thomas Saubers of 23 Sycamore Street, going about this family-sustaining charity with the craft of a master criminal. He was always afraid that his mom would discover what he was up to, object (probably strenuously), and things would go back to the way they had been. Things weren't perfect now, there was still the occasional arkie-barkie, but he supposed things weren't perfect in any family outside those old TV sitcoms on Nick at Nite.

They could watch Nick at Nite, and Cartoon Network, and MTV, and everything else, because, ladies and gentlemen, the cable was *back*.

In May, another good thing happened: Dad got a part-time job with a new real estate company, as something called a "pre-sell investigator." Pete didn't know what that was, and didn't give Shit One. Dad could do it on his phone and the home computer, it brought in a little money, and those were the things that mattered.

Two other things mattered in the months after the money started coming in. Dad's legs were getting better, that was one thing. In June of 2010 (when the perpetrator of the so-called City Center Massacre was finally caught), Tom began walking without his crutches some of the time, and he also began stepping down on the pink pills. The other thing was more difficult to explain, but Pete knew it was there. So did Tina. Dad and Mom felt . . . well . . . *blessed*, and now when they argued they looked guilty as well as mad, as if they were shitting on the mysterious good fortune that had befallen them. Often they would stop and talk about other things before the shit got deep. Often it was the money they talked about, and who could be sending it. These discussions came to nothing, and that was good.

I will not be caught, Pete told himself. I must not, and I will not.

One day in August of that year, Dad and Mom took Tina and Ellen to a petting zoo called Happydale Farm. This was the opportunity Pete had been patiently waiting for, and as soon as they were gone, he went back to the stream with two suitcases.

After making sure the coast was clear, he dug the trunk out of the embankment again and loaded the notebooks into the suitcases. He reburied the trunk and then went back to the house with his booty. In the upstairs hall, he pulled down the ladder and carried the suitcases up to the attic. This was a small, low space, chilly in winter and stifling in summer. The family rarely used it; their extra stuff was still stored in the garage. The few relics up here were probably left over from one of the previous families that had owned 23 Sycamore. There was a dirty baby carriage listing on one wheel, a standing lamp with tropical birds on the shade, old issues of *Redbook* and *Good Housekeeping* tied up with twine, a pile of moldy blankets that smelled like yuck.

Pete piled the notebooks in the farthest corner and covered them with the blankets, but first he grabbed one at random, sat under one of the attic's two hanging lightbulbs, and opened it. The writing was cursive and quite small, but carefully made and easy to read. There were no cross-outs, which Pete thought remarkable. Although he was looking at the first page of the notebook, the small circled number at the top was 482, making him think that this was continued not just from one of the other notebooks, but from half a dozen. Half a dozen, at least.

Chapter 27

The back room of the Drover was the same as it had been five years before; the same smell of ancient beer mingled with the stink of the stockyards and the tang of diesel from the trucking depots that fronted this half of Nebraska's great emptiness. Stew Logan looked the same, too. Here was the same white apron, the same suspiciously black hair, even the same parrots-and-macaws necktie strangling his rosy neck.

"Why, it's Jimmy Gold, as I live and breathe," he said, and smiled in his old dislikeable way that said we don't care for each other, but let's pretend. "Have you come to pay me what you owe, then?"

"I have," Jimmy said, and touched his back pocket where the pistol rested. It felt small and final, a thing capable—if used correctly, and with courage—of paying all debts.

"Then step in," Logan said. "Have a drink. You look dusty."

"I am," Jimmy said, "and along with a drink I could use

A horn honked on the street. Pete jumped and looked around guiltily, as if he had been whacking off instead of reading. What if they'd come home early because that doofus Ellen had gotten carsick, or something? What if they found him up here with the notebooks? Everything could fall apart.

He shoved the one he had been reading under the old blankets (phew, they stank) and crawled back to the trapdoor, sparing a glance for the suitcases. No time for them. Going down the ladder, the change in temperature from boiling hot to August-normal made him shiver. Pete folded the ladder and shoved it up, wincing at the screek and bang the trapdoor made when it snapped shut on its rusty spring.

He went into his bedroom and peered out at the driveway.

Nobody there. False alarm.

Thank God.

He returned to the attic and retrieved the suitcases. He put them back in the downstairs closet, took a shower (once more remembering to clean up the tub afterwards), then dressed in clean clothes and lay down on his bed.

He thought, It's a novel. With that many pages, it's pretty much got to be. And there might be more than one, because no single novel's long enough to fill all those books. Not even the Bible would fill all those books.

Also . . . it was interesting. He wouldn't mind hunting through the notebooks and finding the one where it started. Seeing if it really was good. Because you couldn't tell if a novel was good from just a single page, could you?

Pete closed his eyes and began to drift napward. Ordinarily he wasn't much of a day-sleeper, but it had been a busy morning, the house was empty and quiet, and he decided to let himself go. Why not? Everything was right, at least right now, and that was his doing. He deserved a nap.

That name, though—Jimmy Gold.

Pete could swear he'd heard it before. In class, maybe? Mrs. Swidrowski giving them background on one of the authors they were reading? Maybe. She liked to do that.

Maybe I'll google it later on, Pete thought. I could do that. I could . . .

He slept.

1978

Morris sat on a steel bunk with his throbbing head lowered and his hands dangling between his orange-clad thighs, breathing in a poison atmosphere of piss, puke, and disinfectant. His stomach was a lead ball that seemed to have expanded until it filled him from crotch to Adam's apple. His eyes pulsed in their sockets. His mouth tasted like a dumpster. His gut ached and his face hurt. His sinuses were stuffed. Somewhere a hoarse and despairing voice was chanting, "I need a lover that won't drive me *cray-zee*, I need a lover that won't drive me *cray-zee*, I need a lover that won't drive me *cray-zee* . . ."

"Shut up!" someone shouted. "You're drivin *me* crazy, asshole!"

A pause. Then:

"I need a lover that won't drive me *cray-zee*!"

The lead in Morris's belly liquefied and gurgled. He slid off the bunk, landed on his knees (provoking a fresh bolt of agony in his head), and hung his gaping mouth over the functional steel toilet. For a moment there was nothing. Then everything clenched and he ejected what looked like two gallons of yellow toothpaste. For a moment the pain in his head was so huge that he thought it would simply explode, and in that moment Morris hoped it would. Anything to end the pain.

Instead of dying, he threw up again. A pint instead of a

gallon this time, but it *burned*. The next one was a dry heave. Wait, not completely dry; thick strings of mucus hung from his lips like cobwebs, swinging back and forth. He had to brush them away.

"Somebody's *feelin* it!" a voice shouted.

Shouts and cackles of laughter greeted this sally. To Morris it sounded as if he were locked up in a zoo, and he supposed he was, only this was the kind where the cages held humans. The orange jumpsuit he was wearing proved it.

How had he gotten here?

He couldn't remember, any more than he could remember how he'd gotten into the house he'd trashed in Sugar Heights. What he *could* remember was his own house, on Sycamore Street. And the trunk, of course. Burying the trunk. There had been money in his pocket, two hundred dollars of John Rothstein's money, and he had gone down to Zoney's to get a couple of beers because his head ached and he was feeling lonely. He had talked to the clerk, he was pretty sure of that, but he couldn't remember what they had discussed. Baseball? Probably not. He had a Groundhogs cap, but that was as far as his interest went. After that, almost nothing. All he could be sure of was that something had gone horribly wrong. When you woke up wearing an orange jumpsuit, that was an easy deduction to make.

He crawled back to the bunk, pulled himself up, drew his knees to his chest, and clasped his hands around them. It was cold in the cell. He began to shiver.

I might have asked that clerk what his favorite bar was. One I could get to on the bus. And I went there, didn't I? Went there and got drunk. In spite of all I know about what it does to me. Not just a little loaded, either—standing-up, falling-down shitfaced drunk.

Oh yes, undoubtedly, in spite of all he knew. Which was bad, but he couldn't remember the crazy things afterwards, and that was worse. After the third drink (sometimes only second), he fell down a dark hole and didn't climb back out until he woke up hungover but sober. Blackout drinking was what they called it. And in those blackouts, he almost always got up to . . . well, call it hijinks. Hijinks was how he'd ended up in Riverview Youth Detention, and doubtless how he'd ended up here. Wherever *here* was.

Hijinks.

Fucking hijinks.

Morris hoped it had been a good old-fashioned bar fight and not more breaking and entering. Not a repeat of his Sugar Heights adventure, in other words. Because he was well past his teenage years now and it wouldn't be the reformatory this time, no sir. Still, he would do the time if he had done the crime. Just as long as the crime had nothing to do with the murder of a certain genius American writer, please God. If it did, he would not be breathing free air again for a long time. Maybe never. Because it wasn't just Rothstein, was it? And now a memory *did* arise: Curtis Rogers asking if New Hampshire had the death penalty.

Morris lay on the bunk, shivering, thinking, That can't be why I'm here. It *can't*.

Can it?

He had to admit that it was possible, and not just because the police might have put him together with the dead men in the rest area. He could see himself in a bar or a stripjoint somewhere, Morris Bellamy, the college dropout and self-proclaimed American lit scholar, tossing back bourbon and having an out-of-body experience. Someone starts talking about the murder of John Rothstein, the great writer, the reclusive American *genius*, and Morris Bellamy—drunk off his tits and full of that huge anger he usually kept locked in a cage, that black beast with the yellow eyes—turning to the speaker and saying, He didn't look much like a genius when I blew his head off.

"I would *never*," he whispered. His head was aching worse than ever, and there was something wrong on the left side of his face, too. It *burned*. "I would *never*."

Only how did he know that? When he drank, any day was Anything Can Happen Day. The black beast came out. As a teenager the beast had rampaged through that house in Sugar Heights, tearing the motherfucker pretty much to shreds, and when the cops responded to the silent alarm he had fought them until one belted him unconscious with his nightstick, and when they searched him they found a shitload of jewelry in his pockets, much of it of the costume variety but some, carelessly left out of madame's safe, extraordinarily valuable, and howdy-do, off we go to Riverview, where we will get our tender young buttsky reamed and make exciting new friends.

He thought, The person who put on a shit-show like that is perfectly capable of boasting while drunk about murdering Jimmy Gold's creator, and you know it.

Although it could have been the cops, too. If they had ID'd him and put out an APB. That was just as likely.

"I need a lover who won't drive me *cray-zee!*"

"Shut up!" This time it was Morris himself, and he tried to yell it, but what came out was nothing but a puke-clotted croak. Oh, his head hurt. And his *face*, yow. He ran a hand up his left cheek and stared stupidly at the flakes of dried blood in his palm. He explored again and felt scratches there, at least three of them. Fingernail scratches, and deep. What does that tell us, class? Well, ordinarily—although there are exceptions to every rule—men punch and women scratch. The ladies do it with their nails because more often than not they have nice long ones to scratch with.

Did I try to slap the make on some twist, and she refused me with her nails?

Morris tried to remember and couldn't. He remembered the rain, the poncho, and the flashlight shining on the roots.

He remembered the pick. He *sort* of remembered wanting to hear fast loud music and talking to the clerk at Zoney's Go-Mart. After that? Just darkness.

He thought, Maybe it was the car. That damn Biscayne. Maybe somebody saw it coming out of the rest area on Route 92 with the front end all bloody on the right, and maybe I left something in the glove compartment. Something with my name on it.

But that didn't seem likely. Freddy had purchased the Chevy from a half-drunk bar-bitch in a Lynn taproom, paying with money the three of them had pooled. She had signed over the pink to Harold Fineman, which happened to be the name of Jimmy Gold's best friend in *The Runner*. She had never seen Morris Bellamy, who knew enough to stay out of sight while that particular deal went down. Besides, Morris had done everything but soap PLEASE STEAL ME on the windshield when he left it at the mall. No, the Biscayne was now sitting in a vacant lot somewhere, either in Lowtown or down by the lake, stripped to the axles.

So how did I wind up here? Back to that, like a rat running on a wheel. If some woman marked my face with her nails, did I haul off on her? Maybe break her jaw?

That rang a faint bell behind the blackout curtains. If it were so, then he was probably going to be charged with assault, and he might go up to Waynesville for it; a ride in the big green bus with the wire mesh on the windows. Waynesville would be bad, but he could do a few years for assault if he had to. Assault was not murder.

Please don't let it be Rothstein, he thought. I've got a lot of reading to do, it's stashed away all safe and waiting. The beauty part is I've got money to support myself with while I do it, more than twenty thousand dollars in unmarked twenties and fifties. That will last quite awhile, if I live small. So please don't let it be murder.

"I need a lover who won't drive me *cray-zee*!"

"One more time, motherfucker!" someone shouted. "One more time and I'll pull your asshole right out through your mouth!"

Morris closed his eyes.

Although he was feeling better by noon, he refused the slop that passed for lunch: noodles floating in what appeared to be blood sauce. Then, around two o'clock, a quartet of guards came down the aisle between the cells. One had a clipboard and was shouting names.

"Bellamy! Holloway! McGiver! Riley! Roosevelt! Titgarden! Step forward!"

"That's *Tea*garden, sir," said the large black man in the box next to Morris's.

"I don't give a shit if it's John Q. Motherfucker. If you want to talk to your court-appointed, step forward. If you don't, sit there and stack more time."

The half dozen named prisoners stepped forward. They were the last ones left, at least in this corridor. The others brought in the previous night (mercifully including the fellow who had been butchering John Mellencamp) had either been released or taken to court for the morning arraignment. They were the small fry. Afternoon arraignments, Morris knew, were for more serious shit. He had been arraigned in the afternoon after his little adventure in Sugar Heights. Judge Bukowski, that cunt.

Morris prayed to a God he did not believe in as the door of his holding cell snapped back. Assault, God, okay? Simple, not ag. Just not murder. God, let them know nothing about what went down in New Hampshire, or at a certain rest area in upstate New York, okay? That okay with you?

"Step out, boys," the guard with the clipboard said. "Step out and face right. Arm's length from the upstanding American in front of you. No wedgies and no reach-arounds. Don't fuck with us and we will return the favor."

They went down in an elevator big enough to hold a small herd of cattle, then along another corridor, and then—God knew why, they were wearing sandals and the jumpsuits had no pockets—through a metal detector. Beyond that was a visitor's room with eight walled booths like library carrels. The guard with the clipboard directed Morris to number 3. Morris sat down and faced his court-appointed through Plexiglas that had been smeared often and wiped seldom. The guy on the freedom side was a nerd with a bad haircut and a dandruff problem. He had a coldsore below one nostril and a scuffed briefcase sitting on his lap. He looked like he might be all of nineteen.

This is what I get, Morris thought. Oh Jesus, this is what I get.

The lawyer pointed to the phone on the wall of Morris's booth, and opened his briefcase. From it he removed a single sheet of paper and the inevitable yellow legal pad. Once these were on the counter in front of him, he put his briefcase on the floor and picked up his own phone. He spoke not in the tentative tenor of your usual adolescent, but in a confident, husky baritone that seemed far too big for the chicken chest lurking behind the purple rag of his tie.

"You're in deep shit, Mr."—he looked at the sheet lying on top of his legal pad—"Bellamy. You must prepare for a very long stay in the state penitentiary, I think. Unless you have something to trade, that is."

Morris thought, He's talking about trading the notebooks.

Coldness went marching up his arms like the feet of evil fairies. If they had him for Rothstein, they had him for Curtis and Freddy. That meant life with no possibility of parole. He would never be able to retrieve the trunk, never find out Jimmy Gold's ultimate fate.

"Speak," the lawyer said, as if talking to a dog.

"Then tell me who I'm speaking to."

"Elmer Cafferty, temporarily at your service. You're going to be arraigned in . . ." He looked at his watch, a Timex even cheaper than his suit. "Thirty minutes. Judge Bukowski is very prompt."

A bolt of pain that had nothing to do with his hangover went through Morris's head. "No! Not her! It can't be! That bitch came over on the Ark!"

Cafferty smiled. "I deduce you've had doings with the Great Bukowski before."

"Check your file," Morris said dully. Although it probably wasn't there. The Sugar Heights thing would be under seal, as he had told Andy.

Fucking Andy Halliday. This is more his fault than mine.

"Homo."

Cafferty frowned. "*What* did you say?"

"Nothing. Go on."

"My *file* consists of last night's arrest report. The good news is that your fate will be in some other judge's hands when you come to trial. The better news, for me, at least, is that by that point, someone else will be representing you. My wife and I are moving to Denver and you, Mr. Bellamy, will be just a memory."

Denver or hell, it made no difference to Morris. "Tell me what I'm charged with."

"You don't remember?"

"I was in a blackout."

"Is that so."

"It actually is," Morris said.

Maybe he *could* trade the notebooks, although it hurt him to even consider it. But even if he made the offer—or if Cafferty made it—would a prosecutor grasp the importance of what was in them? It didn't seem likely. Lawyers weren't scholars.

A prosecutor's idea of great literature would probably be Erle Stanley Gardner. Even if the notebooks—all those beautiful Moleskines—did matter to the state's legal rep, what would he, Morris, gain by turning them over? One life sentence instead of three? Whoopee-ding.

I can't, no matter what. I *won't*.

Andy Halliday might have been an English Leather–wearing homo, but he had been right about Morris's motivation. Curtis and Freddy had been in it for cash; when Morris assured them the old guy might have squirreled away as much as a hundred thousand, they had believed him. Rothstein's writings? To those two bumblefucks, the value of Rothstein's output since 1960 was just a misty maybe, like a lost goldmine. It was Morris who cared about the writing. If things had gone differently, he would have offered to trade Curtis and Freddy his share of the money for the written words, and he was sure they would have taken him up on it. If he gave that up now—especially when the notebooks contained the continuation of the Jimmy Gold saga—it would all have been for nothing.

Cafferty rapped his phone on the Plexi, then put it back to his ear. "Cafferty to Bellamy, Cafferty to Bellamy, come in, Bellamy."

"Sorry. I was thinking."

"A little late for that, wouldn't you say? Try to stick with me, if you please. You'll be arraigned on three counts. Your mission, should you choose to accept it, is to plead not guilty to each in turn. Later, when you go to trial, you can change to guilty, should it prove to your advantage to do so. Don't even think about bail, because Bukowski doesn't laugh; she cackles like Witch Hazel."

Morris thought, This is a case of worst fears realized. Rothstein, Dow, and Rogers. Three counts of Murder One.

"Mr. Bellamy? Our time is fleeting, and I'm losing patience."

The phone sagged away from his ear and Morris brought it

back with an effort. Nothing mattered now, and still the lawyer with the guileless Richie Cunningham face and the weird middle-aged baritone voice kept pouring words into his ear, and at some point they began to make sense.

"They'll work up the ladder, Mr. Bellamy, from first to worst. Count one, resisting arrest. For arraignment purposes, you plead not guilty. Count two, aggravated assault—not just the woman, you also got one good one in on the first-responding cop before he cuffed you. You plead not guilty. Count three, aggravated rape. They may add attempted murder later, but right now it's just rape . . . if rape can be called just anything, I suppose. You plead—"

"Wait a minute," Morris said. He touched the scratches on his cheek, and what he felt was . . . hope. "I *raped* somebody?"

"Indeed you did," Cafferty said, sounding pleased. Probably because his client finally seemed to be following him. "After Miss Cora Ann Hooper . . ." He took a sheet of paper from his briefcase and consulted it. "This was shortly after she left the diner where she works as a waitress. She was heading for a bus stop on Lower Marlborough. Says you tackled her and pulled her into an alley next to Shooter's Tavern, where you had spent several hours imbibing Jack Daniel's before kicking the jukebox and being asked to leave. Miss Hooper had a battery-powered Police Alert in her purse and managed to trigger it. She also scratched your face. You broke her nose, held her down, choked her, and proceeded to insert your Johns Hopkins into her Sarah Lawrence. When Officer Philip Ellenton hauled you off, you were still matriculating."

"Rape. Why would I . . ."

Stupid question. Why had he spent three long hours tearing up that home in Sugar Heights, just taking a short break to piss on the Aubusson carpet?

"I have no idea," Cafferty said. "Rape is foreign to my way of life."

And mine, Morris thought. Ordinarily. But I was drinking Jack and got up to hijinks.

"How long will they give me?"

"The prosecution will ask for life. If you plead guilty at trial and throw yourself on the mercy of the court, you might only get twenty-five years."

Morris pleaded guilty at trial. He said he regretted what he'd done. He blamed the booze. He threw himself on the mercy of the court.

And got life.

2013–2014

By the time he was a high school sophomore, Pete Saubers had already figured out the next step: a good college in New England where literature instead of cleanliness was next to godliness. He began investigating online and collecting brochures. Emerson or BC seemed the most likely candidates, but Brown might not be out of reach. His mother and father told him not to get his hopes up, but Pete didn't buy that. He felt that if you didn't have hopes and ambitions when you were a teenager, you'd be pretty much fucked later on.

About majoring in English there was no question. Some of this surety had to do with John Rothstein and the Jimmy Gold novels; so far as Pete knew, he was the only person in the world who had read the final two, and they had changed his life.

Howard Ricker, his sophomore English teacher, had also been life-changing, even though many kids made fun of him, calling him Ricky the Hippie because of the flower-power shirts and bellbottoms he favored. (Pete's girlfriend, Gloria Moore, called him Pastor Ricky, because he had a habit of waving his hands above his head when he got excited.) Hardly anyone cut Mr. Ricker's classes, though. He was entertaining, he was enthusiastic, and—unlike many of the teachers—he seemed to genuinely like the kids, whom he called "my young ladies and gentlemen." They rolled their eyes at his retro clothes and his screechy laugh . . . but the clothes had a certain funky cachet, and the screechy laugh was so amiably weird it made you want to laugh along.

On the first day of sophomore English, he blew in like a cool breeze, welcomed them, and then printed something on the board that Pete Saubers never forgot:

This is stupid!

"What do you make of this, ladies and gentlemen?" he asked. "What on earth can it *mean*?"

The class was silent.

"I'll tell you, then. It happens to be the most common criticism made by young ladies and gentlemen such as yourselves, doomed to a course where we begin with excerpts from *Beowulf* and end with Raymond Carver. Among teachers, such survey courses are sometimes called GTTG: Gallop Through the Glories."

He screeched cheerfully, also waggling his hands at shoulder height in a yowza-yowza gesture. Most of the kids laughed along, Pete among them.

"Class verdict on Jonathan Swift's 'A Modest Proposal'? This is stupid! 'Young Goodman Brown,' by Nathaniel Hawthorne? This is stupid! 'Mending Wall,' by Robert Frost? This is moderately stupid! The required excerpt from *Moby-Dick*? This is *extremely* stupid!"

More laughter. None of them had read *Moby-Dick*, but they all knew it was hard and boring. Stupid, in other words.

"And sometimes!" Mr. Ricker exclaimed, raising one finger and pointing dramatically at the words on the blackboard. "Sometimes, my young ladies and gentlemen, *the criticism is spot-on*. I stand here with my bare face hanging out and admit it. I am required to teach certain antiquities I would rather not teach. I see the loss of enthusiasm in your eyes, and my soul groans. Yes! *Groans!* But I soldier on, because I know that much of what I teach is *not* stupid. Even some of the antiquities to which you feel you cannot relate now or ever will, have deep resonance that will eventually reveal itself. Shall I tell you how you judge the *not-stupid* from the *is-stupid*? Shall I impart this great secret? Since we have forty minutes left in this class and as yet no grist to grind in the mill of our combined intellects, I believe I will."

He leaned forward and propped his hands on the desk, his tie swinging like a pendulum. Pete felt that Mr. Ricker was looking directly at him, as if he knew—or at least intuited—the tremendous secret Pete was keeping under a pile of blankets in the attic of his house. Something far more important than money.

"At some point in this course, perhaps even tonight, you will read something difficult, something you only partially understand, and your verdict will be *this is stupid*. Will I argue when you advance that opinion in class the next day? Why would I do such a useless thing? My time with you is short, only thirty-four weeks of classes, and I will not waste it arguing about the merits of this short story or that poem. Why would I, when all such opinions are subjective, and no final resolution can ever be reached?"

Some of the kids—Gloria was one of them—now looked lost, but Pete understood exactly what Mr. Ricker, aka Ricky the Hippie, was talking about, because since starting the notebooks, he had read dozens of critical essays on John Rothstein. Many of them judged Rothstein to be one of the greatest American writers of the twentieth century, right up there with Fitzgerald, Hemingway, Faulkner, and Roth. There were others—a minority, but a vocal one—who asserted that his work was second-rate and hollow. Pete had read a piece in *Salon* where the writer had called Rothstein "king of the wisecrack and the patron saint of fools."

"Time is the answer," Mr. Ricker said on the first day of Pete's sophomore year. He strode back and forth, antique bell-bottoms swishing, occasionally waving his arms. "Yes! Time mercilessly culls away the *is-stupid* from the *not-stupid*. It is a natural, Darwinian process. It is why the novels of Graham Greene are available in every good bookstore, and the novels of Somerset Maugham are not—those novels still exist, of course, but you must order them, and you would only do that if you knew about them. Most modern readers do not. Raise your hand if you have ever heard of Somerset Maugham. And I'll spell that for you."

No hands went up.

Mr. Ricker nodded. Rather grimly, it seemed to Pete. "Time has decreed that Mr. Greene is *not-stupid* while Mr. Maugham is . . . well, not exactly stupid but forgettable. He wrote some very fine novels, in my opinion—*The Moon and Sixpence* is re-markable, my young ladies and gentlemen, *remarkable*—and he also wrote a great deal of excellent short fiction, but none is included in your textbook.

"Shall I weep over this? Shall I rage, and shake my fists, and proclaim injustice? No. I will not. Such culling is a natural process. It will occur for you, young ladies and gentle-men, although I will be in your rearview mirror by the time it happens. Shall I tell you *how* it happens? You will read something—perhaps 'Dulce et Decorum Est,' by Wilfred Owen. Shall we use that as an example? Why not?"

Then, in a deeper voice that sent chills up Pete's back and tightened his throat, Mr. Ricker cried: "'Bent double, like old beggars under sacks, Knock-kneed, coughing like hags, we cursed through sludge . . .' And so on. Cetra-cetra. Some of you will say, *This is stupid*. Will I break my promise not to argue the point, even though I consider Mr. Owen's poems the greatest to come out of World War I? No! It's just my opinion, you see, and opinions are like assholes: everybody has one."

They all roared at that, young ladies and gentlemen alike.

Mr. Ricker drew himself up. "I may give some of you detentions if you disrupt my class, I have no problem with imposing discipline, but *never* will I disrespect your opinion. And yet! And yet!"

Up went the finger.

"Time will pass! *Tempus* will *fugit*! Owen's poem may fall away from your mind, in which case your verdict of *is-stupid* will have turned out to be correct. For you, at least. But for some of you it will recur. And recur. And recur. Each time it does, the steady march of your maturity will deepen its resonance. Each time that poem steals back into your mind, it will seem a little less stupid and a little more vital. A little more important. Until it *shines*, young ladies and gentlemen. Until it *shines*. Thus endeth my opening day peroration, and I ask you to turn to page sixteen in that most excellent tome *Language and Literature*."

One of the stories Mr. Ricker assigned that year was "The Rocking-Horse Winner," by D. H. Lawrence, and sure enough, many of Mr. Ricker's young ladies and gentlemen (including Gloria Moore, of whom Pete was growing tired, in spite of her really excellent breasts) considered it stupid. Pete did not, in large part because events in his life had already caused him to mature beyond his years. As 2013 gave way to 2014—the year of the famed Polar Vortex, when furnaces all over the upper Midwest went into maximum overdrive, burning money by the bale—that story recurred to him often, and its resonance continued to deepen. And recur.

The family in it seemed to have everything, but they didn't; there was never quite enough, and the hero of the story, a young boy named Paul, always heard the house whispering, "There must be more money! There must be more money!" Pete Saubers guessed that there were kids who considered that stupid. They were the lucky ones who had never been forced to listen to nightly arkie-barkies about which bills to pay. Or the price of cigarettes.

The young protagonist in the Lawrence story discovered a supernatural way to make money. By riding his toy rocking-horse to the make-believe land of luck, Paul could pick horse-race winners in the real world. He made thousands of dollars, and still the house whispered, "There must be more money!"

After one final epic ride on the rocking-horse—and one final big-money pick—Paul dropped dead of a brain hemorrhage or something. Pete didn't have so much as a headache after finding the buried trunk, but it was still his rocking-horse, wasn't it? Yes. His very own rocking-horse. But by 2013, the year he met Mr. Ricker, the rocking-horse was slowing down. The trunk-money had almost run out.

It had gotten his parents through a rough and scary patch when their marriage might otherwise have crashed and burned; this Pete knew, and he never once regretted playing guardian angel. In the words of that old song, the trunk-money had formed a bridge over troubled waters, and things were better—*much*—on the other side. The worst of the recession was over. Mom was teaching full-time again, her salary three thousand a year better than before. Dad now ran his own small business, not real estate, exactly, but something called real estate search. He had several agencies in the city as clients. Pete didn't completely understand how it worked, but he knew it was actually making some money, and might make more in the years ahead, if the housing market continued to trend upward. He was agenting a few properties of his own, too. Best of all, he was drug-free and walking well. The crutches had been in the closet for over a year, and he only used his cane on rainy or snowy days when his bones and joints ached. All good. Great, in fact.

And yet, as Mr. Ricker said at least once in every class. And yet!

There was Tina to think about, that was one very large *and yet*. Many of her friends from the old neighborhood on the West Side, including Barbara Robinson, whom Tina had idolized, were going to Chapel Ridge, a private school that had an excellent record when it came to sending kids on to good colleges. Mom had told Tina that she and Dad didn't see how they could afford to send her there directly from middle school. Maybe she could attend as a sophomore, if their finances continued to improve.

"But I won't know *anybody* by then," Tina had said, starting to cry.

"You'll know Barbara Robinson," Mom said, and Pete (listening from the next room) could tell from the sound of her voice that Mom was on the verge of tears herself. "Hilda and Betsy, too."

But Teens had been a little younger than those girls, and Pete knew only Barbs had been a real friend to his sister back in the West Side days. Hilda Carver and Betsy DeWitt probably didn't even remember her. Neither would Barbara, in another year or two. Their mother didn't seem to remember what a big deal high school was, and how quickly you forgot your little-kid friends once you got there.

Tina's response summed up these thoughts with admirable succinctness. "Yeah, but they won't know *me*."

"Tina—"

"You have that *money*!" Tina cried. "That mystery money that comes every month! Why can't I have some for Chapel Ridge?"

"Because we're still catching up from the bad time, honey."

To this Tina could say nothing, because it was true.

His own college plans were another *and yet*. Pete knew that to some of his friends, maybe most of them, college seemed as far away as the outer planets of the solar system. But if he wanted a good one (*Brown*, his mind whispered, *English Lit at Brown*), that meant making early applications when he was a first-semester senior. The applications themselves cost money, as did the summer class he needed to pick up if he wanted to score at least a 670 on the math part of the SATs. He had a part-time job at the Garner Street Library, but thirty-five bucks a week didn't go far.

Dad's business had grown enough to make a downtown office desirable, that was *and yet* number three. Just a low-rent place on an upper floor, and being close to the action would pay dividends, but it would mean laying out more money, and Pete knew—even though no one said it out loud—that Dad was counting on the mystery cash to carry him through the critical period. They had all come to depend on the mystery cash, and only Pete knew it would be gone before the end of '14.

And yeah, okay, he had spent some on himself. Not a huge amount—that would have raised questions—but a hundred here and a hundred there. A blazer and a pair of loafers for the class trip to Washington. A few CDs. And books. He had become a fool for books since reading the notebooks and falling in love with John Rothstein. He began with Rothstein's Jewish contemporaries, like Philip Roth, Saul Bellow, and Irwin Shaw (he thought *The Young Lions* was fucking awesome, and couldn't understand why it wasn't a classic), and spread out from there. He always bought paperbacks, but even those were twelve or fifteen dollars apiece these days, unless you could find them used.

"The Rocking-Horse Winner" had resonance, all right, big-time resonance, because Pete could hear his own house whispering *There must be more money* . . . and all too soon there would be less. But money wasn't *all* the trunk had contained, was it?

That was another *and yet*. One Pete Saubers thought about more and more as time passed.

• • •

For his end-of-year research paper in Mr. Ricker's Gallop Through the Glories, Pete did a sixteen-page analysis of the Jimmy Gold trilogy, quoting from various reviews and adding in stuff from the few interviews Rothstein had given before retreating to his farm in New Hampshire and going completely dark. He finished by talking about Rothstein's tour of the German death camps as a reporter for the *New York Herald*—this four years before publishing the first Jimmy Gold book.

"I believe that was the most important event of Mr. Rothstein's life," Pete wrote. "Surely the most important event of his life as a writer. Jimmy's search for meaning always goes back to what Mr. Rothstein saw in those camps, and it's why, when Jimmy tries to live the life of an ordinary American citizen, he always feels hollow. For me, this is best expressed when he throws an ashtray through the TV in *The Runner Slows Down*. He does it during a CBS news special about the Holocaust."

When Mr. Ricker returned their papers, a big A+ was scrawled on Pete's cover, which was a computer-scanned photo of Rothstein as a young man, sitting in Sardi's with Ernest Hemingway. Below the A+, Mr. Ricker had written *See me after class*.

When the other kids were gone, Mr. Ricker looked at Pete so fixedly that Pete was momentarily scared his favorite teacher was going to accuse him of plagiarism. Then Mr. Ricker smiled. "That is the best student paper I've read in my twenty-eight years of teaching. Because it was the most confident, and the most deeply felt."

Pete's face heated with pleasure. "Thanks. Really. Thanks a lot."

"I'd argue with your conclusion, though," Mr. Ricker said, leaning back in his chair and lacing his fingers together behind his neck. "The characterization of Jimmy as 'a noble

American hero, like Huck Finn,' is not supported by the concluding book of the trilogy. Yes, he throws an ashtray at the television screen, but it's not an act of heroism. The CBS logo is an eye, you know, and Jimmy's act is a ritual blinding of his inner eye, the one that sees the truth. That's not my insight; it's an almost direct quote from an essay called 'The Runner Turns Away,' by John Crowe Ransom. Leslie Fiedler says much the same in *Love and Death in the American Novel*."

"But—"

"I'm not trying to debunk you, Pete; I'm just saying you need to follow the evidence of any book *wherever* it leads, and that means not omitting crucial developments that run counter to your thesis. What does Jimmy do *after* he throws the ashtray through the TV, and after his wife delivers her classic line, 'You bastard, how will the kids watch Mickey Mouse now?'"

"He goes out and buys another TV set, but—"

"Not just *any* TV set, but *the first color TV set on the block*. And then?"

"He creates the big successful ad campaign for Duzzy-Doo household cleaner. But—"

Mr. Ricker raised his eyebrows, waiting for the but. And how could Pete tell him that a year later, Jimmy steals into the agency late one night with matches and a can of kerosene? That Rothstein foreshadows all the protests about Vietnam and civil rights by having Jimmy start a fire that pretty much destroys the building known as the Temple of Advertising? That he hitchhikes out of New York City without a look back, leaving his family behind and striking out for the territory, just like Huck and Jim? He couldn't say any of that, because it was the story told in *The Runner Goes West*, a novel that existed only in seventeen closely written notebooks that had lain buried in an old trunk for over thirty years.

"Go ahead and but me your buts," Mr. Ricker said equably.

"There's nothing I like better than a good book discussion with someone who can hold up his end of the argument. I imagine you've already missed your bus, but I'll be more than happy to give you a ride home." He tapped the cover sheet of Pete's paper, Johnny R. and Ernie H., those twin titans of American literature, with oversized martini glasses raised in a toast. "Unsupported conclusion aside—which I put down to a touching desire to see light at the end of an extremely dark final novel—this is extraordinary work. Just extraordinary. So go for it. But me your buts."

"But nothing, I guess," Pete said. "You could be right."

Only Mr. Ricker wasn't. Any doubt about Jimmy Gold's capacity to sell out that remained at the end of *The Runner Goes West* was swept away in the last and longest novel of the series, *The Runner Raises the Flag*. It was the best book Pete had ever read. Also the saddest.

"In your paper you don't go into how Rothstein died."

"No."

"May I ask why not?"

"Because it didn't fit the theme, I guess. And it would have made the paper too long. Also . . . well . . . it was such a bummer for him to die that way, getting killed in a stupid burglary."

"He shouldn't have kept cash in the house," Mr. Ricker said mildly, "but he did, and a lot of people knew it. Don't judge him too harshly for that. Many writers have been stupid and improvident about money. Charles Dickens found himself supporting a family of slackers, including his own father. Samuel Clemens was all but bankrupted by bad real estate transactions. Arthur Conan Doyle lost thousands of dollars to fake mediums and spent thousands more on fake photos of fairies. At least Rothstein's major work was done. Unless you believe, as some people do—"

Pete looked at his watch. "Um, Mr. Ricker? I can still catch my bus if I hurry."

Mr. Ricker did that funny yowza-yowza thing with his hands. "Go, by all means go. I just wanted to thank you for such a wonderful piece of work . . . and to offer a friendly caution: when you approach this kind of thing next year—and in college—don't let your good nature cloud your critical eye. The critical eye should always be cold and clear."

"I won't," Pete said, and hurried out.

The last thing he wanted to discuss with Mr. Ricker was the possibility that the thieves who had taken John Rothstein's life had stolen a bunch of unpublished manuscripts as well as money, and maybe destroyed them after deciding they had no value. Once or twice Pete had played with the idea of turning the notebooks over to the police, even though that would almost surely mean his parents would find out where the mystery money had been coming from. The notebooks were, after all, evidence of a crime as well as a literary treasure. But it was an *old* crime, ancient history. Better to leave well enough alone.

Right?

The bus had already gone, of course, and that meant a two-mile walk home. Pete didn't mind. He was still glowing from Mr. Ricker's praise, and he had a lot to think about. Rothstein's unpublished works, mostly. The short stories were uneven, he thought, only a few of them really good, and the poems he'd tried to write were, in Pete's humble opinion, pretty lame. But those last two Jimmy Gold novels were . . . well, gold. Judging by the evidence scattered through them, Pete guessed the last one, where Jimmy raises a burning flag at a Washington peace rally, had been finished around 1973, because Nixon was still president when the story ended. That Rothstein had never published the final Gold books (plus yet another novel, this one about the Civil War) blew Pete's mind. They were so good!

Pete took only one Moleskine at a time down from the attic, reading them with his door closed and an ear cocked for unexpected company when there were other members of his family in the house. He always kept another book handy, and if he heard approaching footsteps, he would slide the notebook under his mattress and pick up the spare. The only time he'd been caught was by Tina, who had the unfortunate habit of walking around in her sock feet.

"What's that?" she'd asked from the doorway.

"None of your beeswax," he had replied, slipping the notebook under his pillow. "And if you say anything to Mom or Dad, you're in trouble with me."

"Is it porno?"

"No!" Although Mr. Rothstein could write some pretty racy scenes, especially for an old guy. For instance the one where Jimmy and these two hippie chicks—

"Then why don't you want me to see it?"

"Because it's private."

Her eyes lit up. "Is it yours? Are you writing a *book*?"

"Maybe. So what if I am?"

"I think that's cool! What's it about?"

"Bugs having sex on the moon."

She giggled. "I thought you said it wasn't porno. Can I read it when you're done?"

"We'll see. Just keep your trap shut, okay?"

She had agreed, and one thing you could say for Teens, she rarely broke a promise. That had been two years ago, and Pete was sure she'd forgotten all about it.

Billy Webber came rolling up on a gleaming ten-speed. "Hey, Saubers!" Like almost everyone else (Mr. Ricker was an exception), Billy pronounced it *Sobbers* instead of *SOW-bers*, but what the hell. It was sort of a dipshit name however you said it. "What you doin this summer?"

"Working at the Garner Street libe."

"Still?"

"I talked em into twenty hours a week."

"Fuck, man, you're too young to be a wage-slave!"

"I don't mind," Pete said, which was the truth. The libe meant free computer-time, among the other perks, with no one looking over your shoulder. "What about you?"

"Goin to our summer place up in Maine. China Lake. Many cute girls in bikinis, man, and the ones from Massachusetts know what to do."

Then maybe they can show you, Pete thought snidely, but when Billy held out his palm, Pete slapped him five and watched him go with mild envy. Ten-speed bike under his ass; expensive Nike kicks on his feet; summer place in Maine. It seemed that some people had already caught up from the bad time. Or maybe the bad time had missed them completely. Not so with the Saubers family. They were doing okay, but—

There must be more money, the house had whispered in the Lawrence story. There must be more money. And honey, that was *resonance*.

Could the notebooks be turned into money? Was there a way? Pete didn't even like to think about giving them up, but at the same time he recognized how wrong it was to keep them hidden away in the attic. Rothstein's work, especially the last two Jimmy Gold books, deserved to be shared with the world. They would remake Rothstein's reputation, Pete was sure of that, but his rep still wasn't that bad, and besides, it wasn't the important part. People would like them, that was the important part. *Love* them, if they were like Pete.

Only, handwritten manuscripts weren't like untraceable twenties and fifties. Pete would be caught, and he might go to jail. He wasn't sure exactly what crime he could be charged with—not receiving stolen property, surely, because he hadn't received it, only found it—but he was positive that trying to sell what wasn't yours had to be *some* kind of crime. Donating the notebooks to Rothstein's alma mater seemed like a possible answer, only he'd have to do it anonymously, or it would all come out and his parents would discover that their son had been supporting them with a murdered man's stolen money. Besides, for an anonymous donation you got zilch.

Although he hadn't written about Rothstein's murder in his term paper, Pete had read all about it, mostly in the computer room at the library. He knew that Rothstein had been shot "execution-style." He knew that the cops had found enough different tracks in the dooryard to believe two, three, or even four people had been involved, and that, based on the size of those tracks, all were probably men. They also thought that two of the men had been killed at a New York rest area not long after.

Margaret Brennan, the author's first wife, had been interviewed in Paris not long after the killing. "Everyone talked about him in that provincial little town where he lived," she said. "What else did they have to talk about? Cows? Some farmer's new manure spreader? To the provincials, John was a big deal. They had the erroneous idea that writers make as much as corporate bankers, and believed he had hundreds of thousands of dollars stashed away on that rundown farm of his. Someone from out of town heard the loose talk, that's all. Closemouthed Yankees, my Irish fanny! I blame the locals as much as the thugs who did it."

When asked about the possibility that Rothstein had squirreled away manuscripts as well as cash, Peggy Brennan had given what the interview called "a cigarette-raspy chuckle."

"More rumors, darling. Johnny pulled back from the world for one reason and one reason only. He was burned out and too proud to admit it."

Lot you knew, Pete thought. He probably divorced you because he got tired of that cigarette-raspy chuckle.

There was plenty of speculation in the newspaper and magazine articles Pete had read, but he himself liked what Mr. Ricker called "the Occam's razor principle." According to that, the simplest and most obvious answer was usually the right one. Three men had broken in, and one of them had killed his partners so he could keep all the swag for himself. Pete had no idea why the guy had come to this city afterwards, or why he'd buried the trunk, but one thing he *was* sure of: the surviving robber was never going to come back and get it.

Pete's math skills weren't the strongest—it was why he needed that summer course to bone up—but you didn't have to be an Einstein to run simple numbers and assess certain possibilities. If the surviving robber had been thirty-five in 1978, which seemed like a fair estimate to Pete, he would have been sixty-seven in 2010, when Pete found the trunk, and around seventy now. Seventy was ancient. If he turned up looking for his loot, he'd probably do so on a walker.

Pete smiled as he turned onto Sycamore Street.

He thought there were three possibilities for why the surviving robber had never come back for his trunk, all equally likely. One, he was in prison somewhere for some other crime. Two, he was dead. Three was a combination of one and two: he had died in prison. Whichever it was, Pete didn't think he had to worry about the guy. The notebooks, though, were a different story. About them he had plenty of worries. Sitting on them was like sitting on a bunch of beautiful stolen paintings you could never sell.

Or a crate filled with dynamite.

In September of 2013—almost exactly thirty-five years from the date of John Rothstein's murder—Pete tucked the last of the trunk-money into an envelope addressed to his father. The final installment amounted to three hundred and forty dollars.

And because he felt that hope which could never be realized was a cruel thing, he added a one-line note:

This is the last of it. I am sorry there's not more.

He took a city bus to Birch Hill Mall, where there was a mailbox between Discount Electronix and the yogurt place. He looked around, making sure he wasn't observed, and kissed the envelope. Then he slipped it through the slot and walked away. He did it Jimmy Gold–style: without looking back.

A week or two after New Year's, Pete was in the kitchen, making himself a peanut butter and jelly sandwich, when he overheard his parents talking to Tina in the living room. It was about Chapel Ridge.

"I thought maybe we *could* afford it," his dad was saying. "If I gave you false hope, I'm just as sorry as can be, Teens."

"It's because the mystery money stopped coming," Tina said. "Right?"

Mom said, "Partly but not entirely. Dad tried for a bank loan, but they wouldn't give it to him. They went over his business records and did something—"

"A two-year profit projection," Dad said. Some of the old post-accident bitterness crept into his voice. "Lots of compliments, because those are free. They said they might be able to make the loan in 2016, if the business grows by five percent. In the meantime, this goddam Polar Vortex thing . . . we're way over your mom's budget on heating expenses. Everyone is, from Maine to Minnesota. I know that's no consolation, but there it is."

"Honey, we're so, so sorry," Mom said.

Pete expected Tina to explode into a full-fledged tantrum—there were lots more of those as she approached the big thirteen—but it didn't happen. She said she understood, and that Chapel Ridge was probably a snooty school, anyway. Then she came out to the kitchen and asked Pete if he would make her a sandwich, because his looked good. He did, and they went into the living room, and all four of them watched TV together and had some laughs over *The Big Bang Theory*.

Later that night, though, he heard Tina crying behind the closed door of her room. It made him feel awful. He went into his own room, pulled one of the Moleskines out from under his mattress, and began rereading *The Runner Goes West*.

He was taking Mrs. Davis's creative writing course that semester, and although he got As on his stories, he knew by February that he was never going to be a fiction-writer. Although he was good with words, a thing he didn't need Mrs. Davis to tell him (although she often did), he just didn't possess that kind of creative spark. His chief interest was in *reading* fiction, then trying to analyze what he had read, fitting it into a larger pattern. He had gotten a taste for this kind of detective work while writing his paper on Rothstein. At the Garner Street Library he hunted out one of the books Mr. Ricker had mentioned, Fiedler's *Love and Death in the American Novel*, and liked it so much that he bought his own copy in order to highlight certain passages and write in the margins. He wanted to major in English more than ever, and teach like Mr. Ricker (except maybe at a university instead of in high school), and at some point write a book like Mr. Fiedler's, getting into the faces of more traditional critics and questioning the established way those traditional critics looked at things.

And yet!

There had to be more money. Mr. Feldman, the guidance counselor, told him that getting a full-boat scholarship to an Ivy League school was "rather unlikely," and Pete knew even that was an exaggeration. He was just another whitebread high school kid from a so-so Midwestern school, a kid with a part-time library job and a few unglamorous extracurriculars like newspaper and yearbook. Even if he did manage to catch a boat, there was Tina to think about. She was basically trudging through her days, getting mostly Bs and Cs, and seemed more interested in makeup and shoes and pop music than school these days. She needed a change, a clean break. He was wise enough, even at not quite seventeen, to know that Chapel Ridge might not fix his little sister . . . but then again, it might. Especially since she wasn't broken. At least not yet.

I need a plan, he thought, only that wasn't precisely what he needed. What he needed was a *story*, and although he was never going to be a great fiction-writer like Mr. Rothstein or Mr. Lawrence, he *was* able to plot. That was what he had to do now. Only every plot stood on an idea, and on that score he kept coming up empty.

He had begun to spend a lot of time at Water Street Books, where the coffee was cheap and even new paperbacks were thirty percent off. He went by one afternoon in March, on his way to his after-school job at the library, thinking he might pick up something by Joseph Conrad. In one of his few interviews, Rothstein had called Conrad "the first great writer of the twentieth century, even though his best work was written before 1900."

Outside the bookstore, a long table had been set up beneath an awning. SPRING CLEANING, the sign said. EVERYTHING ON THIS TABLE 70% OFF! And below it: WHO KNOWS WHAT BURIED TREASURE YOU WILL FIND! This line was flanked by big yellow smiley-faces, to show it was a joke, but Pete didn't think it was funny.

He finally had an idea.

A week later, he stayed after school to talk to Mr. Ricker.

• • •

"Great to see you, Pete." Mr. Ricker was wearing a paisley shirt with billowy sleeves today, along with a psychedelic tie. Pete thought the combination said quite a lot about why the love-and-peace generation had collapsed. "Mrs. Davis says great things about you."

"She's cool," Pete said. "I'm learning a lot." Actually he wasn't, and he didn't think anyone else in her class was, either. She was nice enough, and quite often had interesting things to say, but Pete was coming to the conclusion that creative writing couldn't really be taught, only learned.

"What can I do for you?"

"Remember when you were talking about how valuable a handwritten Shakespeare manuscript would be?"

Mr. Ricker grinned. "I always talk about that during a midweek class, when things get dozy. There's nothing like a little avarice to perk kids up. Why? Have you found a folio, Malvolio?"

Pete smiled politely. "No, but when we were visiting my uncle Phil in Cleveland during February vacation, I went out to his garage and found a whole bunch of old books. Most of them were about Tom Swift. He was this kid inventor."

"I remember Tom and his friend Ned Newton well," Mr. Ricker said. "*Tom Swift and His Motor Cycle, Tom Swift and His Wizard Camera* . . . when I was a kid myself, we used to joke about *Tom Swift and His Electric Grandmother*."

Pete renewed his polite smile. "There were also a dozen or so about a girl detective named Trixie Belden, and another one named Nancy Drew."

"I believe I see where you're going with this, and I hate to disappoint you, but I must. Tom Swift, Nancy Drew, the Hardy Boys, Trixie Belden . . . all interesting relics of a by-gone age, and a wonderful yardstick to judge how much what is called 'YA fiction' has changed in the last eighty years or so, but those books have little or no monetary value, even when found in excellent condition."

"I know," Pete said. "I checked it out later on *Fine Books*. That's a blog. But while I was looking those books over, Uncle Phil came out to the garage and said he had something else that might interest me even more. Because I'd told him I was into John Rothstein. It was a signed hardback of *The Runner*. Not dedicated, just a flat signature. Uncle Phil said some guy named Al gave it to him because he owed my uncle ten dollars from a poker game. Uncle Phil said he'd had it for almost fifty years. I looked at the copyright page, and it's a first edition."

Mr. Ricker had been rocked back in his chair, but now he sat down with a bang. "Whoa! You probably know that Rothstein didn't sign many autographs, right?"

"Yeah," Pete said. "He called it 'defacing a perfectly good book.'"

"Uh-huh, he was like Raymond Chandler that way. And you know signed volumes are worth more when it's just the signature? *Sans* dedication?"

"Yes. It says so on *Fine Books*."

"A signed first of Rothstein's most famous book probably *would* be worth money." Mr. Ricker considered. "On second thought, strike the probably. What kind of condition is it in?"

"Good," Pete said promptly. "Some foxing on the inside cover and title page, is all."

"You *have* been reading up on this stuff."

"More since my uncle showed me the Rothstein."

"I don't suppose you're in possession of this fabulous book, are you?"

I've got something a lot better, Pete thought. If you only knew.

Sometimes he felt the weight of that knowledge, and never more than today, telling these lies.

Necessary lies, he reminded himself.

"I don't, but my uncle said he'd give it to me, if I wanted it. I said I needed to think about it, because he doesn't . . . you know . . ."

"He doesn't have any idea of how much it might really be worth?"

"Yeah. But then I started wondering . . ."

"What?"

Pete dug into his back pocket, took out a folded sheet of paper, and handed it to Mr. Ricker. "I went looking on the Internet for book dealers here in town that buy and sell first editions, and I found these three. I know you're sort of a book collector yourself—"

"Not much, I can't afford serious collecting on my salary, but I've got a signed Theodore Roethke that I intend to hand down to my children. *The Waking*. Very fine poems. Also a Vonnegut, but that's not worth so much; unlike Rothstein, Father Kurt signed everything."

"Anyway, I wondered if you knew any of these, and if you do, which one might be the best. If I decided to let him give me the book . . . and then, you know, sell it."

Mr. Ricker unfolded the sheet, glanced at it, then looked at Pete again. That gaze, both keen and sympathetic, made Pete feel uneasy. This might have been a bad idea, he really *wasn't* much good at fiction, but he was in it now and would have to plow through somehow.

"As it happens, I know all of them. But jeez, kiddo, I also know how much Rothstein means to you, and not just from your paper last year. Annie Davis says you bring him up often in Creative Writing. Claims the Gold trilogy is your Bible."

Pete supposed this was true, but he hadn't realized how blabby he'd been until now. He resolved to stop talking about Rothstein so much. It might be dangerous. People might think back and remember, if—

If.

"It's good to have literary heroes, Pete, especially if you plan to major in English when you get to college. Rothstein is yours—at least for now—and that book could be the beginning of your own library. Are you sure you want to sell it?"

Pete could answer this question with fair honesty, even though it wasn't really a signed book he was talking about. "Pretty sure, yeah. Things have been a little tough at home—"

"I know what happened to your father at City Center, and I'm sorry as hell. At least they caught the psycho before he could do any more damage."

"Dad's better now, and both he and my mom are working again, only I'm probably going to need money for college, see . . ."

"I understand."

"But that's not the biggest thing, at least not now. My sister wants to go to Chapel Ridge, and my parents told her she couldn't, at least not this coming year. They can't quite swing it. Close, but no cigar. And I think she needs a place like that. She's kind of, I don't know, *lagging*."

Mr. Ricker, who had undoubtedly known lots of students who were lagging, nodded gravely.

"But if Tina could get in with a bunch of strivers—especially this one girl, Barbara Robinson, she used to know from when we lived on the West Side—things might turn around."

"It's good of you to think of her future, Pete. Noble, even."

Pete had never thought of himself as noble. The idea made him blink.

Perhaps seeing his embarrassment, Mr. Ricker turned his attention to the list again. "Okay. Grissom Books would have been your best bet when Teddy Grissom was still alive, but his son runs the shop now, and he's a bit of a tightwad. Honest, but close with a buck. He'd say it's the times, but it's also his nature."

"Okay . . ."

"I assume you've checked on the Net to find out how much a signed first-edition *Runner* in good condition is valued at?"

"Yeah. Two or three thousand. Not enough for a year at Chapel Ridge, but a start. What my dad calls earnest money."

Mr. Ricker nodded. "That sounds about right. Teddy Junior would start you at eight hundred. You might get him up to a grand, but if you kept pushing, he'd get his back up and tell you to take a hike. This next one, Buy the Book, is Buddy Franklin's shop. He's also okay—by which I mean honest—but Buddy doesn't have much interest in twentieth-century fiction. His big deal is selling old maps and seventeenth-century atlases to rich guys in Branson Park and Sugar Heights. But if you could talk Buddy into valuing the book, then go to Teddy Junior at Grissom, you might get twelve hundred. I'm not saying you would, I'm just saying it's possible."

"What about Andrew Halliday Rare Editions?"

Mr. Ricker frowned. "I'd steer clear of Halliday. He's got a little shop on Lacemaker Lane, in that walking mall off Lower Main Street. Not much wider than an Amtrak car, but damn near a block long. Seems to do quite well, but there's an odor about him. I've heard it said he's not too picky about the provenance of certain items. Do you know what that is?"

"The line of ownership."

"Right. Ending with a piece of paper that says *you* legally own what you're trying to sell. The only thing I know for sure is that about fifteen years ago, Halliday sold a proof copy of James Agee's *Let Us Now Praise Famous Men*, and it turned out to have been stolen from the estate of Brooke Astor. She was a rich old biddy from New York with a larcenous business manager. Halliday showed a receipt, and his story of how he came by the book was credible, so the investigation was dropped. But receipts can be forged, you know. I'd steer clear of him."

"Thanks, Mr. Ricker," Pete said, thinking that if he went ahead with this, Andrew Halliday Rare Editions would be his first stop. But he would have to be very, very careful, and if Mr. Halliday wouldn't do a cash deal, that would mean *no* deal. Plus, under no circumstances could he know Pete's name. A disguise might be in order, although it wouldn't do to go overboard on that.

"You're welcome, Pete, but if I said I felt good about this, I'd be lying."

Pete could relate. He didn't feel so good about it himself.

He was still mulling his options a month later, and had almost come to the conclusion that trying to sell even one of the notebooks would be too much risk for too little reward. If it went to a private collector—like the ones he had sometimes read about, who bought valuable paintings to hang in secret rooms where only they could look at them—it would be okay. But he couldn't be sure that would happen. He was leaning more and more to the idea of donating them anonymously, maybe mailing them to the New York University Library. The curator of a place like that would understand the value of them, no doubt. But doing that would be a little more public than Pete liked to think about, not at all like dropping the letters with the money inside them into anonymous streetcorner mailboxes. What if someone remembered him at the post office?

Then, on a rainy night in late April of 2014, Tina came to his room again. Mrs. Beasley was long gone, and the footy pajamas had been replaced by an oversized Cleveland Browns football jersey, but to Pete she looked very much like the worried girl who had asked, during the Era of Bad Feelings, if their mother and father were going to get divorced. Her hair was in pigtails, and with her face cleansed of the little makeup Mom let her wear (Pete had an idea she put on fresh layers when she got to school), she looked closer to ten than going on thirteen. He thought, Teens is almost a teen. It was hard to believe.

"Can I come in for a minute?"

"Sure."

He was lying on his bed, reading a novel by Philip Roth called *When She Was Good*. Tina sat on his desk chair, pulling her jersey nightshirt down over her shins and blowing a few errant hairs from her forehead, where a faint scattering of acne had appeared.

"Something on your mind?" Pete asked.

"Um . . . yeah." But she didn't go on.

He wrinkled his nose at her. "Go on, spill it. Some boy you've been crushing on told you to buzz off?"

"You sent that money," she said. "Didn't you?"

Pete stared at her, flabbergasted. He tried to speak and couldn't. He tried to persuade himself she hadn't said what she'd said, and couldn't do that, either.

She nodded as if he had admitted it. "Yeah, you did. It's all over your face."

"It didn't come from me, Teens, you just took me by surprise. Where would I get money like that?"

"I don't know, but I remember the night you asked me what I'd do if I found a buried treasure."

"I did?" Thinking, You were half-asleep. You *can't* remember that.

"Doubloons, you said. Coins from olden days. I said I'd give it to Dad and Mom so they wouldn't fight anymore, and that's just what you did. Only it wasn't pirate treasure, it was regular money."

Pete put his book aside. "Don't you go telling them that. They might actually believe you."

She looked at him solemnly. "I never would. But I need to ask you . . . is it really all gone?"

"The note in the last envelope said it was," Pete replied cautiously, "and there hasn't been any more since, so I guess so."

She sighed. "Yeah. What I figured. But I had to ask." She got up to go.

"Tina?"

"What?"

"I'm really sorry about Chapel Ridge and all. I wish the money *wasn't* gone."

She sat down again. "I'll keep your secret if you keep one Mom and I have. Okay?"

"Okay."

"Last November she took me to Chap—that's what the girls call it—for one of their tour days. She didn't want Dad to know, because she thought he'd be mad, but back then she thought they maybe *could* afford it, especially if I got a need scholarship. Do you know what that is?"

Pete nodded.

"Only the money hadn't stopped coming then, and it was before all the snow and weird cold weather in December and January. We saw some of the classrooms, and the science labs. There's like a jillion computers. We also saw the gym, which is humongous, and the showers. They have private changing booths, too, not just cattle stalls like at Northfield. At least they do for the girls. Guess who my tour group had for a guide?"

"Barbara Robinson?"

She smiled. "It was great to see her again." Then the smile faded. "She said hello and gave me a hug and asked how everyone was, but I could tell she hardly remembered me. Why would she, right? Did you know her and Hilda and Betsy and a couple of other girls from back then were at the 'Round Here concert? The one the guy who ran over Dad tried to blow up?"

"Yeah." Pete also knew that Barbara Robinson's big brother

had played a part in saving Barbara and Barbara's friends and maybe thousands of others. He had gotten a medal or a key to the city, or something. That was real heroism, not sneaking around and mailing stolen money to your parents.

"Did you know I was invited to go with them that night?"

"What? No!"

Tina nodded. "I said I couldn't because I was sick, but I wasn't. It was because Mom said they couldn't afford to buy me a ticket. We moved a couple of months later."

"Jesus, how about that, huh?"

"Yeah, I missed all the excitement."

"So how was the school tour?"

"Good, but not great or anything. I'll be fine at Northfield. Hey, once they find out I'm your sister, they'll probably give me a free ride, Honor Roll Boy."

Pete suddenly felt sad, almost like crying. It was the sweetness that had always been part of Tina's nature combined with that ugly scatter of pimples on her forehead. He wondered if she got teased about those. If she didn't yet, she would.

He held out his arms. "C'mere." She did, and he gave her a strong hug. Then he held her by the shoulders and looked at her sternly. "But that money . . . it wasn't me."

"Uh-huh, okay. So was that notebook you were reading stuck in with the money? I bet it was." She giggled. "You looked so guilty that night when I walked in on you."

He rolled his eyes. "Go to bed, short stuff."

"Okay." At the door she turned back. "I liked those private changing booths, though. And something else. Want to know? You'll think it's weird."

"Go ahead, lay it on me."

"The kids wear uniforms. For the girls it's gray skirts with white blouses and white kneesocks. There are also sweaters, if you want. Some gray like the skirts and some this pretty dark red—hunter red they call it, Barbara said."

"Uniforms," Pete said, bemused. "You like the idea of *uniforms*."

"Knew you'd think it was weird. Because boys don't know how girls are. Girls can be mean if you're wearing the wrong clothes, or even if you wear the right ones too much. You can wear different blouses, or your sneakers on Tuesdays and Thursdays, you can do different things with your hair, but pretty soon they—the mean girls—figure out you've only got three jumpers and six good school skirts. Then they say stuff. But when everyone wears the same thing every day . . . except maybe the sweater's a different color . . ." She blew back those few errant strands again. "Boys don't have the same problem."

"I actually do get it," Pete said.

"Anyway, Mom's going to teach me how to make my own clothes, then I'll have more. Simplicity, Butterick. Also, I've got friends. Plenty of them."

"Ellen, for instance."

"Ellen's okay."

And headed for a rewarding job as a waitress or a drive-thru girl after high school, Pete thought but did not say. If she doesn't get pregnant at sixteen, that is.

"I just wanted to tell you not to worry. If you were."

"I wasn't," Pete said. "I know you'll be fine. And it wasn't me who sent the money. Honest."

She gave him a smile, both sad and complicit, that made her look like anything but a little girl. "Okay. Gotcha."

She left, closing the door gently behind her.

Pete lay awake for a long time that night. Not long after, he made the biggest mistake of his life.

1979–2014

Morris Randolph Bellamy was sentenced to life in prison on January 11th, 1979, and for a brief time things went fast before they went slow. And slow. And slow. His intake at Waynesville State Prison was completed by six PM the day of his sentencing. His cellmate, a convicted murderer named Roy Allgood, raped him for the first time forty-five minutes after lights-out.

"Hold still and don't you shit on my cock, young man," he whispered in Morris's ear. "If you do that, I'll cut your nose. You'll look like a pig been bit by a allygator."

Morris, who had been raped before, held still, biting his forearm to keep from screaming. He thought of Jimmy Gold, as Jimmy had been before he started chasing the Golden Buck. When he had still been an authentic hero. He thought of Harold Fineman, Jimmy's high school friend (Morris had never had a high school friend himself), saying that all good things must end, which implied the converse was also true: bad things must end, too.

This particular bad thing went on for a long time, and while it did, Morris repeated Jimmy's mantra from *The Runner* over and over in his mind: *Shit don't mean shit, shit don't mean shit, shit don't mean shit*. It helped.

A little.

In the weeks that followed, he was ass-raped by Allgood on some nights and mouth-raped on others. On the whole, he preferred taking it up the ass, where there were no tastebuds. Either way, he thought that Cora Ann Hooper, the woman he had so foolishly attacked while in a blackout, was getting what she would probably have considered perfect justice. On the other hand, she'd only had to endure an unwanted invader once.

There was a clothing factory attached to Waynesville. The factory made jeans and the kind of shirts workmen wore. On his fifth day in the dyehouse, one of Allgood's friends took him by the wrist, led Morris around the number three blue-vat, and told him to unbuckle his pants. "You just hold still and let me do the rest," he said. When he was finished, he said, "I ain't a fag, or anything, but I got to get along, same as anyone. Tell anyone I'm a fag and I'll fuckin kill you."

"I won't," Morris said. Shit don't mean shit, he told himself. Shit don't mean shit.

One day in mid-March of 1979, a Hell's Angel type with tattooed slabs of muscle strolled up to Morris in the exercise yard. "Can you write?" this fellow said with an unmistakable Deep-South accent—*kin you raht?* "I hear you can write."

"Yes, I can write," Morris said. He saw Allgood approach, notice who was walking beside Morris, and sheer off toward the basketball court at the far end of the yard.

"I'm Warren Duckworth. Most folks call me Duck."

"I'm Morris Bel—"

"I know who you are. Write purty well, do you?"

"Yes." Morris spoke with no hesitation or false modesty. The way Roy Allgood had suddenly found another place to be wasn't lost on him.

"Could you write a letter to my wife, if I sort of tell you what to say? Only put it in, like, better words?"

"I could do that, and I will, but I've got a little problem."

"I know what your problem is," his new acquaintance said. "You write my wife a letter that'll make her happy, maybe stop her divorce talk, you ain't gonna have no more trouble with that skinny bitchboy in your house."

I'm the skinny bitchboy in my house, Morris thought, but he felt the tiniest glimmer of hope. "Sir, I'm going to write your wife the prettiest letter she ever got in her life."

Looking at Duckworth's huge arms, he thought of something he'd seen on a nature program. There was a kind of bird that lived in the mouths of crocodiles, granted survival on a day-to-day basis by pecking bits of food out of the reptiles' jaws. Morris thought that kind of bird probably had a pretty good deal.

"I'd need some paper." Thinking of the reformatory, where five lousy sheets of Blue Horse was all you ever got, paper with big spots of pulp floating in it like pre-cancerous moles.

"I'll get you paper. All you want. You just write that letter, and at the end say ever' word came from my mouth and you just wrote it down."

"Okay, tell me what would make her most happy to hear."

Duck considered, then brightened. "That she throws a fine fuck?"

"She'll know that already." It was Morris's turn to consider. "What part of her does she say she'd change, if she could?"

Duck's frown deepened. "I dunno, she always says her ass is too big. But you can't say that, it'll make things worse instead of better."

"No, what I'll write is how much you love to put your hands on it and squeeze it."

Duck was smiling now. "Better watch out or I'll be rapin you myself."

"What's her favorite dress? Does she have one?"

"Yeah, a green one. It's silk. Her ma gave it to her last year, just before I went up. She wears that one when we go out dancin." He looked down at the ground. "She better not be dancin now, but she might be. I know that. Maybe I can't write much more than my own fuckin name, but I ain't no stupe."

"I could write how much you like to squeeze her bottom when she's wearing that green dress, how's that? I could say thinking of that gets you hot."

Duck looked at Morris with an expression that was utterly foreign to Morris's Waynesville experience. It was respect. "Say, that's not bad."

Morris was still working on it. Sex wasn't all women thought about when they thought about men; sex wasn't romance. "What color is her hair?"

"Well, right now I don't know. She's what you call a brownette when there ain't no dye in it."

Brown didn't sing, at least not to Morris, but there were ways you could skate around stuff like that. It occurred to him that this was very much like selling a product in an ad agency, and pushed the idea away. Survival was survival. He said, "I'll write how much you like to see the sun shining in her hair, especially in the morning."

Duck didn't reply. He was staring at Morris with his bushy eyebrows furrowed together.

"What? No good?"

Duck seized Morris's arm, and for one terrible moment Morris was sure he was going to break it like a dead branch. HATE was tattooed on the fingers of the big man's knuckles. Duck breathed, "It's like poitry. I'll get you the paper tomorrow. There's lots in the liberry."

That night, when Morris returned to the cellblock after a three-to-nine shift spent blue-dyeing, his house was empty. Rolf Venziano, in the next cell, told Morris that Roy Allgood had been taken to the infirmary. When Allgood returned the next day, both his eyes were black and his nose had been splinted. He looked at Morris from his bunk, then rolled over and faced the wall.

Warren Duckworth was Morris's first client. Over the next thirty-six years, he had many.

Sometimes when he couldn't sleep, lying on his back in his cell (by the early '90s he had a single, complete with a shelf of well-thumbed books), Morris would soothe himself by remembering his discovery of Jimmy Gold. That had been a shaft of bright sunlight in the confused and angry darkness of his adolescence.

By then his parents had been fighting all the time, and although he had grown to heartily dislike both of them, his mother had the better armor against the world, and so he adopted her sarcastic curl of a smile and the superior, debunking attitude that went with it. Except for English, where he got As (when he wanted to), he was a straight-C student. This drove Anita Bellamy into report-card-waving frenzies. He had no friends but plenty of enemies. Three times he suffered beatings. Two were administered by boys who just didn't like his general attitude, but one boy had a more specific issue. This was a hulking senior football player named Pete Womack, who didn't care for the way Morris was checking out his girlfriend one lunch period in the cafeteria.

"What are you looking at, rat-face?" Womack enquired, as the tables around Morris's solitary position grew silent.

"Her," Morris said. He was frightened, and when clear-headed, fright usually imposed at least a modicum of restraint on his behavior, but he had never been able to resist an audience.

"Well, you want to quit it," Womack said, rather lamely. Giving him a chance. Perhaps Pete Womack was aware that he was six-two and two-twenty, while the skinny, red-lipped piece of freshman shit sitting by himself was five-seven and maybe a hundred and forty soaking wet. He might also have been aware that those watching—including his clearly embarrassed girlfriend—would take note of this disparity.

"If she doesn't want to be looked at," Morris said, "why does she dress like that?"

Morris considered this a compliment (of the left-handed variety, granted), but Womack felt differently. He ran around the table, fists raised. Morris got in a single punch, but it was a good one, blacking Womack's eye. Of course after that he got his shit handed to him, and most righteously, but that one punch was a revelation. He *would* fight. It was good to know.

Both boys were suspended, and that night Morris got a twenty-minute lecture on passive resistance from his mother, along with the acid observation that *fighting in cafeteria* was generally not the sort of extracurricular activity the finer colleges looked for on the applications of prospective enrollees.

Behind her, his father raised his martini glass and dropped him a wink. It suggested that, even though George Bellamy mostly resided beneath his wife's thumb and thin smile, he would also fight under certain circumstances. But running was still dear old dad's default position, and during the second semester of Morris's freshman year at Northfield, Georgie-Porgie ran right out of the marriage, pausing only to clean out what was left in the Bellamy bank account. The investments of which he had boasted either didn't exist or had gone tits-up. Anita Bellamy was left with a stack of bills and a rebellious fourteen-year-old son.

Only two assets remained following her husband's departure to parts unknown. One was the framed Pulitzer nomination for that book of hers. The other was the house where Morris had grown up, situated in the nicer section of the North Side. It was mortgage-free because she had steadfastly refused to co-sign the bank papers her husband brought home, for once immune to his rhapsodizing about an investment opportunity that was absolutely not to be missed. She sold it after he was gone, and they moved to Sycamore Street.

"A comedown," she admitted to Morris during the summer between his freshman and sophomore years, "but the financial reservoir will refill. And at least the neighborhood is white." She paused, replaying that remark, and added, "Not that I'm prejudiced."

"No, Ma," Morris said. "Who'd ever believe that?"

Ordinarily she hated being called Ma, and said so, but on that day she kept still, which made it a good day. It was always a good day when he got in a poke at her. There were so few opportunities.

During the early seventies, book reports were still a requirement in sophomore English at Northfield. The students were given a mimeographed list of approved books to choose from. Most looked like dreck to Morris, and, as usual, he wasn't shy about saying so. "Look!" he cried from his spot in the back row. "Forty flavors of American oatmeal!"

Some of the kids laughed. He could make them laugh, and although he couldn't make them like him, that was absolutely okay. They were dead-enders headed for dead-end marriages and dead-end jobs. They would raise dead-end kids and dandle dead-end grandkids before coming to their own dead ends in dead-end hospitals and nursing homes, rocketing off into darkness believing they had lived the American Dream and Jesus would meet them at the gates of heaven with the Welcome Wagon. Morris was meant for better things. He just didn't know what they were.

Miss Todd—then about the age Morris would be when he and his cohorts broke into John Rothstein's house—asked him to stay after class. Morris lounged splay-legged at his desk as the other kids went out, expecting Todd to write him a detention slip. It would not be his first for mouthing off in class, but it would be his first in an English class, and he was sort of sorry about that. A vague thought occurred to him in his father's voice—*You're burning too many bridges, Morrie*—and was gone like a wisp of steam.

Instead of giving him a detention, Miss Todd (not exactly fair of face but with a holy-shit body) reached into her bulging book-bag and brought out a paperback with a red cover. Sketched on it in yellow was a boy lounging against a brick wall and smoking a cigarette. Above him was the title: *The Runner*.

"You never miss a chance to be a smartass, do you?" Miss Todd asked. She sat on the desk next to him. Her skirt was short, her thighs long, her hose shimmery.

Morris said nothing.

"In this case, I saw it coming. Which is why I brought this book today. It's a good-news bad-news thing, my know-it-all friend. You don't get detention, but you don't get to choose, either. You get to read this and only this. It's not on the school-board's Approved List, and I suppose I could get in trouble for giving it to you, but I'm counting on your better nature, which I like to believe is in there somewhere, minuscule though it may be."

Morris glanced at the book, then looked over it at Miss Todd's legs, making no attempt to disguise his interest.

She saw the direction of his gaze and smiled. For a moment Morris glimpsed a whole future for them, most of it spent in bed. He had heard of such things actually happening. *Yummy teacher seeks teenage boy for extracurricular lessons in sex education.*

This fantasy balloon lasted perhaps two seconds. She popped it with her smile still in place. "You and Jimmy Gold will get along. He's a sarcastic, self-hating little shit. A lot like you." She stood up. Her skirt fell back into place two inches above her knees. "Good luck with your book report. And the next time you peek up a woman's skirt, you might remember something Mark Twain said: 'Any idler in need of a haircut can *look*.'"

Morris slunk from the classroom with his face burning, for once not just put in his place but rammed into it and hammered flat. He had an urge to chuck the paperback down a sewer drain as soon as he got off the bus on the corner of Sycamore and Elm, but held on to it. Not because he was afraid of detention or suspension, though. How could she do *anything* to him when the book wasn't on the Approved List? He held on to it because of the boy on the cover. The boy looking through a drift of cigarette smoke with a kind of weary insolence.

He's a sarcastic, self-hating little shit. A lot like you.

His mother wasn't home, and wouldn't be back until after ten. She was teaching adult education classes at City College to make extra money. Morris knew she loathed those classes, believing they were far beneath her skill set, and that was just fine with him. Sit on it, Ma, he thought. Sit on it and spin.

The freezer was stocked with TV dinners. He picked one at random and shoved it in the oven, thinking he'd read until it was done. After supper he might go upstairs, grab one of his father's *Playboy*s from under the bed (*my inheritance from the old man,* he sometimes thought), and choke the chicken for awhile.

He neglected to set the stove timer, and it was the stench of burning beef stew that roused him from the book a full ninety minutes later. He had read the first hundred pages, no longer in this shitty little postwar tract home deep in the Tree Streets but wandering the streets of New York City with Jimmy Gold. Like a boy in a dream, Morris went to the kitchen, donned oven gloves, removed the congealed mass from the oven, tossed it in the trash, and went back to *The Runner*.

I'll have to read it again, he thought. He felt as if he might be running a mild fever. And with a marker. There's so much to underline and remember. So much.

For readers, one of life's most electrifying discoveries is that they *are* readers—not just capable of doing it (which Morris already knew), but in love with it. Hopelessly. Head over heels. The first book that does that is never forgotten, and each page seems to bring a fresh revelation, one that burns and exalts: *Yes! That's how it is! Yes! I saw that, too!* And, of course, *That's what I think! That's what I FEEL!*

Morris wrote a ten-page book report on *The Runner*. It came back from Miss Todd with an A+ and a single comment: *I knew you'd dig it.*

He wanted to tell her it wasn't digging; it was loving. *True* loving. And true love would never die.

The Runner Sees Action was every bit as good as *The Runner*, only instead of being a stranger in New York City, Jimmy was now a stranger in Europe, fighting his way across Germany, watching his friends die, and finally staring with a blankness beyond horror through the barbed wire at one of the concentration camps. *The wandering, skeletal survivors confirmed what Jimmy had suspected for years,* Rothstein wrote. *It was all a mistake.*

Using a stencil kit, Morris copied this line in Roman Gothic print and thumbtacked it to the door of his room, the one that would later be occupied by a boy named Peter Saubers.

His mother saw it hanging there, smiled her sarcastic curl of a smile, and said nothing. At least not then. Their argument over the Gold trilogy came two years later, after she had raced through the books herself. That argument resulted in Morris getting drunk; getting drunk resulted in breaking and entering and common assault; these crimes resulted in nine months at Riverview Youth Detention Center.

But before all that came *The Runner Slows Down*, which Morris read with increasing horror. Jimmy got married to a nice girl. Jimmy got a job in advertising. Jimmy began putting on weight. Jimmy's wife got pregnant with the first of three little Golds, and they moved to the suburbs. Jimmy made friends there. He and his wife threw backyard barbecue parties. Jimmy presided over the grill wearing an apron that said THE CHEF IS ALWAYS RIGHT. Jimmy cheated on his wife, and his wife cheated right back. Jimmy took Alka-Seltzer for his acid indigestion and something called Miltown for his hangovers. Most of all, Jimmy pursued the Golden Buck.

Morris read these terrible developments with ever increasing dismay and growing rage. He supposed he felt the way his mother had when she discovered that her husband, whom she had believed comfortably under her thumb, had been cleaning out all the accounts even as he ran hither and yon, eagerly doing her bidding and never once raising a hand to slap that sarcastic curl of a smile off her overeducated face.

Morris kept hoping that Jimmy would wake up. That he would remember who he was—who he had been, at least—and trash the stupid and empty life he was leading. Instead of that, *The Runner Slows Down* ended with Jimmy celebrating his most successful ad campaign ever—Duzzy-Doo, for God's sake—and crowing *Just wait until next year!*

In the detention center, Morris had been required to see a shrink once a week. The shrink's name was Curtis Larsen. The boys called him Curd the Turd. Curd the Turd always ended their sessions by asking Morris the same question: "Whose fault is it that you're in here, Morris?"

Most boys, even the cataclysmically stupid ones, knew the right answer to that question. Morris did, too, but refused to give it. "My mother's," he said each time the question was asked.

At their final session, shortly before the end of Morris's term, Curd the Turd folded his hands on his desk and looked at Morris for a long space of silent seconds. Morris knew Curd the Turd was waiting for him to drop his eyes. He refused to do it.

"In my game," Curd the Turd finally said, "there's a term for your response. It's called blame avoidance. Will you be back in here if you continue to practice blame avoidance? Almost certainly not. You'll be eighteen in a few months, so the next time you hit the jackpot—and there *will* be a next time—you'll be tried as an adult. Unless, that is, you make a change. So, for the last time: whose fault is it that you're in here?"

"My mother's," Morris said with no hesitation. Because it wasn't blame avoidance, it was the truth. The logic was inarguable.

Between fifteen and seventeen, Morris read the first two books of the Gold trilogy obsessively, underlining and annotating. He reread *The Runner Slows Down* only once, and had to force himself to finish. Every time he picked it up, a ball of lead formed in his gut, because he knew what was going to happen. His resentment of Jimmy Gold's creator grew. For Rothstein to destroy Jimmy like that! To not even allow him to go out in a blaze of glory, but to *live*! To compromise, and cut corners, and believe that sleeping with the Amway-selling slut down the street meant he was still a rebel!

Morris thought of writing Rothstein a letter, asking—no, *demanding*—that he explain himself, but he knew from the *Time* cover story that the sonofabitch didn't even read his fan mail, let alone answer it.

As Ricky the Hippie would suggest to Pete Saubers years later, most young men and women who fall in love with the works of a particular writer—the Vonneguts, the Hesses, the Brautigans and Tolkiens—eventually find new idols. Disenchanted as he was with *The Runner Slows Down*, this might have happened to Morris. Before it could, there came the argument with the bitch who was determined to spoil his life since she could no longer get her hooks into the man who had spoiled hers. Anita Bellamy, with her framed near-miss Pulitzer and her sprayed dome of dyed blond hair and her sarcastic curl of a smile.

During her February vacation in 1973, she raced through all three Jimmy Gold novels in a single day. And they were *his* copies, his *private* copies, filched from his bedroom shelf. They littered the coffee table when he came in, *The Runner Sees Action* soaking up a condensation ring from her wineglass. For one of the few times in his adolescent life, Morris was speechless.

Anita wasn't. "You've been talking about these for well over a year now, so I finally decided I had to see what all the excitement was about." She sipped her wine. "And since I had the week off, I read them. I thought it would take longer than a day, but there's really not much *content* here, is there?"

"You . . ." He choked for a moment. Then: "You went in my room!"

"You've never raised an objection when I go in to change your sheets, or when I return your clothes, all clean and folded. Perhaps you thought the Laundry Fairy did those little chores?"

"Those books are mine! They were on my special shelf! You had no right to take them!"

"I'll be happy to put them back. And don't worry, I didn't disturb the magazines under your bed. I know boys need . . . amusement."

He stepped forward on legs that felt like stilts and gathered up the paperbacks with hands that felt like hooks. The back cover of *The Runner Sees Action* was soaking from her goddam glass, and he thought, If one volume of the trilogy had to get wet, why couldn't it have been *The Runner Slows Down*?

"I'll admit they're interesting artifacts." She had begun speaking in her judicious lecture-hall voice. "If nothing else, they show the growth of a marginally talented writer. The first two are painfully jejune, of course, the way *Tom Sawyer* is jejune when compared to *Huckleberry Finn*, but the last one— although no *Huck Finn*—*does* show growth."

"The last one *sucks*!" Morris shouted.

"You needn't raise your voice, Morris. You needn't *roar*. You can defend your position without doing that." And here was that smile he hated, so thin and so sharp. "We're having a discussion."

"I don't *want* to have a fucking discussion!"

"But we *should* have one!" Anita cried, smiling. "Since I've spent my day—I won't say *wasted* my day—trying to understand my self-centered and rather pretentiously intellectual son, who is currently carrying a C average in his classes."

She waited for him to respond. He didn't. There were traps everywhere. She could run rings around him when she wanted to, and right now she wanted to.

"I notice that the first two volumes are tattered, almost falling out of their bindings, nearly read to death. There are copious underlinings and notes, some of which show the budding—I won't say *flowering*, it can't really be called that, can it, at least not yet—of an acute critical mind. But the third one looks almost new, and there are no underlinings at all. You don't like what happened to him, do you? You don't care for your Jimmy once he—and, by logical transference, the author—grew up."

"He sold out!" Morris's fists were clenched. His face was hot and throbbing, as it had been after Womack tuned up on him that day in the caff with everyone watching. But Morris had gotten in that one good punch, and he wanted to get one in now. He needed to. "Rothstein *let* him sell out! If you can't see that, you're *stupid*!"

"No," she said. The smile was gone now. She leaned forward, set her glass on the coffee table, looking at him steadily all the while. "That's the core of your misunderstanding. A good novelist does not lead his characters, he follows them. A good novelist does not create events, he watches them happen and then writes down what he sees. A good novelist realizes he is a secretary, not God."

"That wasn't Jimmy's character! Fucking Rothstein changed him! He made Jimmy into a joke! He made him into . . . into everyone!"

Morris hated how weak that sounded, and he hated that his mother had baited him into defending a position that didn't need defending, that was self-evident to anyone with half a brain and any feelings at all.

"Morris." Very softly. "Once I wanted to be the female version of Jimmy, just as you want to be Jimmy now. Jimmy Gold, or someone like him, is the island of exile where most teenagers go to wait until childhood becomes adulthood. What you need to see—what Rothstein finally saw, although it took him three books to do it—is that most of us become everyone. I certainly did." She looked around. "Why else would we be living here on Sycamore Street?"

"Because you were stupid and let my father rob us blind!"

She winced at that (*a hit, a palpable hit,* Morris exulted), but then the sarcastic curl resurfaced. Like a piece of paper charring in an ashtray. "I admit there's an element of truth in what you say, although you're unkind to task me with it. But have you asked yourself *why* he robbed us blind?"

Morris was silent.

"Because he refused to grow up. Your father is a potbellied Peter Pan who's found some girl half his age to play Tinker Bell in bed."

"Put my books back or throw them in the trash," Morris said in a voice he barely recognized. To his horror, it sounded like his father's voice. "I don't care which. I'm getting out of here, and I'm not coming back."

"Oh, I think you will," she said, and she was right about that, but it was almost a year before he did, and by then she no longer knew him. If she ever had. "And you should read this third one a few more times, I think."

She had to raise her voice to say the rest, because he was

plunging down the hall, in the grip of emotions so strong he was almost blind. "Find some pity! Mr. Rothstein did, *and it's the last book's saving grace!*"

The slam of the front door cut her off.

Morris stalked to the sidewalk with his head down, and when he reached it, he began to run. There was a strip mall with a liquor store in it three blocks away. When he got there, he sat on the bike rack outside Hobby Terrific and waited. The first two guys he spoke to refused his request (the second with a smile Morris longed to punch off his face), but the third was wearing thrift-shop clothes and walking with a pronounced list to port. He agreed to buy Morris a pint for two dollars, or a quart for five. Morris opted for the quart, and began drinking it beside the stream running through the undeveloped land between Sycamore and Birch Streets. By then the sun was going down. He had no memory of making his way to Sugar Heights in the boosted car, but there was no doubt that once he was there, he'd gotten into what Curd the Turd liked to call a mega jackpot.

Whose fault is it that you're in here?

He supposed a little of the blame could go to the wino who'd bought an underage kid a quart of whiskey, but mostly it was his mother's fault, and one good thing had come of it: when he was sentenced, there had been no sign of that sarcastic curl of a smile. He had finally wiped it off her face.

During prison lockdowns (there was at least one a month), Morris would lie on his bunk with his hands crossed behind his head and think about the fourth Jimmy Gold novel, wondering if it contained the redemption he had so longed for after closing *The Runner Slows Down*. Was it possible Jimmy had regained his old hopes and dreams? His old fire? If only he'd had two more days with it! Even one!

Although he doubted if even John Rothstein could have

made a thing like that believable. Based on Morris's own observations (his parents being his prime exemplars), when the fire went out, it usually went out for good. Yet some people *did* change. He remembered once bringing up that possibility to Andy Halliday, while they were having one of their many lunch-hour discussions. This was at the Happy Cup, just down the street from Grissom Books, where Andy worked, and not long after Morris had left City College, deciding what passed for higher education there was fucking pointless.

"Nixon changed," Morris said. "The old Commie-hater opened trade relations with China. And Lyndon Johnson pushed the Civil Rights Bill through Congress. If an old racist hyena like him could change his spots, I suppose anything is possible."

"Politicians." Andy sniffed, as at a bad smell. He was a skinny, crewcut fellow only a few years older than Morris. "*They* change out of expediency, not idealism. Ordinary people don't even do that. They can't. If they refuse to behave, they're punished. Then, after punishment, they say okay, yes sir, and get with the program like the good little drones they are. Look at what happened to the Vietnam War protestors. Most of them are now living middle-class lives. Fat, happy, and voting Republican. Those who refused to knuckle under are in jail. Or on the run, like Katherine Ann Power."

"How can you call Jimmy Gold *ordinary?*" Morris cried.

Andy had given him a patronizing look. "Oh, please. His entire story is an epic journey out of exceptionalism. The purpose of American culture is to create a *norm*, Morris. That means that extraordinary people must be leveled, and it happens to Jimmy. He ends up working in *advertising*, for God's sake, and what greater agent of the norm is there in this fucked-up country? It's Rothstein's main point." He shook his head. "If you're looking for optimism, buy a Harlequin Romance."

Morris thought Andy was basically arguing for the sake of

argument. A zealot's eyes burned behind his nerdy hornrims, but even then Morris was getting the man's measure. His zeal was for books as objects, not for the stories and ideas inside them.

They had lunch together two or three times a week, usually at the Cup, sometimes across the street from Grissom's on the benches in Government Square. It was during one of these lunches that Andrew Halliday first mentioned the persistent rumor that John Rothstein had continued to write, but that his will specified all the work be burned upon his death.

"No!" Morris had cried, genuinely wounded. "That could never happen. Could it?"

Andy shrugged. "If it's in the will, anything he's written since he dropped out of sight is as good as ashes."

"You're just making it up."

"The stuff about the will might just be a rumor, I grant you that, but it's well accepted in bookstore circles that Rothstein never stopped writing."

"Bookstore circles," Morris had said doubtfully.

"We have our own grapevine, Morris. Rothstein's housekeeper does his shopping, okay? Not just groceries, either. Once every month or six weeks, she goes into White River Books in Berlin, which is the closest town of any size, to pick up books he's ordered by phone. She's told the people who work there that he writes every day from six in the morning until two in the afternoon. The owner told some other dealers at the Boston Book Fair, and the word got around."

"Holy shit," Morris had breathed. This conversation had taken place in June of 1976. Rothstein's last published story, "The Perfect Banana Pie," had been published in 1960. If what Andy was saying was true, it meant that John Rothstein had been piling up fresh fiction for sixteen years. At even eight hundred words a day, that added up to . . . Morris couldn't begin to do the math in his head, but it was a lot.

"Holy shit is right," Andy said.

"If he really wants all that burned when he dies, he's *crazy*!"

"Most writers are." Andy had leaned forward, smiling, as if what he said next were a joke. Maybe it was. To him, at least. "Here's what I think—someone should mount a rescue mission. Maybe you, Morris. After all, you're his number one fan."

"Not me," Morris said, "not after what he did to Jimmy Gold."

"Cool it, guy. You can't blame a man for following his muse."

"Sure I can."

"Then steal em," Andy said, still smiling. "Call it theft as a protest on behalf of English literature. Bring em to me. I'll sit on em awhile, then sell em. If they're not senile gibberish, they might fetch as much as a million dollars. I'll split with you. Fifty-fifty, even-Steven."

"They'd catch us."

"Don't think so," Andy Halliday had replied. "There are ways."

"How long would you have to wait before you could sell them?"

"A few years," Andy had replied, waving his hand as if he were talking about a couple of hours. "Five, maybe."

A month later, heartily sick of living on Sycamore Street and haunted by the idea of all those manuscripts, Morris packed his beat-up Volvo and drove to Boston, where he got hired by a contractor building a couple of housing developments out in the burbs. The work had nearly killed him at first, but he had muscled up a little (not that he was ever going to look like Duck Duckworth), and after that he'd done okay. He even made a couple of friends: Freddy Dow and Curtis Rogers.

Once he called Andy. "Could you *really* sell unpublished Rothstein manuscripts?"

"No doubt," Andy Halliday said. "Not right away, as I believe I said, but so what? We're young. He's not. Time would be on our side."

Yes, and that would include time to read everything Rothstein had written since "The Perfect Banana Pie." Profit—even half a million dollars—was incidental. I am not a mercenary, Morris told himself. I am not interested in the Golden Buck. That shit don't mean shit. Give me enough to live on—sort of like a grant—and I'll be happy.

I am a *scholar*.

On the weekends, he began driving up to Talbot Corners, New Hampshire. In 1977, he began taking Curtis and Freddy with him. Gradually, a plan began to take shape. A simple one, the best kind. Your basic smash-and-grab.

Philosophers have debated the meaning of life for centuries, rarely coming to the same conclusion. Morris studied the subject himself over the years of his incarceration, but his inquiries were practical rather than cosmic. He wanted to know the meaning of life in a legal sense. What he found was pretty schizo. In some states, life meant exactly that. You were supposedly in until you died, with no possibility of parole. In some states, parole was considered after as little as two years. In others, it was five, seven, ten, or fifteen. In Nevada, parole was granted (or not) based on a complicated point system.

By the year 2001, the average life sentence of a man in the American prison system was thirty years and four months.

In the state where Morris was stacking time, lawmakers had created their own arcane definition of life, one based on demographics. In 1979, when Morris was convicted, the average American male lived to the age of seventy. Morris was twenty-three at the time, therefore he could consider his debt to society paid in forty-seven years.

Unless, that is, he were granted parole.

He became eligible the first time in 1990. Cora Ann Hooper appeared at the hearing. She was wearing a neat blue suit. Her graying hair was pulled back in a bun so tight it screeched. She held a large black purse in her lap. She recounted how Morris Bellamy had grabbed her as she passed the alley beside Shooter's Tavern and told her of his intention to "rip off a piece." She told the five-member Parole Board how he had punched her and broken her nose when she managed to trigger the Police Alert device she kept in her purse. She told the board about the reek of alcohol on his breath and how he had gouged her stomach with his nails when he ripped off her underwear. She told them how Morris was "still choking me and hurting me with his organ" when Officer Ellenton arrived and pulled him off. She told the board that she had attempted suicide in 1980, and was still under the care of a psychiatrist. She told the board that she was better since accepting Jesus Christ as her personal savior, but she still had nightmares. No, she told the board, she had never married. The thought of sex gave her panic attacks.

Parole was not granted. Several reasons were given on the green sheet passed to him through the bars that evening, but the one at the top was clearly the PB's major consideration: *Victim states she is still suffering.*

Bitch.

Hooper appeared again in 1995, and again in 2000. In '95, she wore the same blue suit. In the millennium year—by then she had gained at least forty pounds—she wore a brown one. In 2005, the suit was gray, and a large white cross hung on the growing shelf of her bosom. She held what appeared to be the same large black purse in her lap at each appearance. Presumably her Police Alert was inside. Maybe a can of Mace, as well. She was not summoned to these hearings; she volunteered.

And told her story.

Parole was not granted. Major reason given on the green sheet: *Victim states she is still suffering.*

Shit don't mean shit, Morris told himself. Shit don't mean shit.

Maybe not, but *God*, he wished he'd killed her.

By the time of his third turndown, Morris's work as a writer was much in demand—he was, in the small world of Waynesville, a bestselling author. He wrote love letters to wives and girlfriends. He wrote letters to the children of inmates, a few of which confirmed the reality of Santa Claus in touching prose. He wrote job applications for prisoners whose release dates were coming up. He wrote themes for prisoners taking online college courses or working to get their GEDs. He was no jailhouse lawyer, but he did write letters to real lawyers on behalf of inmates from time to time, cogently explaining each case at hand and laying out the basis for appeal. In some cases lawyers were impressed by these letters, and—mindful of the money to be made from wrongful imprisonment suits that were successful—came on board. As DNA became of overriding importance in the appeals process, he wrote often to Barry Scheck and Peter Neufeld, the founders of the Innocence Project. One of those letters ultimately led to the release of an auto mechanic and part-time thief named Charles Roberson, who had been in Waynesville for twenty-seven years. Roberson got his freedom; Morris got Roberson's eternal gratitude and nothing else . . . unless you counted his own growing reputation, and that was *far* from nothing. It had been a long time since he had been raped.

In 2004, Morris wrote his best letter ever, laboring over four drafts to get it exactly right. This letter was to Cora Ann Hooper. In it he told her that he lived with terrible remorse for what he had done, and promised that if he were granted parole, he would spend the rest of his life atoning for his one violent act, committed during an alcohol-induced blackout.

"I attend AA meetings four times a week here," he wrote, "and now sponsor half a dozen recovering alcoholics and drug addicts. I would continue this work on the outside, at the St. Patrick's Halfway House on the North Side. I had a spiritual awakening, Ms. Hooper, and have allowed Jesus into my life. You will understand how important this is, because I know you have also accepted Christ as your Savior. 'Forgive us our trespasses,' He said, 'as we forgive those who trespass against us.' Won't you please forgive my trespass against you? I am no longer the man who hurt you so badly that night. I have had a soul conversion. I pray that you respond to my letter."

Ten days later, his prayer for a response was answered. There was no return address on the envelope, but *C.A. Hooper* had been printed neatly on the back flap. Morris didn't need to tear it open; some screw in the front office, assigned the duty of checking inmate mail, had already taken care of that. Inside was a single sheet of deckle-edged stationery. In the upper right corner and the lower left, fluffy kittens played with gray balls of twine. There was no salutation. A single line had been printed halfway down the page:

I hope you rot in there.

The bitch appeared at his hearing the following year, legs now clad in support hose, ankles slopping over her sensible shoes. She was like some overweight, vengeful swallow returning to the prison version of Capistrano. She once more told her story, and parole was once more not granted. Morris had been a model prisoner, and now there was just a single reason given on the inmate green sheet: *Victim states she is still suffering.*

Morris assured himself that shit did not mean shit and went back to his cell. Not exactly a penthouse apartment, just six by eight, but at least there were books. Books were escape. Books were freedom. He lay on his cot, imagining how pleasant it would be to have fifteen minutes alone with Cora Ann Hooper, and a power nailer.

Morris was by then working in the library, which was a wonderful change for the better. The guards didn't much care how he spent his paltry budget, so it was no problem to subscribe to *The American Bibliographer's Newsletter*. He also got a number of catalogues from rare book dealers around the country, which were free. Books by John Rothstein came up for sale frequently, offered at ever steeper prices. Morris found himself rooting for this the way some prisoners rooted for sports teams. The value of most writers went down after they died, but a fortunate few trended upward. Rothstein had become one of those. Once in awhile a signed Rothstein showed up in one of the catalogues. In the 2007 edition of Bauman's Christmas catalogue, a copy of *The Runner* signed to Harper Lee—a so-called association copy—went for $17,000.

Morris also kept an eye on the city newspaper during his years of incarceration, and then, as the twenty-first century wrought its technological changes, various city websites. The land between Sycamore Street and Birch Street was still mired in that unending legal suit, which was just the way Morris liked it. He would get out eventually, and his trunk would be there, with the roots of that overhanging tree wrapped firmly around it. That the worth of those notebooks must by now be astronomical mattered less and less to him.

Once he had been young, and he supposed he would have enjoyed all the things young men chased after when their legs were strong and their balls were tight: travel and women, cars and women, big homes like the ones in Sugar Heights and women. Now he rarely even dreamed of such things, and the last woman with whom he'd had sex remained largely instrumental in keeping him locked up. The irony wasn't lost on him. But that was okay. The things of the world fell by the wayside, you lost your speed and your eyesight and your fucking Electric Boogaloo, but literature was eternal, and that was what was waiting for him: a lost geography as yet seen by no eye but its creator's. If he didn't get to see that geography himself until he was seventy, so be it. There was the money, too—all those cash envelopes. Not a fortune by any means, but a nice little nest egg.

I have something to live for, he told himself. How many men in here can say that, especially once their thighs go flabby and their cocks only stand up when they need to pee?

Morris wrote several times to Andy Halliday, who now *did* have his own shop—Morris knew that from *American Bibliographer's Newsletter*. He also knew that his old pal had gotten into trouble at least once, for trying to sell a stolen copy of James Agee's most famous book, but had skated. Too bad. Morris would have dearly loved to welcome that cologne-wearing homo to Waynesville. There were plenty of bad boys here who would have been all too willing to put a hurt on him for Morrie Bellamy. Just a daydream, though. Even if Andy had been convicted, it probably would have been just a fine. At worst, he would have gotten sent to the country club at the west end of the state, where the white-collar thieves went.

None of Morris's letters to Andy were answered.

In 2010, his personal swallow once more returned to Capistrano, wearing a black suit again, as if dressed for her own funeral. Which will be soon if she doesn't lose some weight, Morris thought nastily. Cora Ann Hooper's jowls now hung down at the sides of her neck in fleshy flapjacks, her eyes were all but buried in pouches of fat, her skin was sallow. She had replaced the black purse with a blue one, but everything else was the same. Bad dreams! Endless therapy! Life ruined thanks to the horrible beast who sprang out of the alley that night! So on and so forth, blah-blah-blah.

Aren't you over that lousy rape yet? Morris thought. Aren't you *ever* going to move on?

Morris went back to his cell thinking Shit don't mean shit. It don't mean fucking *shit*.

That was the year he turned fifty-five.

One day in March of 2014, a turnkey came to get Morris from the library, where he was sitting behind the main desk, reading *American Pastoral* for the third time. (It was by far Philip Roth's best book, in Morris's opinion.) The turnkey told him he was wanted in Admin.

"What for?" Morris asked, getting up. Trips to Admin were not ordinarily good news. Usually it was cops wanting you to roll on somebody, and threatening you with all kinds of dark shit if you refused to cooperate.

"PB hearing."

"No," Morris said. "It's a mistake. The board doesn't hear me again until next year."

"I only do what they tell me," the turnkey said. "If you don't want me to give you a mark, find somebody to take the desk and get the lead out of your ass."

The Parole Board—now three men and three women—was convened in the conference room. Philip Downs, the Board's legal counsel, made lucky seven. He read a letter from Cora Ann Hooper. It was an amazing letter. The bitch had cancer. That was good news, but what followed was even better. She was dropping all objections to Morris Bellamy's parole. She said she was sorry she had waited so long. Downs then read a letter from the Midwest Culture and Arts Center, locally known as the MAC. They had hired many Waynesville parolees over the years, and were willing to take Morris Bellamy on as a part-time file clerk and computer operator starting in May, should parole be granted.

"In light of your clean record over the past thirty-five years, and in light of Ms. Hooper's letter," Downs said, "I felt that putting the subject of your parole before the board a year early was the right thing to do. Ms. Hooper informs us that she doesn't have much time, and I'm sure she'd like to get closure on this matter." He turned to them. "How say you, ladies and gentlemen?"

Morris already knew how the ladies and gentlemen would say; otherwise he never would have been brought here. The vote was 6–0 in favor of granting him parole.

"How do you feel about that, Morris?" Downs asked.

Morris, ordinarily good with words, was too stunned to say anything, but he didn't have to. He burst into tears.

Two months later, after the obligatory pre-release counseling and shortly before his job at the MAC was scheduled to begin, he walked through Gate A and back into the free world. In his pocket were his earnings from thirty-five years in the dyehouse, the furniture workshop, and the library. It amounted to twenty-seven hundred dollars and change.

The Rothstein notebooks were finally within reach.

PART 2: OLD PALS

1

Kermit William Hodges—plain old Bill, to his friends—drives along Airport Road with the windows rolled down and the radio turned up, singing along with Dylan's "It Takes a Lot to Laugh, It Takes a Train to Cry." He's sixty-six, no spring chicken, but he looks pretty good for a heart attack survivor. He's lost forty pounds since the vapor-lock, and has quit eating the junk food that was killing him a little with each mouthful.

Do you want to live to see seventy-five? the cardiologist asked him. This was at his first full checkup, a couple of weeks after the pacemaker went in. If you do, give up the pork rinds and doughnuts. Make friends with salads.

As advice goes, it's not up there with love thy neighbor as thyself, but Hodges has taken it to heart. There's a salad in a white paper bag on the seat beside him. He'll have plenty of time to eat it, with Dasani to wash it down, if Oliver Madden's plane is on time. And if Madden comes at all. Holly Gibney has assured him that Madden is already on the way—she got his flight plan from a computer site called AirTracker—but it's always possible that Madden will smell something downwind and head in another direction. He has been out there doing dirt for quite some time now, and guys like that have very educated sniffers.

Hodges passes the feeder road to the main terminals and short-term parking and continues on, following the signs that read AIR FREIGHT and SIGNATURE AIR and THOMAS ZANE AVIATION. He turns in at this last. It's an independent fixed-based operator, huddled—almost literally—in the shadow of the much bigger Signature Air FBO next door. There are weeds sprouting from the cracked asphalt of the little parking lot, which is empty except for the front row. That has been reserved for a dozen or so rental cars. In the middle of the economies and mid-sizes, and hulking above them, is a black Lincoln Navigator with smoked glass windows. Hodges takes this as a good sign. His man *does* like to go in style, a common trait among dirtbags. And although his man may wear thousand-dollar suits, he is still very much a dirtbag.

Hodges bypasses the parking lot and pulls into the turnaround out front, stopping in front of a sign reading LOADING AND UNLOADING ONLY.

Hodges hopes to be loading.

He checks his watch. Quarter to eleven. He thinks of his mother saying, You must always arrive early on important occasions, Billy, and the memory makes him smile. He takes his iPhone off his belt and calls the office. It rings just once.

"Finders Keepers," Holly says. She always says the name of the company, no matter who's calling; it's one of her little tics. She has many little tics. "Are you there, Bill? Are you at the airport? Are you?"

Little tics aside, this Holly Gibney is very different from the one he first met four years ago, when she came to town for her aunt's funeral, and the changes are all for the better. Although she's sneaking the occasional cigarette again; he has smelled them on her breath.

"I'm here," he says. "Tell me I'm gonna get lucky."

"Luck has nothing to do with it," she says. "AirTracker is a very good website. You might like to know that there are currently six thousand, four hundred and twelve flights in U.S. airspace. Isn't that interesting?"

"Totally fascinating. Is Madden's ETA still eleven thirty?"

"Eleven thirty-seven, to be exact. You left your skim milk

on your desk. I put it back in the fridge. Skim milk goes over very rapidly on hot days, you know. Even in an air-conditioned environment, which this is. Now." She nagged Hodges into the air-conditioning. Holly is a very good nagger, when she puts her mind to it.

"Chug-a-lug, Holly," he says. "I have a Dasani."

"No, thank you, I'm drinking my Diet Coke. Barbara Robinson called. She wanted to talk to you. She was all serious. I told her she could call you later this afternoon. Or you'd call her." Uncertainty creeps into her voice. "Was that all right? I thought you'd want your phone available for the time being."

"That's fine, Holly. Did she say what she was all serious about?"

"No."

"Call her back and tell her I'll be in touch as soon as this is wrapped up."

"You'll be careful, won't you?"

"I always am." Although Holly knows that's not exactly true; he damned near got himself, Barbara's brother, Jerome, and Holly herself blown to kingdom come four years ago . . . and Holly's cousin *was* blown up, although that came earlier. Hodges, who had been more than halfway to in love with Janey Patterson, still mourns her. And still blames himself. These days he takes care of himself *for* himself, but he also does it because he believes it's what Janey would have wanted.

He tells Holly to hold the fort and returns his iPhone to the place on his belt where he used to carry his Glock before he became a Det-Ret. In retirement he always used to forget his cell, but those days are gone. What he's doing these days isn't quite the same as carrying a badge, but it's not bad. In fact, it's pretty good. Most of the fish Finders Keepers nets are minnows, but today's is a bluefin tuna, and Hodges is stoked. He's looking at a big payday, but that's not the main thing. He's *engaged*, that's the main thing. Nailing bad boys like Oliver

Madden is what he was made to do, and he intends to keep on doing it until he no longer can. With luck, that might be eight or nine years, and he intends to treasure every day. He believes Janey would have wanted that for him, too.

Yeah, he can hear her say, wrinkling her nose at him in that funny way she had.

Barbara Robinson was also nearly killed four years ago; she was at the fateful concert with her mother and a bunch of friends. Barbs was a cheerful, happy kid then and is a cheerful, happy teenager now—he sees her when he takes the occasional meal at the Robinson home, but he does that less often now that Jerome is away at school. Or maybe Jerome's back for the summer. He'll ask Barbara when he talks to her. Hodges hopes she's not in some kind of jam. It seems unlikely. She's your basic good kid, the kind who helps old ladies across the street.

Hodges unwraps his salad, douses it with lo-cal French, and begins to snark it up. He's hungry. It's good to be hungry. Hunger is a sign of health.

2

Morris Bellamy isn't hungry at all. A bagel with cream cheese is the most he can manage for lunch, and not much of that. He ate like a pig when he first got out—Big Macs, funnel cakes, pizza by the slice, all the stuff he had longed for while in prison—but that was before a night of puking after an ill-advised visit to Senor Taco in Lowtown. He never had a problem with Mexican when he was young, and youth seems like just hours ago, but a night spent on his knees praying to the porcelain altar was all it took to drive home the truth: Morris Bellamy is fifty-nine, on the doorstep of old age. The best years of his life were spent dyeing bluejeans, varnishing tables and chairs to be sold in the Waynesville Outlet Shop, and writing letters for an unending stream of dead-end Charlies in prison overalls.

Now he's in a world he hardly recognizes, one where movies show on bloated screens called IMAX and everyone on the street is either wearing phones in their ears or staring at tiny screens. There are television cameras watching inside every shop, it seems, and the prices of the most ordinary items—bread, for instance, fifty cents a loaf when he went up—are so high they seem surreal. Everything has changed; he feels glare-blind. He is way behind the curve, and he knows his prison-oriented brain will never catch up. Nor his body. It's stiff when he gets out of bed in the morning, achy when he goes to bed at night; a touch of arthritis, he supposes. After that night of vomiting (and when he wasn't doing that, he was shitting brown water), his appetite just died.

For food, at least. He has thought of women—how could he not, when they're everywhere, the young ones barely dressed in the early summer heat?—but at his age, he'd have to buy one younger than thirty, and if he went to one of the places where such transactions are made, he would be violating his parole. If he were caught, he'd find himself back in Waynesville with the Rothstein notebooks still buried in that patch of waste ground, unread by anyone except the author himself.

He knows they're still there, and that makes it worse. The urge to dig them up and have them at last has been a maddening constant, like a snatch of music (*I need a lover that won't drive me cray-zee*) that gets into your head and simply won't leave, but so far he has done almost everything by the book, waiting for his PO to relax and let up a little. This was the gospel according to Warren "Duck" Duckworth, handed down when Morris first became eligible for parole.

"You gotta be super-careful to start with," Duck had said. This was before Morris's first board hearing and the first vengeful appearance of Cora Ann Hooper. "Like you're walking on eggs. 'Cause, see, the bastard will show up when you least expect it. You can take that to the bank. If you get the idea to do something that might get you marked up on Doubtful Behavior—that's a category they have—wait until *after* your PO makes a surprise visit. Then you prob'ly be all right. Get me?"

Morris did.

And Duck had been right.

3

After not even one hundred hours as a free man (well, *semi*-free), Morris came back to the old apartment building where he now lived to find his PO sitting on the stoop and smoking a cigarette. The graffiti-decorated cement-and-breezeblock pile, called Bugshit Manor by the people who lived there, was a state-subsidized fish tank stocked with recovering druggies, alcoholics, and parolees like himself. Morris had seen his PO just that noon, and been sent on his way after a few routine questions and a *Seeya next week*. This was not next week, this was not even the next *day*, but here he was.

Ellis McFarland was a large black gentleman with a vast sloping gut and a shining bald head. Tonight he was dressed in an acre of bluejeans and a Harley-Davidson tee-shirt, size XXL. Beside him was a battered old knapsack. "Yo, Morrie," he said, and patted the cement next to one humongous haunch. "Take a pew."

"Hello, Mr. McFarland."

Morris sat, heart beating so hard it was painful. Please just a Doubtful Behavior, he thought, even though he couldn't think what he'd done that was doubtful. Please don't send me back, not when I'm so close.

"Where you been, homie? You finish work at four. It's now after six."

"I . . . I stopped and had a sandwich. I got it at the Happy Cup. I couldn't believe the Cup was still there, but it is." Babbling. Not able to stop himself, even though he knew babbling was what people did when they were high on something.

"Took you two hours to eat a sandwich? Fucker must have been three feet long."

"No, it was just regular. Ham and cheese. I ate it on one of the benches in Government Square, and fed some of the crusts to the pigeons. I used to do that with a friend of mine, back in the day. And I just . . . you know, lost track of the time."

All perfectly true, but how lame it sounded!

"Enjoying the air," McFarland suggested. "Digging the freedom. That about the size of it?"

"Yes."

"Well, you know what? I think we ought to go upstairs and then I think you ought to drop a urine. Make sure you haven't been digging the wrong kind of freedom." He patted the knapsack. "Got my little kit right here. If the pee don't turn blue, I'll get out of your hair and let you get on with your evening. You don't have any objection to that plan, do you?"

"No." Morris was almost giddy with relief.

"And I'll watch while you make wee-wee in the little plastic cup. Any objection to that?"

"No." Morris had spent over thirty-five years pissing in front of other people. He was used to it. "No, that's fine, Mr. McFarland."

McFarland flipped his cigarette into the gutter, grabbed his knapsack, and stood up. "In that case, I believe we'll forgo the test."

Morris gaped.

McFarland smiled. "You're okay, Morrie. For now, at least. So what do you say?"

For a moment Morris couldn't think what he should say. Then it came to him. "Thank you, Mr. McFarland."

McFarland ruffled the hair of his charge, a man twenty years older than himself, and said, "Good boy. Seeya next week."

Later, in his room, Morris replayed that indulgent, patronizing *good boy* over and over, looking at the few cheap furnishings and the few books he was allowed to bring with him out of purgatory, listening to the animal-house yells and gawps and thumps of his fellow housemates. He wondered if McFarland had any idea how much Morris hated him, and supposed McFarland did.

Good boy. I'll be sixty soon, but I'm Ellis McFarland's good boy.

He lay on his bed for awhile, then got up and paced, thinking of the rest of the advice Duck had given him: *If you get the idea to do something that might get you marked up on Doubtful Behavior, wait until* after *your PO makes a surprise visit. Then you prob'ly be all right.*

Morris came to a decision and yanked his jeans jacket on. He rode down to the lobby in the piss-smelling elevator, walked two blocks to the nearest bus stop, and waited for one with NORTHFIELD in the destination window. His heart was beating double-time again, and he couldn't help imagining Mr. McFarland somewhere near. McFarland thinking, *Ah, now that I've lulled him, I'll double back. See what that bad boy's really up to.* Unlikely, of course; McFarland was probably home by now, eating dinner with his wife and three kids as humongous as he was. Still, Morris couldn't help imagining it.

And if he *should* double back and ask where I went? I'd tell him I wanted to look at my old house, that's all. No taverns or titty bars in that neighborhood, just a couple of convenience stores, a few hundred houses built after the Korean War, and a bunch of streets named after trees. Nothing but over-the-hill suburbia in that part of Northfield. Plus one block-sized patch of overgrown land caught in an endless, Dickensian lawsuit.

He got off the bus on Garner Street, near the library where

he had spent so many hours as a kid. The libe had been his safe haven, because big kids who might want to beat you up avoided it like Superman avoids kryptonite. He walked nine blocks to Sycamore, then actually did idle past his old house. It still looked pretty rundown, all the houses in this part of town did, but the lawn had been mowed and the paint looked fairly new. He looked at the garage where he had stowed the Biscayne thirty-six years ago, away from Mrs. Muller's prying eyes. He remembered lining the secondhand trunk with plastic so the notebooks wouldn't get damp. A very good idea, considering how long they'd had to stay in there.

Lights were on inside Number 23; the people who lived here—their name was Saubers, according to computer research he'd done in the prison library—were home. He looked at the upstairs window on the right, the one overlooking the driveway, and wondered who was in his old room. A kid, most likely, and in degenerate times like these, one probably a lot more interested in playing games on his phone than reading books.

Morris moved on, turning the corner onto Elm Street, then walking up to Birch. When he got to the Birch Street Rec (closed for two years now due to budget cuts, a thing he also knew from his computer research), he glanced around, saw the sidewalks were deserted on both sides, and hurried up the Rec's brick flank. Once behind it, he broke into a shambling jog, crossing the outside basketball courts—rundown but still used, by the look—and the weedy, overgrown baseball field.

The moon was out, almost full and bright enough to cast his shadow beside him. Ahead of him now was an untidy tangle of bushes and runty trees, their branches entwined and fighting for space. Where was the path? He thought he was in the right location, but he wasn't seeing it. He began to course back and forth where the baseball field's right field had been, like a dog trying to catch an elusive scent. His heart was up to full speed again, his mouth dry and coppery. Revisiting the old neighborhood was one thing, but being here, behind the abandoned Rec, was another. This was Doubtful Behavior for sure.

He was about to give up when he saw a potato chip bag fluttering from a bush. He swept the bush aside and bingo, there was the path, although it was just a ghost of its former self. Morris supposed that made sense. Some kids probably still used it, but the number would have dropped after the Rec closed. That was a good thing. Although, he reminded himself, for most of the years he'd been in Waynesville, the Rec would have been open. Plenty of foot traffic passing near his buried trunk.

He made his way up the path, moving slowly, stopping completely each time the moon dove behind a cloud and moving on again when it came back out. After five minutes, he heard the soft chuckle of the stream. So that was still there, too.

Morris stepped out on the bank. The stream was open to the sky, and with the moon now directly overhead, the water shone like black silk. He had no problem picking out the tree on the other bank, the one he had buried the trunk under. The tree had both grown and tilted toward the stream. He could see a couple of gnarled roots poking out below it and then diving back into the earth, but otherwise it all looked the same.

Morris crossed the stream in the old way, going from stone to stone and hardly getting his shoes wet. He looked around once—he knew he was alone, if there had been anyone else in the area he would have heard them, but the old Prison Peek was second nature—and then knelt beneath the tree. He could hear his breath rasping harshly in his throat as he tore at weeds with one hand and held on to a root for balance with the other.

He cleared a small circular patch and then began digging, tossing aside pebbles and small stones. He was in almost halfway to the elbow when his fingertips touched something hard and smooth. He rested his burning forehead against a gnarled elbow of protruding root and closed his eyes.

Still here.

His trunk was still here.

Thank you, God.

It was enough, at least for the time being. The best he could manage, and ah God, such a relief. He scooped the dirt back into the hole and scattered it with last fall's dead leaves from the bank of the stream. Soon the weeds would be back—weeds grew fast, especially in warm weather—and that would complete the job.

Once upon a freer time, he would have continued up the path to Sycamore Street, because the bus stop was closer when you went that way, but not now, because the backyard where the path came out belonged to the Saubers family. If any of them saw him there and called 911, he'd likely be back in Waynesville tomorrow, probably with another five years tacked on to his original sentence, just for good luck.

He doubled back to Birch Street instead, confirmed the sidewalks were still empty, and walked to the bus stop on Garner Street. His legs were tired and the hand he'd been digging with was scraped and sore, but he felt a hundred pounds lighter. Still there! He had been sure it would be, but confirmation was *so* sweet.

Back at Bugshit Manor, he washed the dirt from his hands, undressed, and lay down. The place was noisier than ever, but not as noisy as D Wing at Waynesville, especially on nights like tonight, with the moon big in the sky. Morris drifted toward sleep almost at once.

Now that the trunk was confirmed, he had to be careful: that was his final thought.

More careful than ever.

4

For almost a month he *has* been careful; has turned up for his day job on the dot every morning and gotten in early at Bugshit Manor every night. The only person from Waynesville he'll see is Charlie Roberson, who got out on DNA with Morris's help, and Charlie doesn't rate as a known associate, because Charlie was innocent all along. At least of the crime he was sent up for.

Morris's boss at the MAC is a fat, self-important asshole, barely computer literate but probably making sixty grand a year. Sixty at least. And Morris? Eleven bucks an hour. He's on food stamps and living in a ninth-floor room not much bigger than the cell where he spent the so-called "best years of his life." Morris isn't positive his office carrel is bugged, but he wouldn't be surprised. It seems to him that *everything* in America is bugged these days.

It's a crappy life, and whose fault is that? He told the Parole Board time after time, and with no hesitation, that it was his; he had learned how to play the blame game from his sessions with Curd the Turd. Copping to bad choices was a necessity. If you didn't give them the old *mea culpa* you'd never get out, no matter what some cancer-ridden bitch hoping to curry favor with Jesus might put in a letter. Morris didn't need Duck to tell him that. He might have been born at night, as the saying went, but it wasn't last night.

But had it *really* been his fault?

Or the fault of that asshole right over yonder?

Across the street and about four doors down from the bench where Morris is sitting with the remains of his unwanted bagel, an obese baldy comes sailing out of Andrew Halliday Rare Editions, where he has just flipped the sign on the door from OPEN to CLOSED. It's the third time Morris has ob-

served this lunchtime ritual, because Tuesdays are his afternoon days at the MAC. He'll go in at one and busy himself
until four, working to bring the ancient filing system up-to-
date. (Morris is sure the people who run the place know a lot
about art and music and drama, but they know fuckall about
Mac Office Manager.) At four, he'll take the crosstown bus
back to his crappy ninth-floor room.

In the meantime, he's here.

Watching his old pal.

Assuming this is like the other two midday Tuesdays—
Morris has no reason to think it won't be, his old pal always
was a creature of habit—Andy Halliday will walk (well,
waddle) down Lacemaker Lane to a café called Jamais Toujours.
Stupid fucking name, means absolutely nothing, but sounds
pretentious. Oh, but that was Andy all over, wasn't it?

Morris's old pal, the one with whom he had discussed
Camus and Ginsberg and John Rothstein during many coffee breaks and pickup lunches, has put on at least a hundred
pounds, the hornrims have been replaced by pricey designer
spectacles, his shoes look like they cost more than all the
money Morris made in his thirty-five years of prison toil, but
Morris feels quite sure his old pal hasn't changed inside. As
the twig is bent the bough is shaped, that was another old
saying, and once a pretentious asshole, always a pretentious
asshole.

The owner of Andrew Halliday Rare Editions is walking away from Morris rather than toward him, but Morris
wouldn't have been concerned if Andy had crossed the street
and approached. After all, what would he see? An elderly gent
with narrow shoulders and bags under his eyes and thinning
gray hair, wearing an el cheapo sport jacket and even cheaper
gray pants, both purchased at Chapter Eleven. His old pal
would accompany his growing stomach past him without a
first look, let alone a second.

I told the Parole Board what they wanted to hear, Morris thinks. I had to do that, but the loss of all those years is really your fault, you conceited homo cocksucker. If it had been Rothstein and my partners I'd been arrested for, that would be different. But it wasn't. I was never even questioned about Mssrs. Rothstein, Dow, and Rogers. I lost those years because of a forced and unpleasant act of sexual congress I can't even remember. And why did that happen? Well, it's sort of like the house that Jack built. I was in the alley instead of the tavern when the Hooper bitch came by. I got booted out of the tavern because I kicked the jukebox. I kicked the jukebox for the same reason I was in the tavern in the first place: because I was pissed at *you*.

Why don't you try me on those notebooks around the turn of the twenty-first century, if you still have them?

Morris watches Andy waddle away from him and clenches his fists and thinks, You were like a girl that day. The hot little virgin you get in the backseat of your car and she's all *yes, honey, oh yes, oh yes, I love you so much.* Until you get her skirt up to her waist, that is. Then she clamps her knees together almost hard enough to break your wrist and it's all *no, oh no, unhand me, what kind of girl do you think I am?*

You could have been a little more diplomatic, at least, Morris thinks. A little diplomacy could have saved all those wasted years. But you couldn't spare me any, could you? Not so much as an attaboy, that must have taken guts. All I got was *don't try to lay this off on me.*

His old pal walks his expensive shoes into Jamais Toujours, where he will no doubt have his expanding ass kissed by the maître d'. Morris looks at his bagel and thinks he should finish it—or at least use his teeth to scrape the cream cheese into his mouth—but his stomach is too knotted up to accept it. He will go to the MAC instead, and spend the afternoon trying to impose some order on their tits-up, bass-ackwards digital filing system. He knows he shouldn't come back here to Lacemaker Lane—no longer even a street but a kind of pricey, open-air mall from which vehicles are banned—and knows he'll probably be on the same bench next Tuesday. And the Tuesday after that. Unless he's got the notebooks. That would break the spell. No need to bother with his old pal then.

He gets up and tosses the bagel into a nearby trash barrel. He looks down toward Jamais Toujours and whispers, "You suck, old pal. You really suck. And for two cents—"

But no.

No.

Only the notebooks matter, and if Charlie Roberson will help him out, he's going after them tomorrow night. And Charlie *will* help him. He owes Morris a large favor, and Morris means to call it in. He knows he should wait longer, until Ellis McFarland is absolutely sure Morris is one of the good ones and turns his attention elsewhere, but the pull of the trunk and what's inside it is just too strong. He'd love to get some payback from the fat sonofabitch now feeding his face with fancy food, but revenge isn't as important as that fourth Jimmy Gold novel. There might even be a fifth! Morris knows that isn't likely, but it's possible. There was a lot of writing in those books, a mighty lot. He walks toward the bus stop, sparing one baleful glance back at Jamais Toujours and thinking, You'll never know how lucky you were.

Old pal.

5

Around the time Morris Bellamy is chucking his bagel and heading for the bus stop, Hodges is finishing his salad and thinking he could eat two more just like it. He puts the Styrofoam box and plastic spork back in the carryout bag and tosses it in the passenger footwell, reminding himself to dispose of his litter later. He likes his new car, a Prius that has yet to turn ten thousand miles, and does his best to keep it clean and neat. The car was Holly's pick. "You'll burn less gas and be kind to the environment," she told him. The woman who once hardly dared to step out of her house now runs many aspects of his life. She might let up on him a little if she had a boyfriend, but Hodges knows that's not likely. He's as close to a boyfriend as she's apt to get.

It's a good thing I love you, Holly, he thinks, or I'd have to kill you.

He hears the buzz of an approaching plane, checks his watch, and sees it's eleven thirty-four. It appears that Oliver Madden is going to be johnny-on-the-spot, and that's lovely. Hodges is an on-time man himself. He grabs his sportcoat from the backseat and gets out. It doesn't hang just right because there's heavy stuff in the front pockets.

A triangular overhang juts out above the entrance doors, and it's at least ten degrees cooler in its shade. Hodges takes his new glasses from the jacket's inner pocket and scans the sky to the west. The plane, now on its final approach, swells from a speck to a blotch to an identifiable shape that matches the pictures Holly has printed out: a 2008 Beechcraft KingAir 350, red with black piping. Only twelve hundred hours on the clock, and exactly eight hundred and five landings. The one he's about to observe will be number eight-oh-six. Rated selling price, four million and change.

A man in a coverall comes out through the main door. He looks at Hodges's car, then at Hodges. "You can't park there," he says.

"You don't look all that busy today," Hodges says mildly.

"Rules are rules, mister."

"I'll be gone very shortly."

"Shortly is not the same as now. The front is for pickups and deliveries. You need to use the parking lot."

The KingAir floats over the end of the runway, now only feet from Mother Earth. Hodges jerks a thumb at it. "Do you see that plane, sir? The man flying it is an extremely dirty dog. A number of people have been looking for him for a number of years, and now here he is."

The guy in the coverall considers this as the extremely dirty dog lands the plane with nothing more than a small blue-gray puff of rubber. They watch as it disappears behind the Zane Aviation building. Then the man—probably a mechanic— turns back to Hodges. "Are you a cop?"

"No," Hodges says, "but I'm in that neighborhood. Also, I know presidents." He holds out his loosely curled hand, palm down. A fifty-dollar bill peeps from between the knuckles.

The mechanic reaches for it, then reconsiders. "Is there going to be trouble?"

"No," Hodges says.

The man in the coverall takes the fifty. "I'm supposed to bring that Navigator around for him. Right where you're parked. That's the only reason I gave you grief about it."

Now that Hodges thinks of it, that's not a bad idea. "Why don't you go on and do that? Pull it up behind my car, nice and tight. Then you might have business somewhere else for fifteen minutes or so."

"Always stuff to do in Hangar A," the man in the coverall agrees. "Hey, you're not carrying a gun, are you?"

"No."

"What about the guy in the KingAir?"

"He won't have one, either." This is almost certainly true, but in the unlikely event Madden *does* have one, it will probably be in his carryall. Even if it's on his person, he won't have a chance to pull it, let alone use it. Hodges hopes he never gets

too old for excitement, but he has absolutely no interest in OK
Corral shit.

Now he can hear the steady, swelling beat of the KingAir's
props as it taxies toward the building. "Better bring that
Navigator around. Then . . ."

"Hangar A, right. Good luck."

Hodges nods his thanks. "You have a good day, sir."

6

Hodges stands to the left of the doors, right hand in his sportcoat pocket, enjoying both the shade and the balmy summer
air. His heart is beating a little faster than normal, but that's
okay. That's just as it should be. Oliver Madden is the kind
of thief who robs with a computer rather than a gun (Holly
has discovered the socially engaged motherfucker has eight
different Facebook pages, each under a different name), but
it doesn't do to take things for granted. That's a good way to
get hurt. He listens as Madden shuts the KingAir down and
imagines him walking into the terminal of this small, almost-
off-the-radar FBO. No, not just walking, *striding*. With a
bounce in his step. Going to the desk, where he will arrange
for his expensive turboprop to be hangared. And fueled? Probably not today. He's got plans in the city. This week he's buying casino licenses. Or so he thinks.

The Navigator pulls up, chrome twinkling in the sun,
smoked gangsta glass reflecting the front of the building . . .
and Hodges himself. Whoops! He sidles farther to the left.
The man in the coverall gets out, tips Hodges a wave, and
heads for Hangar A.

Hodges waits, wondering what Barbara might want, what
a pretty girl with lots of friends might consider important
enough to make her reach out to a man old enough to be her

grandpa. Whatever she needs, he'll do his best to supply it. Why wouldn't he? He loves her almost as much as he loves Jerome and Holly. The four of them were in the wars together.

That's for later, he tells himself. Right now Madden's the priority. Keep your eyes on the prize.

The doors open and Oliver Madden walks out. He's whistling, and yes, he's got that Mr. Successful bounce in his step. He's at least four inches taller than Hodges's not inconsiderable six-two. Broad shoulders in a summerweight suit, the shirt open at the collar, the tie hanging loose. Handsome, chiseled features that fall somewhere between George Clooney and Michael Douglas. He's got a briefcase in his right hand and an overnight bag slung over his left shoulder. His haircut's the kind you get in one of those places where you have to book a week ahead.

Hodges steps forward. He can't decide between morning and afternoon, so just wishes Madden a good day.

Madden turns, smiling. "The same back to you, sir. Do I know you?"

"Not at all, Mr. Madden," Hodges says, returning the smile. "I'm here for the plane."

The smile withers a bit at the corners. A frown line appears between Madden's manicured brows. "I beg your pardon?"

"The plane," Hodges says. "Three-fifty Beech KingAir? Seating for ten? Tail number November-one-one-four-Delta-Kilo? Actually belongs to Dwight Cramm, of El Paso, Texas?"

The smile stays on, but boy, it's struggling. "You've mistaken me, friend. My name's Mallon, not Madden. James Mallon. As for the plane, mine's a King, all right, but the tail is N426LL, and it belongs to no one but little old me. You probably want Signature Air, next door."

Hodges nods as if Madden might be right. Then he takes out his phone, reaching crossdraw so he can keep his right hand in his pocket. "Why don't I just put through a call to Mr.

Cramm? Clear this up. I believe you were at his ranch just last week? Gave him a bank check for two hundred thousand dollars? Drawn on First of Reno?"

"I don't know what you're talking about." Smile all gone.

"Well, you know what? He knows you. As James Mallon rather than Oliver Madden, but when I faxed him a photo six-pack, he had no trouble circling you."

Madden's face is entirely expressionless now, and Hodges sees he's not handsome at all. Or ugly, for that matter. He's nobody, extra tall or not, and that's how he's gotten by as long as he has, pulling one scam after another, taking in even a wily old coyote like Dwight Cramm. He's *nobody*, and that makes Hodges think of Brady Hartsfield, who almost blew up an auditorium filled with kids not so long ago. A chill goes up his back.

"Are you police?" Madden asks. He looks Hodges up and down. "I don't think so, you're too old. But if you are, let me see your ID."

Hodges repeats what he told the guy in the coverall: "Not exactly police, but in the neighborhood."

"Then good luck to you, Mr. In The Neighborhood. I've got appointments, and I'm running a bit late."

He starts toward the Navigator, not running but moving fast.

"You were actually right on time," Hodges says amiably, falling in step. Keeping up with him would have been hard after his retirement from the police. Back then he was living on Slim Jims and taco chips, and would have been wheezing after the first dozen steps. Now he does three miles a day, either walking or on the treadmill.

"Leave me alone," Madden says, "or I'll call the real police."

"Just a few words," Hodges says, thinking, Damn, I sound like a Jehovah's Witness. Madden is rounding the Navigator's rear end. His overnight bag swings back and forth like a pendulum.

"No words," Madden says. "You're a nut."

"You know what they say," Hodges replies as Madden reaches for the driver's-side door. "Sometimes you feel like a nut, sometimes you don't."

Madden opens the door. This is really working out well, Hodges thinks as he pulls his Happy Slapper from his coat pocket. The Slapper is a knotted sock. Below the knot, the sock's foot is loaded with ball bearings. Hodges swings it, connecting with Oliver Madden's left temple. It's a Goldilocks blow, not too hard, not too soft, just right.

Madden staggers and drops his briefcase. His knees bend but don't quite buckle. Hodges seizes him above the elbow in the strong come-along grip he perfected as a member of this city's MPD and helps Madden into the driver's seat of the Navigator. The man's eyes have the floaty look of a fighter who's been tagged hard and can only hope for the round to end before his opponent follows up and puts him down for good.

"Upsa-daisy," Hodges says, and when Madden's ass is on the leather upholstery of the bucket seat, he bends and lifts in the trailing left leg. He takes his handcuffs from the left pocket of his sportcoat and has Madden tethered to the steering wheel in a trice. The Navigator's keys, on a big yellow Hertz fob, are in one of the cupholders. Hodges takes them, slams the driver's door, grabs the fallen briefcase, and walks briskly around to the passenger side. Before getting in, he tosses the keys onto the grass verge near the sign reading LOADING AND UN-LOADING ONLY. A good idea, because Madden has recovered enough to be punching the SUV's start button over and over again. Each time he does it, the dashboard flashes KEY NOT DETECTED.

Hodges slams the passenger door and regards Madden cheerfully. "Here we are, Oliver. Snug as two bugs in a rug."

"You can't do this," Madden says. He sounds pretty good for a man who should still have cartoon birdies flying in circles around his head. "You assaulted me. I can press charges. Where's my briefcase?"

Hodges holds it up. "Safe and sound. I picked it up for you."

Madden reaches with his uncuffed hand. "Give it to me."

Hodges puts it in the footwell and steps on it. "For the time being, it's in protective custody."

"What do you want, asshole?" The growl is in stark contrast to the expensive suit and haircut.

"Come on, Oliver, I didn't hit you that hard. The plane. Cramm's plane."

"He sold it to me. I have a bill of sale."

"As James Mallon."

"That's my name. I had it changed legally four years ago."

"Oliver, you and legal aren't even kissing cousins. But that's beside the point. Your check bounced higher than Iowa corn in August."

"That's impossible." He yanks his cuffed wrist. "Get this off me!"

"We can discuss the cuff after we discuss the check. Man, that was slick. First of Reno is a real bank, and when Cramm called to verify your check, the Caller ID said First of Reno was what he was calling. He got the usual automated answering service, welcome to First of Reno where the customer is king, blah-de-blah, and when he pushed the right number, he got somebody claiming to be an accounts manager. I'm thinking that was your brother-in-law, Peter Jamieson, who was arrested early this morning in Fields, Virginia."

Madden blinks and recoils, as if Hodges has suddenly thrust a hand at his face. Jamieson really is Madden's brother-in-law, but he hasn't been arrested. At least not to Hodges's knowledge.

"Calling himself Fred Dawlings, Jamieson assured Mr. Cramm that you had over twelve million dollars in First of Reno in several different accounts. I'm sure he was convincing, but the Caller ID thing was the clincher. It's a fiddle accomplished with a highly illegal computer program. My assistant is good with computers, and she figured that part out. The use of that alone could get you sixteen to twenty months in a Club Fed. But there's so much more. Five years ago, you and Jamieson hacked your way into the General Accounting Office and managed to steal almost four million dollars."

"You're insane."

"For most people, four million split two ways would be enough. But you're not one to rest on your laurels. You're just a big old thrill-seeker, aren't you, Oliver?"

"I'm not talking to you. You assaulted me and you're going to jail for it."

"Give me your wallet."

Madden stares at him, wide-eyed, genuinely shocked. As if he himself hasn't lifted the wallets and bank accounts of God knows how many people. Don't like it when the shoe's on the other foot, do you? Hodges thinks. Isn't that just tough titty.

He holds out his hand. "Give it."

"Fuck you."

Hodges shows Madden his Happy Slapper. The loaded toe hangs down, a sinister teardrop. "Give it, asshole, or I'll darken your world and take it. The choice is yours."

Madden looks into Hodges's eyes to see if he means it. Then he reaches into his suitcoat's inner pocket—slowly, reluctantly—and brings out a bulging wallet.

"Wow," Hodges says. "Is that ostrich?"

"As a matter of fact, it is."

Hodges understands that Madden wants him to reach for it. He thinks of telling Madden to lay it on the console between the seats, then doesn't. Madden, it seems, is a slow learner in need of a refresher course on who's in charge here. So he reaches for the wallet, and Madden grabs his hand in a powerful, knuckle-grinding grip, and Hodges whacks the back of

Madden's hand with the Slapper. The knuckle-grinding stops at once.

"Ow! *Ow! Shit!*"

Madden's got his hand to his mouth. Above it, his incredulous eyes are welling tears of pain.

"One must not grasp what one cannot hold," Hodges says. He picks up the wallet, wondering briefly if the ostrich is an endangered species. Not that this moke would give a shit, one way or the other.

He turns to the moke in question.

"That was your second courtesy-tap, and two is all I ever give. This is not a police-and-suspect situation. You make another move on me and I'll beat you like a rented mule, chained to the wheel or not. Do you understand?"

"Yes." The word comes through lips still tightened with pain.

"You're wanted by the FBI for the GAO thing. Do you know that?"

A long pause while Madden eyes the Slapper. Then he says yes again.

"You're wanted in California for stealing a Rolls-Royce Silver Wraith, and in Arizona for stealing half a million dollars' worth of construction equipment which you then resold in Mexico. Do you also know those things?"

"Are you wearing a wire?"

"No."

Madden decides to take Hodges's word for it. "Okay, yes. Although I got pennies on the dollar for those front-end loaders and bulldozers. It was a damn swindle."

"If anyone would know a swindle when it walks up and says howdy, it would be you."

Hodges opens the wallet. There's hardly any cash inside, maybe eighty bucks total, but Madden doesn't need cash; he's got at least two dozen credit cards in at least six different names. Hodges looks at Madden with honest curiosity. "How do you keep them all straight?"

Madden doesn't reply.

With that same curiosity, Hodges says: "Are you never ashamed?"

Still looking straight ahead, Madden says: "That old bastard in El Paso is worth a hundred and fifty million dollars. He made most of it selling worthless oil leases. All right, I flew off with his plane. Left him nothing but his Cessna 172 and his Lear 35. Poor baby."

Hodges thinks, If this guy had a moral compass, it would always point due south. Talking is no use . . . but when was it ever?

He hunts through the wallet and finds a bill of particulars in the matter of the KingAir: two hundred thousand down, the rest held in escrow at First of Reno, to be paid after a satisfactory test flight. The paper is worthless in a practical sense—the plane was bought under a false name, with nonexistent money—but Hodges isn't always practical, and he's not too old to count coup and take scalps.

"Did you lock it up or leave the key at the desk so they could do it after they put it in the hangar?"

"At the desk."

"Okay, good." Hodges regards Madden earnestly. "Here comes the important part of our little talk, Oliver, so listen closely. I was hired to find the plane and take possession of it. That's all, end of story. I'm not FBI, MPD, or even a private dick. My sources are good, though, and I know you're on the verge of making a deal to buy a controlling interest in a couple of casinos out on the lake, one on Grande Belle Coeur Island and one on P'tit Grand Coeur." He taps the briefcase with his foot. "I'm sure the paperwork is in here, as I'm sure that if you want to remain a free man, it's never going to be signed."

"Oh now wait a minute!"

"Shut your hole. There's a ticket in the James Mallon name

at the Delta terminal. It's one-way to Los Angeles. Leaves in—" he looked at his watch—"in about ninety minutes. Which gives you just time enough to go through all the security shit. Be on that plane or you'll be in jail tonight. Do you understand?"

"I can't—"

"*Do you understand?*"

Madden—who is also Mallon, Morton, Mason, Dillon, Callen, and God knows how many others—thinks over his options, decides he has none, and gives a sullen nod.

"Great! I'll unlock you now, take my cuffs, and exit your vehicle. If you try making a move on me while I do either, I'll knock you into next week. Are you clear on that?"

"Yes."

"Your car key's on the grass. Big yellow Hertz fob, can't miss it. For now, both hands on the wheel. Ten and two, just like Dad taught you."

Madden puts both hands on the wheel. Hodges unlocks the cuffs, slips them back in his left pocket, and exits the Navigator. Madden doesn't move.

"You have a good day, now," Hodges says, and shuts the door.

7

He gets into his Prius, drives to the end of the Zane Aviation turnaround, parks, and watches Madden grub the Navigator's key out of the grass. He waves as Madden drives past him. Madden doesn't wave back, which doesn't even come close to breaking Hodges's heart. He follows the Navigator along the airport feeder road, not quite tailgating but close. When Madden turns off toward the main terminals, Hodges flashes a so-long with his lights.

Half a mile farther up, he pulls into the lot of Midwest Airmotive and calls Pete Huntley, his old partner. He gets a civil enough "Hey, Billy, how you doin," but nothing you'd call effusive. Since Hodges went his own way in the matter of the so-called Mercedes Killer (and barely escaped serious legal trouble as a result), his relationship with Pete has frosted over. Maybe this will thaw it out a bit. Certainly he feels no remorse about lying to the moke now heading for the Delta terminal; if ever there was a guy who deserved a heaping spoonful of his own medicine, it's Oliver Madden.

"How would you like to bag an extremely tasty turkey, Pete?"

"How tasty?" Still cool, but on the interested side of cool now.

"FBI Ten Most Wanted, that tasty enough? He's currently checking in at Delta, scheduled to leave for LA on Flight One-nineteen at one forty-five PM. Going under James Mallon, but his real name is Oliver Madden. He stole a bunch of money from the Feds five years ago as Oliver Mason, and you know how Uncle Sam feels about getting his pocket picked." He adds a few of the more colorful details on Madden's résumé.

"You know he's at Delta how?"

"Because I bought the ticket. I'm leaving the airport now. I just repo'd his plane. Which was not his plane, because he made the down payment with a rubber check. Holly will call Zane Aviation and give them all the details. She loves that part of the job."

A long moment of silence. Then: "Aren't you ever going to retire, Billy?"

That sort of hurts. "You could say thanks. It wouldn't kill you."

Pete sighs. "I'll call airport security, then get on out there myself." A pause. Then: "Thank you. *Kermit.*"

Hodges grins. It's not much, but it might be a start in repairing what has been, if not broken, then badly sprained. "Thank Holly. She's the one who tracked him down. She's still jumpy with people she doesn't know, but when she's on the computer, she kills."

"I'll be sure to do that."

"And say hi to Izzy." Isabelle Jaynes has been Pete's partner since Hodges pulled the pin. She's one dynamite redhead, and plenty smart. It occurs to Hodges, almost as a shock, that soon enough she'll be working with a new partner; Pete himself will be retiring ere long.

"I'll pass that on, too. Want to give me this guy's description for the airport security guys?"

"He's hard to miss. Six and a half feet tall, light brown suit, probably looking a little woozy just about now."

"You clocked him?"

"I *soothed* him."

Pete laughs. It's good to hear him do that. Hodges ends the call and heads back to the city, well on the way to being twenty thousand dollars richer, courtesy of a crusty old Texan named Dwight Cramm. He'll call and give Cramm the good news after he finds out what the Barbster wants.

8

Drew Halliday (Drew is what he prefers to be called now, among his small circle of friends) eats eggs Benedict at his usual corner table in Jamais Toujours. He ingests slowly, pacing himself, although he could gobble everything in four large gulps, then pick up the plate and lick the tasty yellow sauce like a dog licking its bowl. He has no close relatives, his lovelife has been in the rearview mirror for over fifteen years now, and—face it—his small circle of friends are really no more than acquaintances. The only things he cares about these days are books and food.

Well, no.

These days there's a third thing.

John Rothstein's notebooks have made a reappearance in his life.

The waiter, a young fellow in a white shirt and tight black pants, glides over. Longish dark blond hair, clean and tied back at the nape so his elegant cheekbones show. Drew has been in a little theater group for thirty years now (funny how time glides away . . . only not really), and he thinks William would make a perfectly adequate Romeo, always assuming he could act. And good waiters always can, a little.

"Will there be anything else, Mr. Halliday?"

Yes! he thinks. Two more of these, followed by two crème brûlées and a strawberry shortcake!

"Another cup of coffee, I think."

William smiles, exposing teeth that have received nothing but the best of dental care. "I'll be back with it in two shakes of a lamb's tail."

Drew pushes his plate away regretfully, leaving the last smear of yolk and hollandaise behind. He takes out his appointment book. It's a Moleskine, of course, the pocket-sized one. He pages past four months' worth of jottings—addresses, reminders to self, prices of books he's ordered or will order for various clients. Near the end, on a blank page all its own, are two names. The first is James Hawkins. He wonders if it's a coincidence or if the boy picked it deliberately. Do boys still read Robert Louis Stevenson these days? Drew tends to think this one did; after all, he claims to be a lit major, and Jim Hawkins is the hero-narrator of *Treasure Island*.

The name written below James Hawkins is Peter Saubers.

9

Saubers—aka Hawkins—came into the shop for the first time two weeks ago, hiding behind a ridiculous adolescent moustache that hadn't had a chance to grow out much. He was wearing black hornrims like the ones Drew (then Andy) affected back in the days when Jimmy Carter was president. Teenagers did not as a rule come into the shop, and that was fine with Drew; he might still be attracted to the occasional young male—William the Waiter being a case in point—but teens tended to be careless with valuable books, handling them roughly, reshelving them upside down, even dropping them. Also, they had a regrettable tendency to shoplift.

This one looked as if he would turn and sprint for the door if Drew so much as said boo. He was wearing a City College jacket, although the day was too warm for it. Drew, who'd read his share of Sherlock Holmes, put it together with the moustache and studious hornrims and deduced that here was a lad attempting to look older, as if he were trying to get into one of the dance clubs downtown instead of a bookshop specializing in rare volumes.

You want me to take you for at least twenty-one, Drew thought, but if you're a day past seventeen, I'll eat my hat. You're not here to browse, either, are you? I believe you are a young man on a mission.

Under his arm, the boy carried a large book and a manila envelope. Drew's first thought was that the kid wanted an appraisal on some moldy old thing he'd found in the attic, but as Mr. Moustache drew hesitantly closer, Drew saw a purple sticker he recognized at once on the spine of the book.

Drew's first impulse was to say Hello, son, but he quashed it. Let the kid have his college-boy disguise. What harm?

"Good afternoon, sir. May I help you?"

For a moment young Mr. Moustache said nothing. The dark brown of his new facial hair was in stark contrast to the pallor of his cheeks. Drew realized he was deciding whether to stay or mutter *Guess not* and get the hell out. One word would probably be enough to turn him around, but Drew suffered the not unusual antiquarian disease of curiosity. So he favored the boy with his most pleasant wouldn't-hurt-a-fly smile, folded his hands, and kept silent.

"Well . . ." the boy said at length. "Maybe."

Drew raised his eyebrows.

"You buy rarities as well as sell them, right? That's what your website says."

"I do. If I feel I can sell them at a profit, that is. It's the nature of the business."

The boy gathered his courage—Drew could almost see him doing it—and stepped all the way up to the desk, where the circular glow of an old-fashioned Anglepoise lamp spotlighted a semi-organized clutter of paperwork. Drew held out his hand. "Andrew Halliday."

The boy shook it briefly and then withdrew, as if fearful of being grabbed. "I'm James Hawkins."

"Pleased to meet you."

"Uh-huh. I think . . . I have something you might be interested in. Something a collector might pay a lot for. If it was the right collector."

"Not the book you're carrying, is it?" Drew could see the title now: *Dispatches from Olympus*. The subtitle wasn't on the spine, but Drew had owned a copy for many years and knew it well: *Letters from 20 Great American Writers in Their Own Hand*.

"Gosh, no. Not this one." James Hawkins gave a small, nervous laugh. "This is just for comparison."

"Very well, say on."

For a moment "James Hawkins" seemed unsure how to do that. Then he tucked his manila envelope more firmly under his arm and began to hurry through the glossy pages of *Dispatches from Olympus*, passing a note from Faulkner scolding an Oxford, Mississippi, feed company about a misplaced order, a gushy letter from Eudora Welty to Ernest Hemingway, a scrawl about who knew what from Sherwood Anderson, and a

grocery list Robert Penn Warren had decorated with a doodle
of two dancing penguins, one of them smoking a cigarette.

At last he found what he wanted, set the book on the desk,
and turned it to face Drew. "Here," he said. "Look at this."

Drew's heart jumped as he read the heading: *John Rothstein
to Flannery O'Connor*. The carefully photographed note had
been written on lined paper tattered down the lefthand side
where it had been torn from a dimestore notebook. Rothstein's
small, neat handwriting, very unlike the scrawl of so many
writers, was unmistakable.

February 19, 1953

My dear Flannery O'Connor,

　I am in receipt of your wonderful novel, Wise Blood, *which
you have so kindly inscribed to me. I can say* <u>wonderful</u> *because I
purchased a copy as soon as it came out, and read it immediately. I
am delighted to have a signed copy, as I am sure you are delighted
to have the royalty accruing from one more sold volume! I enjoyed
the entire motley cast of characters, especially Hazel Motes and
Enoch Emery, a zookeeper I'm sure my own Jimmy Gold would
have enjoyed and befriended. You have been called a "connoisseur of
grotesqueries," Miss O'Connor, yet what the critics miss—probably
because they have none themselves—is your lunatic sense of humor,
which takes no prisoners. I know you are physically unwell, but I
hope you will persevere in your work in spite of that. It is* <u>important</u>
work! Thanking you again,

John Rothstein

PS: I still laugh about the Famous Chicken!!!

Drew scanned the letter longer than necessary, to calm himself, then looked up at the boy calling himself James Hawkins.
"Do you understand the reference to the Famous Chicken?
I'll explain, if you like. It's a good example of what Rothstein
called her lunatic sense of humor."

"I looked it up. When Miss O'Connor was six or seven, she had—or claimed she had—a chicken that walked backwards. Some newsreel people came and filmed it, and the chicken was in the movies. She said it was the high point of her life, and everything afterwards was an anticlimax."

"Exactly right. Now that we've covered the Famous Chicken, what can I do for you?"

The boy took a deep breath and opened the clasp on his manila envelope. From inside he took a photocopy and laid it beside Rothstein's letter in *Dispatches from Olympus*. Drew Halliday's face remained placidly interested as he looked from one to the other, but beneath the desk, his fingers interlaced so tightly that his closely clipped nails dug into the backs of his hands. He knew what he was looking at immediately. The squiggles on the tails of the *y*s, the *b*s that always stood by themselves, the *h*s that stood high and the *g*s that dipped low. The question now was how much "James Hawkins" knew. Maybe not a lot, but almost certainly more than a little. Otherwise he would not be hiding behind a new moustache and specs looking suspiciously like the clear-glass kind that could be purchased in a drugstore or costume shop.

At the top of the page, circled, was the number 44. Below it was a fragment of poetry.

> *Suicide is circular, or so I think;*
> *you may have your own opinion.*
> *In the meantime, meditate on this.*
>
> *A plaza just after sunrise,*
> *You could say in Mexico.*
> *Or Guatemala, if you like.*
> *Anyplace where the rooms still come*
> *with wooden ceiling fans.*

In any case it's blanco up to the blue sky
except for the ragged mops of palms and
rosa where the boy outside the café
is washing cobbles, half asleep.
On the corner, waiting for the first

It ended there. Drew looked up at the boy.

"It goes on about the first bus of the day," James Hawkins said. "The kind that runs on wires. A *trolebus*, he calls it. It's Spanish for trolley. The wife of the man narrating the poem, or maybe it's his girlfriend, is sitting dead in the corner of the room. She shot herself. He's just found her."

"It doesn't strike me as deathless poesy," Drew said. In his current gobsmacked state, it was all he could *think* of to say. Regardless of its quality, the poem was the first new work by John Rothstein to appear in over half a century. No one had seen it but the author, this boy, and Drew himself. Unless Morris Bellamy had happened to glimpse it, which seemed unlikely given the great number of notebooks he claimed to have stolen.

The great number.

My God, the great number of notebooks.

"No, it's sure not Wilfred Owen or T. S. Eliot, but I don't think that's the point. Do you?"

Drew was suddenly aware that "James Hawkins" was watching him closely. And seeing what? Probably too much. Drew was used to playing them close to the vest—you had to in a business where lowballing the seller was as important as highballing potential buyers—but this was like the *Titanic* suddenly floating to the surface of the Atlantic Ocean, dinged-up and rusty, but *there*.

Okay, then, admit it.

"No, probably not." The photocopy and the letter to O'Connor were still side by side, and Drew couldn't help moving his pudgy finger back and forth between points of comparison. "If it's a forgery, it's a damned good one."

"It's not." No lack of confidence there.

"Where did you get it?"

The boy then launched into a bullshit story Drew barely listened to, something about how his uncle Phil in Cleveland had died and willed his book collection to young James, and there had been six Moleskine notebooks packed in with the paperbacks and Book of the Month Club volumes, and it turned out, hidey-ho, that these six notebooks, filled with all sorts of interesting stuff—mostly poetry, along with some essays and a few fragmentary short stories—were the work of John Rothstein.

"How did you know it was Rothstein?"

"I recognized his style, even in the poems," Hawkins said. It was a question he had prepared for, obviously. "I'm majoring in American Lit at CC, and I've read most of his stuff. But there's more. For instance, this one is about Mexico, and Rothstein spent six months wandering around there after he got out of the service."

"Along with a dozen other American writers of note, including Ernest Hemingway and the mysterious B. Traven."

"Yeah, but look at this." The boy drew a second photocopy from his envelope. Drew told himself not to reach for it greedily . . . and reached for it greedily. He was behaving as though he'd been in this business for three years instead of over thirty, but who could blame him? This was big. This was *huge*. The difficulty was that "James Hawkins" seemed to know it was.

Ah, but he doesn't know what *I* know, which includes where they came from. Unless Morrie is using him as a cat's paw, and how likely is that with Morrie rotting in Waynesville State Prison?

The writing on the second photocopy was clearly from the same hand, but not as neat. There had been no scratch-outs and marginal notes on the fragment of poetry, but there were plenty here.

"I think he might have written it while he was drunk," the boy said. "He drank a lot, you know, then quit. Cold turkey. Read it. You'll see what it's about."

The circled number at the top of this page was 77. The writing below it started in mid-sentence.

never anticipated. While good reviews are always sweet desserts in the short term, one finds they lead to indigestion—insomnia, night-mares, even problems taking that ever-more-important afternoon shit—in the long term. And the stupiddity is even more remark-able in the good notices than in the bad ones. To see Jimmy Gold as some sort of benchmark, a HERO, even, is like calling someone like Billy the Kid (or Charles Starkweather, his closest 20th century avatar) an American icon. Jimmy is as Jimmy is, even as I am or you are; he is modeled not on Huck Finn but Etienne Lantier, the greatest character in 19th century fiction! If I have withdrawn from the public eye, it is because that eye is infected and there is no reason to put more materiel before it. As Jimmy himself would say, "Shit don't

It ended there, but Drew knew what came next, and he was sure Hawkins did, too. It was Jimmy's famous motto, still sometimes seen on tee-shirts all these years later.

"He misspelled *stupidity*." It was all Drew could think of to say.

"Uh-huh, and *material*. Real mistakes, not cleaned up by some copyeditor." The boy's eyes glowed. It was a glow Drew had seen often, but never in one so young. "It's *alive*, that's what I think. Alive and breathing. You see what he says about Étienne Lantier? That's the main character of *Germinal*, by Émile Zola. And it's new! Do you get it? It's a new insight into a character everybody knows, and from the author himself! I bet some collectors would pay big bucks for the original of this, and all the rest of the stuff I have."

"You say there are six notebooks in your possession?"

"Uh-huh."

Six. Not a hundred or more. If six was all the kid had, then he certainly wasn't acting on Bellamy's behalf, unless Morris had for some reason split his haul up. Drew couldn't see his old pal doing that.

"They're the medium-sized ones, eighty pages in each. That's four hundred and eighty pages. A lot of white space—with poems there always is—but they're not all poems. There are those short stories, too. One is about Jimmy Gold as a kid."

But here was a question: did he, Drew, really *believe* there were only six? Was it possible the boy was holding back the good stuff? And if so, was he holding back because he wanted to sell the rest later, or because he didn't want to sell it at all? To Drew, the glow in his eyes suggested the latter, although the boy might not yet know it consciously.

"Sir? Mr. Halliday?"

"Sorry. Just getting used to the idea that this really might be new Rothstein material."

"It is," the boy said. There was no doubt in his voice. "So how much?"

"How much would *I* pay?" Drew thought *son* would be okay now, because they were about to get down to the dickering. "Son, I'm not exactly made of money. Nor am I completely convinced these aren't forgeries. A hoax. I'd have to see the real items."

Drew could see Hawkins biting his lip behind the nascent moustache. "I wasn't talking about how much *you'd* pay, I was talking about private collectors. You must know some who are willing to spend big money for special items."

"I know a couple, yes." He knew a dozen. "But I wouldn't even write to them on the basis of two photocopied pages. As for getting authentication from a handwriting expert . . . that might be dicey. Rothstein was murdered, you know, which makes these stolen property."

"Not if he gave them to someone before he was killed," the boy countered swiftly, and Drew had to remind himself again that the kid had prepared for this encounter. But I have experience on my side, he thought. Experience and craft.

"Son, there's no way to prove that's what happened."

"There's no way to prove it wasn't, either."

So: impasse.

Suddenly the boy grabbed the two photocopies and jammed them back into the manila envelope.

"Wait a minute," Drew said, alarmed. "Whoa. Hold on."

"No, I think it was a mistake coming here. There's a place in Kansas City, Jarrett's Fine Firsts and Rare Editions. They're one of the biggest in the country. I'll try there."

"If you can hold off a week, I'll make some calls," Drew said. "But you have to leave the photocopies."

The boy hovered, unsure. At last he said, "How much could you get, do you think?"

"For almost five hundred pages of unpublished—hell, *unseen*—Rothstein material? The buyer would probably want at least a computer handwriting analysis, there are a couple of good programs that do that, but assuming that proved out, perhaps . . ." He calculated the lowest possible figure he could throw out without sounding absurd. "Perhaps fifty thousand dollars."

James Hawkins either accepted this, or seemed to. "And what would your commission be?"

Drew laughed politely. "Son . . . James . . . no dealer would take a *commission* on a deal like this one. Not when the creator—known as the proprietor, in legalese—was murdered and the material might have been stolen. We'd split right down the middle."

"No." The boy said it at once. He might not yet be able to grow the biker moustache he saw in his dreams, but he had balls as well as smarts. "Seventy-thirty. My favor."

Drew could give in on this, get maybe a quarter of a million for the six notebooks and give the boy seventy percent of fifty K, but wouldn't "James Hawkins" expect him to dicker, at least a little? Wouldn't he be suspicious if he didn't?

"Sixty-forty. My last offer, and of course contingent on finding a buyer. That would be thirty thousand dollars for something you found crammed into a cardboard box along with old copies of *Jaws* and *The Bridges of Madison County*. Not a bad return, I'd say."

The boy shifted from foot to foot, saying nothing but clearly conflicted.

Drew reverted to the wouldn't-hurt-a-fly smile. "Leave the photocopies with me. Come back in a week and I'll tell you how we stand. And here's some advice—stay away from Jarrett's place. The man will pick your pockets."

"I'd want cash."

Drew thought, Don't we all.

"You're getting way ahead of yourself, son."

The boy came to a decision and put the manila envelope down on the cluttered desk. "Okay. I'll come back."

Drew thought, I'm sure you will. And I believe my bargaining position will be much stronger when you do.

He held out his hand. The boy shook it again, as briefly as he could while still being polite. As if he were afraid of leaving fingerprints. Which in a way he had already done.

Drew sat where he was until "Hawkins" went out, then dropped into his office chair (it gave out a resigned groan) and woke up his sleeping Mac. There were two security cameras mounted above the front door, one pointing each way along Lacemaker Lane. He watched the kid turn the corner onto Crossway Avenue and disappear from sight.

The purple sticker on the spine of *Dispatches from Olympus*, that was the key. It marked the volume as a library book, and Drew knew every branch in the city. Purple meant a reference volume from the Garner Street Library, and reference volumes weren't supposed to circulate. If the kid had tried to smuggle it out under his City College jacket, the security gate would have buzzed when he went through, because that purple sticker was also an antitheft device. Which led to another Holmesian deduction, once you added in the kid's obvious book-smarts.

Drew went to the Garner Street Library's website, where all sorts of choices were displayed: SUMMER HOURS, KIDS & TEENS, UPCOMING EVENTS, CLASSIC FILM SERIES, and, last but far from least: MEET OUR STAFF.

Drew Halliday clicked on this and needed to click no farther, at least to begin with. Above the thumbnail bios was a photo of the staff, roughly two dozen in all, gathered on the library lawn. The statue of Horace Garner, open book in hand, loomed behind them. They were all smiles, including his boy, sans moustache and bogus spectacles. Second row, third from the left. According to the bio, young Mr. Peter Saubers was a student at Northfield High, currently working part-time. He hoped to major in English, with a minor in Library Science.

Drew continued his researches, aided by the fairly unusual surname. He was sweating lightly, and why not? Six notebooks already seemed like a pittance, a tease. *All* of them— some containing a fourth Jimmy Gold novel, if his psycho friend had been right all those years ago—might be worth as much as fifty million dollars, if they were broken up and sold to different collectors. The fourth Jimmy Gold alone might fetch twenty. And with Morrie Bellamy safely tucked away in prison, all that stood in his way was one teenage boy who couldn't even grow a proper moustache.

10

William the Waiter returns with Drew's check, and Drew tucks his American Express card into the leather folder. It will not be refused, he's confident of that. He's less sure about the other two cards, but he keeps the Amex relatively clean, because it's the one he uses in business transactions.

Business hasn't been so good over the last few years, although God knew it *should* have been. It should have been terrific, especially between 2008 and 2012, when the American economy fell into a sinkhole and couldn't seem to climb back out. In such times the value of precious commodities—real things, as opposed to computer boops and bytes on the New York Stock Exchange—always went up. Gold and diamonds, yes, but also art, antiques, and rare books. Fucking Michael Jarrett in KC is now driving a Porsche. Drew has seen it on his Facebook page.

His thoughts turn to his second meeting with Peter Saubers. He wishes the kid hadn't found out about the third mortgage; that had been a turning point. Maybe *the* turning point.

Drew's financial woes go back to that damned James Agee book, *Let Us Now Praise Famous Men.* Gorgeous copy, mint condition, signed by Agee *and* Walker Evans, the man who'd taken the photographs. How was Drew supposed to know it had been stolen?

All right, he probably *did* know, certainly all the red flags were there and flying briskly, and he should have steered clear, but the seller had had no idea of the volume's actual worth, and Drew had let down his guard a little. Not enough to get fined or thrown in jail, and thank Christ for that, but the results have been long-term. Ever since 1999 he's carried a certain *aroma* with him to every convention, symposium, and book auction. Reputable dealers and buyers tend to give him a miss, unless—here is the irony—they've got something just a teensy bit sketchy they'd like to turn over for a quick profit. Sometimes when he can't sleep, Drew thinks, *They are pushing me to the dark side. It's not my fault. Really, I'm the victim here.*

All of which makes Peter Saubers even more important.

William comes back with the leather folder, face solemn. Drew doesn't like that. Maybe the card has been refused after all. Then his favorite waiter smiles, and Drew releases the breath he's been holding in a soft sigh.

"Thanks, Mr. Halliday. Always great to see you."

"Likewise, William. Likewise, I'm sure." He signs with a flourish and slides his Amex—a bit bowed but not broken—back into his wallet.

On the street, walking toward his shop (the thought that he might be waddling never crosses his mind), his thoughts turn to the boy's second visit, which went *fairly* well, but not nearly as well as Drew had hoped and expected. At their first meeting, the boy had been so uneasy that Drew worried he might be tempted to destroy the priceless trove of manuscript he'd stumbled across. But the glow in his eyes had argued against that, especially when he talked about that second photocopy, with its drunken ramblings about the critics.

It's alive, Saubers had said. *That's what I think.*

And can the boy kill it? Drew asks himself as he enters his shop and turns the sign from CLOSED to OPEN. *I don't think so. Any more than he could let the authorities take all that treasure away, despite his threats.*

Tomorrow is Friday. The boy has promised to come in immediately after school so they can conclude their business. The boy thinks it will be a negotiating session. He thinks he's still holding some cards. Perhaps he is . . . but Drew's are higher.

The light on his answering machine is blinking. It's probably someone wanting to sell him insurance or an extended warranty on his little car (the idea of Jarrett driving a Porsche around Kansas City pinches momentarily at his ego), but you can never tell until you check. Millions are within his reach, but until they are actually in his grasp, it's business as usual.

Drew goes to see who called while he was having his lunch, and recognizes Saubers's voice from the first word.

His fists clench as he listens.

11

When the artist formerly known as Hawkins came in on the Friday following his first visit, the moustache was a trifle fuller but his step was just as tentative—a shy animal approaching a bit of tasty bait. By then Drew had learned a great deal about him and his family. And about the notebook pages, those too. Three different computer apps had confirmed that the letter to Flannery O'Connor and the writing on the photocopies were the work of the same man. Two of these apps compared handwriting. The third—not entirely reliable, given the small size of the scanned-in samples—pointed out certain stylistic similarities, most of which the boy had already seen. These results were tools laid by for the time when Drew would approach prospective buyers. He himself had no doubts, having seen one of the notebooks with his own eyes thirty-six years ago, on a table outside the Happy Cup.

"Hello," Drew said. This time he didn't offer to shake hands.

"Hi."

"You didn't bring the notebooks."

"I need a number from you first. You said you'd make some calls."

Drew had made none. It was still far too early for that. "If you recall, I gave *you* a number. I said your end would come to thirty thousand dollars."

The boy shook his head. "That's not enough. And sixty-forty isn't enough, either. It would have to be seventy-thirty. I'm not stupid. I know what I have."

"I know things, too. Your real name is Peter Saubers. You don't go to City College; you go to Northfield High and work part-time at the Garner Street Library."

The boy's eyes widened. His mouth fell open. He actually swayed on his feet, and for a moment Drew thought he might faint.

"How—"

"The book you brought. *Dispatches from Olympus*. I recognized the Reference Room security sticker. After that it was easy. I even know where you live—on Sycamore Street." Which made perfect, even divine sense. Morris Bellamy had lived on Sycamore Street, in the same house. Drew had never been there—because Morris didn't want him to meet his vampire of a mother, Drew suspected—but city records proved it. Had the notebooks been hidden behind a wall in the basement, or buried beneath the floor of the garage? Drew was betting it was one or the other.

He leaned as far forward as his paunch would allow and engaged the boy's dismayed eyes.

"Here's some more. Your father was seriously injured in the City Center Massacre back in '09. He was there because he became unemployed after the downturn in '08. There was a feature story in the Sunday paper a couple of years ago, about how some of the people who survived were doing. I looked it up, and it made for interesting reading. Your family moved to the North Side after your father got hurt, which must have been a considerable comedown, but you Sauberses landed on your feet. A nip here and a tuck there with just your mom working, but plenty of people did worse. American success story. Get knocked down? Arise, brush yourself off, and get

back in the race! Except the story never really said how your
family managed that. Did it?"

The boy wet his lips, tried to speak, couldn't, cleared his
throat, tried again. "I'm leaving. Coming here was a big mistake."

He turned away from the desk.

"Peter, if you walk out that door, I can just about guarantee
you'll be in jail by tonight. What a shame that would be, with
your whole life ahead of you."

Saubers turned back, eyes wide, mouth open and trembling.

"I researched the Rothstein killing, too. The police believed
that the thieves who murdered him only took the notebooks
because they were in his safe along with his money. According
to the theory, they broke in for what thieves usually break in
for, which is cash. Plenty of people in the town where he lived
knew the old guy kept cash in the house, maybe a lot of it.
Those stories circulated in Talbot Corners for years. Finally the
wrong someones decided to find out if the stories were true.
And they were, weren't they?"

Saubers returned to the desk. Slowly. Step by step.

"You found his stolen notebooks, but you also found some
stolen money, that's what I think. Enough to keep your family
solvent until your dad could get back on his feet again. Literally on his feet, because the story said he was busted up quite
badly. Do your folks know, Peter? Are they in on it? Did Mom
and Dad send you here to sell the notebooks now that the
money's gone?"

Most of this was guesswork—if Morris had said anything
about money that day outside the Happy Cup, Drew couldn't
remember it—but he observed each of his guesses hit home
like hard punches to the face and midsection. Drew felt any
detective's delight in seeing he had followed a true trail.

"I don't know what you're talking about." The boy sounded more like a phone answering machine than a human being.

"And as for there only being six notebooks, that really doesn't compute. Rothstein went dark in 1960, after publishing his last short story in *The New Yorker*. He was murdered in 1978. Hard to believe he only filled six eighty-page notebooks in eighteen years. I bet there were more. A *lot* more."

"You can't prove anything." Still in that same robotic monotone. Saubers was teetering; two or three more punches and he'd fall. It was rather thrilling.

"What would the police find if they came to your house with a search warrant, my young friend?"

Instead of falling, Saubers pulled himself together. If it hadn't been so annoying, it would have been admirable. "What about you, Mr. Halliday? You've already been in trouble once about selling what wasn't yours to sell."

Okay, that was a hit . . . but only a glancing blow. Drew nodded cheerfully.

"It's why you came to me, isn't it? You found out about the Agee business and thought I might help you do something illegal. Only my hands were clean then and they're clean now." He spread them to demonstrate. "I'd say I took some time to make sure that what you were trying to sell was the real deal, and once I was, I did my civic duty and called the police."

"But that's not true! It's not and you know it!"

Welcome to the real world, Peter, Drew thought. He said nothing, just let the kid explore the box he was in.

"I could burn them." Saubers seemed to be speaking to himself rather than Drew, trying the idea on for size. "I could go h . . . to where they are, and just burn them."

"How many are there? Eighty? A hundred and twenty? A hundred and *forty*? They'd find residue, son. The ashes. Even if they didn't, I have the photocopied pages. They'd start asking questions about just how your family *did* manage to get through the big recession as well as it did, especially with your father's injuries and all the medical bills. I think a competent accountant might find that your family's outlay extended its income by quite a bit."

Drew had no idea if this was true, but the kid didn't, either. He was close to panic now, and that was good. Panicked people never thought clearly.

"There's no proof." Saubers could hardly talk above a whisper. "The money is gone."

"I'm sure it is, or you wouldn't be here. But the financial trail remains. And who will follow it besides the police? The IRS! Who knows, Peter, maybe your mother and dad can also go to jail, for tax evasion. That would leave your sister—Tina, I believe?—all alone, but perhaps she has a kind old auntie she can live with until your folks get out."

"What do you want?"

"Don't be dense. I want the notebooks. *All* of them."

"If I give them to you, what do I get?"

"The knowledge that you're free and clear. Which, given your situation, is priceless."

"Are you *serious*?"

"Son—"

"Don't call me that!" The boy clenched his fists.

"Peter, think it through. If you refuse to turn the notebooks over to me, I'm going to turn *you* over to the police. But once you hand them over, my hold on you vanishes, because I have received stolen property. You'll be safe."

While he spoke, Drew's right index finger hovered near the silent alarm button beneath his desk. Pushing it was the last thing in the world he wanted to do, but he didn't like those clenched fists. In his panic, it might occur to Saubers that there was one other way to shut Drew Halliday's mouth. They were currently being recorded on security video, but the boy might not have realized that.

"And you walk away with hundreds and thousands of dollars," Saubers said bitterly. "Maybe even millions."

"You got your family through a tough time," Drew said. He thought of adding *why be greedy*, but under the circumstances, that might sound a little . . . off. "I think you should be content with that."

The boy's face offered a wordless reply: *Easy for you to say.*

"I need time to think."

Drew nodded, but not in agreement. "I understand how you feel, but no. If you walk out of here now, I can promise a police car waiting for you when you get home."

"And you lose your big payday."

Drew shrugged. "It wouldn't be the first." Although never one of this size, that was true.

"My dad's in real estate, did you know that?"

The sudden change in direction put Drew off his stride a bit. "Yes, I saw that when I was doing my research. Has his own little business now, and good for him. Although I have an idea that John Rothstein's money might have paid for some of the start-up costs."

"I asked him to research all the bookstores in town," Saubers said. "I told him I was doing a paper on how e-books are impacting traditional bookstores. This was before I even came to see you, while I was still making up my mind if I should take the chance. He found out you took a third mortgage on this place last year, and said you only got it because of the location. Lacemaker Lane being pretty upscale and all."

"I don't think that has anything to do with the subject under discus—"

"You're right, we went through a really bad time, and you know something? That gives a person a nose for people who are in trouble. Even if you're a kid. Maybe especially if you're a kid. I think you're pretty strapped yourself."

Drew raised the finger that had been poised near the silent alarm button and pointed it at Saubers. "Don't fuck with me, kid."

Saubers's color had come back in big hectic patches, and Drew saw something he didn't like and certainly hadn't intended: he had made the boy angry.

"I know you're trying to rush me into this, and it's not going to work. Yes, okay, I've got his notebooks. There's a hundred and sixty-five. Not all of them are full, but most of them are. And guess what? It was never the Gold trilogy, it was the Gold *cycle*. There are two more novels, both in the notebooks. First drafts, yeah, but pretty clean."

The boy was talking faster and faster, figuring out everything Drew had hoped he would be too frightened to see even as he was speaking.

"They're hidden away, but I guess you're right, if you call the police, they'll find them. Only my parents never knew, and I think the police will believe that. As for me . . . I'm still a minor." He even smiled a little, as if just realizing this. "They won't do much to me, since I never stole the notebooks or the money in the first place. I wasn't even born. You'll come out clean, but you also won't have anything to show for it. When the bank takes this place—my dad says they will, sooner or later—and there's an Au Bon Pain here instead, I'll come in and eat a croissant in your honor."

"That's quite a speech," Drew said.

"Well, it's over. I'm leaving."

"I warn you, you're being very foolish."

"I told you, I need time to think."

"How long?"

"A week. You need to think, too, Mr. Halliday. Maybe we can still work something out."

"I hope so, son." Drew used the word deliberately. "Because if we can't, I'll make that call. I am not bluffing."

The boy's bravado collapsed. His eyes filled with tears. Before they could fall, he turned and walked out.

12

Now comes this voicemail, which Drew listens to with fury but also with fear, because the boy sounds so cold and composed on top and so desperate underneath.

"I can't come tomorrow like I said I would. I completely forgot the junior-senior retreat for class officers, and I got elected vice president of the senior class next year. I know that sounds like an excuse, but it's not. I guess it entirely slipped my mind, what with you threatening to send me to jail and all."

Erase this right away, Drew thinks, his fingernails biting into his palms.

"It's at River Bend resort, up in Victor County. We leave on a bus at eight tomorrow morning—it's a teacher in-service day, so there's no school—and come back Sunday night. Twenty of us. I thought about begging off, but my parents are already worried about me. My sister, too. If I skip the retreat, they'll know something's wrong. I think my mom thinks I might have gotten some girl pregnant."

The boy voices a brief, semi-hysterical laugh. Drew thinks there's nothing more terrifying than boys of seventeen. You have absolutely no idea what they'll do.

"I'll come on Monday afternoon instead," Saubers resumes. "If you wait that long, maybe we can work something out. A compromise. I've got an idea. And if you think I'm just shining you on about the retreat, call the resort and check the reservation. Northfield High School Student Government. Maybe I'll see you on Monday. If not, not. Goodb—"

That's where the message-time—extra-long, for clients who call after-hours, usually from the West Coast—finally runs out. *Beep*.

Drew sits down in his chair (ignoring its despairing squeal, as always), and stares at the answering machine for nearly a full minute. He feels no need to call the River Bend Resort . . . which is, amusingly enough, only six or seven miles upriver from the penitentiary where the original notebook thief is now serving a life sentence. Drew is sure Saubers was telling the truth about the retreat, because it's so easy to check. About his reasons for not ditching it he's far less sure. Maybe Saubers has decided to call Drew's bluff about bringing the police into it. Except it's not a bluff. He has no intention of letting Saubers have what Drew can't have himself. One way or another, the little bastard is going to give those notebooks up.

I'll wait until Monday afternoon, Drew thinks. I can afford to wait that long, but then this situation is going to be resolved, one way or the other. I've already given him too much rope.

He reflects that the Saubers boy and his old friend Morris Bellamy, although at opposite ends of the age-spectrum, are very much alike when it comes to the Rothstein notebooks. They lust for what's *inside* them. It's why the boy only wanted to sell him six, and probably the six he judged least interesting. Drew, on the other hand, cares little about John Rothstein. He read *The Runner*, but only because Morrie was bonkers on the subject. He never bothered with the other two, or the book of short stories.

That's your Achilles' heel, son, Drew thinks. That collector's lust. While I, on the other hand, only care about money, and money simplifies everything. So go ahead. Enjoy your weekend of pretend politics. When you come back, we'll play some hardball.

Drew leans over his paunch and erases the message.

13

Hodges gets a good whiff of himself on his way back into the city and decides to divert to his house long enough for a veggie burger and a quick shower. Also a change of clothes. Harper Road isn't much out of his way, and he'll be more comfortable in a pair of jeans. Jeans are one of the major perks of self-employment, as far as he's concerned.

Pete Huntley calls as he's heading out the door, to inform his old partner that Oliver Madden is in custody. Hodges congratulates Pete on the collar and has just settled behind the wheel of his Prius when his phone rings again. This time it's Holly.

"Where *are* you, Bill?"

Hodges looks at his watch and sees it's somehow gotten all the way to three fifteen. How the time flies when you're having fun, he thinks.

"My house. Just leaving for the office."

"What are you doing *there*?"

"Stopped for a shower. Didn't want to offend your delicate olfactories. And I didn't forget about Barbara. I'll call as soon as I—"

"You won't have to. She's here. With a little chum named Tina. They came in a taxi."

"A taxi?" Ordinarily, kids don't even *think* of taxis. Maybe whatever Barbara wants to discuss is a little more serious than he believed.

"Yes. I put them in your office." Holly lowers her voice. "Barbara's just worried, but the other one acts scared to death. I think she's in some kind of jam. You should get here as soon as you can, Bill."

"Roger that."

"Please hurry. You know I'm not good with strong emotions. I'm working on that with my therapist, but right now I'm just *not*."

"On my way. There in twenty."

"Should I go across the street and get them Cokes?"

"I don't know." The light at the bottom of the hill turns yellow. Hodges puts on speed and scoots through it. "Use your judgment."

"But I have so little," Holly mourns, and before he can reply, she tells him again to hurry and hangs up.

14

While Bill Hodges was explaining the facts of life to the dazed Oliver Madden and Drew Halliday was settling in to his eggs Benedict, Pete Saubers was in the nurse's office at Northfield High, pleading a migraine headache and asking to be dismissed from afternoon classes. The nurse wrote the slip with no hesitation, because Pete is one of the good ones: Honor Roll, lots of school activities (although no sports), near-perfect attendance. Also, he *looked* like someone suffering a migraine. His face was far too pale, and there were dark circles under his eyes. She asked if he needed a ride home.

"No," Pete said, "I'll take the bus."

She offered him Advil—it's all she's allowed to dispense for headaches—but he shook his head, telling her he had special pills for migraines. He forgot to bring one that day, but said he'd take one as soon as he got home. He felt okay about this story, because he really did have a headache. Just not the physical kind. His headache was Andrew Halliday, and one of his mother's Zomig tablets (she's the migraine sufferer in the family) wouldn't cure it.

Pete knew he had to take care of that himself.

15

He has no intention of taking the bus. The next one won't be along for half an hour, and he can be on Sycamore Street in fifteen minutes if he runs, and he will, because this Thursday afternoon is all he has. His mother and father are at work and won't be home until at least four. Tina won't be home at all. She *says* she has been invited to spend a couple of nights with her old friend Barbara Robinson on Teaberry Lane, but Pete thinks she might actually have invited herself. If so, it probably means his sister hasn't given up her hopes of attending Chapel Ridge. Pete thinks he might still be able to help her with that, but only if this afternoon goes perfectly. That's a very big if, but he has to do *something*. If he doesn't, he'll go crazy.

He's lost weight since foolishly making the acquaintance of Andrew Halliday, the acne of his early teens is enjoying a return engagement, and of course there are those dark circles under his eyes. He's been sleeping badly, and what sleep he's managed has been haunted by bad dreams. After awakening from these—often curled in a fetal position, pajamas damp with sweat—Pete has lain awake, trying to think his way out of the trap he's in.

He genuinely forgot the class officers' retreat, and when Mrs. Gibson, the chaperone, reminded him of it yesterday, it shocked his brain into a higher gear. That was after period five French, and before he got to his calculus class, only two doors down, he has the rough outline of a plan in his head. It partly depends on an old red wagon, and even more on a certain set of keys.

Once out of sight of the school, Pete calls Andrew Halliday Rare Editions, a number he wishes he did not have on speed dial. He gets the answering machine, which at least saves him another arkie-barkie. The message he leaves is a long one, and the machine cuts him off as he's finishing, but that's okay.

If he can get those notebooks out of the house, the police will find nothing, search warrant or no search warrant. He's confident his parents will keep quiet about the mystery money, as they have all along. As Pete slips his cell back into the pocket of his chinos, a phrase from freshman Latin pops into his head. It's a scary one in any language, but it fits this situation perfectly.

Alea iacta est.

The die is cast.

16

Before going into his house, Pete ducks into the garage to make sure Tina's old Kettler wagon is still there. A lot of their stuff went in the yard sale they had before moving from their old house, but Teens had made such a fuss about the Kettler, with its old-fashioned wooden sides, that their mother relented. At first Pete doesn't see it and gets worried. Then he spots it in the corner and lets out a sigh of relief. He remembers Teens trundling back and forth across the lawn with all her stuffed toys packed into it (Mrs. Beasley holding pride of place, of course), telling them that they were going on a nik-nik in the woods, with devil-ham samwitches and ginger-snap tooties for children who could behave. Those had been good days, before the lunatic driving the stolen Mercedes had changed everything.

No more nik-niks after that.

Pete lets himself into the house and goes directly to his father's tiny home office. His heart is pounding furiously, because this is the crux of the matter. Things might go wrong even if he finds the keys he needs, but if he doesn't, this will be over before it gets started. He has no Plan B.

Although Tom Saubers's business mostly centers on real estate search—finding likely properties that are for sale or might come up for sale, and passing these prospects on to small companies and independent operators—he has begun creeping back into primary sales again, albeit in a small way, and only here on the North Side. That didn't amount to much in 2012, but over the last couple of years, he's bagged several decent commissions, and has an exclusive on a dozen properties in the Tree Streets neighborhood. One of these—the irony wasn't lost on any of them—is 49 Elm Street, the house that had belonged to Deborah Hartsfield and her son, Brady, the so-called Mercedes Killer.

"I may be awhile selling that one," Dad said one night at dinner, then actually laughed.

A corkboard is mounted on the wall to the left of his father's computer. The keys to the various properties he's currently agenting are thumbtacked to it, each on its own ring. Pete scans the board anxiously, sees what he wants—what he *needs*—and punches the air with a fist. The label on this keyring reads BIRCH STREET REC.

"Unlikely I can move a brick elephant like that," Tom Saubers said at another family dinner, "but if I do, we can kiss this place goodbye and move back to the Land of the Hot Tub and BMW." Which is what he always calls the West Side.

Pete shoves the keys to the Rec into his pocket along with his cell phone, then pelts upstairs and gets the suitcases he used when he brought the notebooks to the house. This time he wants them for short-term transport only. He climbs the pull-down ladder to the attic and loads in the notebooks (treating them with care even in his haste). He lugs the suitcases down to the second floor one by one, unloads the notebooks onto his bed, returns the suitcases to his parents' closet, and then races *downstairs*, all the way to the cellar. He's sweating freely from his exertions and probably smells like the monkey house at the zoo, but there will be no time to shower until later. He ought to change his shirt, though. He has a Key Club polo that will be perfect for what comes next. Key Club is always doing community service shit.

His mother keeps a good supply of empty cartons in the cellar. Pete grabs two of the bigger ones and goes back upstairs, first detouring into his father's office again to grab a Sharpie.

Remember to put that back when you return the keys, he cautions himself. Remember to put *everything* back.

He packs the notebooks into the cartons—all but the six he still hopes to sell to Andrew Halliday—and folds down the lids. He uses the Sharpie to print **KITCHEN SUPPLIES** on each, in big capital letters. He looks at his watch. Doing okay for time . . . as long as Halliday doesn't listen to his message and blow the whistle on him, that is. Pete doesn't believe that's likely, but it isn't out of the question, either. This is unknown territory. Before leaving his bedroom, he hides the six remaining notebooks behind the loose baseboard in his closet. There's just enough room, and if all goes well, they won't be there long.

He carries the cartons out to the garage and puts them in Tina's old wagon. He starts down the driveway, remembers he forgot to change into the Key Club polo shirt, and pelts back up the stairs again. As he's pulling it over his head, a cold realization hits him: he left the notebooks sitting in the driveway. They are worth a huge amount of money, and there they are, out in broad daylight where anyone could come along and take them.

Idiot! he scolds himself. Idiot, idiot, fucking idiot!

Pete sprints back downstairs, the new shirt already sweat-stuck to his back. The wagon is there, of course it is, who would bother stealing boxes marked kitchen supplies? Duh! But it was still a stupid thing to do, some people will steal anything that's not nailed down, and it raises a valid question: How many other stupid things is he doing?

He thinks, I never should have gotten into this, I should have called the police and turned in the money and the notebooks as soon as I found them.

But because he has the uncomfortable habit of being honest with himself (most of the time, at least), he knows that if he had it all to do over again, he would probably do most of it the same way, because his parents had been on the verge of breaking up, and he loved them too much not to at least try to prevent that.

And it worked, he thinks. The bonehead move was not quitting while I was ahead.

But.

Too late now.

17

His first idea had been to put the notebooks back in the buried trunk, but Pete rejected that almost immediately. If the police came with the search warrant Halliday had threatened, where might they try next when they didn't find the notebooks in the house? All they'd have to do was go into the kitchen and see that undeveloped land beyond the backyard. The perfect spot. If they followed the path and saw a patch of freshly turned ground by the stream, it would be ballgame over. No, this way is better.

Scarier, though.

He pulls Tina's old wagon down the sidewalk and turns left onto Elm. John Tighe, who lives on the corner of Sycamore and Elm, is out mowing his lawn. His son Bill is tossing a Frisbee to the family dog. It sails over the dog's head and lands in the wagon, coming to rest between the two boxes.

"Hum it!" Billy Tighe shouts, cutting across the lawn. His brown hair bounces. "Hum it *hard*!"

Pete does so, but waves Billy off when he goes to throw him another. Someone honks at him when he turns onto Birch, and Pete almost jumps out of his skin, but it's only Andrea Kellogg, the woman who does Linda Saubers's hair once a month. Pete gives her a thumbs-up and what he hopes is a sunny grin. At least she doesn't want to play Frisbee, he thinks.

And here is the Rec, a three-story brick box with a sign out front reading FOR SALE and CALL THOMAS SAUBERS REAL ESTATE, followed by his dad's cell number. The first-floor windows have been blocked with plywood to keep kids from breaking them, but otherwise it still looks pretty good. A couple of tags on the bricks, sure, but the Rec was prime tagger territory even when it was open. The lawn in front is mowed. That's Dad's doing, Pete thinks with some pride. He probably hired some kid to do it. I would've done it for free, if he'd asked.

He parks the wagon at the foot of the steps, lugs the cartons up one at a time, and is pulling the keys out of his pocket when a beat-up Datsun pulls over. It's Mr. Evans, who used to coach Little League when there was still a league on this side of town. Pete played for him when Mr. Evans coached the Zoney's Go-Mart Zebras.

"Hey, Centerfield!" He's leaned over to roll down the passenger window.

Shit, Pete thinks. Shit-shit-shit.

"Hi, Coach Evans."

"What're you doing? They opening the Rec up again?"

"I don't think so." Pete has prepared a story for this eventuality, but hoped he wouldn't have to use it. "It's some kind of political thing next week. League of Women Voters? Maybe a debate? I don't know for sure."

It's at least plausible, because this is an election year with primaries just a couple of weeks away and municipal issues up the wazoo.

"Plenty to argue about, that's for sure." Mr. Evans—overweight, friendly, never much of a strategist but big on team spirit and always happy to pass out sodas after games and practices—is wearing his old Zoney Zebras cap, now faded and lapped with sweat-stains. "Need a little help?"

Oh please no. *Please.*

"Nah, I got it."

"Hey, I'm happy to lend a hand." Pete's old coach turns off the Datsun's engine and begins horsing his bulk across the seat, ready to jump out.

"Really, Coach, I'm okay. If you help me, I'll be done too soon and have to go back to class."

Mr. Evans laughs and slides back under the wheel. "I get that." He keys the engine and the Datsun farts blue smoke. "But you be sure and lock up tight once you're done, y'hear?"

"Right," Pete says. The keys to the Rec slip through his sweaty fingers and he bends to pick them up. When he straightens, Mr. Evans is pulling away.

Thank you, God. And please don't let him call up my dad to congratulate him on his civic-minded son.

The first key Pete tries won't fit the lock. The second one does, but won't turn. He wiggles it back and forth as sweat streams down his face and trickles, stinging, into his left eye. No joy. He's thinking he may have to unbury the trunk after all—which will mean going back to the garage for tools—when the balky old lock finally decides to cooperate. He pushes open the door, carries the cartons inside, then goes back for the wagon. He doesn't want anyone wondering what it's doing sitting there at the foot of the steps.

The Rec's big rooms have been almost completely cleaned out, which makes them seem even bigger. It's hot inside with no air-conditioning, and the air tastes stale and dusty. With the windows blocked up, it's also gloomy. Pete's footfalls echo as he carries the cartons through the big main room where kids used to play boardgames and watch TV, then into the kitchen. The door leading down to the basement is also locked, but the key he tried first out front opens it, and at least the power is still on. A good thing, because he never thought to bring a flashlight.

He carries the first carton downstairs and sees something delightful: the basement is loaded with crap. Dozens of card tables are stacked against one wall, at least a hundred folding chairs are leaning in rows against another, there are old stereo components and outdated video game consoles, and, best of all, dozens of cartons pretty much like his. He looks in a few and sees old sports trophies, framed photos of intramural teams from the eighties and nineties, a set of beat-to-shit catcher's gear, a jumble of LEGOs. Good God, there are even a few marked KITCHEN! Pete puts his cartons with these, where they look right at home.

Best I can do, he thinks. And if I can just get out of here without anyone coming in to ask me what the hell I'm up to, I think it will be good enough.

He locks the basement, then returns to the main door, listening to the echo of his footfalls and remembering all the times he brought Tina here so she wouldn't have to listen to their parents argue. So neither of them would.

He peeps out at Birch Street, sees it's empty, and lugs Tina's wagon back down the steps. He returns to the main door, locks it, then heads back home, making sure to wave again to Mr. Tighe. Waving is easier this time; he even gives Billy Tighe a couple of Frisbee throws. The dog steals the second one, making them all laugh. With the notebooks stored in the basement of the abandoned Rec, hidden among all those legitimate cartons, laughing is also easy. Pete feels fifty pounds lighter.

Maybe a hundred.

18

When Hodges lets himself into the outer office of the tiny suite on the seventh floor of the Turner Building on lower Marlborough Street, Holly is pacing worry-circles with a Bic jutting from her mouth. She stops when she sees him. "At last!"

"Holly, we spoke on the phone just fifteen minutes ago." He gently takes the pen from her mouth and observes the bite marks incised on the cap.

"It seems much longer. They're in there. I'm pretty sure Barbara's friend has been crying. Her eyes were all red when I brought them the Cokes. Go, Bill. Go go go."

He won't try to touch Holly, not when she's like this. She'd jump out of her skin. Still, she's so much better than when he first met her. Under the patient tutelage of Tanya Robinson, Jerome and Barbara's mother, she's even developed something approximating clothes sense.

"I will," he says, "but I wouldn't mind a head start. Do you have any idea what it's about?" There are many possibilities, because good kids aren't *always* good kids. It could be minor shoplifting or weed. Maybe school bullying, or an uncle with Roman hands and Russian fingers. At least he can be sure (*fairly* sure, nothing is impossible) that Barbara's friend hasn't murdered anyone.

"It's about Tina's brother. Tina, that's Barbara's friend's name, did I tell you that?" Holly misses his nod; she's looking longingly at the pen. Denied it, she goes to work on her lower lip. "Tina thinks her brother stole some money."

"How old is the brother?"

"In high school. That's all I know. May I have my pen back?"

"No. Go outside and smoke a cigarette."

"I don't do that anymore." Her eyes shift up and to the left, a tell Hodges saw many times in his life as a cop. Oliver Madden even did it once or twice, come to think of it, and when it came to lying, Madden was a pro. "I qui—"

"Just one. It'll calm you down. Did you get them anything to eat?"

"I didn't think of it. I'm sor—"

"No, that's okay. Go back across the street and get some snacks. NutraBars, or something."

"NutraBars are *dog treats*, Bill."

Patiently, he says, "Energy bars, then. Healthy stuff. No chocolate."

"Okay."

She leaves in a swirl of skirts and low heels. Hodges takes a deep breath and goes into his office.

19

The girls are on the couch. Barbara is black and her friend Tina is white. His first amused thought is salt and pepper in matching shakers. Only the shakers don't quite match. Yes, they are wearing their hair in almost identical ponytails. Yes, they are wearing similar sneakers, whatever happens to be the in thing for tweenage girls this year. And yes, each of them is holding a magazine from his coffee table: *Pursuit*, the skip-tracing trade, hardly the usual reading material for young girls, but that's okay, because it's pretty clear that neither of them is actually reading.

Barbara is wearing her school uniform and looks relatively composed. The other one is wearing black slacks and a blue tee with a butterfly appliquéd on the front. Her face is pale, and her red-rimmed eyes look at him with a mixture of hope and terror that's hard on the heart.

Barbara jumps up and gives him a hug, where once she would have dapped him, knuckles to knuckles, and called it good. "Hi, Bill. It's great to see you." How adult she sounds, and how tall she's grown. Can she be fourteen yet? Is it possible?

"Good to see you, too, Barbs. How's Jerome? Is he going to be home this summer?" Jerome is a Harvard man these days, and his alter ego—the jive-talking Tyrone Feelgood Delight—seems to have been retired. Back when Jerome was in high school and doing chores for Hodges, Tyrone used to be a regular visitor. Hodges doesn't miss him much, Tyrone was always sort of a juvenile persona, but he misses Jerome.

Barbara wrinkles her nose. "Came back for a week, and now he's gone again. He's taking his girlfriend, she's from Pennsylvania somewhere, to a *cotillion*. Does that sound racist to you? It does to me."

Hodges is not going there. "Introduce me to your friend, why don't you?"

"This is Tina. She used to live on Hanover Street, just around the block from us. She wants to go to Chapel Ridge with me next year. Tina, this is Bill Hodges. He can help you."

Hodges gives a little bow in order to hold out his hand to the white girl still sitting on the couch. She cringes back at first, then shakes it timidly. As she lets go, she begins to cry. "I shouldn't have come. Pete is going to be *so mad* at me."

Ah, shit, Hodges thinks. He grabs a handful of tissues from the box on the desk, but before he can give them to Tina, Barbara takes them and wipes the girl's eyes. Then she sits down on the couch again and hugs her.

"Tina," Barbara says, and rather sternly, "you came to me and said you wanted help. This is help." Hodges is amazed at how much she sounds like her mother. "All you have to do is tell him what you told me."

Barbara turns her attention on Hodges.

"And you can't tell my folks, Bill. Neither can Holly. If you tell my dad, he'll tell Tina's dad. Then her brother really will be in trouble."

"Let's put that aside for now." Hodges works his swivel chair out from behind the desk—it's a tight fit, but he manages. He doesn't want a desk between himself and Barbara's frightened friend; he'd look too much like a school principal. He sits down, clasps his hands between his knees, and gives Tina a smile. "Let's start with your full name."

"Tina Annette Saubers."

Saubers. That tinkles a faint bell. Some old case? Maybe.

"What's troubling you, Tina?"

"My brother stole some money." Whispering it. Eyes welling again. "Maybe a lot of money. And he can't give it back, because it's gone. I told Barbara because I knew her brother helped stop the crazy guy who hurt our dad when the crazy guy tried to blow up a concert at the MAC. I thought maybe Jerome could help me, because he got a special medal for bravery and all. He was on TV."

"Yes," Hodges says. Holly should have been on TV, too—she was just as brave, and they sure wanted her—but during that phase of her life, Holly Gibney would have swallowed drain-cleaner rather than step in front of television cameras and answer questions.

"Only Barbs said Jerome was in Pennsylvania and I should talk to you instead, because you used to be a policeman." She looks at him with huge, welling eyes.

Saubers, Hodges muses. Yeah, okay. He can't remember the man's first name, but the last one is hard to forget, and he knows why that little bell tinkled. Saubers was one of those badly hurt at City Center, when Hartsfield plowed into the job fair hopefuls.

"At first I was going to talk to you on my own," Barbara adds. "That's what me and Tina agreed on. Kind of, you know, feel you out and see if you'd be willing to help. But then Teens came to my school today and she was all upset—"

"Because he's *worse* now!" Tina bursts out. "I don't know what happened, but since he grew that stupid moustache, he's *worse*! He talks in his sleep—I hear him—and he's losing weight and he's got pimples again, which in Health class the teacher says can be from stress, and . . . and . . . I think sometimes he *cries*." She looks amazed at this, as if she can't quite get her head around the idea of her big brother crying. "What if he kills himself? That's what I'm really scared of, because teen suicide is a *big problem*!"

More fun facts from Health class, Hodges thinks. Not that it isn't true.

"She's not making it up," Barbara says. "It's an amazing story."

"Then let's hear it," Hodges says. "From the beginning."

Tina takes a deep breath and begins.

20

If asked, Hodges would have said he doubted that a thirteen-year-old's tale of woe could surprise, let alone amaze him, but he's amazed, all right. Fucking astounded. And he believes every word; it's too crazy to be a fantasy.

By the time Tina has finished, she's calmed down considerably. Hodges has seen this before. Confession may or may not be good for the soul, but it's undoubtedly soothing to the nerves.

He opens the door to the outer office and sees Holly sitting at her desk, playing computer solitaire. Beside her is a bag filled with enough energy bars to feed the four of them during a zombie siege. "Come in here, Hols," he says. "I need you. And bring those."

Holly steps in tentatively, checks Tina Saubers out, and seems relieved by what she sees. Each of the girls takes an energy bar, which seems to relieve her even more. Hodges takes one himself. The salad he had for lunch seems to have gone down the hatch a month ago, and the veggie burger hasn't really stuck to his ribs, either. Sometimes he still dreams of going to Mickey D's and ordering everything on the menu.

"This is good," Barbara says, munching. "I got raspberry. What'd you get, Teens?"

"Lemon," she says. "It *is* good. Thank you, Mr. Hodges. Thank you, Ms. Holly."

"Barb," Holly says, "where does your mom think you are now?"

"Movies," Barbara says. "*Frozen* again, the sing-along version. It plays every afternoon at Cinema Seven. It's been there like for-*ev*-er." She rolls her eyes at Tina, who rolls hers in complicity. "Mom said we could take the bus home, but we have to be back by six at the very latest. Tina's staying over."

That gives us a little time, Hodges thinks. "Tina, I want you to tell it all again, so Holly can hear. She's my assistant, and she's smart. Plus, she can keep a secret."

Tina goes through it again, and in more detail now that she's calmer. Holly listens closely, her Asperger's-like tics mostly disappearing as they always do when she's fully engaged. All that remains are her restlessly moving fingers, tapping her thighs as if she's working at an invisible keyboard.

When Tina has come to the end, Holly asks, "The money started coming in February of 2010?"

"February or March," Tina says. "I remember, because our folks were fighting a lot then. Daddy lost his job, see . . . and his legs were all hurt . . . and Mom used to yell at him about smoking, how much his cigarettes cost . . ."

"I hate yelling," Holly says matter-of-factly. "It makes me sick in my stomach."

Tina gives her a grateful look.

"The conversation about the doubloons," Hodges puts in. "Was that before or after the money-train started to roll?"

"Before. But not *long* before." She gives the answer with no hesitation.

"And it was five hundred every month," Holly says.

"Sometimes the time was a little shorter than that, like three weeks, and sometimes it was a little longer. When it was more than a month, my folks would think it was over. Once I think it was like six weeks, and I remember Daddy saying to Mom, 'Well, it was good while it lasted.'"

"When was that?" Holly's leaning forward, eyes bright, fingers no longer tapping. Hodges loves it when she's like this.

"Mmm . . ." Tina frowns. "Around my birthday, for sure. When I was twelve. Pete wasn't there for my party. It was spring vacation, and his friend Rory invited him to go to Disney World with their family. That was a bad birthday, because I was so jealous he got to go and I . . ."

She stops, looking first at Barbara, then at Hodges, finally at Holly, upon whom she seems to have imprinted as Mama Duck. "That's *why* it was late that time! Isn't it? *Because he was in Florida!*"

Holly glances at Hodges with just the slightest smile edging her lips, then returns her attention to Tina. "Probably. Always twenties and fifties?"

"Yes. I saw it lots of times."

"And it ran out when?"

"Last September. Around the time school started. There was a note that time. It said something like, 'This is the last of it, I'm sorry there isn't more.'"

"And how long after that was it when you told your brother you thought he was the one sending the money?"

"Not very long. And he never exactly admitted it, but I know it was him. And maybe this is all my fault because I kept talking to him about Chapel Ridge . . . and he said he wished the money wasn't all gone so I could go . . . and maybe he did something stupid and now he's sorry, and it's too l-l-late!"

She starts crying again. Barbara enfolds her and makes comforting sounds. Holly's finger-tapping resumes, but she shows no other signs of distress; she's lost in her thoughts. Hodges can almost see the wheels turning. He has his own questions, but for the time being, he's more than willing to let Holly take the lead.

When Tina's weeping is down to sniffles, Holly says, "You said you came in one night and he had a notebook he acted guilty about. He put it under his pillow."

"That's right."

"Was that near the end of the money?"

"I think so, yeah."

"Was it one of his school notebooks?"

"No. It was black, and looked expensive. Also, it had an elastic strap that went around the outside."

"Jerome has notebooks like that," Barbara said. "They're made of moleskin. May I have another energy bar?"

"Knock yourself out," Hodges tells her. He grabs a pad from his desk and jots *Moleskine*. Then, returning his attention to Tina: "Could it have been an accounts book?"

Tina frowns in the act of peeling the wrapper from her own energy bar. "I don't get you."

"It's possible he was keeping a record of how much he'd paid out and how much was left."

"Maybe, but it looked more like a fancy diary."

Holly is looking at Hodges. He tips her a nod: *Continue.*

"This is all good, Tina. You're a terrific witness. Don't you think so, Bill?"

He nods.

"So, okay. When did he grow his moustache?"

"Last month. Or maybe it was the end of April. Mom and

Daddy both told him it was silly, Daddy said he looked like a drugstore cowboy, whatever that is, but he wouldn't shave it off. I thought it was just something he was going through." She turns to Barbara. "You know, like when we were little and you tried to cut your hair yourself to look like Hannah Montana's."

Barbara grimaces. "Please don't talk about that." And to Hodges: "My mother hit the *roof*."

"And since then, he's been upset," Holly says. "Since the moustache."

"Not so much at first, although I could tell he was nervous even then. It's really only been the last couple of weeks that he's been scared. And now *I'm* scared! *Really* scared!"

Hodges checks to see if Holly has more. She gives him a look that says *Over to you.*

"Tina, I'm willing to look into this, but it has to begin with talking to your brother. You know that, right?"

"Yes," she whispers. She carefully places her second energy bar, with only one bite gone, on the arm of the sofa. "Oh my God, he'll be so mad at me."

"You might be surprised," Holly says. "He might be relieved that someone finally forced the issue."

Holly, Hodges knows, is the voice of experience in this regard.

"Do you think so?" Tina asks. Her voice is small.

"Yes." Holly gives a brisk nod.

"Okay, but you can't this weekend. He's going up to River Bend Resort. It's a thing for class officers, and he got elected vice president next year. If he's still in school next year, that is." Tina puts the palm of her hand to her forehead in a gesture of distress so adult that it fills Hodges with pity. "If he isn't in *jail* next year. For *robbery*."

Holly looks as distressed as Hodges feels, but she's not a

toucher and Barbara is too horrified by this idea to be motherly. It's up to him. He reaches over and takes Tina's small hands in his big ones.

"I don't think that's going to happen. But I *do* think Pete might need some help. When does he come back to the city?"

"S-Sunday night."

"Suppose I were to meet him after school on Monday. Would that work?"

"I guess so." Tina looks utterly drained. "He mostly rides the bus, but you could probably catch him when he leaves."

"Are *you* going to be all right this weekend, Tina?"

"I'll make sure she is," Barbara says, and plants a smack on her friend's cheek. Tina responds with a wan smile.

"What's next for you two?" Hodges asks. "It's probably too late for the movie."

"We'll go to my house," Barbara decides. "Tell my mom we decided to skip it. That's not exactly lying, is it?"

"No," Hodges agrees. "Do you have enough for another taxi?"

"I can drive you if you don't," Holly offers.

"We'll take the bus," Barbara says. "We both have passes. We only took a taxi here because we were in a hurry. Weren't we, Tina?"

"Yes." She looks at Hodges, then back to Holly. "I'm so worried about him, but you can't tell our folks, at least not yet. Do you promise?"

Hodges promises for both of them. He can't see the harm in it, if the boy is going to be out of the city over the weekend with a bunch of his classmates. He asks Holly if she'll go down with the girls and make sure they get on to the West Side bus okay.

She agrees. And makes them take the leftover energy bars. There are at least a dozen.

21

When Holly comes back, she's got her iPad. "Mission accomplished. They're off to Teaberry Lane on the Number Four."

"How did the Saubers girl seem?"

"Much better. She and Barbara were practicing some dance step they learned on TV while we waited for the bus. They tried to get me to do it with them."

"And did you?"

"No. Homegirl don't dance."

She doesn't smile when she says this, but she still might be joking. He knows she sometimes does these days, but it's always hard to tell. Much of Holly Gibney is still a mystery to Hodges, and he guesses that will always be the case.

"Will Barb's mom get the story out of them, do you think? She's pretty perceptive, and a weekend can be a long time when you're sitting on a big secret."

"Maybe, but I don't think so," Holly says. "Tina was a lot more relaxed once she got it off her chest."

Hodges smiles. "If she was dancing at the bus stop, I guess she was. So what do you think, Holly?"

"About which part?"

"Let's start with the money."

She taps at her iPad, brushing absently at her hair to keep it out of her eyes. "It started coming in February of 2010, and stopped in September of last year. That's forty-four months. If the brother—"

"Pete."

"If Pete sent his parents five hundred dollars a month over that period, that comes to twenty-two thousand dollars. Give or take. Not exactly a fortune, but—"

"But a mighty lot for a kid," Hodges finishes. "Especially if he started sending it when he was Tina's age."

They look at each other. That she will sometimes meet his gaze like this is, in a way, the most extraordinary part of her change from the terrified woman she was when he first met her. After a silence of perhaps five seconds, they speak at the same time.

"So—" "How did—"

"You first," Hodges says, laughing.

Without looking at him (it's a thing she can only do in short bursts, even when she's absorbed by some problem), Holly says, "That conversation he had with Tina about buried treasure—gold and jewels and doubloons. I think that's important. I don't think he stole that money. I think he *found* it."

"Must have. Very few thirteen-year-olds pull bank jobs, no matter how desperate they are. But where does a kid stumble across that kind of loot?"

"I don't know. I can craft a computer search with a timeline and get a dump of cash robberies, I suppose. We can be pretty sure it happened before 2010, if he found the money in February of that year. Twenty-two thousand dollars is a large enough haul to have been reported in the papers, but what's the search protocol? What are the parameters? How far back should I go? Five years? Ten? I bet an info dump going back to just oh-five would be pretty big, because I'd need to search the whole tristate area. Don't you think so?"

"You'd only get a partial catch even if you searched the whole Midwest." Hodges is thinking of Oliver Madden, who probably conned hundreds of people and dozens of organizations during the course of his career. He was an expert when it came to creating false bank accounts, but Hodges is betting that Ollie didn't put much trust in banks when it came to his own money. No, he would have wanted a cushy cash reserve.

"Why only partial?"

"You're thinking about banks, check-cashing joints, fast credit outfits. Maybe the dog track or the concession take from a Groundhogs game. But it might not have been public money. The thief or thieves could have knocked over a high-stakes poker game or ripped off a meth dealer over on Edgemont Avenue in Hillbilly Heaven. For all we know, the cash could have come from a home invasion in Atlanta or San Diego or anyplace in between. Cash from that kind of theft might not even have been reported."

"Especially if it was never reported to Internal Revenue in the first place," Holly says. "Right right right. So where does that leave us?"

"Needing to talk to Peter Saubers, and frankly, I can't wait. I thought I'd seen it all, but I've never seen anything like this."

"You could talk to him tonight. He's not going on his class trip until tomorrow. I took Tina's phone number. I could call her and get her brother's."

"No, let's let him have his weekend. Hell, he's probably left already. Maybe it will calm him down, give him time to think. And let Tina have hers. Monday afternoon will be soon enough."

"What about the black notebook she saw? The Moleskine? Any ideas about that?"

"Probably has nothing at all to do with the money. Could be his *50 Shades of Fun* fantasy journal about the girl who sits behind him in homeroom."

Holly makes a *hmph* sound to show what she thinks of that and begins to pace. "You know what bugs me? The lag."

"The lag?"

"The money stopped coming last September, along with a note that said he's sorry there isn't more. But as far as we know, Peter didn't start getting weird until April or May of this year. For seven months he's fine, then he grows a moustache and starts exhibiting symptoms of anxiety. What happened? Any ideas on that?"

One possibility stands out. "He decided he wanted more money, maybe so his sister could go to Barbara's school. He thought he knew a way to get it, but something went wrong."

"Yes! That's what I think, too!" She crosses her arms over her breasts and cups her elbows, a self-comforting gesture Hodges has seen often. "I wish Tina had seen what was in that notebook, though. The Moleskine notebook."

"Is that a hunch, or are you following some chain of logic I don't see?"

"I'd like to know why he was so anxious for her not to see it, that's all." Having successfully evaded Hodges's question, she heads for the door. "I'm going to build a computer search on robberies between 2001 and 2009. I know it's a longshot, but it's a place to start. What are you going to do?"

"Go home. Think this over. Tomorrow I'm repo'ing cars and looking for a bail-jumper named Dejohn Frasier, who is almost certainly staying with his stepmom or ex-wife. Also, I'll watch the Indians and possibly go to a movie."

Holly lights up. "Can I go to the movies with you?"

"If you like."

"Can I pick?"

"Only if you promise not to drag me to some idiotic romantic comedy with Jennifer Aniston."

"Jennifer Aniston is a very fine actress and a badly underrated comedienne. Did you know she was in the original *Leprechaun* movie, back in 1993?"

"Holly, you're a font of information, but you're dodging the issue here. Promise me no rom-com, or I go on my own."

"I'm sure we can find something mutually agreeable," Holly says, not quite meeting his eyes. "Will Tina's brother be all right? You don't think he'd really try to kill himself, do you?"

"Not based on his actions. He put himself way out on a limb for his family. Guys like that, ones with empathy, usually aren't suicidal. Holly, does it seem strange to you that the little girl figured out Peter was behind the money, and their parents don't seem to have a clue?"

The light in Holly's eyes goes out, and for a moment she looks very much like the Holly of old, the one who spent most of her adolescence in her room, the kind of neurotic isolate the Japanese call *hikikomori*.

"Parents can be very stupid," she says, and goes out.

Well, Hodges thinks, yours certainly were, I think we can agree on that.

He goes to the window, clasps his hands behind his back, and stares out at lower Marlborough, where the afternoon rush hour traffic is building. He wonders if Holly has considered the second plausible source of the boy's anxiety: that the mokes who hid the money have come back and found it gone.

And have somehow found out who took it.

22

Statewide Motorcycle & Small Engine Repair isn't statewide or even citywide; it's a ramshackle zoning mistake made of rusty corrugated metal on the South Side, a stone's throw from the minor league stadium where the Groundhogs play. Out front there's a line of cycles for sale under plastic pennants fluttering lackadaisically from a sagging length of cable. Most of the bikes look pretty sketchy to Morris. A fat guy in a leather vest is sitting against the side of the building, swabbing road rash with a handful of Kleenex. He looks up at Morris and says nothing. Morris says nothing right back. He had to walk here from Edgemont Avenue, over a mile in the hot morning sun, because the buses only come out this far when the Hogs are playing.

He goes into the garage and there's Charlie Roberson, sit-

ting on a grease-smeared car seat in front of a half-disassembled
Harley. He doesn't see Morris at first; he's holding the Harley's
battery up and studying it. Morris, meanwhile, studies him.
Roberson is still a muscular fireplug of a man, although he
has to be over seventy, bald on top with a graying fringe. He's
wearing a cut-off tee, and Morris can read a fading prison tat-
too on one of his biceps: WHITE POWER 4EVER.

One of my success stories, Morris thinks, and smiles.

Roberson was doing life in Waynesville for bludgeoning a
rich old lady to death on Wieland Avenue in Branson Park.
She supposedly woke up and caught him creeping her house.
He also raped her, possibly before the bludgeoning, perhaps
after, as she lay dying on the floor of her upstairs hall. The case
was a slam-dunk. Roberson had been seen in the area on several occasions leading up to the robbery, he had been photographed by the security camera outside the rich old lady's gate
a day prior to the break-in, he had discussed the possibility of
creeping that particular crib and robbing that particular lady
with several of his lowlife friends (all given ample reason to
testify by the prosecution, having legal woes of their own), and
he had a long record of robbery and assault. Jury said guilty;
judge said life without parole; Roberson swapped motorcycle
repair for stitching bluejeans and varnishing furniture.

"I done plenty, but I didn't do that," he told Morris time
and time again. "I *woulda*, I had the fuckin security code, but
someone else beat me to the punch. I know who it was, too,
because there was only one guy I told those numbers to. He
was one of the ones who fuckin testified against me, and if I
ever get out of here, that man is gonna die. Trust me."

Morris neither believed nor disbelieved him—his first two
years in the Ville had shown him that it was filled with men
claiming to be as innocent as morning dew—but when Charlie
asked him to write Barry Scheck, Morris was willing. It was
what he did, his real job.

Turned out the robber-bludgeoner-rapist had left semen in the old lady's underpants, the underpants were still in one of the city's cavernous evidence rooms, and the lawyer the Innocence Project sent out to investigate Charlie Roberson's case found them. DNA testing unavailable at the time of Charlie's conviction showed the jizz wasn't his. The lawyer hired an investigator to track down several of the prosecution's witnesses. One of them, dying of liver cancer, not only recanted his testimony but copped to the crime, perhaps in hopes that doing so would earn him a pass through the pearly gates.

"Hey, Charlie," Morris says. "Guess who."

Roberson turns, squints, gets to his feet. "Morrie? Is that Morrie Bellamy?"

"In the flesh."

"Well, I'll be fucked."

Probably not, Morris thinks, but when Roberson puts the battery down on the seat of the Harley and comes forward with his arms outstretched, Morris submits to the obligatory back-pounding bro-hug. Even gives it back to the best of his ability. The amount of muscle beneath Roberson's filthy tee-shirt is mildly alarming.

Roberson pulls back, showing his few remaining teeth in a grin. "Jesus Christ! Parole?"

"Parole."

"Old lady took her foot off your neck?"

"She did."

"God-*dam*, that's great! Come on in the office and have a drink! I got bourbon."

Morris shakes his head. "Thanks, but booze doesn't agree with my system. Also, the man might come around anytime and ask me to drop a urine. I called in sick at work this morning, that's risky enough."

"Who's your PO?"

"McFarland."

"Big buck nigger, isn't he?"

"He's black, yes."

"Ah, he ain't the worst, but they watch you close to begin with, no doubt. Come on in the office, anyway, I'll drink yours. Hey, did you hear Duck died?"

Morris has indeed heard this, got the news shortly before his parole came through. Duck Duckworth, his first protector, the one who stopped the rapes by Morris's cellie and his cellie's friends. Morris felt no special grief. People came; people went; shit didn't mean shit.

Roberson shakes his head as he takes a bottle from the top shelf of a metal cabinet filled with tools and spare parts. "It was some kind of brain thing. Well, you know what they say—in the midst of fuckin life we're in fuckin death." He pours bourbon into a cup with WORLD'S BEST HUGGER on the side, and lifts it. "Here's to ole Ducky." He drinks, smacks his lips, and raises the cup again. "And here's to you. Morrie Bellamy, out on the street again, rollin and trollin. What they got you doin? Some kind of paperwork'd be my guess."

Morris tells him about his job at the MAC, and makes chitchat while Roberson helps himself to another knock of bourbon. Morris doesn't envy Charlie his freedom to drink, he lost too many years of his life thanks to high-tension booze, but he feels Roberson will be more amenable to his request if he's a little high.

When he judges the time is right, he says, "You told me to come to you if I ever got out and needed a favor."

"True, true . . . but I never thought you'd get out. Not with that Jesus-jumper you nailed ridin you like a motherfuckin pony." Roberson chortles and pours himself a fresh shot.

"I need you to loan me a car, Charlie. Short-term. Not even twelve hours."

"When?"

"Tonight. Well . . . this evening. Tonight's when I need it. I can return it later on."

Roberson has stopped laughing. "That's a bigger risk than takin a drink, Morrie."

"Not for you; you're out, free and clear."

"No, not for me, I'd just get a slap on the wrist. But drivin without a license is a big parole violation. You might go back inside. Don't get me wrong, I'm willin to help you out, just want to be sure you understand the stakes."

"I understand them."

Roberson tops up his glass and sips it as he considers. Morris wouldn't want to be the owner of the bike Charlie is going to be putting back together once their little palaver is done.

At last Roberson says, "You be okay with a truck instead of a car? One I'm thinking of is a small panel job. And it's an automatic. Says 'Jones Flowers' on the side, but you can hardly read it anymore. It's out back. I'll show it to you, if you want."

Morris wants, and one look makes him decide the little black panel truck is a gift from God . . . assuming it runs all right. Roberson assures him that it does, even though it's on its second trip around the clock.

"I shut up shop early on Fridays. Around three. I could put in some gas and leave the keys under the right front tire."

"That's perfect," Morris says. He can go in to the MAC, tell his fat fuck of a boss that he had a stomach bug but it passed, work until four like a good little office drone, then come back out here. "Listen, the Groundhogs play tonight, don't they?"

"Yeah, they got the Dayton Dragons. Why? You hankerin to take in a game? Because I could be up for that."

"Another time, maybe. What I'm thinking is I could return the truck around ten, park it in the same place, then take a stadium bus back into town."

"Same old Morrie," Roberson says, and taps his temple. His

eyes have become noticeably bloodshot. "You are one thinking cat."

"Remember to put the keys under the tire." The last thing Morris needs is for Roberson to get shitfaced on cheap bourbon and forget.

"I will. Owe you a lot, buddy. Owe you the motherfuckin *world*."

This sentiment necessitates another bro-hug, redolent of sweat, bourbon, and cheap aftershave. Roberson squeezes so tightly that Morris finds it hard to breathe, but at last he's released. He accompanies Charlie back into the garage, thinking that tonight—in twelve hours, maybe less—the Rothstein notebooks will once more be in his possession. With such an intoxicating prospect as that, who needs bourbon?

"You mind me asking why you're working here, Charlie? I thought you were going to get a boatload of cash from the state for false imprisonment."

"Aw, man, they threatened to bring up a bunch of old charges." Roberson resumes his seat in front of the Harley he's been working on. He picks up a wrench and taps it against the grease-smeared leg of his pants. "Including a bad one in Missouri, could have put me away down there for the rest of my life. Three-strikes rule or some shit. So we kinda worked out a trade."

He regards Morris with his bloodshot eyes, and in spite of his meaty biceps (it's clear he never lost the prison workout habit), Morris can see he's really old, and will soon be unhealthy, as well. If he isn't already.

"They fuck you in the end, buddy. Right up the ass. Rock the boat and they fuck you even harder. So you take what you can get. This is what I got, and it's enough for me."

"Shit don't mean shit," Morris says.

Roberson bellows laughter. "What you always said! And it's the fuckin truth!"

"Just don't forget to leave the keys."

"I'll leave em." Roberson levels a grease-blackened finger at Morris. "And don't get caught. Listen to your daddy."

I won't get caught, Morris thinks. *I've waited too long.*

"One other thing?"

Roberson waits for it.

"I don't suppose I could get a gun." Morris sees the look on Charlie's face and adds hastily, "Not to use, just as insurance."

Roberson shakes his head. "No gun. I'd get a lot more than a slap on the wrist for that."

"I'd never say it came from you."

The bloodshot eyes regard Morris shrewdly. "Can I be honest? You're too jail-bit for guns. Probably shoot yourself in the nutsack. The truck, okay. I owe you that. But if you want a gun, find it somewhere else."

23

At three o'clock that Friday afternoon, Morris comes within a whisker of trashing twelve million dollars' worth of modern art.

Well, no, not really, but he *does* come close to erasing the records of that art, which include the provenance and the background info on a dozen rich MAC donors. He's spent weeks creating a new search protocol that covers all of the Arts Center's acquisitions since the beginning of the twenty-first century. That protocol is a work of art in itself, and this afternoon, instead of sliding the biggest of the subfiles into the master file, he has moused it into the trash along with a lot of other dreck he needs to get rid of. The MAC's lumbering, outdated computer system is overloaded with useless shit, including a ton of stuff that's no longer even in the building. Said ton got moved to the Metropolitan Museum of Art in

New York back in '05. Morris is on the verge of emptying the trash to make room for more dreck, his finger is actually on the trigger, when he realizes he's about to send a very valuable live file to data heaven.

For a moment he's back in Waynesville, trying to hide contraband before a rumored cell inspection, maybe nothing more dangerous than a snack-pack of Keebler cookies but enough to get him marked down if the screw is in a pissy mood. He looks at his finger, hovering less than an eighth of an inch over that damned delete button, and pulls his hand back to his chest, where he can feel his heart thumping fast and hard. What in God's name was he thinking?

His fat fuck of a boss chooses that moment to poke his head into Morris's closet-sized workspace. The cubicles where the other office drones spend their days are papered with pictures of boyfriends, girlfriends, families, even the fucking family dog, but Morris has put up nothing but a postcard of Paris, which he has always wanted to visit. Like *that's* ever going to happen.

"Everything all right, Morris?" the fat fuck asks.

"Fine," Morris says, praying that his boss won't come in and look at his screen. Although he probably wouldn't know what he was looking at. The obese bastard can send emails, he even seems to have a vague grasp of what Google is for, but beyond that he's lost. Yet he's living out in the suburbs with the wife and kiddies instead of in Bugshit Manor, where the crazies yell at invisible enemies in the middle of the night.

"Good to hear. Carry on."

Morris thinks, Carry your fat ass on out of here.

The fat fuck does, probably headed down to the canteen to feed his fat fuck face. When he's gone, Morris clicks on the trash icon, grabs what he almost deleted, and moves it back into the master file. This isn't much of an operation, but when it's finished he blows out his breath like a man who has just defused a bomb.

Where was your head? he scolds himself. What were you thinking?

Rhetorical questions. He was thinking about the Rothstein notebooks, now so close. Also about the little panel truck, and how scary it's going to feel, driving again after all those years inside. All he needs is one fender-bender . . . one cop who thinks he looks suspicious . . .

I have to keep it together a little longer, Morris thinks. I have to.

But his brain feels overloaded, running in the red zone. He thinks he'll be all right once the notebooks are actually in his possession (also the money, although that's far less important). Get those puppies hidden away at the back of the closet in his room on the ninth floor of Bugshit Manor and he can relax, but right now the stress is killing him. It's also being in a changed world and working an actual job and having a boss who doesn't wear a gray uniform but still has to be kowtowed to. On top of all that, there's the stress of having to drive an unregistered vehicle without a license tonight.

He thinks, By ten PM, things will be better. In the meantime, strap down and tighten up. Shit don't mean shit.

"Right," Morris whispers, and wipes a prickle of sweat from the skin between his mouth and nose.

24

At four o'clock he saves his work, closes out the apps he's been running, and shuts down. He walks into the MAC's plush lobby and standing there like a bad dream made real, feet apart and hands clasped behind his back, is Ellis McFarland. His PO is studying an Edward Hopper painting like the art aficionado he surely isn't.

Without turning (Morris realizes the man must have seen

his reflection in the glass covering the painting, but it's still eerie), McFarland says, "Yo, Morrie. How you doin, homie?"

He knows, Morris thinks. Not just about the panel truck, either. About everything.

Not true, and he knows it isn't, but the part that's still in jail and always will be assures him it *is* true. To McFarland, Morris Bellamy's forehead is a pane of glass. Everything inside, every turning wheel and overheated whirling cog, is visible to him.

"I'm all right, Mr. McFarland."

Today McFarland is wearing a plaid sportcoat approximately the size of a living room rug. He looks Morris up and down, and when his eyes return to Morris's face, it's all Morris can do to hold them.

"You don't *look* all right. You're pale, and you got those dark whack-off circles under your eyes. Been using something you hadn't oughtta been using, Morrie?"

"No, sir."

"Doing something you hadn't oughtta be doing?"

"No." Thinking of the panel truck with **JONES FLOWERS** still visible on the side, waiting for him on the South Side. The keys probably already under the tire.

"No what?"

"No, sir."

"Uh-huh. Maybe it's the flu. Because, frankly speaking, you look like ten pounds of shit in a five-pound bag."

"I almost made a mistake," Morris says. "It could have been rectified—probably—but it would have meant bringing in an outside I-T guy, maybe even shutting down the main server. I would have been in trouble."

"Welcome to the workaday world," McFarland says, with zero sympathy.

"Well, it's different for me!" Morris bursts out, and oh God, it's such a *relief* to burst out, and to do it about something safe.

"If anyone should know that, it's you! Someone else who did that would just get a reprimand, but not me. And if they fired me—for a lapse in attention, not anything I did on purpose—I'd end up back inside."

"Maybe," McFarland says, turning back to the picture. It shows a man and a woman sitting in a room and apparently working hard not to look at each other. "Maybe not."

"My boss doesn't like me," Morris says. He knows he sounds like he's whining, probably he *is* whining. "I know four times as much as he does about how the computer system in this place works, and it pisses him off. He'd love to see me gone."

"You sound a weensy bit paranoid," McFarland says. His hands are again clasped above his truly awesome buttocks, and all at once Morris understands why McFarland is here. McFarland followed him to the motorcycle shop where Charlie Roberson works and has decided he's up to something. Morris knows this isn't so. He knows it is.

"What are they doing, anyway, letting a guy like me screw with their files? A parolee? If I do the wrong thing, and I almost did, I could cost them a lot of money."

"What did you think you'd be doing on the outside?" McFarland says, still examining the Hopper painting, which is called *Apartment 16-A*. He seems fascinated by it, but Morris isn't fooled. McFarland is watching his reflection again. Judging him. "You're too old and too soft to shift cartons in a warehouse or work on a gardening crew."

He turns around.

"It's called mainstreaming, Morris, and I didn't make the policy. If you want to wah-wah-wah about it, find somebody who gives a shit."

"Sorry," Morris says.

"Sorry *what*?"

"Sorry, Mr. McFarland."

"Thank you, Morris, that's better. Now let's step into the

men's room, where you will pee in the little cup and prove to me that your paranoia isn't drug-induced."

The last stragglers of the office staff are leaving. Several glance at Morris and the big black man in the loud sportcoat, then quickly glance away. Morris feels an urge to shout *That's right, he's my parole officer, get a good look!*

He follows McFarland into the men's, which is empty, thank God. McFarland leans against the wall, arms crossed on his chest, watching as Morris unlimbers his elderly thingama-jig and produces a urine sample. When it doesn't turn blue after thirty seconds, McFarland hands the little plastic cup back to Morris. "Congratulations. Dump that, homie."

Morris does. McFarland is washing his hands methodically, lathering all the way to his wrists.

"I don't have AIDS, you know. If that's what you're worried about. I had to take the test before they let me out."

McFarland carefully dries his big hands. He studies himself in the mirror for a moment (maybe wishing he had some hair to comb), then turns to Morris. "You may be substance-free, but I really don't like the way you look, Morrie."

Morris keeps silent.

"Let me tell you something eighteen years in this job has taught me. There are two types of parolees, and two only: wolves and lambs. You're too old to be a wolf, but I'm not entirely sure you're hip to that. You may not have *internalized* it, as the shrinks say. I don't know what wolfish shit you might have on your mind, maybe it's nothing more than stealing paper clips from the supply room, but whatever it is, you need to forget about it. You're too old to howl and *much* too old to run."

Having imparted this bit of wisdom, he leaves. Morris heads for the door himself, but his legs turn to rubber before he can get there. He wheels around, grasps a washbasin to keep from falling, and blunders into one of the stalls. There he sits down and lowers his head until it almost touches his knees. He closes his eyes and takes long deep breaths. When the roaring in his head subsides, he gets up and leaves.

He'll still be here, Morris thinks. Staring at that damned picture with his hands clasped behind his back.

But this time the lobby is empty save for the security guard, who gives Morris a suspicious look as he passes.

25

The Hogs-Dragons game doesn't start until seven, but the buses with BASEBALL GAME 2NITE in their destination windows start running at five. Morris takes one to the park, then walks back to Statewide Motorcycle, aware of each car that passes and cursing himself for losing his shit in the men's room after McFarland departed. If he'd gotten out sooner, maybe he could have seen what the sonofabitch was driving. But he didn't, and now any one of these cars might be Mc-Farland's. The PO would be easy enough to spot, given the size of him, but Morris doesn't dare look at any of the passing cars too closely. There are two reasons for this. First, he'd look guilty, wouldn't he? Yes indeed, like a man who's got wolf-ish shit on his mind and has to keep checking his perimeter. Second, he might see McFarland even if McFarland isn't there, because he's edging ever closer to a nervous breakdown. It isn't surprising, either. A man could only stand so much stress.

What are you, twenty-two? Rothstein had asked him. *Twenty-three?*

That was a good guess by an observant man. Morris *had* been twenty-three. Now he's on the cusp of sixty, and the years between have disappeared like smoke in a breeze. He has heard people say sixty is the new forty, but that's bullshit. When you've spent most of your life in prison, sixty is the new seventy-five. Or eighty. Too old to be a wolf, according to McFarland.

Well, we'll see about that, won't we?

He turns into the yard of Statewide Motorcycle—the shades pulled, the bikes that were out front this morning locked away—and expects to hear a car door slam behind him the moment he transgresses private property. Expects to hear McFarland saying *Yo, homie, what you doing in there?*

But the only sound is the traffic passing on the way to the stadium, and when he gets around to the back lot, the invisible band that's been constricting his chest eases a little. There's a high wall of corrugated metal cutting off this patch of yard from the rest of the world, and walls comfort Morris. He doesn't like that, knows it isn't natural, but there it is. A man is the sum of his experiences.

He goes to the panel truck—small, dusty, blessedly nondescript—and feels beneath the right front tire. The keys are there. He gets in, and is gratified when the engine starts on the first crank. The radio comes on in a blare of rock. Morris snaps it off.

"I can do this," he says, first adjusting the seat and then gripping the wheel. "I can do this."

And, it turns out, he can. It's like riding a bike. The only hard part is turning against the stream of traffic headed for the stadium, and even that isn't too bad; after a minute's wait, one of the BASEBALL GAME 2NITE buses stops, and the driver waves for Morris to go. The northbound lanes are nearly empty, and he's able to avoid downtown by using the new city bypass. He almost enjoys driving again. *Would* enjoy it, if not for the nagging suspicion that McFarland is tailing him. Not busting him yet, though; he won't do that until he sees what his old pal—his *homie*—is up to.

Morris stops at the Bellows Avenue Mall and goes into Home Depot. He strolls around beneath the glaring fluorescents, taking his time; he can't do his business until after dark, and in June the evening light lasts until eight thirty or nine. In the gardening section he buys a spade and also a hatchet, in case he has to chop some roots—that tree overhanging the bank looks like it might have his trunk in a pretty tight grip. In the aisle marked CLEARANCE, he grabs a pair of Tuff Tote duffels, on sale for twenty bucks each. He stows his purchases in the back of the truck and heads around to the driver's door.

"Hey!" From behind him.

Morris freezes, listening to the approaching footsteps and waiting for McFarland to grab his shoulder.

"Do you know if there's a supermarket in this mall?"

The voice is young. And white. Morris discovers he can breathe again. "Safeway," he says, without turning. He has no idea if there's a supermarket in the mall or not.

"Oh. Okay. Thanks."

Morris gets into the truck and starts the engine. I can do this, he thinks.

I can and I will.

26

Morris cruises slowly through the Northfield tree streets that were his old stomping grounds—not that he ever did much stomping; usually he had his nose in a book. It's still too early, so he parks on Elm for awhile. There's a dusty old map in the glove compartment, and he pretends to read it. After twenty minutes or so, he drives over to Maple and does the same thing. Then down to the local Zoney's Go-Mart, where he bought snacks as a kid. Also cigarettes for his father. That was back in the day when a pack cost forty cents and kids buying smokes for their parents was taken for granted. He gets a Slushie and makes it last. Then he moves onto Palm Street and goes back to pretend map reading. The shadows are lengthening, but oh so slowly.

Should have brought a book, he thinks, then thinks No—a man with a map looks okay, somehow, but a man reading a book in an old truck would probably look like a potential child molester.

Is that paranoid or smart? He can no longer tell. All he knows for sure is that the notebooks are close now. They're pinging like a sonar blip.

Little by little, the long light of this June evening mellows to dusk. The kids who've been playing on sidewalks and front lawns go inside to watch TV or play video games or spend an educational evening texting various misspelled messages and dumbass emoticons to their friends.

Confident that McFarland is nowhere near (although not *completely* confident), Morris keys the panel truck's engine and drives slowly to his final destination: the Birch Street Rec, where he used to go when the Garner Street branch of the library was closed. Skinny, bookish, with a regrettable tendency to run his mouth, he rarely got picked for the outdoor games, and almost always got yelled at on the few occasions when he did: hey butterfingers, hey dumbo, hey fumblebutt. Because of his red lips, he earned the nickname Revlon. When he went to the Rec, he mostly stayed indoors, reading or maybe putting together a jigsaw puzzle. Now the city has shut the old brick building down and put it up for sale in the wake of municipal budget cuts.

A few boys toss up a few final baskets on the weedy courts out back, but there are no longer outside lights and they beat feet when it's too dark to see, yelling and dribbling and shooting passes back and forth. When they're gone, Morris starts the truck and pulls into the driveway running alongside the building. He does it without turning on his headlights, and the little black truck is exactly the right color for this kind of work.

He snuggles it up to the rear of the building, where a faded sign still reads RESERVED FOR REC DEPT. VEHICLES. He kills the engine, gets out, and smells the June air, redolent of grass and clover. He can hear crickets, and the drone of traffic on the city bypass, but otherwise the newly fallen night is his.

Fuck you, Mr. McFarland, he thinks. Fuck you very much.

He gets his tools and Tuff Totes from the back of the truck and starts toward the tangle of unimproved ground beyond the baseball field where he dropped so many easy pop flies. Then an idea strikes him and he turns back. He braces a palm on the old brick, still warm from the heat of the day, slides down to a crouch, and pulls some weeds so he can peer through one of the basement windows. These haven't been boarded up. The moon has just risen, orange and full. It lends enough light for him to see folding chairs, card tables, and heaps of boxes.

Morris has planned on bringing the notebooks back to his room in Bugshit Manor, but that's risky; Mr. McFarland can search his room anytime he pleases, it's part of the deal. The Rec is a lot closer to where the notebooks are buried, and the basement, where all sorts of useless bric-a-brac has already been stored, would be the perfect hiding place. It might be possible to rathole most of them here, only taking a few at a time back to his room, where he could read them. Morris is skinny enough to fit through this window, although he might have to wriggle a bit, and how hard could it be to bust the thumb-lock he sees on the inside of the window and pry it up? A screwdriver would probably do the trick. He doesn't have one, but there are plenty at Home Depot. He even saw a small display of tools when he was in Zoney's.

He leans closer to the dirty window, studying it. He knows to look for alarm tapes (the state penitentiary is a very educational place when it comes to breaking and entering), but he doesn't see any. Only suppose the alarm uses contact points, instead? He wouldn't see those, and he might not hear the alarm, either. Some of them are silent.

Morris looks a little longer, then reluctantly gets to his feet. It doesn't seem likely to him that an old building like this one is alarmed—the valuable stuff has no doubt been moved elsewhere long ago—but he doesn't dare take the chance.

Better to stick with the original plan.

He grabs his tools and his duffel bags and once more starts for the overgrown waste ground, careful to skirt the ballfield. He's not going there, uh-uh, no way. The moon will help him once he's in the undergrowth, but out in the open, the world looks like a brightly lighted stage.

The potato chip bag that helped him last time is gone, and it takes awhile to find the path again. Morris beats back and forth through the undergrowth beyond right field (the site of several childhood humiliations), finally rediscovers it, and sets off. When he hears the faint chuckle of the stream, he has to restrain himself from breaking into a run.

Times have been hard, he thinks. *There could be people sleeping in here, homeless people. If one of them sees me—*

If one of them sees him, he'll use the hatchet. No hesitation. Mr. McFarland may think he's too old to be a wolf, but what his parole officer doesn't know is that Morris has already killed three people, and driving a car isn't the only thing that's like riding a bike.

27

The trees are runty, choking each other in their struggle for space and sun, but they are tall enough to filter the moonlight. Two or three times Morris loses the path and blunders around, trying to find it again. This actually pleases him. He has the sound of the stream to guide him if he really does lose his way, and the path's faintness confirms that fewer kids use it now than back in his day. Morris just hopes he's not walking through poison ivy.

The sound of the stream is very close when he finds the path for the last time, and less than five minutes later, he's standing on the bank opposite the landmark tree. He stops there for a bit in the moon-dappled shade, looking for any sign of human habitation: blankets, a sleeping bag, a shopping cart, a piece of plastic draped over branches to create a makeshift tent. There's nothing. Just the water purling along in its stony bed, and the tree tilting over the far side of the stream. The tree that has faithfully guarded his treasure all these years.

"Good old tree," Morris whispers, and steps his way across the stream.

He kneels and puts aside the tools and the duffel bags for a moment of meditation. "Here I am," he whispers, and places his palms on the ground, as if feeling for a heartbeat.

And it seems that he *does* feel one. It's the heartbeat of John Rothstein's genius. The old man turned Jimmy Gold into a sellout joke, but who can say Rothstein didn't redeem Jimmy during his years of solitary composition? If he did that . . . *if* . . . then everything Morris has gone through has been worthwhile.

"Here I am, Jimmy. Here I finally am."

He grabs the spade and begins digging. It doesn't take long to get to the trunk again, but the roots have embraced it, all right, and it's almost an hour before Morris can chop through enough of them to pull it out. It's been years since he did hard manual labor, and he's exhausted. He thinks of all the cons he knew—Charlie Roberson, for example—who worked out constantly, and how he sneered at them for what he considered obsessive-compulsive behavior (in his mind, at least; never on his face). He's not sneering now. His thighs ache, his back aches, and worst of all, his head is throbbing like an infected tooth. A little breeze has sprung up, which cools the sweat sliming his skin, but it also causes the branches to sway, creating moving shadows that make him afraid. They make him think of McFarland again. McFarland making his way up the path, moving with the eerie quiet some big men, soldiers and ex-athletes, mostly, are able to manage.

When he's got his breath and his heartbeat has slowed a little, Morris reaches for the handle at the end of the trunk and finds it's no longer there. He leans forward on his splayed palms, peering into the hole, wishing he'd remembered to bring a flashlight.

The handle *is* still there, only it's hanging in two pieces.

That's not right, Morris thinks. Is it?

He casts his mind back across all those years, trying to remember if either trunk handle was broken. He doesn't think so. In fact, he's almost sure. But then he remembers tipping the trunk endwise in the garage, and exhales a sigh of relief strong enough to puff out his cheeks. It must have broken when he put the trunk on the dolly. Or maybe while he was bumping and thumping his way along the path to this very location. He had dug the hole in a hurry and muscled the trunk in as fast as he could. Wanting to get out of there and much too busy to notice a little thing like a broken handle. That was it. Had to be. After all, the trunk hadn't been new when he bought it.

He grasps the sides, and the trunk slides out of its hole so easily that Morris overbalances and flops on his back. He lies there, staring up at the bright bowl of the moon, and tries to tell himself nothing is wrong. Only he knows better. He might be able to talk himself out of the broken handle, but not out of this new thing.

The trunk is too light.

Morris scrambles back to a sitting position with smears of dirt now sticking to his damp skin. He brushes his hair off his forehead with a shaking hand, leaving a fresh streak.

The trunk is too light.

He reaches for it, then draws back.

I can't, he thinks. I can't. If I open it and the notebooks aren't there, I'll just . . . *snap*.

But why would anyone take a bunch of notebooks? The money, yes, but the notebooks? There wasn't even any space left to write in most of them; in most, Rothstein had used it all.

What if someone took the money and then *burned* the notebooks? Not understanding their incalculable value, just wanting to get rid of something a thief might see as evidence?

"No," Morris whispers. "No one would do that. They're still in there. They have to be."

But the trunk is too light.

He stares at it, a small exhumed coffin tilted on the bank in the moonlight. Behind it is the hole, gaping like a mouth that has just vomited something up. Morris reaches for the trunk again, hesitates, then lunges forward and snaps the latches up, praying to a God he knows cares nothing for the likes of him.

He looks in.

The trunk is not quite empty. The plastic he lined it with is still there. He pulls it out in a crackling cloud, hoping that a few of the notebooks are left underneath—two or three, or oh please God even just one—but there are just a few small trickles of dirt caught in the corners.

Morris puts his filthy hands to his face—once young, now deeply lined—and begins to cry in the moonlight.

28

He promised to return the truck by ten, but it's after midnight when he parks it behind Statewide Motorcycle and puts the keys back under the right front tire. He doesn't bother with the tools or the empty Tuff Totes that were supposed to be full; let Charlie Roberson have them if he wants them.

The lights of the minor league field four blocks over have been turned off an hour ago. The stadium buses have stopped running, but the bars—in this neighborhood there are a lot of them—are roaring away with live bands and jukebox music, their doors open, men and women in Groundhogs tee-shirts and caps standing out on the sidewalks, smoking cigarettes and drinking from plastic cups. Morris plods past them without looking, ignoring a couple of friendly yells from inebriated baseball fans, high on beer and a home team win, asking him if he wants a drink. Soon the bars are behind him.

He has stopped obsessing about McFarland, and the thought of the three mile walk back to Bugshit Manor never crosses his mind. He doesn't care about his aching legs, either. It's as if they belong to someone else. He feels as empty as that old trunk in the moonlight. Everything he's lived for during the last thirty-six years has been swept away like a shack in a flood.

He comes to Government Square, and that's where his legs finally give out. He doesn't so much sit on one of the benches as collapse there. He glances around dully at the empty expanse of concrete, realizing that he'd probably look mighty suspicious to any cops passing in a squad car. He's not supposed to be out this late anyway (like a teenager, he has a *curfew*), but what does that matter? Shit don't mean shit. Let them send him back to Waynesville. Why not? At least there he won't have to deal with his fat fuck boss anymore. Or pee while Ellis McFarland watches.

Across the street is the Happy Cup, where he had so many pleasant conversations about books with Andrew Halliday. Not to mention their *last* conversation, which was far from pleasant. *Stay clear of me,* Andy had said. That was how the last conversation had ended.

Morris's brains, which have been idling in neutral, suddenly engage again and the dazed look in his eyes begins to clear. *Stay clear of me or I'll call the police myself,* Andy had said . . . but that wasn't *all* he said that day. His old pal had also given him some advice.

Hide them somewhere. Bury them.

Had Andy Halliday really said that, or was it only his imagination?

"He said it," Morris whispers. He looks at his hands and sees they have rolled themselves into grimy fists. "He said it, all right. Hide them, he said. *Bury* them." Which leads to certain questions.

Like who was the only person who knew he had the Rothstein notebooks?

Like who was the only person who had actually *seen* one of the Rothstein notebooks?

Like who knew where he had lived in the old days?

And—here was a big one—who knew about that stretch of undeveloped land, an overgrown couple of acres caught in an endless lawsuit and used only by kids cutting across to the Birch Street Rec?

The answer to all these questions is the same.

Maybe we can revisit this in ten years, his old pal had said. *Maybe in twenty.*

Well, it had been a fuck of a lot longer than ten or twenty, hadn't it? Time had gone slip-sliding away. Enough for his old pal to meditate on those valuable notebooks, which had never turned up—not when Morris was arrested for rape and not later on, when the house was sold.

Had his old pal at some point decided to visit Morris's old neighborhood? Perhaps to stroll any number of times along the path between Sycamore Street and Birch? Had he perhaps made those strolls with a metal detector, hoping it would sense the trunk's metal fittings and start to beep?

Did Morris even *mention* the trunk that day?

Maybe not, but what else could it be? What else made sense? Even a large strongbox would be too small. Paper or canvas bags would have rotted. Morris wonders how many holes Andy had to dig before he finally hit paydirt. A dozen? Four dozen? Four dozen was a lot, but back in the seventies, Andy had been fairly trim, not a waddling fat fuck like he was now. And the motivation would have been there. Or maybe he didn't have to dig any holes at all. Maybe there had been a spring flood or something, and the bank had eroded enough to reveal the trunk in its cradle of roots. Wasn't that possible?

Morris gets up and walks on, now thinking about McFarland again and occasionally glancing around to make sure he isn't there. It matters again now, because now he has something to live for again. A goal. It's possible that his old pal has sold the notebooks, selling is his business as sure as it was Jimmy Gold's in *The Runner Slows Down*, but it's just as possible that he's still sitting on some or all of them. There's only one sure way to find out, and only one way to find out if the old wolf still has some teeth. He has to pay his *homie* a visit.

His old pal.

PART 3: PETER AND THE WOLF

1

It's Saturday afternoon in the city, and Hodges is at the movies with Holly. They engage in a lively negotiation while looking at the showtimes in the lobby of the AMC City Center 7. His suggestion of *The Purge: Anarchy* is rejected as too scary. Holly enjoys scary movies, she says, but only on her computer, where she can pause the film and walk around for a few minutes to release the tension. Her counter-suggestion of *The Fault in Our Stars* is rejected by Hodges, who says it will be too sentimental. What he actually means is too emotional. A story about someone dying young will make him think of Janey Patterson, who left the world in an explosion meant to kill him. They settle on *22 Jump Street*, a comedy with Jonah Hill and Channing Tatum. It's pretty good. They laugh a lot and share a big tub of popcorn, but Hodges's mind keeps returning to Tina's story about the money that helped her parents through the bad years. Where in God's name could Peter Saubers have gotten his hands on over twenty thousand dollars?

As the credits are rolling, Holly puts her hand over Hodges's, and he is a little alarmed to see tears standing in her eyes. He asks her what's wrong.

"Nothing. It's just nice to have someone to go to the movies with. I'm glad you're my friend, Bill."

Hodges is more than touched. "And I'm glad you're mine. What are you going to do with the rest of your Saturday?"

"Tonight I'm going to order in Chinese and binge on *Orange Is the New Black*," she says. "But this afternoon I'm going online to look at more robberies. I've already got quite a list."

"Do any of them look likely to you?"

She shakes her head. "I'm going to keep looking, but I think it's something else, although I don't have any idea what it could be. Do you think Tina's brother will tell you?"

At first he doesn't answer. They're making their way up the aisle, and soon they'll be away from this oasis of make-believe and back in the real world.

"Bill? Earth to Bill?"

"I certainly hope so," he says at last. "For his own sake. Because money from nowhere almost always spells trouble."

2

Tina and Barbara and Barbara's mother spend that Saturday afternoon in the Robinson kitchen, making popcorn balls, an operation both messy and hilarious. They are having a blast, and for the first time since she came to visit, Tina doesn't seem troubled. Tanya Robinson thinks that's good. She doesn't know what the deal is with Tina, but a dozen little things—like the way the girl jumps when a draft slams an upstairs door shut, or the suspicious I've-been-crying redness of her eyes—tells Tanya that something is wrong. She doesn't know if that something is big or little, but one thing she's sure of: Tina Saubers can use a little hilarity in her life just about now.

They are finishing up—and threatening each other with syrup-sticky hands—when an amused voice says, "Look at all these womenfolk dashing around the kitchen. I do declare."

Barbara whirls, sees her brother leaning in the kitchen doorway, and screams "*Jerome!*" She runs to him and leaps. He catches her, whirls her around twice, and sets her down.

"I thought you were going to a *cotillion*!"

Jerome smiles. "Alas, my tux went back to the rental place unworn. After a full and fair exchange of views, Priscilla and I have agreed to break up. It's a long story, and not very interesting. Anyway, I decided to drive home and get some of my ma's cooking."

"Don't call me Ma," Tanya says. "It's vulgar." But she also looks mightily pleased to see Jerome.

He turns to Tina and gives a small bow. "Pleased to meet you, little ma'am. Any friend of Barbara's, and so forth."

"I'm Tina."

She manages to say this in a tone of voice that's almost normal, but doing so isn't easy. Jerome is tall, Jerome is broad-shouldered, Jerome is extremely handsome, and Tina Saubers falls in love with him immediately. Soon she will be calculating how old she'll need to be before he might look upon her as something more than a little ma'am in an oversized apron, her hands all sticky from making popcorn balls. For the time being, however, she's too stunned by his beauty to run the numbers. And later that evening, it doesn't take much urging from Barbara for Tina to tell him everything. Although it's not always easy for her to keep her place in the story, with his dark eyes on her.

3

Pete's Saturday afternoon isn't nearly as good. In fact, it's fairly shitty.

At two o'clock, class officers and officers-elect from three high schools crowd into the River Bend Resort's largest conference room to listen as one of the state's two U.S. senators gives a long and boring talk titled "High School Governance: Your Introduction to Politics and Service." This fellow, who's wearing a three-piece suit and sporting a luxuriant, swept-back head of white hair (what Pete thinks of as "soap opera villain hair"), seems ready to go on until dinnertime. Possibly longer. His thesis seems to be something about how they are the NEXT GENERATION, and being class officers will prepare them to deal with pollution, global warming, diminishing resources, and, perhaps, first contact with aliens from Proxima Centauri. Each minute of this endless Saturday afternoon dies a slow and miserable death as he drones on.

Pete couldn't care less about assuming the mantle of student vice president at Northfield High this coming September. As far as he's concerned, September might as well be out there on Proxima Centauri with the aliens. The only future that matters is this coming Monday afternoon, when he will confront Andrew Halliday, a man he now wishes most heartily that he had never met.

But I can work my way out of this, he thinks. If I can hold my nerve, that is. And keep in mind what Jimmy Gold's elderly aunt says in *The Runner Raises the Flag*.

Pete has decided he'll begin his conversation with Halliday by quoting that line: *They say half a loaf is better than none, Jimmy, but in a world of want, even a single slice is better than none.*

Pete knows what *Halliday* wants, and will offer more than a single slice, but not half a loaf, and certainly not the whole thing. That is simply not going to happen. With the notebooks safely hidden away in the basement of the Birch Street Rec, he can afford to negotiate, and if Halliday wants anything at all out of this, he'll have to negotiate, too.

No more ultimatums.

I'll give you three dozen notebooks, Pete imagines saying. *They contain poems, essays, and nine complete short stories. I'm even going to split fifty-fifty, just to be done with you.*

He *has* to insist on getting money, although with no way of verifying how much Halliday actually receives from his buyer or buyers, Pete supposes he'll be cheated out of his fair share, and cheated badly. But that's okay. The important thing is making sure Halliday knows he's serious. That he's not going to be, in Jimmy Gold's pungent phrase, anyone's birthday fuck. Even more important is not letting Halliday see how scared he is.

How terrified.

The senator winds up with a few ringing phrases about how the VITAL WORK of the NEXT GENERATION begins in AMERICA'S HIGH SCHOOLS, and how they, the chosen few, must carry forward THE TORCH OF DEMOCRACY. The applause is enthusiastic, possibly because the lecture is finally over and they get to leave. Pete wants desperately to get out of here, go for a long walk, and check his plan a few more times, looking for loopholes and stumbling blocks.

Only they don't get to leave. The high school principal who has arranged this afternoon's endless chat with greatness steps forward to announce that the senator has agreed to stay another hour and answer their questions. "I'm sure you have lots," she says, and the hands of the butt-lickers and grade-grubbers—there seem to be plenty of both in attendance—shoot up immediately.

Pete thinks, This shit don't mean shit.

He looks at the door, calculates his chances of slipping through it without being noticed, and settles back into his seat. A week from now, all this will be over, he tells himself.

The thought brings him some comfort.

4

A certain recent parolee wakes up as Hodges and Holly are leaving their movie and Tina is falling in love with Barbara's brother. Morris has slept all morning and part of the afternoon following a wakeful, fretful night, only dropping off as the first light of that Saturday morning began to creep into his room. His dreams have been worse than bad. In the one that woke him, he opened the trunk to find it full of black widow spiders, thousands of them, all entwined and gorged with poison and pulsing in the moonlight. They came streaming out, pouring over his hands and clittering up his arms.

Morris gasps and chokes his way back into the real world, hugging his chest so tightly he can barely breathe.

He swings his legs out of bed and sits there with his head down, the same way he sat on the toilet after McFarland exited the MAC men's room the previous afternoon. It's the not knowing that's killing him, and that uncertainty cannot be laid to rest too soon.

Andy *must* have taken them, he thinks. Nothing else makes sense. And you better still have them, pal. God help you if you don't.

He puts on a fresh pair of jeans and takes a crosstown bus over to the South Side, because he's decided he wants at least one of his tools, after all. He'll also take back the Tuff Totes. Because you had to think positive.

Charlie Roberson is once more seated in front of the Harley, now so torn down it hardly looks like a motorcycle at all. He doesn't seem terribly pleased at this reappearance of the man who helped get him out of jail. "How'd it go last night? Did you do what you needed to do?"

"Everything's fine," Morris says, and offers a smile that feels too wide and loose to be convincing. "Four-oh."

Roberson doesn't smile back. "As long as *five*-o isn't involved. You don't look so great, Morrie."

"Well, you know. Things rarely get taken care of all at once. I've got a few more details to iron out."

"If you need the truck again—"

"No, no. I left a couple of things in it, is all. Okay if I grab them?"

"It's nothing that's going to come back on me later, is it?"

"Absolutely not. Just a couple of bags."

And the hatchet, but he neglects to mention that. He could buy a knife, but there's something scary about a hatchet. Morris drops it into one of the Tuff Totes, tells Charlie so long, and heads back to the bus stop. The hatchet slides back and forth in the bag with each swing of his arms.

Don't make me use it, he will tell Andy. *I don't want to hurt you.*

But of course part of him *does* want to use it. Part of him *does* want to hurt his old pal. Because—notebooks aside—he's owed a payback, and payback's a bitch.

5

Lacemaker Lane and the walking mall of which it is a part is busy on this Saturday afternoon. There are hundreds of shops with cutie-poo names like Deb and Buckle and Forever 21. There's also one called Lids, which sells nothing but hats. Morris stops in there and buys a Groundhogs cap with an extra-long brim. A little closer to Andrew Halliday Rare Editions, he stops again and purchases a pair of shades at a Sunglass Hut kiosk.

Just as he spots the sign of his old pal's business establishment, with its scrolled gold leaf lettering, a dismaying thought occurs to him: What if Andy closes early on Saturday? All the other shops seem to be open, but some rare bookstores keep lazy hours, and wouldn't that be just his luck?

But when he walks past, swinging the totes (*clunk* and *bump* goes the hatchet), secure behind his new shades, he sees the OPEN sign hanging in the door. He sees something else, as well: cameras peeking left and right along the sidewalk. There are probably more inside, too, but that's okay; Morris has done decades of postgraduate work with thieves.

He idles up the street, looking in the window of a bakery and scanning the wares of a souvenir vendor's cart (although

Morris can't imagine who'd want a souvenir of this dirty little lakefront city). He even pauses to watch a mime who juggles colored balls and then pretends to climb invisible stairs. Morris tosses a couple of quarters into the mime's hat. For good luck, he tells himself. Pop music pours down from street-corner loudspeakers. There's a smell of chocolate in the air.

He walks back. He sees a couple of young men come out of Andy's bookshop and head off down the sidewalk. This time Morris pauses to look in the display window, where three books are open on stands beneath pinspots: *To Kill a Mockingbird*, *The Catcher in the Rye*, and—surely it's an omen—*The Runner Sees Action*. The shop beyond the window is narrow and high-ceilinged. He sees no other customers, but he *does* see his old pal, the one and only Andy Halliday, sitting at the desk halfway down, reading a paperback.

Morris pretends to tie his shoe and unzips the Tuff Tote with the hatchet inside. Then he stands and, with no hesitation, opens the door of Andrew Halliday Rare Editions.

His old pal looks up from his book and scopes the sunglasses, the long-brimmed cap, the tote bags. He frowns, but only a little, because *everyone* in this area is carrying bags, and the day is warm and bright. Morris sees caution but no signs of real alarm, which is good.

"Would you mind putting your bags under the coatrack?" Andy asks. He smiles. "Store policy."

"Not at all," Morris says. He puts the Tuff Totes down, removes his sunglasses, folds the bows, and slides them into his shirt pocket. Then he takes off his new hat and runs a hand through the short scruff of his white hair. He thinks, See? Just an elderly geezer who's come in to get out of the hot sun and do a little browsing. Nothing to worry about here. "Whew! It's hot outside today." He puts his cap back on.

"Yes, and they say tomorrow's going to be even hotter. Can I help you with something special?"

"Just browsing. Although . . . I *have* been looking for a rather rare book called *The Executioners*. It's by a mystery novelist named John D. MacDonald." MacDonald's books were very popular in the prison library.

"Know him well!" Andy says jovially. "Wrote all those Travis McGee stories. The ones with colors in the titles. Paperback writer for the most part, wasn't he? I don't deal in paperbacks, as a rule; very few of collectible quality."

What about notebooks? Morris thinks. Moleskines, to be specific. Do you deal in those, you fat, thieving fuck?

"*The Executioners* was published in hardcover," he says, examining a shelf of books near the door. He wants to stay close to the door for the time being. And the bag with the hatchet in it. "It was the basis of a movie called *Cape Fear*. I'd buy a copy of that, if you happened to have one in mint condition. What I believe you people call very fine as new. And if the price was right, of course."

Andy looks engaged now, and why not? He has a fish on the line. "I'm sure I don't have it in stock, but I could check Book-Finder for you. That's a database. If it's listed, and a MacDonald hardcover probably is, especially if it was made into a film . . . *and* if it's a first edition . . . I could probably have it for you by Tuesday. Wednesday at the latest. Would you like me to look?"

"I would," Morris says. "But the price has to be right."

"Naturally, naturally." Andy's chuckle is as fat as his gut. He lowers his eyes to the screen of his laptop. As soon as he does this, Morris flips the sign hanging in the door from OPEN to CLOSED. He bends down and takes the hatchet from the open duffel bag. He moves up the narrow central aisle with it held beside his leg. He doesn't hurry. He doesn't have to hurry. Andy is clicking away at his laptop and absorbed by whatever he's seeing on the screen.

"Found it!" his old pal exclaims. "James Graham has one, very fine as new, for just three hundred dol—"

He ceases speaking as the blade of the hatchet floats first into his peripheral vision, then front and center. He looks up, his face slack with shock.

"I want your hands where I can see them," Morris says. "There's probably an alarm button in the kneehole of your desk. If you want to keep all your fingers, don't reach for it."

"What do you want? Why are you—"

"Don't recognize me, do you?" Morris doesn't know whether to be amused by this or infuriated. "Not even right up close and personal."

"No, I . . . I . . ."

"Not surprising, I guess. It's been a long time since the Happy Cup, hasn't it?"

Halliday stares into Morris's lined and haggard face with dreadful fascination. Morris thinks, He's like a bird looking at a snake. This is a pleasant thought, and makes him smile.

"Oh my God," Andy says. His face has gone the color of old cheese. "It can't be you. You're in jail."

Morris shakes his head, still smiling. "There's probably a database for parolees as well as rare books, but I'm guessing you never checked it. Good for me, not so good for you."

One of Andy's hands is creeping away from the keyboard of his laptop. Morris wiggles the hatchet.

"Don't do that, Andy. I want to see your hands on either side of your computer, palms down. Don't try to hit the button with your knee, either. I'll know if you try, and the consequences for you will be unpleasant in the extreme."

"What do you want?"

The question makes him angry, but his smile widens. "As if you don't know."

"I don't, Morrie, my God!" Andy's mouth is lying but his eyes tell the truth, the whole truth, and nothing but the truth.

"Let's go in your office. I'm sure you have one back there."

"No!"

Morris wiggles the hatchet again. "You can come out of this whole and intact, or with some of your fingers lying on the desk. Believe me on this, Andy. I'm not the man you knew."

Andy gets up, his eyes never leaving Morris's face, but Morris isn't sure his old pal is actually seeing him anymore. He sways as if to invisible music, on the verge of passing out. If he does that, he won't be able to answer questions until he comes around. Also, Morris would have to *drag* him to the office. He's not sure he can do that; if Andy doesn't tip the scales at three hundred, he's got to be pushing it.

"Take a deep breath," he says. "Calm down. All I want is a few answers. Then I'm gone."

"You promise?" Andy's lower lip is pushed out, shining with spit. He looks like a fat little boy who's in dutch with his father.

"Yes. Now breathe."

Andy breathes.

"Again."

Andy's massive chest rises, straining the buttons of his shirt, then lowers. A bit of his color comes back.

"Office. Now. Do it."

Andy turns and lumbers to the back of the store, weaving his way between boxes and stacks of books with the finicky grace some fat men possess. Morris follows. His anger is growing. It's something about the girlish flex and sway of Andy's buttocks, clad in gray gabardine trousers, that fuels it.

There's a keypad beside the door. Andy punches in four numbers—9118—and a green light flashes. As he enters, Morris reads his mind right through the back of his bald head.

"You're not quick enough to slam the door on me. If you try, you're going to lose something that can't be replaced. Count on it."

Andy's shoulders, which have risen as he tenses to make just this attempt, slump again. He steps in. Morris follows and closes the door.

The office is small, lined with stuffed bookshelves, lit by hanging globes. On the floor is a Turkish rug. The desk in here is much nicer—mahogany or teak or some other expensive wood. On it is a lamp with a shade that looks like real Tiffany glass. To the left of the door is a sideboard with four heavy crystal decanters on it. Morris doesn't know about the two containing clear liquid, but he bets the others hold scotch and bourbon. The good stuff, too, if he knows his old pal. For toasting big sales, no doubt.

Morris remembers the only kinds of booze available in the joint, prunejack and raisinjack, and even though he only imbibed on rare occasions like his birthday (and John Rothstein's, which he always marked with a single jolt), his anger grows. Good booze to drink and good food to gobble—that's what Andy Halliday had while Morris was dyeing bluejeans, inhaling varnish fumes, and living in a cell not much bigger than a coffin. He was in the joint for rape, true enough, but he never would have been in that alley, in a furious drunken blackout, if this man had not denied him and sent him packing. *Morris, I shouldn't even be seen with you.* That's what he said that day. And then called him batshit-crazy.

"Luxy accommodations, my friend."

Andy looks around as if noting the luxy accommodations for the first time. "It looks that way," he admits, "but appearances can be deceiving, Morrie. The truth is, I'm next door to broke. This place never came back from the recession, and from certain . . . allegations. You have to believe that."

Morris rarely thinks about the money envelopes Curtis Rogers found along with the notebooks in Rothstein's safe that night, but he thinks about them now. His old pal got the cash as well as the notebooks. For all Morris knows, that money paid for the desk, and the rug, and the fancy crystal decanters of booze.

At this, the balloon of rage finally bursts and Morris slings the hatchet in a low sideways arc, his cap tumbling from his head. The hatchet bites through gray gabardine and buries itself in the bloated buttock beneath with a *chump* sound. Andy screams and stumbles forward. He breaks his fall on the edge of his desk with his forearms, then goes to his knees. Blood pours through a six-inch slit in his pants. He claps a hand over it and more blood runs through his fingers. He falls on his side, then rolls over on the Turkish rug. With some satisfaction, Morris thinks, You'll never get *that* stain out, homie.

Andy squalls, "You said you wouldn't hurt me!"

Morris considers this and shakes his head. "I don't believe I ever said that in so many words, although I suppose I might have implied it." He stares into Andy's contorted face with serious sincerity. "Think of it as DIY liposuction. And you can still come out of this alive. All you have to do is give me the notebooks. Where are they?"

This time Andy doesn't pretend not to know what Morris is talking about, not with his ass on fire and blood seeping out from beneath one hip. "I don't have them!"

Morris drops to one knee, careful to avoid the growing pool of blood. "I don't believe you. They're gone, nothing left but the trunk they were in, and nobody knew I had them but you. So I'm going to ask you again, and if you don't want to get a close look at your own guts and whatever you ate for lunch, you should be careful how you answer. *Where are the notebooks?*"

"A kid found them! It wasn't me, it was a kid! He lives in your old house, Morrie! He must have found them buried in the basement, or something!"

Morris stares into his old pal's face. He's looking for a lie, but he's also trying to cope with this sudden rearrangement of what he thought he knew. It's like a hard left turn in a car doing sixty.

"Please, Morrie, please! His name is Peter Saubers!"

It's the convincer, because Morris knows the name of the family now living in the house where he grew up. Besides, a man with a deep gash in his ass could hardly make up such specifics on the spur of the moment.

"How do you know that?"

"*Because he's trying to sell them to me!* Morrie, I need a doctor! I'm bleeding like a stuck pig!"

You *are* a pig, Morris thinks. But don't worry, old pal, pretty soon you'll be out of your misery. I'm going to send you to that big bookstore in the sky. But not yet, because Morris sees a bright ray of hope.

He's trying, Andy said, not *He tried.*

"Tell me everything," Morris says. "Then I'll leave. You'll have to call for an ambulance yourself, but I'm sure you can manage that."

"How do I know you're telling the truth?"

"Because if the kid has the notebooks, I have no more interest in you. Of course, you have to promise not to tell them who hurt you. It was a masked man, wasn't it? Probably a drug addict. He wanted money, right?"

Andy nods eagerly.

"It had nothing to do with the notebooks, right?"

"No, nothing! You think I want my name involved with this?"

"I suppose not. But if you tried making up some story—and if my name was in that story—I'd have to come back."

"I won't, Morrie, I won't!" Next comes a declaration as childish as that pushed-out, spit-shiny lower lip: "Honest injun!"

"Then tell me everything."

Andy does. Saubers's first visit, with photocopies from the notebooks and *Dispatches from Olympus* for comparison. Andy's identification of the boy calling himself James Hawkins, using no more than the library sticker on the spine of *Dispatches*. The boy's second visit, when Andy turned the screws on him. The voicemail about the weekend class-officer trip to River Bend Resort, and the promise to come in Monday afternoon, just two days from now.

"What time on Monday?"

"He . . . he didn't say. After school, I'd assume. He goes to Northfield High. Morrie, I'm still bleeding."

"Yes," Morris says absently. "I guess you are." He's thinking furiously. The boy claims to have all the notebooks. He might be lying about that, but probably not. The number of them that he quoted to Andy sounds right. *And he's read them.* This ignites a spark of poison jealousy in Morris Bellamy's head and lights a fire that quickly spreads to his heart. The Saubers boy has read what was meant for Morris and Morris alone. This is a grave injustice, and must be addressed.

He leans closer to Andy and says, "Are you gay? You are, aren't you?"

Andy's eyes flutter. "Am I . . . what does that matter? Morrie, I need an *ambulance*!"

"Do you have a partner?"

His old pal is hurt, but not stupid. He can see what such a question portends. "Yes!"

No, Morris thinks, and swings the hatchet: *chump.*

Andy screams and begins to writhe on the bloody rug. Morris swings again and Andy screams again. Lucky the room's lined with books, Morris thinks. Books make good insulation.

"Hold still, damn you," he says, but Andy doesn't. It takes four blows in all. The last one comes down above the bridge of Andy's nose, splitting both of his eyes like grapes, and at last the writhing stops. Morris pulls the hatchet free with a low squall of steel on bone and drops it on the rug beside one of Andy's outstretched hands. "There," he says. "All finished."

The rug is sodden with blood. The front of the desk is beaded with it. So is one of the walls, and Morris himself. The inner office is your basic abattoir. This doesn't upset Morris much; he's pretty calm. It's probably shock, he thinks, but so what if it is? He *needs* to be calm. Upset people forget things.

There are two doors behind the desk. One opens on his old pal's private bathroom, the other on a closet. There are plenty of clothes in the closet, including two suits that look expensive. They're of no use to Morris, though. He'd float in them.

He wishes the bathroom had a shower, but if wishes were horses, et cetera, et cetera. He'll make do with the basin. As he strips off his bloody shirt and washes up, he tries to replay everything he touched since entering the shop. He doesn't believe there's much. He will have to remember to wipe down the sign hanging in the front door, though. Also the doorknobs of the closet and this bathroom.

He dries off and goes back into the office, dropping the towel and bloody shirt by the body. His jeans are also spattered, a problem that's easily solved by what he finds on a shelf in the closet: at least two dozen tee-shirts, neatly folded with tissue paper between them. He finds an XL that will cover his jeans halfway down his thighs, where the worst of the spotting is, and unfolds it. ANDREW HALLIDAY RARE EDITIONS is printed on the front, along with the shop's telephone number, website address, and an image of an open book. Morris thinks, He probably gives these away to big-money customers. Who take them, say thank you, and never wear them.

He starts to put the tee-shirt on, decides he really doesn't want to be walking around wearing the location of his latest murder on his chest, and turns it inside-out. The lettering shows through a little, but not enough for anyone to read it, and the book could be any rectangular object.

His Dockers are a problem, though. The tops are splattered with blood and the soles are smeared with it. Morris studies his old pal's feet, nods judiciously, and returns to the closet. Andy's waist size may be almost twice Morris's, but their shoe sizes look approximately the same. He selects a pair of loafers and tries them on. They pinch a little, and may leave a blister or two, but blisters are a small price to pay for what he has learned, and the long-delayed revenge he has exacted.

Also, they're damned fine-looking shoes.

He adds his own footwear to the pile of gooey stuff on the rug, then examines his cap. Not so much as a single spot. Good luck there. He puts it on and circles the office, wiping the surfaces he knows he touched and the ones he might have touched.

He kneels by the body one last time and searches the pockets, aware that he's getting blood on his hands again and will have to wash them again. Oh well, so it goes.

That's Vonnegut, not Rothstein, he thinks, and laughs. Literary allusions always please him.

Andy's keys are in a front pocket, his wallet tucked against the buttock Morris didn't split with the hatchet. More good luck. Not much in the way of cash, less than thirty dollars, but a penny saved is a penny et cetera. Morris tucks the bills away along with the keys. Then he re-washes his hands and re-wipes the faucet handles.

Before leaving Andy's sanctum sanctorum, he regards the hatchet. The blade is smeared with gore and hair. The rubber handle clearly bears his palmprint. He should probably take it along in one of the Tuff Totes with his shirt and shoes, but some intuition—too deep for words but very powerful—tells him to leave it, at least for the time being.

Morris picks it up, wipes the blade and the handle to get rid of the fingerprints, then sets it gently down on the fancy desk. Like a warning. Or a calling card.

"Who says I'm not a wolf, Mr. McFarland?" he asks the empty office. "Who says?"

Then he leaves, using the blood-streaked towel to turn the knob.

6

In the shop again, Morris deposits the bloody stuff in one of the bags and zips it closed. Then he sits down to investigate Andy's laptop.

It's a Mac, much nicer than the one in the prison library but basically the same. Since it's still wide awake, there's no need to waste time hunting for a password. There are lots of business files on the screen, plus an app marked SECURITY in the bar at the bottom. He'll want to investigate that, and closely, but first he opens a file marked JAMES HAWKINS, and yes, here is the information he wants: Peter Saubers's address (which he knows), and also Peter Saubers's cell phone number, presumably gleaned from the voicemail his old pal mentioned. His father is Thomas. His mother is Linda. His sister is Tina. There's even a picture of young Mr. Saubers, aka James Hawkins, standing with a bunch of librarians from the Garner Street branch, a branch Morris knows well. Below this information—which may come in handy, who knows, who knows—is a John Rothstein bibliography, which Morris only glances at; he knows Rothstein's work by heart.

Except for the stuff young Mr. Saubers is sitting on, of course. The stuff he stole from its rightful owner.

There's a notepad by the computer. Morris jots down the boy's cell number and sticks it in his pocket. Next he opens the security app and clicks on CAMERAS. Six views appear. Two show Lacemaker Lane in all its consumer glory. Two look down on the shop's narrow interior. The fifth shows this very desk, with Morris sitting behind it in his new tee-shirt. The sixth shows Andy's inner office, and the body sprawled on the

Turkish rug. In black-and-white, the splashes and splatters of
blood look like ink.

Morris clicks on this image, and it fills the screen. Arrow
buttons appear on the bottom. He clicks the double arrow for
rewind, waits, then hits play. He watches, engrossed, as he
murders his old pal all over again. Fascinating. Not a home
movie he wants anyone to see, however, which means the laptop is coming with him.

He unplugs the various cords, including the one leading
from a shiny box stamped VIGILANT SECURITY SYS-
TEMS. The cameras feed directly to the laptop's hard drive,
and so there are no automatically made DVDs. That makes
sense. A system like that would be a little too pricey for a
small business like Andrew Halliday Rare Editions. But one
of the cords he unplugged went to a disc-burner add-on, so his
old pal could have made DVDs from stored security footage if
he had desired.

Morris hunts methodically through the desk, looking for
them. There are five drawers in all. He finds nothing of interest in the first four, but the kneehole is locked. Morris finds
this suggestive. He sorts through Andy's keys, selects the
smallest, unlocks the drawer, and strikes paydirt. He has no
interest in the six or eight graphic photos of his old pal fel-
lating a squat young man with a lot of tattoos, but there's
also a gun. It's a prissy, overdecorated P238 SIG Sauer, red
and black, with gold-inlaid flowers scrolling down the barrel.
Morris drops the clip and sees it's full. There's even one in the
pipe. He puts the clip back in and lays the gun on the desk—
something else to take along. He searches deep into the drawer
and finds an unmarked white envelope at the very back, the
flap tucked under rather than sealed. He opens it, expecting
more dirty pix, and is delighted to find money instead—at
least five hundred dollars. His luck is still running. He puts
the envelope next to the SIG.

There's nothing else, and he's about decided that if there *are* DVDs, Andy's locked them in a safe somewhere. Yet Lady Luck is not quite done with Morris Bellamy. When he gets up, his shoulder bumps an overloaded shelf to the left of the desk. A bunch of old books go tumbling to the floor, and behind them is a slim stack of plastic DVD cases bound together with rubber bands.

"How do you do," Morris says softly. "How *do* you do."

He sits back down and goes through them rapidly, like a man shuffling cards. Andy has written a name on each in black Sharpie. Only the last one means anything to him, and it's the one he was looking for. "HAWKINS" is printed on the shiny surface.

He's had plenty of breaks this afternoon (possibly to make up for the horrible disappointment he suffered last night), but there's no point in pushing things. Morris takes the computer, the gun, the envelope with the money in it, and the HAWKINS disc to the front of the store. He tucks them into one of his totes, ignoring the people passing back and forth in front. If you look like you belong in a place, most people think you do. He exits with a confident step, and locks the door behind him. The CLOSED sign swings briefly, then settles. Morris pulls down the long visor of his Groundhogs cap and walks away.

He makes one more stop before returning to Bugshit Manor, at a computer café called Bytes 'N Bites. For twelve of Andy Halliday's dollars, he gets an overpriced cup of shitty coffee and twenty minutes in a carrel, at a computer equipped with a DVD player. It takes less than five minutes to be sure of what he has: his old pal talking to a boy who appears to be wearing fake glasses and his father's moustache. In the first clip, Saubers has a book that has to be *Dispatches from Olympus* and an envelope containing several sheets of paper that have to be the photocopies Andy mentioned. In the second clip, Saubers and Andy appear to be arguing. There's no sound in either of these black-and-white mini-movies, which is fine. The boy could be saying anything. In the second one, the argument one, he could even be saying The next time I come, I'll bring my hatchet, you fat fuck.

As he leaves Bytes 'N Bites, Morris is smiling. The man behind the counter smiles back and says, "I guess you had a good time."

"Yes," says the man who has spent well over two-thirds of his life in prison. "But your coffee sucks, nerdboy. I ought to pour it on your fucking head."

The smile dies on the counterman's face. A lot of the people who come in here are crackpots. With those folks, it's best to just keep quiet and hope they never come back.

7

Hodges told Holly he intended to spend at least part of his weekend crashed out in his La-Z-Boy watching baseball, and on Sunday afternoon he does watch the first three innings of the Indians game, but then a certain restlessness takes hold and he decides to pay a call. Not on an old pal, but certainly an old acquaintance. After each of these visits he tells himself Okay, that's the end, this is pointless. He means it, too. Then—four weeks later, or eight, maybe ten—he'll take the ride again. Something nags him into it. Besides, the Indians are already down to the Rangers by five, and it's only the third inning.

He zaps off the television, pulls on an old Police Athletic League tee-shirt (in his heavyset days he used to steer clear of tees, but now he likes the way they fall straight, with hardly any belly-swell above the waist of his pants), and locks up the house. Traffic is light on Sunday, and twenty minutes later he's sliding his Prius into a slot on the third deck of the visitors' parking garage, adjacent to the vast and ever metastasizing concrete sprawl of John M. Kiner Hospital. As he walks to the parking garage elevator, he sends up a prayer as he almost always does, thanking God that he's here as a visitor rather than as a paying customer. All too aware, even as he says this very proper thank-you, that most people *become* customers sooner or later, here or at one of the city's four other fine and not-so-fine sickbays. No one rides for free, and in the end, even the most seaworthy ship goes down, blub-blub-blub. The only way to balance that off, in Hodges's opinion, is to make the most of every day afloat.

But if that's true, what is he doing here?

The thought recalls to mind a snatch of poetry, heard or read long ago and lodged in his brain by virtue of its simple rhyme: *Oh do not ask what is it, let us go and make our visit.*

8

It's easy to get lost in any big city hospital, but Hodges has made this trip plenty of times, and these days he's more apt to give directions than ask for them. The garage elevator takes him down to a covered walkway; the walkway takes him to a lobby the size of a train terminal; the Corridor A elevator takes him up to the third floor; a skyway takes him across Kiner Boulevard to his final destination, where the walls are painted a soothing pink and the atmosphere is hushed. The sign above the reception desk reads:

**WELCOME TO LAKES REGION
TRAUMATIC BRAIN INJURY CLINIC
NO CELL PHONES OR TELECOMMUNICATIONS
DEVICES ALLOWED
HELP US MAINTAIN A QUIET ENVIRONMENT
WE APPRECIATE YOUR COOPERATION**

Hodges goes to the desk, where his visitor's badge is already waiting. The head nurse knows him; after four years, they are almost old friends.

"How's your family, Becky?"

She says they are fine.

"Son's broken arm mending?"

She says it is. The cast is off and he'll be out of the sling in another week, two at most.

"That's fine. Is my boy in his room or physical therapy?"

She says he's in his room.

Hodges ambles down the hall toward Room 217, where a certain patient resides at state expense. Before Hodges gets there, he meets the orderly the nurses call Library Al. He's in his sixties, and—as usual—he's pushing a trolley cart packed with paperbacks and newspapers. These days there's a new addition to his little arsenal of diversions: a small plastic tub filled with handheld e-readers.

"Hey, Al," Hodges says. "How you doin?"

Although Al is ordinarily garrulous, this afternoon he seems half asleep, and there are purple circles under his eyes. Somebody had a hard night, Hodges thinks with amusement. He knows the symptoms, having had a few hard ones himself. He thinks of snapping his fingers in front of Al's eyes, sort of like a stage hypnotist, then decides that would be mean. Let the man suffer the tail end of his hangover in peace. If it's this bad in the afternoon, Hodges hates to think of what it must have been like this morning.

But Al comes to and smiles before Hodges can pass by. "Hey there, Detective! Haven't seen your face in the place for awhile."

"It's just plain old mister these days, Al. You feeling okay?"

"Sure. Just thinking about . . ." Al shrugs. "Jeez, I dunno what I was thinking about." He laughs. "Getting old is no job for sissies."

"You're not old," Hodges says. "Somebody forgot to give you the news—sixty's the new forty."

Al snorts. "Ain't *that* a crock of you-know-what."

Hodges couldn't agree more. He points to the cart. "Don't suppose my boy ever asks for a book, does he?"

Al gives another snort. "Hartsfield? He couldn't read a Berenstain Bears book these days." He taps his forehead gravely. "Nothing left but oatmeal up top. Although sometimes he does hold out his hand for one of these." He picks up a Zappit e-reader. It's a bright girly pink. "These jobbies have games on em."

"He plays games?" Hodges is astounded.

"Oh God no. His motor control is shot. But if I turn on one of the demos, like Barbie Fashion Walk or Fishin' Hole, he stares at it for hours. The demos do the same thing over and over, but does he know that?"

"I'm guessing not."

"Good guess. I think he likes the noises, too—the beeps and boops and goinks. I come back two hours later, the reader's layin on his bed or windowsill, screen dark, battery flat as a pancake. But what the hell, that don't hurt em, three hours on the charger and they're ready to go again. *He* don't recharge, though. Probably a good thing." Al wrinkles his nose, as at a bad smell.

Maybe, maybe not, Hodges thinks. As long as he's not better, he's here, in a nice hospital room. Not much of a view, but there's air-conditioning, color TV, and every now and then a bright pink Zappit to stare at. If he was compos mentis—able to assist in his own defense, as the law has it—he'd have to stand trial for a dozen offenses, including nine counts of murder. Ten, if the DA decided to add in the asshole's mother, who died of poisoning. Then it would be Waynesville State Prison for the rest of his life.

No air-conditioning there.

"Take it easy, Al. You look tired."

"Nah, I'm fine, Detective Hutchinson. Enjoy your visit."

Al rolls on, and Hodges looks after him, brow furrowed. Hutchinson? Where the hell did *that* come from? Hodges has been coming here for years now, and Al knows his name perfectly well. Or did. Jesus, he hopes the guy isn't suffering from early-onset dementia.

For the first four months or so, there were two guards on the door of 217. Then one. Now there are none, because guarding Brady is a waste of time and money. There's not much danger of escape when the perp can't even make it to the bathroom by himself. Each year there's talk of transferring him to a cheaper institution upstate, and each year the prosecutor reminds all and sundry that this gentleman, brain-damaged or not, is technically still awaiting trial. It's easy to keep him here because the clinic foots a large portion of the bills. The neurological team—especially Dr. Felix Babineau, the Head of Department—finds Brady Hartsfield an extremely interesting case.

This afternoon he sits by the window, dressed in jeans and a checked shirt. His hair is long and needs cutting, but it's been washed and shines golden in the sunlight. Hair some girl would love to run her fingers through, Hodges thinks. If she didn't know what a monster he was.

"Hello, Brady."

Hartsfield doesn't stir. He's looking out the window, yes, but is he seeing the brick wall of the parking garage, which is his only view? Does he know it's Hodges in the room with him? Does he know *anybody* is in the room with him? These are questions to which a whole team of neuro guys would like answers. So would Hodges, who sits on the end of the bed, thinking *Was* a monster? Or still is?

"Long time no see, as the landlocked sailor said to the chorus girl."

Hartsfield makes no reply.

"I know, that's an oldie. I got hundreds, ask my daughter. How are you feeling?"

Hartsfield makes no reply. His hands are in his lap, the long white fingers loosely clasped.

In April of 2009, Brady Hartsfield stole a Mercedes-Benz belonging to Holly's aunt, and deliberately drove at high speed into a crowd of job-seekers at City Center. He killed eight and seriously injured twelve, including Thomas Saubers, father of Peter and Tina. He got away with it, too. Hartsfield's mistake was to write Hodges, by then retired, a taunting letter.

The following year, Brady killed Holly's cousin, a woman with whom Hodges had been falling in love. Fittingly, it was Holly herself who stopped Brady Hartsfield's clock, almost literally bashing his brains out with Hodges's own Happy Slapper before Hartsfield could detonate a bomb that would have killed thousands of kids at a pop concert.

The first blow from the Slapper had fractured Hartsfield's skull, but it was the second one that did what was considered to be irreparable damage. He was admitted to the Traumatic Brain Injury Clinic in a deep coma from which he was unlikely to ever emerge. So said Dr. Babineau. But on a dark and stormy night in November of 2011, Hartsfield opened his eyes and spoke to the nurse changing his IV bag. (When considering that moment, Hodges always imagines Dr. Frankenstein screaming, "It's alive! It's alive!") Hartsfield said he had a headache, and asked for his mother. When Dr. Babineau was fetched, and asked his patient to follow his finger to check his extraocular movements, Hartsfield was able to do so.

Over the thirty months since then, Brady Hartsfield has spoken on many occasions (although never to Hodges). Mostly he asks for his mother. When he's told she is dead, he sometimes nods as if he understands . . . but then a day or a week later, he'll repeat the request. He is able to follow simple instructions in the PT center, and can sort of walk again, although it's actually more of an orderly-assisted shamble. On good days he's able to feed himself, but cannot dress himself. He is classed as a semicatatonic. Mostly he sits in his room, either looking out the window at the parking garage, or at a picture of flowers on the wall of his room.

But there have been certain peculiar occurrences around Brady Hartsfield over the last year or so, and as a result he has become something of a legend in the Brain Injury Clinic. There are rumors and speculations. Dr. Babineau scoffs at these, and refuses to talk about them . . . but some of the orderlies and other nurses will, and a certain retired police detective has proved to be an avid listener over the years.

Hodges leans forward, hands dangling between his knees, and smiles at Hartsfield.

"Are you faking, Brady?"

Brady makes no reply.

"Why bother? You're going to be locked up for the rest of your life, one way or the other."

Brady makes no reply, but one hand rises slowly from his lap. He almost pokes himself in the eye, then gets what he was aiming for and brushes a lock of hair from his forehead.

"Want to ask about your mother?"

Brady makes no reply.

"She's dead. Rotting in her coffin. You fed her a bunch of gopher poison. She must have died hard. Did she die hard? Were you there? Did you watch?"

No reply.

"Are you in there, Brady? Knock, knock. Hello?"

No reply.

"I think you are. I hope you are. Hey, tell you something. I used to be a big drinker. And do you know what I remember best about those days?"

Nothing.

"The hangovers. Struggling to get out of bed with my head pounding like a hammer on an anvil. Pissing the morning quart and wondering what I did the night before. Sometimes not even knowing how I got home. Checking my car for dents. It was like being lost inside my own fucking mind, looking for the door so I could get out of there and not finding it until maybe noon, when things would finally start going back to normal."

This makes him think briefly of Library Al.

"I hope that's where you are right now, Brady. Wandering around inside your half-busted brain and looking for a way out. Only for you there isn't one. For you the hangover just goes on and on. Is that how it is? Man, I hope so."

His hands hurt. He looks down at them and sees his fingernails digging into his palms. He lets up and watches the white crescents there fill in red. He refreshes his smile. "Just sayin, buddy. Just sayin. You want to say anything back?"

Hartsfield says nothing back.

Hodges stands up. "That's all right. You sit right there by the window and try to find that way out. The one that isn't there. While you do that, I'll go outside and breathe some fresh air. It's a beautiful day."

On the table between the chair and the bed is a photograph Hodges first saw in the house on Elm Street where Hartsfield lived with his mother. This is a smaller version, in a plain silver frame. It shows Brady and his mom on a beach somewhere, arms around each other, cheeks pressed together, looking more like boyfriend and girlfriend than mother and son. As Hodges turns to go, the picture falls over with a toneless *clack* sound.

He looks at it, looks at Hartsfield, then looks back at the facedown picture.

"Brady?"

No answer. There never is. Not to him, anyway.

"Brady, did you do that?"

Nothing. Brady is staring down at his lap, where his fingers are once more loosely entwined.

"Some of the nurses say . . ." Hodges doesn't finish the thought. He sets the picture back up on its little stand. "If you did it, do it again."

Nothing from Hartsfield, and nothing from the picture. Mother and son in happier days. Deborah Ann Hartsfield and her honeyboy.

"All right, Brady. Seeya later, alligator. Leaving the scene, jellybean."

He does so, closing the door behind him. As he does, Brady Hartsfield looks up briefly. And smiles.

On the table, the picture falls over again.

Clack.

9

Ellen Bran (known as Bran Stoker by students who have taken the Northfield High English Department's Fantasy and Horror class) is standing by the door of a schoolbus parked in the River Bend Resort reception area. Her cell phone is in her hand. It's four PM on Sunday afternoon, and she is about to call 911 to report a missing student. That's when Peter Saubers comes around the restaurant side of the building, running so fast that his hair flies back from his forehead.

Ellen is unfailingly correct with her students, always staying on the teacher side of the line and never trying to buddy up, but on this one occasion she casts propriety aside and enfolds Pete in a hug so strong and frantic that it nearly stops his breath. From the bus, where the other NHS class officers and officers-to-be are waiting, there comes a sarcastic smatter of applause.

Ellen lets up on the hug, grabs his shoulders, and does another thing she's never done to a student before: gives him a good shaking. "Where *were* you? You missed all three morning seminars, you missed lunch, I was on the verge of calling the *police*!"

"I'm sorry, Ms. Bran. I was sick to my stomach. I thought the fresh air would help me."

Ms. Bran—chaperone and adviser on this weekend trip because she teaches American Politics as well as American History—decides she believes him. Not just because Pete is one of her best students and has never caused her trouble before, but because the boy *looks* sick.

"Well . . . you should have informed me," she says. "I thought you'd taken it into your head to hitchhike back to town, or something. If anything had happened to you, I'd be blamed. Don't you realize you kids are my responsibility when we're on a class trip?"

"I lost track of the time. I was vomiting, and I didn't want to do it inside. It must have been something I ate. Or one of those twenty-four-hour bugs."

It wasn't anything he ate and he doesn't have a bug, but the vomiting part is true enough. It's nerves. Unadulterated fright, to be more exact. He's terrified about facing Andrew Halliday tomorrow. It could go right, he knows there's a chance for it to go right, but it will be like threading a moving needle. If it goes wrong, he'll be in trouble with his parents and in trouble with the police. College scholarships, need-based or otherwise? Forget them. He might even go to jail. So he has spent the day wandering the paths that crisscross the thirty acres of resort property, going over the coming confrontation again and again. What he will say; what Halliday will say; what he will say in return. And yes, he lost track of time.

Pete wishes he had never seen that fucking trunk.

He thinks, But I was only trying to do the right thing. Goddammit, that's all I was trying to do!

Ellen sees the tears standing in the boy's eyes, and notices for the first time—perhaps because he's shaved off that silly singles-bar moustache—how thin his face has become. Really just half a step from gaunt. She drops her cell back into her purse and comes out with a packet of tissues. "Wipe your face," she says.

A voice from the bus calls out, "Hey Saubers! D'ja get any?"

"Shut up, Jeremy," Ellen says without turning. Then, to Pete: "I should give you a week's detention for this little stunt, but I'm going to cut you some slack."

Indeed she is, because a week's detention would necessitate an oral report to NHS Assistant Principal Waters, who is also School Disciplinarian. Waters would inquire into her own actions, and want to know why she had not sounded the alarm earlier, especially if she were forced to admit that she hadn't actually seen Pete Saubers since dinner in the restaurant the night before. He had been out of her sight and supervision for nearly a full day, and that was far too long for a school-mandated trip.

"Thank you, Ms. Bran."

"Do you think you're done throwing up?"

"Yes. There's nothing left."

"Then get on the bus and let's go home."

There's more sarcastic applause as Pete comes up the steps and makes his way down the aisle. He tries to smile, as if everything is okay. All he wants is to get back to Sycamore Street and hide in his room, waiting for tomorrow so he can get this nightmare over with.

10

When Hodges gets home from the hospital, a good-looking young man in a Harvard tee-shirt is sitting on his stoop, reading a thick paperback with a bunch of fighting Greeks or Romans on the cover. Sitting beside him is an Irish setter wearing the sort of happy-go-lucky grin that seems to be the default expression of dogs raised in friendly homes. Both man and dog rise when Hodges pulls into the little lean-to that serves as his garage.

The young man meets him halfway across the lawn, one fisted hand held out. Hodges bumps knuckles with him, thus acknowledging Jerome's blackness, then shakes his hand, thereby acknowledging his own WASPiness.

Jerome stands back, holding Hodges's forearms and giving him a once-over. "Look at you!" he exclaims. "Skinny as ever was!"

"I walk," Hodges says. "And I bought a treadmill for rainy days."

"Excellent! You'll live forever!"

"I wish," Hodges says, and bends down. The dog extends a paw and Hodges shakes it. "How you doing, Odell?"

Odell woofs, which presumably means he's doing fine.

"Come on in," Hodges says. "I have Cokes. Unless you'd prefer a beer."

"Coke's fine. I bet Odell would appreciate some water. We walked over. Odell doesn't walk as fast as he used to."

"His bowl's still under the sink."

They go in and toast each other with icy glasses of Coca-Cola. Odell laps water, then stretches out in his accustomed place beside the TV. Hodges was an obsessive television watcher during the first months of his retirement, but now the box rarely goes on except for Scott Pelley on *The CBS Evening News*, or the occasional Indians game.

"How's the pacemaker, Bill?"

"I don't even know it's there. Which is just the way I like it. What happened to the big country club dance you were going to in Pittsburgh with what's-her-name?"

"That didn't work out. As far as my parents are concerned, what's-her-name and I discovered that we are not compatible in terms of our academic and personal interests."

Hodges raises his eyebrows. "Sounds a tad lawyerly for a philosophy major with a minor in ancient cultures."

Jerome sips his Coke, sprawls his long legs out, and grins. "Truth? What's-her-name—aka Priscilla—was using me to tweak the jealous-bone of her high school boyfriend. And it worked. Told me how sorry she was to get me down there on false pretenses, hopes we can still be friends, so on and so forth. A little embarrassing, but probably all for the best." He pauses. "She still has all her Barbies and Bratz on a shelf in her room, and I must admit that gave me pause. I guess I wouldn't mind *too* much if my folks found out I was the stick she stirred her pot of love-soup with, but if you tell the Barbster, I'll never hear the end of it."

"Mum's the word," Hodges says. "So what now? Back to Massachusetts?"

"Nope, I'm here for the summer. Got a job down on the docks swinging containers."

"That is not work for a Harvard man, Jerome."

"It is for this one. I got my heavy equipment license last winter, the pay is excellent, and Harvard ain't cheap, even with a partial scholarship." Tyrone Feelgood Delight makes a mercifully brief guest appearance. "Dis here black boy goan tote dat barge an' lift dat bale, Massa Hodges!" Then back to Jerome, just like that. "Who's mowing your lawn? It looks pretty good. Not Jerome Robinson quality, but pretty good."

"Kid from the end of the block," Hodges says. "Is this just a courtesy call, or . . . ?"

"Barbara and her friend Tina told me one hell of a story," Jerome says. "Tina was reluctant to spill it at first, but Barbs talked her into it. She's good at stuff like that. Listen, you know Tina's father was hurt in the City Center thing, right?"

"Yes."

"If her big brother was really the one sending cash to keep the fam afloat, good for him . . . but where did it come from? I can't figure that one out no matter how hard I try."

"Nor can I."

"Tina says you're going to ask him."

"After school tomorrow, is the plan."

"Is Holly involved?"

"To an extent. She's doing background."

"Cool!" Jerome grins big. "How about I come with you tomorrow? Get the band back together, man! Play all the hits!"

Hodges considers. "I don't know, Jerome. One guy—a golden oldie like me—might not upset young Mr. Saubers too much. *Two* guys, though, especially when one of them's a badass black dude who stands six-four—"

"Fifteen rounds and I'm still pretty!" Jerome proclaims, waving clasped hands over his head. Odell lays back his ears. "Still pretty! That bad ole bear Sonny Liston never touched me! I float like a butterfly, I sting like a . . ." He assesses Hodges's patient expression. "Okay, sorry, sometimes I get carried away. Where are you going to wait for him?"

"Out front was the plan. You know, where the kids actually exit the building?"

"Not all of them come out that way, and he might not, especially if Tina lets on she talked to you." He sees Hodges about to speak and raises a hand. "She says she won't, but big brothers know little sisters, you can take that from a guy who's got one. If he knows somebody wants to ask him questions, he's apt to go out the back and cut across the football field to Westfield Street. I could park there, give you a call if I see him."

"Do you know what he looks like?"

"Uh-huh, Tina had a picture in her wallet. Let me be a part

of this, Bill. Barbie likes that chick. I liked her too. And it took guts for her to come to you, even with my sister snapping the whip."

"I know."

"Also, I'm curious as hell. Tina says the money started coming when her bro was only thirteen. A kid that young with access to that much money . . ." Jerome shakes his head. "I'm not surprised he's in trouble."

"Me either. I guess if you want to be in, you're in."

"My man!"

This cry necessitates another fist-bump.

"You went to Northfield, Jerome. Is there any other way he could go out, besides the front and Westfield Street?"

Jerome thinks it over. "If he went down to the basement, there's a door that takes you out to one side, where the smoking area used to be, back in the day. I guess he could go across that, then cut through the auditorium and come out on Garner Street."

"I could put Holly there," Hodges says thoughtfully.

"Excellent idea!" Jerome cries. "Gettin the band back together! What I said!"

"But no approach if you see him," Hodges says. "Just call. *I* get to approach. I'll tell Holly the same thing. Not that she'd be likely to."

"As long as we get to hear the story."

"If I get it, you'll get it," Hodges says, hoping he has not just made a rash promise. "Come by my office in the Turner Building around two, and we'll move out around two fifteen. Be in position by two forty-five."

"You're sure Holly will be okay with this?"

"Yes. She's fine with watching. It's confrontation that gives her problems."

"Not always."

"No," Hodges says, "not always."

They are both thinking of one confrontation—at the MAC, with Brady Hartsfield—that Holly handled just fine.

Jerome glances at his watch. "I have to go. Promised I'd take the Barbster to the mall. She wants a Swatch." He rolls his eyes.

Hodges grins. "I love your sis, Jerome."

Jerome grins back. "Actually, so do I. Come on, Odell. Let's shuffle."

Odell rises and heads for the door. Jerome grasps the knob, then turns back. His grin is gone. "Have you been where I think you've been?"

"Probably."

"Does Holly know you visit him?"

"No. And you're not to tell her. She'd find it vastly upsetting."

"Yes. She would. How is he?"

"The same. Although . . ." Hodges is thinking of how the picture fell over. That *clack* sound.

"Although what?"

"Nothing. He's the same. Do me one favor, okay? Tell Barbara to get in touch if Tina calls and says her brother found out the girls talked to me on Friday."

"Will do. See you tomorrow."

Jerome leaves. Hodges turns on the TV, and is delighted to see the Indians are still on. They've tied it up. The game is going into extra innings.

11

Holly spends Sunday evening in her apartment, trying to watch *The Godfather Part II* on her computer. Usually this would be a very pleasant occupation, because she considers it one of the two or three best movies ever made, right up there with *Citizen Kane* and *Paths of Glory*, but tonight she keeps pausing it so she can pace worry-circles around the living room of her apartment. There's a lot of room to pace. This apartment isn't as glitzy as the lakeside condo she lived in for awhile when she first moved to the city, but it's in a good neighborhood and plenty big. She can afford the rent; under the terms of her cousin Janey's will, Holly inherited half a million dollars. Less after taxes, of course, but still a very nice nest egg. And, thanks to her job with Bill Hodges, she can afford to let the nest egg grow.

As she paces, she mutters some of her favorite lines from the movie.

"I don't have to wipe everyone out, just my enemies.

"How do you say banana daiquiri?

"Your country ain't your blood, remember that."

And, of course, the one everyone remembers: "I know it was you, Fredo. You broke my heart."

If she was watching another movie, she would be incanting a different set of quotes. It is a form of self-hypnosis that she has practiced ever since she saw *The Sound of Music* at the age of seven. (Favorite line from that one: "I wonder what grass tastes like.")

She's really thinking about the Moleskine notebook Tina's brother was so quick to hide under his pillow. Bill believes it has nothing to do with the money Pete was sending his parents, but Holly isn't so sure.

She has kept journals for most of her life, listing all the movies she's seen, all the books she's read, the people she's talked to, the times she gets up, the times she goes to bed. Also her bowel movements, which are coded (after all, someone may see her journals after she's dead) as WP, which stands for *Went Potty*. She knows this is OCD behavior—she and her therapist have discussed how obsessive listing is really just another form of magical thinking—but it doesn't hurt anyone, and if she prefers to keep her lists in Moleskine notebooks, whose business is that besides her own? The point is, she *knows* from Moleskines, and therefore knows they're not cheap. Two-fifty will get you a spiral-bound notebook in Walgreens, but a Moleskine with the same number of pages goes for ten bucks. Why would a kid want such an expensive notebook, especially when he came from a cash-strapped family?

"Doesn't make sense," Holly says. Then, as if just following this train of thought: "Leave the gun. Take the cannoli." That's from the original *Godfather*, but it's still a good line. One of the best.

Send the money. Keep the notebook.

An *expensive* notebook that got shoved under the pillow when the little sister appeared unexpectedly in the room. The more Holly thinks about it, the more she thinks there might be something there.

She restarts the movie but can't follow its well-worn and well-loved path with this notebook stuff rolling around in her head, so Holly does something almost unheard of, at least before bedtime: she turns her computer off. Then she resumes pacing, hands locked together at the small of her back.

Send the money. Keep the notebook.

"And the lag!" she exclaims to the empty room. "Don't forget that!"

Yes. The seven months of quiet time between when the money ran out and when the Saubers boy started to get his underpants all in a twist. Because it took him seven months to think up a way to get *more* money? Holly thinks yes. Holly thinks he got an idea, but it wasn't a *good* idea. It was an idea that got him in trouble.

"What gets people in trouble when it's about money?" Holly asks the empty room, pacing faster than ever. "Stealing does. So does blackmail."

Was that it? Did Pete Saubers try to blackmail somebody about something in the Moleskine notebook? Something about the stolen money, maybe? Only how could Pete black-mail someone about that money when he must have stolen it himself?

Holly goes to the telephone, reaches for it, then pulls her hand back. For almost a minute she just stands there, gnaw-ing her lips. She's not used to taking the initiative in things. Maybe she should call Bill first, and ask him if it's okay?

"Bill doesn't think the notebook's important, though," she tells her living room. "I think different. And I can think dif-ferent if I want to."

She snatches her cell from the coffee table and calls Tina Saubers before she can lose her nerve.

"Hello?" Tina asks cautiously. Almost whispering. "Who's this?"

"Holly Gibney. You didn't see my number come up because it's unlisted. I'm very careful about my number, although I'll be happy to give it to you, if you want. We can talk any-time, because we're friends and that's what friends do. Is your brother back home from his weekend?"

"Yes. He came in around six, while we were finishing up dinner. Mom said there was still plenty of pot roast and pota-toes, she'd heat them up if he wanted, but he said they stopped at Denny's on the way back. Then he went up to his room. He didn't even want any strawberry shortcake, and he loves that. I'm really worried about him, Ms. Holly."

"You can just call me Holly, Tina." She hates Ms., thinks it sounds like a mosquito buzzing around your head.

"Okay."

"Did he say anything to you?"

"Just hi," Tina says in a small voice.

"And you didn't tell him about coming to the office with Barbara on Friday?"

"God, no!"

"Where is he now?"

"Still in his room. Listening to the Black Keys. I hate the Black Keys."

"Yes, me too." Holly has no idea who the Black Keys are, although she could name the entire cast of *Fargo*. (Best line in that one, delivered by Steve Buscemi: "Smoke a fuckin peace pipe.")

"Tina, does Pete have a special friend he might have talked to about what's bothering him?"

Tina thinks it over. Holly takes the opportunity to snatch a Nicorette from the open pack beside her computer and pop it into her mouth.

"I don't think so," Tina says at last. "I guess he has friends at school, he's pretty popular, but his only close friend was Bob Pearson, from down the block? And they moved to Denver last year."

"What about a girlfriend?"

"He used to spend a lot of time with Gloria Moore, but they broke up after Christmas. Pete said she didn't like to read, and he could never get tight with a girl who didn't like books." Wistfully, Tina adds: "I liked Gloria. She showed me how to do my eyes."

"Girls don't need eye makeup until they're in their thirties," Holly says authoritatively, although she has never actually worn any herself. Her mother says only sluts wear eye makeup.

"Really?" Tina sounds astonished.

"What about teachers? Did he have a favorite teacher he might have talked to?" Holly doubts if an older brother would have talked to his kid sister about favorite teachers, or if the kid sister would have paid any attention even if he did. She asks because it's the only other thing she can think of.

But Holly doesn't even hesitate. "Ricky the Hippie," she says, and giggles.

Holly stops in mid-pace. "Who?"

"Mr. Ricker, that's his real name. Pete said some of the kids call him Ricky the Hippie because he wears these old-time flower-power shirts and ties. Pete had him when he was a freshman. Or maybe a sophomore. I can't remember. He said Mr. Ricker knew what good books were all about. Ms. . . . I mean Holly, is Mr. Hodges still going to talk to Pete tomorrow?"

"Yes. Don't worry about that."

But Tina is plenty worried. She sounds on the verge of tears, in fact, and this makes Holly's stomach contract into a tight little ball. "Oh boy. I hope he doesn't hate me."

"He won't," Holly says. She's chewing her Nicorette at warp speed. "Bill will find out what's wrong and fix it. Then your brother will love you more than ever."

"Do you promise?"

"Yes! *Ouch!*"

"What's wrong?"

"Nothing." She wipes her mouth and looks at a smear of blood on her fingers. "I bit my lip. I have to go, Tina. Will you call me if you think of anyone he might have talked to about the money?"

"There's no one," Tina says forlornly, and starts to cry.

"Well . . . okay." And because something else seems required: "Don't bother with eye makeup. Your eyes are very pretty as they are. Goodbye."

She ends the call without waiting for Tina to say anything else and resumes pacing. She spits the wad of Nicorette into the wastebasket by her desk and blots her lip with a tissue, but the bleeding has already stopped.

No close friends and no steady girl. No names except for that one teacher.

Holly sits down and powers up her computer again. She opens Firefox, goes to the Northfield High website, clicks OUR FACULTY, and there is Howard Ricker, wearing a flower-patterned shirt with billowy sleeves, just like Tina said. Also a very ridiculous tie. Is it really so impossible that Pete Saubers said something to his favorite English teacher, especially if it had to do with whatever he was writing (or reading) in a Moleskine notebook?

A few clicks and she has Howard Ricker's telephone number on her computer screen. It's still early, but she can't bring herself to cold-call a complete stranger. Phoning Tina was hard enough, and that call ended in tears.

I'll tell Bill tomorrow, she decides. He can call Ricky the Hippie if he thinks it's worth doing.

She goes back to her voluminous movie folder and is soon once more lost in *The Godfather Part II*.

12

Morris visits another computer café that Sunday night, and does his own quick bit of research. When he's found what he wants, he fishes out the piece of notepaper with Peter Saubers's cell number on it, and jots down Andrew Halliday's address. Coleridge Street is on the West Side. In the seventies, that was a middle-class and mostly white enclave where all the houses tried to look a little more expensive than they actually were, and as a result all ended up looking pretty much the same.

A quick visit to several local real estate sites shows Morris that things over there haven't changed much, although an upscale shopping center has been added: Valley Plaza. Andy's car may still be parked at his house out there. Of course it might be in a space behind his shop, Morris never checked (Christ, you can't check *everything*, he thinks), but that seems unlikely. Why would you put up with the hassle of driving three miles into the city every morning and three miles back every night, in rush-hour traffic, when you could buy a thirty-day bus-pass for ten dollars, or a six-month's pass for fifty? Morris has the keys to his old pal's house, although he'd never try using them; the house is a lot more likely to be alarmed than the Birch Street Rec.

But he also has the keys to Andy's car, and a car might come in handy.

He walks back to Bugshit Manor, convinced that McFarland will be waiting for him there, and not content just to make Morris pee in the little cup. No, not this time. This time he'll also want to toss his room, and when he does he'll find the Tuff Tote with the stolen computer and the bloody shirt and shoes inside. Not to mention the envelope of money he took from his old pal's desk.

I'd kill him, thinks Morris—who is now (in his own mind, at least) Morris the Wolf.

Only he couldn't use the gun, plenty of people in Bugshit Manor know what a gunshot sounds like, even a polite *ka-pow* from a little faggot gun like his old pal's P238, and he left the hatchet in Andy's office. That might not do the job even if he did have it. McFarland is big like Andy, but not all puddly-fat like Andy. McFarland looks *strong*.

That's okay, Morris tells himself. That shit don't mean shit. Because an old wolf is a crafty wolf, and that's what I have to be now: crafty.

McFarland isn't waiting on the stoop, but before Morris can breathe a sigh of relief, he becomes convinced that his PO will be waiting for him upstairs. Not in the hall, either. He's probably got a passkey that lets him into every room in this fucked-up, piss-smelling place.

Try me, he thinks. You just try me, you sonofabitch.

But the door is locked, the room is empty, and it doesn't look like it's been searched, although he supposes if McFarland did it carefully . . . *craftily*—

But then Morris calls himself an idiot. If McFarland had

searched his room, he would have been waiting with a couple of cops, and the cops would have handcuffs.

Nevertheless, he snatches open the closet door to make sure the Tuff Totes are where he left them. They are. He takes out the money and counts it. Six hundred and forty dollars. Not great, not even close to what was in Rothstein's safe, but not bad. He puts it back, zips the bag shut, then sits on his bed and holds up his hands. They are shaking.

I have to get that stuff out of here, he thinks, and I have to do it tomorrow morning. But get it out to where?

Morris lies down on his bed and looks up at the ceiling, thinking. At last he falls asleep.

13

Monday dawns clear and warm, the thermometer in front of City Center reading seventy before the sun is even fully over the horizon. School is still in session and will be for the next two weeks, but today is going to be the first real sizzler of the summer, the kind of day that makes people wipe the backs of their necks and squint at the sun and talk about global warming.

When Hodges gets to his office at eight thirty, Holly is already there. She tells him about her conversation with Tina last night, and asks if Hodges will talk to Howard Ricker, aka Ricky the Hippie, if he can't get the story of the money from Pete himself. Hodges agrees to this, and tells Holly that was good thinking (she glows at this), but privately believes talking to Ricker won't be necessary. If he can't crack a seventeen-year-old kid—one who's probably dying to tell someone what's been weighing him down—he needs to quit working and move to Florida, home of so many retired cops.

He asks Holly if she'll watch for the Saubers boy on Garner

Street when school lets out this afternoon. She agrees, as long as she doesn't have to talk to him herself.

"You won't," Hodges assures her. "If you see him, all you need to do is call me. I'll come around the block and cut him off. Have we got pix of him?"

"I've downloaded half a dozen to my computer. Five from the yearbook and one from the Garner Street Library, where he works as a student aide, or something. Come and look."

The best photo—a portrait shot in which Pete Saubers is wearing a tie and a dark sportcoat—identifies him as CLASS OF '15 STUDENT VICE PRESIDENT. He's dark-haired and good-looking. The resemblance to his kid sister isn't striking, but it's there, all right. Intelligent blue eyes look levelly out at Hodges. In them is the faintest glint of humor.

"Can you email these to Jerome?"

"Already done." Holly smiles, and Hodges thinks—as he always does—that she should do it more often. When she smiles, Holly is almost beautiful. With a little mascara around her eyes, she probably would be. "Gee, it'll be good to see Jerome again."

"What have I got this morning, Holly? Anything?"

"Court at ten o'clock. The assault thing."

"Oh, right. The guy who tuned up on his brother-in-law. Belson the Bald Beater."

"It's not nice to call people names," Holly says.

This is probably true, but court is always an annoyance, and having to go there today is particularly trying, even though it will probably take no more than an hour, unless Judge Wiggins has slowed down since Hodges was on the cops. Pete Huntley used to call Brenda Wiggins FedEx, because she always delivered on time.

The Bald Beater is James Belson, whose picture should probably be next to *white trash* in the dictionary. He's a resident of the city's Edgemont Avenue district, sometimes referred to as Hillbilly Heaven. As part of his contract with one of the city's car dealerships, Hodges was hired to repo Belson's Acura MDX, on which Belson had ceased making payments some months before. When Hodges arrived at Belson's ramshackle house, Belson wasn't there. Neither was the car. Mrs. Belson— a lady who looked rode hard and put away still damp—told him the Acura had been stolen by her brother Howie. She gave him the address, which was also in Hillbilly Heaven.

"I got no love for Howie," she told Hodges, "but you might ought to get over before Jimmy kills him. When Jimmy's mad, he don't believe in talk. He goes right to beatin."

When Hodges arrived, James Belson was indeed beating on Howie. He was doing this work with a rake-handle, his bald head gleaming with sweat in the sunlight. Belson's brother-in-law was lying in his weedy driveway by the rear bumper of the Acura, kicking ineffectually at Belson and trying to shield his bleeding face and broken nose with his hands. Hodges stepped up behind Belson and soothed him with the Happy Slapper. The Acura was back on the car dealership's lot by noon, and Belson the Bald Beater was now up on assault.

"His lawyer is going to try to make you look like the bad guy," Holly says. "He's going to ask how you subdued Mr. Belson. You need to be ready for that, Bill."

"Oh, for goodness sake," Hodges says. "I thumped him one to keep him from killing his brother-in-law, that's all. Applied acceptable force and practiced restraint."

"But you used a weapon to do it. A sock loaded with ball bearings, to be exact."

"True, but Belson doesn't know that. His back was turned. And the other guy was semiconscious at best."

"Okay . . ." But she looks worried and her teeth are working at the spot she nipped while talking to Tina. "I just don't want you to get in trouble. Promise me you'll keep your temper and not *shout*, or wave your *arms*, or—"

"Holly." He takes her by the shoulders. Gently. "Go out-side. Smoke a cigarette. Chillax. All will be well in court this morning and with Pete Saubers this afternoon."

She looks up at him, wide-eyed. "Do you promise?"

"Yes."

"All right. I'll just smoke *half* a cigarette." She heads for the door, rummaging in her bag. "We're going to have *such* a busy day."

"I suppose we are. One other thing before you go."

She turns back, questioning.

"You should smile more often. You're beautiful when you smile."

Holly blushes all the way to her hairline and hurries out. But she's smiling again, and that makes Hodges happy.

14

Morris is also having a busy day, and busy is good. As long as he's in motion, the doubts and fears don't have a chance to creep in. It helps that he woke up absolutely sure of one thing: this is the day he becomes a wolf for real. He's all done patching up the Culture and Arts Center's outdated computer filing system so his fat fuck of a boss can look good to *his* boss, and he's done being Ellis McFarland's pet lamb, too. No more baa-ing *yes sir* and *no sir* and *three bags full sir* each time McFarland shows up. Parole is finished. As soon as he has the Rothstein notebooks, he's getting the hell out of this pisspot of a city. He has no interest in going north to Canada, but that leaves the whole lower forty-eight. He thinks maybe he'll opt for New England. Who knows, maybe even New Hamp-shire. Reading the notebooks there, near the same mountains Rothstein must have looked at while he was writing—that had a certain novelistic roundness, didn't it? Yes, and that was the great thing about novels: that roundness. The way things always balanced out in the end. He should have known Rothstein couldn't leave Jimmy working for that fucking ad agency, because there was no roundness in that, just a big old scoop of ugly. Maybe, deep down in his heart, Morris *had* known it. Maybe it was what kept him sane all those years.

He's never felt saner in his life.

When he doesn't show up for work this morning, his fat fuck boss will probably call McFarland. That, at least, is what he's supposed to do in the event of an unexplained absence. So Morris has to disappear. Duck under the radar. Go dark.

Fine.

Terrific, in fact.

At eight this morning, he takes the Main Street bus, rides all the way to its turnaround point where Lower Main ends, and then strolls down to Lacemaker Lane. Morris has put on his only sportcoat and his only tie, and they're good enough for him to not look out of place here, even though it's too early for any of the fancy-schmancy stores to have opened. He turns down the alley between Andrew Halliday Rare Editions and the shop next door, La Bella Flora Children's Boutique. There are three parking spaces in the small courtyard behind the buildings, two for the clothing shop and one for the bookshop. There's a Volvo in one of the La Bella Flora spots. The other one is empty. So is the space reserved for Andrew Halliday.

Also fine.

Morris leaves the courtyard as briskly as he came, pauses for a comforting look at the CLOSED sign hanging inside the bookshop door, and then strolls back to Lower Main, where he catches an uptown bus. Two changes later, he's stepping off in front of the Valley Plaza Shopping Center, just two blocks from the late Andrew Halliday's home.

He walks briskly again, no strolling now. As if he knows where he is, where he's going, and has every right to be here.

Coleridge Street is nearly deserted, which doesn't surprise
him. It's quarter past nine (his fat fuck of a boss will by now
be looking at Morris's unoccupied desk and fuming). The kids
are in school; the workadaddies and workamommies are off
busting heavies to keep up with their credit card debt; most
delivery and service people won't start cruising the neighborhood until ten. The only better time would be the dozy hours
of mid-afternoon, and he can't afford to wait that long. Too
many places to go, too many things to do. This is Morris Bellamy's big day. His life has taken a long, long detour, but he's
almost back on the mainline.

15

Tina starts feeling sick around the time Morris is strolling up
the late Drew Halliday's driveway and seeing his old pal's car
parked inside his garage. Tina hardly slept at all last night because she's so worried about how Pete will take the news that
she ratted him out. Her breakfast is sitting in her belly like a
lump, and all at once, while Mrs. Sloan is performing "Anna-
bel Lee" (Mrs. Sloan *never* just reads), that lump of undigested
food starts to crawl up her throat and toward the exit.

She raises her hand. It seems to weigh at least ten pounds,
but she holds it up until Mrs. Sloan raises her eyes. "Yes, Tina,
what is it?"

She sounds annoyed, but Tina doesn't care. She's beyond
caring. "I feel sick. I need to go to the girls'."

"Then go, by all means, but hurry back."

Tina scuttles from the room. Some of the girls are giggling—
at thirteen, unscheduled bathroom visits are always amusing—
but Tina is too concerned with that rising lump to feel embarrassed. Once in the hall she breaks into a run, heading for the
bathroom halfway down the hall as fast as she can, but the lump

is faster and she doubles over before she can get there and vomits her breakfast all over her sneakers.

Mr. Haggerty, the school's head janitor, is just coming up the stairs. He sees her stagger backward from the steaming puddle of whoopsie and trots toward her, his toolbelt jingling.

"Hey, girl, you okay?"

Tina gropes for the wall with an arm that feels made of plastic. The world is swimming. Part of that is because she has vomited hard enough to bring tears to her eyes, but not all. She wishes with all her heart that she hadn't let Barbara persuade her into talking to Mr. Hodges, that she had left Pete alone to work out whatever was wrong. What if he never speaks to her again?

"I'm fine," she says. "I'm sorry I made a m—"

But the swimming gets worse before she can finish. She doesn't exactly faint, but the world pulls away from her, becomes something she's looking at through a smudged window rather than something she's actually *in*. She slides down the wall, amazed by the sight of her own knees, clad in green tights, coming up to meet her. That is when Mr. Haggerty scoops her up and carries her downstairs to the school nurse's office.

16

Andy's little green Subaru is perfect, as far as Morris is concerned—not apt to attract a first glance, let alone a second. There are only thousands just like it. He backs down the driveway and sets off for the North Side, keeping an eye out for cops and obeying every speed limit.

At first it's almost a replay of Friday night. He stops once more at the Bellows Avenue Mall and once more visits Home

Depot. He goes to the tools section, where he picks out a screwdriver with a long blade and a chisel. Then he drives on to the square brick hulk that used to be the Birch Street Recreation Center and once more parks in the space marked RESERVED FOR REC DEPT. VEHICLES.

It's a good spot in which to do dirty business. There's a loading dock on one side and a high hedge on the other. He's visible only from behind—the baseball field and crumbling basketball courts—but with school in session, those areas are deserted. Morris goes to the basement window he noticed before, squats, and rams the blade of his screwdriver into the crack at the top. It goes in easily, because the wood is rotten. He uses the chisel to widen the crack. The glass rattles in its frame but doesn't break, because the putty is old and there's plenty of give. The possibility that this hulk of a building has alarm protection is looking slimmer all the time.

Morris swaps the chisel for the screwdriver again. He chivvies it through the gap he's made, catches the thumb-lock, and pushes. He looks around to make sure he's still unobserved—it's a good spot, yes, but breaking and entering in broad daylight is still a scary proposition—and sees nothing but a crow perched on a telephone pole. He inserts the chisel at the bottom of the window, beating it in as deep as it will go with the heel of his hand, then bears down on it. For a moment there's nothing. Then the window slides up with a squall of wood and a shower of dirt. Bingo. He wipes sweat from his face as he peers in at the stored chairs, card tables, and boxes of junk, verifying that it will be easy to slide in and drop to the floor.

But not quite yet. Not while there's the slightest possibility that a silent alarm is lighting up somewhere.

Morris takes his tools back to the little green Subaru, and drives away.

17

Linda Saubers is monitoring the mid-morning activity period at Northfield Elementary School when Peggy Moran comes in and tells her that her daughter has been taken sick at Dorton Middle, some three miles away.

"She's in the nurse's office," Peggy says, keeping her voice low. "I understand she vomited and then sort of passed out for a few minutes."

"Oh my God," Linda says. "She looked pale at breakfast, but when I asked her if she was okay, she said she was."

"That's the way they are," Peggy says, rolling her eyes. "It's either melodrama or *I'm fine, Mom, get a life.* Go get her and take her home. I'll cover this, and Mr. Jablonski has already called a sub."

"You're a saint." Linda is gathering up her books and putting them into her briefcase.

"It's probably a stomach thing," Peggy says, sliding into the seat Linda has just vacated. "I guess you could take her to the nearest Doc in the Box, but why bother spending thirty bucks? That stuff's going around."

"I know," Linda says . . . but she wonders.

She and Tom have been slowly but surely digging themselves out of two pits: a money pit and a marriage pit. The year after Tom's accident, they came perilously close to breaking up. Then the mystery cash started coming, a kind of miracle, and things started to turn around. They aren't all the way out of either hole even yet, but Linda has come to believe they *will* get out.

With their parents focused on brute survival (and Tom, of course, had the additional challenge of recovering from his injuries), the kids have spent far too much time flying on autopilot.

It's only now, when she feels she finally has room to breathe and time to look around her, that Linda clearly senses something not right with Pete and Tina. They're good kids, *smart* kids, and she doesn't think either of them has gotten caught in the usual teenage traps—drink, drugs, shoplifting, sex—but there's *something*, and she supposes she knows what it is. She has an idea Tom does, too.

God sent manna from heaven when the Israelites were starving, but cash drops from more prosaic sources: banks, friends, an inheritance, relatives who are in a position to help out. The mystery money didn't come from any of those sources. Certainly not from relatives. Back in 2010, all their kinfolk were just as strapped as Tom and Linda themselves. Only kids are relatives, too, aren't they? It's easy to overlook that because they're so close, but they are. It's absurd to think the cash came from Tina, who'd only been nine years old when the envelopes started arriving, and who couldn't have kept a secret like that, anyway.

Pete, though . . . he's the closemouthed one. Linda remembers her mother saying when Pete was only five, "That one's got a lock on his lips."

Only where could a kid of thirteen have come by that kind of money?

As she drives to Dorton Middle to pick up her ailing daughter, Linda thinks, We never asked *any* questions, not really, because we were afraid to. No one who didn't go through those terrible months after Tommy's accident could get that, and I'm not going to apologize for it. We had reasons to be cowardly. Plenty of them. The two biggest were living right under our roof, and counting on us to support them. But it's time to ask who was supporting whom. If it was Pete, if Tina found out and that's what's troubling her, I need to stop being a coward. I need to open my eyes.

I need some answers.

18

Mid-morning.

Hodges is in court, and on best behavior. Holly would be proud. He answers the questions posed by the Bald Beater's attorney with crisp succinctness. The attorney gives him plenty of opportunity to be argumentative, and although this was a trap Hodges sometimes fell into during his detective days, he avoids it now.

Linda Saubers is driving her pale, silent daughter home from school, where she will give Tina a glass of ginger ale to settle her stomach and then put her to bed. She is finally ready to ask Tina what she knows about the mystery money, but not until the girl feels better. The afternoon will be time enough, and she should make Pete a part of that conversation when he gets home from school. It will be just the three of them, and probably that's best. Tom and a group of his real estate clients are touring an office complex, recently vacated by IBM, fifty miles north of the city, and won't be back until seven. Even later, if they stop for dinner on the return trip.

Pete is in period three Advanced Physics, and although his eyes are trained on Mr. Norton, who is rhapsodizing about the Higgs boson and the CERN Large Hadron Collider in Switzerland, the mind behind those eyes is much closer to home. He is going over his script for this afternoon's meeting yet again, and reminding himself that just because he *has* a script doesn't mean Halliday will follow it. Halliday has been in this business a long time, and he's probably been skirting the edges of the law for much of it. Pete is just a kid, and it absolutely will not do to forget that. He must be careful, and allow for his inexperience. He must think before he speaks, every time.

Above all, he must be brave.

He tells Halliday: Half a loaf is better than none, but in a world of want, even a single slice is better than none. I'm offering you three dozen slices. You need to think about that.

He tells Halliday: I'm not going to be anyone's birthday fuck, you better think about that, too.

He tells Halliday: If you think I'm bluffing, go on and try me. But if you do, we both wind up with nothing.

He thinks, If I can hold my nerve, I can get out of this. And I will hold it. I will. I have to.

Morris Bellamy parks the stolen Subaru two blocks from Bugshit Manor and walks back. He lingers in the doorway of a secondhand store to make sure Ellis McFarland isn't in the vicinity, then scurries to the miserable building and plods up the nine flights of stairs. Both elevators are busted today, which is par for the course. He scrambles random clothes into one of the Tuff Totes and then leaves his crappy room for the last time. All the way down to the first corner his back feels hot, his neck as stiff as an ironing board. He carries one Tuff Tote in each hand, and they seem to weigh a hundred pounds apiece. He keeps waiting for McFarland to call his name. To step out from beneath a shadowed awning and ask him why he's not at work. To ask him where he thinks he's going. To ask him what he's got in those bags. And then to tell him he's going back to prison: Do not pass Go, do not collect two hundred dollars. Morris doesn't relax until Bugshit Manor is out of sight for good.

Tom Saubers is walking his little pack of real estate agents through the empty IBM facility, pointing out the various features and encouraging them to take pictures. They're all excited by the possibilities. Come the end of the day, his surgically repaired legs and hips will ache like all the devils of hell, but for the time being, he's feeling fine. This abandoned office and manufacturing complex could be a big deal for him. Life is finally turning around.

Jerome has popped into Hodges's office to surprise Holly, who squeals with joy when she sees him, then with apprehension when he seizes her by the waist and swings her around as he likes to do with his little sister. They talk for an hour or more, catching up, and she gives him her views on the Saubers affair. She's happy when Jerome takes her concerns about the Moleskine notebook seriously, and happier still to find out he has seen *22 Jump Street*. They drop the subject of Pete Saubers and discuss the movie at great length, comparing it to others in Jonah Hill's filmography. Then they move on to a discussion of various computer apps.

Andrew Halliday is the only one not occupied. First editions no longer matter to him, nor do young waiters in tight black pants. Oil and water are the same as wind and air to him now. He's sleeping the big sleep in a patch of congealed blood, drawing flies.

19

Eleven o'clock. It's eighty degrees in the city, and the radio says the mercury's apt to touch ninety before subsiding. *Got* to be global warming, people tell each other.

Morris cruises past the Birch Street Rec twice, and is happy (though not really surprised) to see it's as deserted as ever, just an empty brick box baking under the sun. No police; no security cars. Even the crow has departed for cooler environs. He circles the block, noting that there's now a trim little Ford Focus parked in the driveway of his old house. Mr. or Mrs. Saubers has knocked off early. Hell, maybe both of them. It's nothing to Morris. He heads back to the Rec and this time turns in, going around to the rear of the building and parking in what he's now begun to think of as his spot.

He's confident that he's unobserved, but it's still a good idea to do this quickly. He carries his bags to the window he's forced up and drops them to the basement floor, where they land with a flat clap and twin puffs of dust. He takes a quick look around, then slides feet first through the window on his stomach.

A wave of dizziness runs through his head as he takes his first deep breath of the cool, musty air. He staggers a little, and puts his arms out for balance. It's the heat, he thinks. You've been too busy to realize it, but you're dripping with sweat. Also, you ate no breakfast.

Both true, but the main thing is simpler and self-evident: he's not as young as he used to be, and it's been years since the physical exertions of the dyehouse. He's got to pace himself. Over by the furnace are a couple of good-sized cartons with **KITCHEN SUPPLIES** printed on the sides. Morris sits down on one of these until his heartbeat slows and the dizziness passes. Then he unzips the tote with Andy's little automatic inside, tucks the gun into the waistband of his pants at the small of his back, and blouses his shirt over it. He takes a hundred dollars of Andy's money, just in case he runs into any unforeseen expenses, and leaves the rest for later. He'll be back here this evening, may even spend the night. It sort of depends on the kid who stole his notebooks, and what measures Morris needs to employ in order to get them back.

Whatever it takes, cocksucker, he thinks. Whatever it takes.

Right now it's time to move on. As a younger man, he could have pulled himself out of that basement window easily, but not now. He drags over one of the **KITCHEN SUPPLIES** cartons—it's surprisingly heavy, probably some old busted appliance inside—and uses it as a step. Five minutes later, he's headed for Andrew Halliday Rare Editions, where he will park his old pal's car in his old pal's space and then spend the rest of the day soaking up the air-conditioning and waiting for the young notebook thief to arrive.

James Hawkins indeed, he thinks.

20

Quarter past two.

Hodges, Holly, and Jerome are on the move, headed for their positions around Northfield High: Hodges out front, Jerome on the corner of Westfield Street, Holly beyond the high school's auditorium, on Garner Street. When they are in position, they'll let Hodges know.

In the bookshop on Lacemaker Lane, Morris adjusts his tie, turns the hanging sign from CLOSED to OPEN, and unlocks the door. He goes back to the desk and sits down. If a customer should come in to browse—not terribly likely at such a slack time of the day, but possible—he will be happy to help. If there's a customer here when the kid arrives, he'll think of something. Improvise. His heart is beating hard, but his hands are steady. The shakes are gone. *I am a wolf*, he tells himself. *I'll bite if I have to.*

Pete is in his creative writing class. The text is Strunk and White's *The Elements of Style*, and today they are discussing the famous Rule 13: *Omit needless words*. They have been assigned Hemingway's short story "The Killers," and it has provoked a lively class discussion. Many words are spoken on the subject of how Hemingway omits needless words. Pete barely hears any of them. He keeps looking at the clock, where the hands march steadily toward his appointment with Andrew Halliday. And he keeps going over his script.

At twenty-five past two, his phone vibrates against his leg. He slips it out and looks at the screen.

Mom: Come right home after school, we need to talk.

His stomach cramps and his heart kicks into a higher gear. It might be no more than some chore that needs doing, but

Pete doesn't believe it. *We need to talk* is Momspeak for *Houston, we have a problem*. It could be the money, and in fact that seems likely to him, because problems come in bunches. If it is, then Tina let the cat out of the bag.

All right. If that's how it is, all right. He will go home, and they will talk, but he needs to resolve the Halliday business first. His parents aren't responsible for the jam he's in, and he won't *make* them responsible. He won't blame himself, either. He did what he had to do. If Halliday refuses to cut a deal, if he calls the police in spite of the reasons Pete can give him not to, then the less his parents know, the better. He doesn't want them charged as accessories, or something.

He thinks about switching his phone off and decides not to. If she texts him again—or if Tina does—it's better to know. He looks up at the clock and sees it's twenty to three. Soon the bell will ring, and he'll leave school.

Pete wonders if he'll ever be back.

21

Hodges parks his Prius fifty feet or so down from the high school's main entrance. He's on a yellow curb, but he has an old POLICE CALL card in his glove compartment, which he saves for just such parking problems. He places it on the dashboard. When the bell rings, he gets out of the car and leans against the hood with his arms folded, watching the bank of doors. Engraved above the entrance is the school's motto: EDUCATION IS THE LAMP OF LIFE. Hodges has his phone in one hand, ready to either make or receive a call, depending on who comes out or doesn't.

The wait isn't long, because Pete Saubers is among the first group of students to burst into the June day and come hurrying down the wide granite steps. Most of the kids are with friends. The Saubers boy is alone. Not the only one flying solo, of course, but there's a set look to his face, as if he's living in the future instead of the here and now. Hodges's eyes are as good as they ever were, and he thinks that could be the face of a soldier going into battle.

Or maybe he's just worried about finals.

Instead of heading toward the yellow buses parked beside the school on the left, he turns right, toward where Hodges is parked. Hodges ambles to meet him, speed-dialing Holly as he goes. "I've got him. Tell Jerome." He cuts the call without waiting for her to answer.

The boy angles to go around Hodges on the street side. Hodges steps in front of him. "Hey, Pete, got a minute?"

The kid's eyes snap front and center. He's good-looking, but his face is too thin and his forehead is spotted with acne. His lips are pressed so tightly together that his mouth is almost gone. "Who are you?" he asks. Not *Yes sir* or *Can I help you*. Just *Who are you*. The voice as tight-wired as the face.

"My name is Bill Hodges. I'd like to talk to you."

Kids are passing them, chattering, elbowing, laughing, shooting the shit, adjusting backpacks. A few glance at Pete and the man with the thinning white hair, but none show any interest. They have places to go and things to do.

"About what?"

"In my car would be better. So we can have some privacy." He points at the Prius.

The boy repeats, "About what?" He doesn't move.

"Here's the deal, Pete. Your sister Tina is friends with Barbara Robinson. I've known the Robinson family for years, and Barb persuaded Tina to come and talk to me. She's very worried about you."

"Why?"

"If you're asking why Barb suggested me, it's because I used to be a police detective."

Alarm flashes in the boy's eyes.

"If you're asking why Tina's worried, that's something we'd really be better off not discussing on the street."

Just like that the look of alarm is gone and the boy's face is expressionless again. It's the face of a good poker player. Hodges has questioned suspects who are able to wipe their faces like that, and they are usually the ones who are toughest to crack. If they crack at all.

"I don't know what Tina said to you, but she's got nothing to worry about."

"If what she told me is true, she might." Hodges gives Pete his best smile. "Come on, Pete. I'm not going to kidnap you. Swear to God."

Pete nods reluctantly. When they reach the Prius, the kid stops dead. He's reading the yellow card on the dashboard. "*Used* to be a police detective, or still are?"

"Used to be," Hodges says. "That card . . . call it a souvenir. Comes in handy sometimes. I've been off the force and collecting my pension for five years. Please get in so we can talk. I'm here as a friend. If we stand out here much longer, I'm going to melt."

"And if I don't?"

Hodges shrugs. "Then you're off."

"Okay, but only for a minute," Pete says. "I have to walk home today so I can stop at the drugstore for my father. He takes this stuff, Vioxx. Because he got hurt a few years ago."

Hodges nods. "I know. City Center. That was my case."

"Yeah?"

"Yeah."

Pete opens the passenger door and gets into the Prius. He doesn't seem nervous about being in a strange man's car. Careful and cautious, but not nervous. Hodges, who has done roughly ten thousand suspect and witness interviews over the years, is pretty sure the boy has come to a decision, although he can't tell if it's to spill what's on his mind or keep it to himself. Either way, it won't take long to find out.

He goes around and gets in behind the wheel. Pete is okay with that, but when Hodges starts the engine, he tenses up and grabs the doorhandle.

"Relax. I only want the air-conditioning. It's damn hot, in case you didn't notice. Especially for so early in the year. Probably global warm—"

"Let's get this over with so I can pick up my dad's scrip and go home. What did my sister tell you? You know she's only thirteen, right? I love her to death, but Mom calls her Tina the Drama Queen-a." And then, as if this explains everything, "She and her friend Ellen never miss *Pretty Little Liars*."

Okay, so the initial decision is not to talk. Not all that surprising. The job now is to change his mind.

"Tell me about the cash that came in the mail, Pete."

No tensing up; no *uh-oh* look flashing across the kid's face. He knew that was it, Hodges thinks. He knew as soon as his sister's name came up. He might even have had advance warning. Tina could have had a change of heart and texted him.

"You mean the mystery money," Pete says. "That's what we call it."

"Yeah. That's what I mean."

"It started coming four years ago, give or take. I was about the age Tina is now. There'd be an envelope addressed to my dad every month or so. Never any letter with it, just the money."

"Five hundred dollars."

"Once or twice it might have been a little less or a little more, I guess. I wasn't always there when it came, and after the first couple of times, Mom and Dad didn't talk about it very much."

"Like talking about it might jinx it?"

"Yeah, like that. And at some point, Teens got the idea I was the one sending it. Like as if. Back then I didn't even get an allowance."

"If you didn't do it, who did?"

"I don't know."

It seems he will stop there, but then he goes on. Hodges listens peacefully, hoping Pete will say too much. The boy is obviously intelligent, but sometimes even the intelligent ones say too much. If you let them.

"You know how every Christmas they have stories on the news about some guy giving out hundred-dollar bills in Walmart or wherever?"

"Sure."

"I think it was that type of deal. Some rich guy decided to play Secret Santa with one of the people who got hurt that day at City Center, and he picked my dad's name out of a hat." He turns to face Hodges for the first time since they got in the car, eyes wide and earnest and totally untrustworthy. "For all I know, he's sending money to some of the others, too. Probably the ones who got hurt the worst, and couldn't work."

Hodges thinks, That's good, kiddo. It actually makes a degree of sense.

"Giving out a thousand dollars to ten or twenty random shoppers at Christmas is one thing. Giving well over twenty grand to one family over four years is something else. If you add in other families, you'd be talking about a small fortune."

"He could be a hedge fund dude," Pete says. "You know, one of those guys who got rich while everyone else was getting poor and felt guilty about it."

He's not looking at Hodges anymore, now he's looking straight out of the windshield. There's an aroma coming off him, or so it seems to Hodges; not sweat but fatalism. Again he thinks of soldiers preparing to go into battle, knowing the chances are at least fifty-fifty that they'll be killed or wounded.

"Listen to me, Pete. I don't care about the money."

"I didn't send it!"

Hodges pushes on. It's the thing he was always best at. "It was a windfall, and you used it to help your folks out of a tough spot. That's not a bad thing, it's an admirable thing."

"Lots of people might not think so," Pete says. "If it was true, that is."

"You're wrong about that. Most people *would* think so. And I'll tell you something you can take as a hundred percent dead-red certainty, because it's based on forty years of experience as a cop. No prosecutor in this city, no prosecutor in the whole *country*, would try bringing charges against a kid who found some money and used it to help his family after his dad first lost his job and then got his legs crushed by a lunatic. The press would crucify a man or woman who tried to prosecute *that* shit."

Pete is silent, but his throat is working, as if he's holding back a sob. He wants to tell, but something is holding him back. Not the money, but related to the money. Has to be. Hodges is curious about where the cash in those monthly envelopes came from—anyone would be—but he's far more curious about what's going on with this kid now.

"You sent them the money—"

"For the last time, I *didn't*!"

"—and that went smooth as silk, but then you got into some kind of jackpot. Tell me what it is, Pete. Let me help you fix it. Let me help you make it right."

For a moment the boy trembles on the brink of revelation. Then his eyes shift to his left. Hodges follows them and sees the card he put on the dashboard. It's yellow, the color of caution. The color of danger. POLICE CALL. He wishes to Christ he'd left it in the glove compartment and parked a hundred yards farther down the street. Jesus Christ, he walks every day. A hundred yards would have been easy.

"There's nothing wrong," Pete says. He now speaks as mechanically as the computer-generated voice that comes out of Hodges's dashboard GPS, but there's a pulse beating in his temples and his hands are clasped tightly in his lap and there's sweat on his face in spite of the air-conditioning. "I didn't send the money. I have to get my dad's pills."

"Pete, listen. Even if I was still a cop, this conversation would be inadmissible in court. You're a minor, and there's no responsible adult present to counsel you. In addition I never gave you the words—the Miranda warning—"

Hodges sees the boy's face slam shut like a bank vault door. All it took was two words: *Miranda warning*.

"I appreciate your concern," Pete says in that same polite robot voice. He opens the car door. "But there's nothing wrong. Really."

"There is, though," Hodges says. He takes one of his cards from his breast pocket and holds it out. "Take this. Call me if you change your mind. Whatever it is, I can hel—"

The door closes. Hodges watches Pete Saubers walk swiftly away, puts the card back in his pocket, and thinks, Fuck me, I blew it. Six years ago, maybe even two, I would have had him.

But blaming his age is too easy. A deeper part of him, more analytical and less emotional, knows he was never really close. Thinking he might have been was an illusion. Pete has geared himself up for battle so completely that he's psychologically incapable of standing down.

The kid reaches City Drug, takes his father's prescription out of his back pocket, and goes inside. Hodges speed-dials Jerome.

"Bill! How did it go?"

"Not so good. You know City Drug?"

"Sure."

"He's getting a scrip filled there. Haul ass around the block as fast as you can. He told me he's going home, and maybe he is, but if he's not, I want to know where he *does* go. Do you think you can tail him? He knows my car. He won't know yours."

"No prob. I'm on my way."

Less than three minutes later Jerome is coming around the corner. He nips into a space just vacated by a mom picking up a couple of kids that look way too shrimpy to be in high school. Hodges pulls out, gives Jerome a wave, and heads for Holly's position on Garner Street, punching in her number as he goes. They can wait for Jerome's report together.

22

Pete's father does take Vioxx, has ever since he finally kicked the OxyContin, but he currently has plenty. The folded sheet of paper Pete takes from his back pocket and glances at before going into City Drug is a stern note from the assistant principal reminding juniors that Junior Skip Day is a myth, and the office will examine all absences that day with particular care.

Pete doesn't brandish the note; Bill Hodges may be retired, but he sure didn't seem retarded. No, Pete just looks at it for a moment, as if making sure he has the right thing, and goes inside. He walks rapidly to the prescription counter at the back, where Mr. Pelkey throws him a friendly salute.

"Yo, Pete. What can I get you today?"

"Nothing, Mr. Pelkey, we're all fine, but there are a couple of kids after me because I wouldn't let them copy some answers from our take-home history test. I wondered if you could help me."

Mr. Pelkey frowns and starts for the swing-gate. He likes Pete, who is always cheerful even though his family has gone through incredibly tough times. "Point them out to me. I'll tell them to get lost."

"No, I can handle it, but tomorrow. After they have a chance to cool off. Just, you know, if I could slip out the back . . ."

Mr. Pelkey drops a conspiratorial wink that says he was a kid once, too. "Sure. Come through the gate."

He leads Pete between shelves filled with salves and pills, then into the little office at the back. Here is a door with a big red sign on it reading ALARM WILL SOUND. Mr. Pelkey shields the code box next to it with one hand and punches in some numbers with the other. There's a buzz.

"Out you go," he tells Pete.

Pete thanks him, nips out onto the loading dock behind the drugstore, and jumps down to the cracked cement. An alley takes him to Frederick Street. He looks both ways for the ex-detective's Prius, doesn't see it, and breaks into a run. It takes him twenty minutes to reach Lower Main Street, and although he never spots the blue Prius, he makes a couple of sudden diversions along the way, just to be safe. He's just turning onto Lacemaker Lane when his phone vibrates again. This time the text is from his sister.

Tina: Did u talk 2 Mr. Hodges? Hope u did. Mom knows. I didn't tell she KNEW. Please don't be mad at me. ☹

As if I could, Pete thinks. Were they two years closer in age, maybe they could have gotten that sibling rivalry thing going, but maybe not even then. Sometimes he gets irritated with her, but really mad has never happened, even when she's being a brat.

The truth about the money is out, but maybe he can say money was *all* he found, and hide the fact that he tried to sell a murdered man's most private property just so his sister could go to a school where she wouldn't have to shower in a pack. And where her dumb friend Ellen would be in the rearview mirror.

He knows his chances of getting out of this clean are slim approaching none, but at some point—maybe this very afternoon, watching the hands of the clock move steadily toward the hour of three—that has become of secondary importance. What he really wants is to send the notebooks, especially the ones containing the last two Jimmy Gold novels, to NYU. Or maybe *The New Yorker*, since they published almost all of Rothstein's short stories in the fifties. And stick it to Andrew Halliday. Yes, and hard. All the way up. No way can Halliday be allowed to sell *any* of Rothstein's later work to some rich crackpot collector who will keep it in a climate-controlled secret room along with his Renoirs or Picassos or his precious fifteenth-century Bible.

When he was a kid, Pete saw the notebooks only as buried treasure. *His* treasure. He knows better now, and not just because he's fallen in love with John Rothstein's nasty, funny, and sometimes wildly moving prose. The notebooks were never just his. They were never just Rothstein's, either, no matter what he might have thought, hidden away in his New Hampshire farmhouse. They deserve to be seen and read by everyone. Maybe the little landslide that exposed the trunk on that winter day had been nothing but happenstance, but Pete doesn't believe it. He believes that, like the blood of Abel, the notebooks cried out from the ground. If that makes him a dipshit romantic, so be it. Some shit *does* mean shit.

Halfway down Lacemaker Lane, he spots the bookshop's old-fashioned scrolled sign. It's like something you might see outside an English pub, although this one reads Andrew Halliday Rare Editions instead of The Plowman's Rest, or whatever. Looking at it, Pete's last doubts disappear like smoke.

He thinks, John Rothstein is not your birthday fuck, either, Mr. Halliday. Not now and never was. You get none of the notebooks. *Bupkes*, honey, as Jimmy Gold would say. If you go to the police, I'll tell them everything, and after that business you went through with the James Agee book, we'll see who they believe.

A weight—invisible but very heavy—slips from his shoulders. Something in his heart seems to have come back into true for the first time in a long time. Pete starts for Halliday's at a fast walk, unaware that his fists are clenched.

23

At a few minutes past three—around the time Pete is getting into Hodges's Prius—a customer *does* come into the bookshop. He's a pudgy fellow whose thick glasses and gray-flecked goatee do not disguise his resemblance to Elmer Fudd.

"Can I help you?" Morris asks, although what first occurs to him is *Ehhh, what's up, Doc?*

"I don't know," Elmer says dubiously. "Where is Drew?"

"There was sort of a family emergency in Michigan." Morris knows Andy came from Michigan, so that's okay, but he'll have to be cagey about the family angle; if Andy ever talked about relatives, Morris has forgotten. "I'm an old friend. He asked if I'd mind the store this afternoon."

Elmer considers this. Morris's left hand, meanwhile, creeps around to the small of his back and touches the reassuring shape of the little automatic. He doesn't want to shoot this guy, doesn't want to risk the noise, but he will if he has to. There's plenty of room for Elmer back there in Andy's private office.

"He was holding a book for me, on which I have made a deposit. A first edition of *They Shoot Horses, Don't They?* It's by—"

"Horace McCoy," Morris finishes for him. The books on the shelf to the left of the desk—the ones the security DVDs were hiding behind—had slips sticking out of them, and since entering the bookstore today, Morris has examined them all.

They're customer orders, and the McCoy is among them. "Fine copy, signed. Flat signature, no dedication. Some foxing on the spine."

Elmer smiles. "That's the one."

Morris takes it down from the shelf, sneaking a glance at his watch as he does. 3:13. Northfield High classes end at three, which means the boy should be here by three thirty at the latest.

He pulls the slip and sees *Irving Yankovic, $750.* He hands the book to Elmer with a smile. "I remember this one especially. Andy—I guess he prefers Drew these days—told me he's only going to charge you five hundred. He got a better deal on it than he expected, and wanted to pass the savings along."

Any suspicion Elmer might have felt at finding a stranger in Drew's customary spot evaporates at the prospect of saving two hundred and fifty dollars. He takes out his checkbook. "So . . . with the deposit, that comes to . . ."

Morris waves a magnanimous hand. "He neglected to tell me what the deposit was. Just deduct it. I'm sure he trusts you."

"After all these years, he certainly ought to." Elmer bends over the counter and begins writing the check. He does this with excruciating slowness. Morris checks the clock. 3:16. "Have you read *They Shoot Horses*?"

"No," Morris says. "I missed that one."

What will he do if the kid comes in while this pretentious goateed asshole is still dithering over his checkbook? He won't be able to tell Saubers that Andy's in back, not after he's told Elmer Fudd he's in Michigan. Sweat begins to trickle out of his hairline and down his cheeks. He can feel it. He used to sweat like that in prison, while he was waiting to be raped.

"Marvelous book," Elmer says, pausing with his pen poised over the half-written check. "Marvelous noir, and a piece of social commentary to rival *The Grapes of Wrath*." He pauses, thinking instead of writing, and now it's 3:18. "Well . . . perhaps not *Grapes*, that might be going too far, but it certainly rivals *In Dubious Battle*, which is more of a socialist tract than a novel, don't you agree?"

Morris says he does. His hands feel numb. If he has to pull out the gun, he's apt to drop it. Or shoot himself straight down the crack of his ass. This makes him yawp a sudden laugh, a startling sound in this narrow, book-lined space.

Elmer looks up, frowning. "Something funny? About Steinbeck, perhaps?"

"Absolutely not," Morris says. "It's . . . I have a medical condition." He runs a hand down one damp cheek. "It makes me sweat, and then I start laughing." The look on Elmer Fudd's face makes him laugh again. He wonders if Andy and Elmer ever had sex, and the thought of that bouncing, slapping flesh makes him laugh some more. "I'm sorry, Mr. Yankovic. It's not you. And by the way . . . are you related to the noted popular-music humorist Weird Al Yankovic?"

"No, not at all." Yankovic scribbles his signature in a hurry, rips the check loose from his checkbook, and passes it to Morris, who is grinning and thinking that this is a scene John Rothstein could have written. During the exchange, Yankovic takes care that their fingers should not touch.

"Sorry about the laughing," Morris says, laughing harder. He's remembering that they used to call the noted popular-musical humorist Weird Al Yank-My-Dick. "I really can't control it." The clock now reads 3:21, and even that is funny.

"I understand." Elmer is backing away with the book clutched to his chest. "Thank you."

He hurries toward the door. Morris calls after him, "Make sure you tell Andy I gave you the discount. When you see him."

This makes Morris laugh harder than ever, because that's a good one. When you see him! Get it?

When the fit finally passes, it's 3:25, and for the first time it occurs to Morris that maybe he hurried Mr. Irving "Elmer Fudd" Yankovic out for no reason at all. Maybe the boy has changed his mind. Maybe he's not coming, and there's nothing funny about that.

Well, Morris thinks, if he doesn't show up here, I'll just have to pay a house call. Then the joke will be on him. Won't it?

24

Twenty to four.

There's no need to park on a yellow curb now; the parents who clogged the area around the high school earlier, waiting to pick up their kids, have all departed. The buses are gone, too. Hodges, Holly, and Jerome are in a Mercedes sedan that once belonged to Holly's cousin Olivia. It was used as a murder weapon at City Center, but none of them is thinking about that now. They have other things in mind, chiefly Thomas Saubers's son.

"The kid may be in trouble, but you have to admit he's a quick thinker," Jerome says. After ten minutes parked down the street from City Drug, he went inside and ascertained that the boy he was tasked to follow had departed. "A pro couldn't have done much better."

"True," Hodges says. The boy has turned into a challenge, certainly more of a challenge than the airplane-stealing Mr. Madden. Hodges hasn't questioned the pharmacist himself and doesn't need to. Pete's been getting prescriptions filled there for years, he knows the pharmacist and the pharmacist knows him. The kid made up some bullshit story, the pharmacist let him use the back door, and pop goes the weasel. They never covered Frederick Street, because there seemed to be no need.

"Now what?" Jerome asks.

"I think we should go over to the Saubers house. We had a slim chance of keeping his parents out of this, per Tina's request, but I think that just went by the boards."

"They must already have some idea it was him," Jerome says. "I mean, they're his *folks*."

Hodges thinks of saying *There are none so blind as those who will not see*, and shrugs instead.

Holly has contributed nothing to the discussion so far, has just sat behind the wheel of her big boat of a car, arms crossed over her bosom, fingers tapping lightly at her shoulders. Now she turns to Hodges, who is sprawled in the backseat. "Did you ask Peter about the notebook?"

"I never got a chance," Hodges says. Holly's got a bee in her hat about that notebook, and he *should* have asked, just to satisfy her, but the truth is, it never even crossed his mind. "He decided to go, and boogied. Wouldn't even take my card."

Holly points to the school. "I think we should talk to Ricky the Hippie before we leave." And when neither of them replies: "Peter's *house* will still *be* there, you know. It's not going to *fly away*, or anything."

"Guess it wouldn't hurt," Jerome says.

Hodges sighs. "And tell him what, exactly? That one of his students found or stole a stack of money and doled it out to his parents like a monthly allowance? The parents should find that out before some teacher who probably doesn't know jackshit about anything. And Pete should be the one to tell them. It'll let his sister off the hook, for one thing."

"But if he's in some kind of jam he doesn't want them to know about, and he still wanted to talk to someone . . . you know, an adult . . ." Jerome is four years older than he was when he helped Hodges with the Brady Hartsfield mess, old enough to vote and buy legal liquor, but still young enough to remember how it is to be seventeen and suddenly realize you've gotten in over your head with something. When that happens, you want to talk to somebody who's been around the block a few times.

"Jerome's right," Holly says. She turns back to Hodges. "Let's talk to the teacher and find out if Pete asked for advice about anything. If he asks why we want to know—"

"Of *course* he'll want to know why," Hodges says, "and I can't exactly claim confidentiality. I'm not a lawyer."

"Or a priest," Jerome adds, not helpfully.

"You can tell him we're friends of the family," Holly says firmly. "And that's true." She opens her door.

"You have a hunch about this," Hodges says. "Am I right?"

"Yes," she says. "It's a Holly-hunch. Now come on."

25

As they are walking up the wide front steps and beneath the motto EDUCATION IS THE LAMP OF LIFE, the door of Andrew Halliday Rare Editions opens again and Pete Saubers steps inside. He starts down the main aisle, then stops, frowning. The man behind the desk isn't Mr. Halliday. He is in most ways the exact *opposite* of Mr. Halliday, pale instead of florid (except for his lips, which are weirdly red), white-haired instead of bald, and thin instead of fat. Almost gaunt. Jesus. Pete expected his script to go out the window, but not this fast.

"Where's Mr. Halliday? I had an appointment to see him."

The stranger smiles. "Yes, of course, although he didn't give me your name. He just said a young man. He's waiting for you in his office at the back of the shop." This is actually true. In a way. "Just knock and go in."

Pete relaxes a little. It makes sense that Halliday wouldn't want to have such a crucial meeting out here, where anybody looking for a secondhand copy of *To Kill a Mockingbird* could walk in and interrupt them. He's being careful, thinking ahead. If Pete doesn't do the same, his slim chance of coming out of this okay will go out the window.

"Thanks," he says, and walks between tall bookcases toward the back of the shop.

As soon as he goes by the desk, Morris rises and goes quickly and quietly to the front of the shop. He flips the sign in the door from OPEN to CLOSED.

Then he turns the bolt.

26

The secretary in the main office of Northfield High looks curiously at the trio of after-school visitors, but asks no questions. Perhaps she assumes they are family members come to plead the case of some failing student. Whatever they are, it's Howie Ricker's problem, not hers.

She checks a magnetic board covered with multicolored tags and says, "He should still be in his homeroom. That's three-oh-nine, on the third floor, but please peek through the window and make sure he's not with a student. He has conferences today until four, and with school ending in a couple of weeks, plenty of kids stop by to ask for help on their final papers. Or plead for extra time."

Hodges thanks her and they go up the stairs, their heels echoing. From somewhere below, a quartet of musicians is playing "Greensleeves." From somewhere above, a hearty male voice cries jovially, "You *suck*, Malone!"

Room 309 is halfway down the third-floor corridor, and Mr. Ricker, dressed in an eye-burning paisley shirt with the collar unbuttoned and the tie pulled down, is talking to a girl who is gesturing dramatically with her hands. Ricker glances up, sees he has visitors, then returns his attention to the girl.

The visitors stand against the wall, where posters advertise summer classes, summer workshops, summer holiday destinations, an end-of-year dance. A couple of girls come bopping down the hall, both wearing softball jerseys and caps. One is tossing a catcher's mitt from hand to hand, playing hot potato with it.

Holly's phone goes off, playing an ominous handful of notes from the "Jaws" theme. Without slowing, one of the girls says, "You're gonna need a bigger boat," and they both laugh.

Holly looks at her phone, then puts it away. "A text from Tina," she says.

Hodges raises his eyebrows.

"Her mother knows about the money. Her father will too, as soon as he gets home from work." She nods toward the closed door of Mr. Ricker's room. "No reason to hold back now."

27

The first thing Pete becomes aware of when he opens the door to the darkened inner office is the billowing stench. It's both metallic and organic, like steel shavings mixed with spoiled cabbage. The next thing is the sound, a low buzzing. Flies, he thinks, and although he can't see what's in there, the smell and the sound come together in his mind with a thud like a heavy piece of furniture falling over. He turns to flee.

The clerk with the red lips is standing there beneath one of the hanging globes that light the back of the store, and in his hand is a strangely jolly gun, red and black with inlaid gold curlicues. Pete's first thought is Looks fake. They never look fake in the movies.

"Keep your head, Peter," the clerk says. "Don't do anything foolish and you won't get hurt. This is just a discussion."

Pete's second thought is You're lying. I can see it in your eyes.

"Turn around, take a step forward, and turn on the light. The switch is to the left of the door. Then go in, but don't try to slam the door, unless you want a bullet in the back."

Pete steps forward. Everything inside him from the chest on down feels loose and in motion. He hopes he won't piss his pants like a baby. Probably that wouldn't be such a big deal—surely he wouldn't be the first person to spray his Jockeys when a gun is pointed at him—but it *seems* like a big deal. He fumbles with his left hand, finds the switch, and flips it. When he sees the thing lying on the sodden carpet, he tries to scream, but the muscles in his diaphragm aren't working and all that comes out is a watery moan. Flies are buzzing and lighting on what remains of Mr. Halliday's face. Which is not much.

"I know," the clerk says sympathetically. "Not very pretty, is he? Object lessons rarely are. He pissed me off, Pete. Do you want to piss me off?"

"No," Pete says in a high, wavering voice. It sounds more like Tina's than his own. "I don't."

"Then you have learned your lesson. Go on in. Move very slowly, but feel free to avoid the mess."

Pete steps in on legs he can barely feel, edging to his left along one of the bookcases, trying to keep his loafers on the part of the rug that hasn't been soaked. There isn't much. His initial panic has been replaced by a glassy sheet of terror. He keeps thinking of those red lips. Keeps imagining the big bad wolf telling Red Riding Hood, *The better to kiss you with, my dear*.

I have to think, he tells himself. I have to, or I'm going to die in this room. Probably I will anyway, but if I can't think, it's for sure.

He keeps skirting the blotch of blackish-purple until a cherrywood sideboard blocks his path, and there he stops. To go farther would mean stepping onto the bloody part of the rug, and it might still be wet enough to *squelch*. On the sideboard are crystal decanters of booze and a number of squat glasses. On the desk he sees a hatchet, its blade throwing back a reflection of the overhead light. That is surely the weapon the man with the red lips used to kill Mr. Halliday, and Pete supposes it should scare him even more, but instead the sight of it clears his mind like a hard slap.

The door clicks shut behind him. The clerk who probably isn't a clerk leans against it, pointing the jolly little gun at Pete. "All right," he says, and smiles. "Now we can talk."

"Wh-Wh—" He clears his throat, tries again, this time sounds a little more like himself. "What? Talk about what?"

"Don't be disingenuous. The notebooks. The ones you stole."

It all comes together in Pete's mind. His mouth falls open.

The clerk who isn't a clerk smiles. "Ah. The penny drops, I see. Tell me where they are, and you might get out of this alive."

Pete doesn't think so.

He thinks he already knows too much for that.

28

When the girl emerges from Mr. Ricker's homeroom, she's smiling, so her conference must have gone all right. She even twiddles her fingers in a little wave—perhaps to all three of them, more likely just to Jerome—as she hurries off down the hall.

Mr. Ricker, who has accompanied her to the door, looks at Hodges and his associates. "Can I help you, lady and gentlemen?"

"Not likely," Hodges says, "but worth a try. May we come in?"

"Of course."

They sit at desks in the first row like attentive students.

Ricker plants himself on the edge of his desk, an informality he eschewed when talking to his young conferee. "I'm pretty sure you're not parents, so what's up?"

"It's about one of your students," Hodges says. "A boy named Peter Saubers. We think he may be in trouble."

Ricker frowns. "Pete? That doesn't seem likely. He's one of the best students I've ever had. Demonstrates a genuine love of literature, especially American literature. Honor Roll every quarter. What kind of trouble do you think he's in?"

"That's the thing—we don't know. I asked, but he stone-walled me."

Ricker's frown deepens. "That doesn't sound like the Pete Saubers I know."

"It has to do with some money he seems to have come into a few years back. I'd like to fill you in on what we know. It won't take long."

"Please say it has nothing to do with drugs."

"It doesn't."

Ricker looks relieved. "Good. Seen too much of that, and the smart kids are just as much at risk as the dumb ones. More, in some cases. Tell me. I'll help if I can."

Hodges starts with the money that began arriving at the Saubers house in what was, almost literally, the family's darkest hour. He tells Ricker about how, seven months after the monthly deliveries of mystery cash ceased, Pete began to seem stressed and unhappy. He finishes with Tina's conviction that her brother tried to get some more money, maybe from the same source the mystery cash came from, and is in his current jam as a result.

"He grew a moustache," Ricker muses when Hodges has finished. "He's in Mrs. Davis's Creative Writing course now, but I saw him in the hall one day and joshed him about it."

"How did he take the joshing?" Jerome asks.

"Not sure he even heard me. He seemed to be on another

planet. But that's not uncommon with teenagers, as I'm sure
you know. Especially when summer vacation's right around
the corner."

Holly asks, "Did he ever mention a notebook to you? A
Moleskine?"

Ricker considers it while Holly looks at him hopefully.

"No," he says at last. "I don't think so."

She deflates.

"Did he come to you about *anything*?" Hodges asks. "Anything at all that was troubling him, no matter how minor? I
raised a daughter, and I know they sometimes talk about their
problems in code. Probably you know that, too."

Ricker smiles. "The famous friend-who."

"Beg pardon?"

"As in 'I have a friend who might have gotten his girlfriend
pregnant.' Or 'I have a friend who knows who spray-painted
anti-gay slogans on the wall in the boys' locker room.' After
a couple of years on the job, every teacher knows about the
famous friend-who."

Jerome asks, "Did Pete Saubers have a friend-who?"

"Not that I can recall. I'm very sorry. I'd help you if I
could."

Holly asks, in a small and not very hopeful voice, "Never a
friend who kept a secret diary or maybe found some valuable
information in a notebook?"

Ricker shakes his head. "No. I'm really sorry. Jesus, I hate
to think of Pete in trouble. He wrote one of the finest term
papers I've ever gotten from a student. It was about the Jimmy
Gold trilogy."

"John Rothstein," Jerome says, smiling. "I used to have a
tee-shirt that said—"

"Don't tell me," Ricker says. "Shit don't mean shit."

"Actually, no. It was the one about not being anyone's birthday . . . uh, present."

"Ah," Ricker says, smiling. "*That* one."

Hodges gets up. "I'm more of a Michael Connelly man. Thanks for your time." He holds out his hand. Ricker shakes it. Jerome is also getting up, but Holly remains seated.

"John Rothstein," she says. "He wrote that book about the kid who got fed up with his parents and ran away to New York City, right?"

"That was the first novel in the Gold trilogy, yes. Pete was crazy about Rothstein. Probably still is. He may discover new heroes in college, but when he was in my class, he thought Rothstein walked on water. Have you read him?"

"I never have," Holly says, also getting up. "But I'm a big movie fan, so I always go to a website called Deadline. To read the latest Hollywood news? They had an article about how all these producers wanted to make a movie out of *The Runner*. Only no matter how much money they offered, he told them to go to hell."

"That sounds like Rothstein, all right," Ricker says. "A famous curmudgeon. Hated the movies. Claimed they were art for idiots. Sneered at the word *cinema*. Wrote an essay about it, I think."

Holly has brightened. "Then he got *murdered* and there was no *will* and they still can't make a movie because of all the *legal* problems."

"Holly, we ought to go," Hodges says. He wants to get over to the Saubers home. Wherever Pete is now, he'll turn up there eventually.

"Okay . . . I guess . . ." She sighs. Although in her late forties, and even with the mood-levelers she takes, Holly still spends too much time on an emotional rollercoaster. Now the light in her eyes is going out and she looks terribly downcast. Hodges feels bad for her, wants to tell her that, even though not many hunches pan out, you shouldn't stop playing them. Because the few that do pan out are pure gold. Not exactly a pearl of wisdom, but later, when he has a private moment with her, he'll pass it on. Try to ease the sting a little.

"Thank you for your time, Mr. Ricker." Hodges opens the door. Faintly, like music heard in a dream, comes the sound of "Greensleeves."

"Oh my gosh," Ricker says. "Hold the phone."

They turn back to him.

"Pete *did* come to me about something, and not so long ago. But I see so many students . . ."

Hodges nods understandingly.

"And it wasn't a big deal, no adolescent Sturm und Drang, it was actually a very pleasant conversation. It only came to mind now because it was about that book you mentioned, Ms. Gibney. *The Runner*." He smiles a little. "Pete didn't have a friend-who, though. He had an uncle-who."

Hodges feels a spark of something bright and hot, like a lit fuse. "What was it about Pete's uncle that made him worth discussing?"

"Pete said the uncle had a signed first edition of *The Runner*. He offered it to Pete because Pete was a Rothstein fan—that was the story, anyway. Pete told me he was interested in selling it. I asked him if he was sure he wanted to part with a book signed by his literary idol, and he said he was considering it very seriously. He was hoping to help send his sister to one of the private schools, I can't remember which one—"

"Chapel Ridge," Holly says. The light in her eyes has returned.

"I think that's right."

Hodges walks slowly back to the desk. "Tell me . . . *us* . . . everything you remember about that conversation."

"That's really all, except for one thing that kind of nudged my bullshit meter. He said his uncle won the book in a poker game. I remember thinking that's the kind of thing that happens in novels or movies, but rarely in real life. But of course, sometimes life *does* imitate art."

Hodges frames the obvious question, but Jerome gets there first. "Did he ask you about booksellers?"

"Yes, that's really why he came to me. He had a short list of local dealers, probably gleaned from the Internet. I steered him away from one of them. Bit of a shady reputation there."

Jerome looks at Holly. Holly looks at Hodges. Hodges looks at Howard Ricker and asks the obvious follow-up question. He's locked in now, the fuse in his head burning brightly.

"What's this shady book dealer's name?"

29

Pete sees only one chance to go on living. As long as the man with the red lips and pasty complexion doesn't know where the Rothstein notebooks are, he won't pull the trigger of the gun, which is looking less jolly all the time.

"You're Mr. Halliday's partner, aren't you?" he says, not exactly looking at the corpse—it's too awful—but lifting his chin in that direction. "In cahoots with him."

Red Lips utters a brief chuckle, then does something that shocks Peter, who believed until that moment he was beyond shock. He spits on the body.

"He was *never* my partner. Although he had his chance, once upon a time. Long before you were even a twinkle in your father's eye, Peter. And while I find your attempt at a diversion admirable, I must insist that we keep to the subject at hand. Where are the notebooks? In your house? Which used to be *my* house, by the way. Isn't that an interesting co-inky-dink?"

Here is another shock. "*Your—*"

"More ancient history. Never mind. Is that where they are?"

"No. They were for awhile, but I moved them."

"And should I believe that? I think not."

"Because of him." Pete again lifts his chin toward the body. "I tried to sell him some of the notebooks, and he threatened to tell the police. I *had* to move them."

Red Lips considers this, then gives a nod. "All right, I can see that. It fits with what he told me. So where did you put them? Out with it, Peter. Fess up. We'll both feel better, especially you. If 'twere to be done, 'twere well it were done quickly. *Macbeth*, act one."

Pete does not fess up. To fess up is to die. This is the man who stole the notebooks in the first place, he knows that now. Stole the notebooks and murdered John Rothstein over thirty years ago. And now he's murdered Mr. Halliday. Will he scruple at adding Pete Saubers to his list?

Red Lips has no trouble reading his mind. "I don't have to kill you, you know. Not right away, at least. I can put a bullet in your leg. If that doesn't loosen your lips, I'll put one in your balls. With those gone, a young fellow like you wouldn't have much to live for, anyway. Would he?"

Pushed into a final corner, Pete has nothing left but the burning, helpless outrage only adolescents can feel. "You killed him! *You killed John Rothstein!*" Tears are welling in his eyes; they run down his cheeks in warm trickles. "The best writer of the twentieth century and you broke into his house and killed him! For money! Just for money!"

"*Not* for money!" Red Lips shouts back. "*He sold out!*"

He takes a step forward, the muzzle of the gun dipping slightly.

"He sent Jimmy Gold to hell and called it advertising! And by the way, who are you to be high and mighty? You tried to sell the notebooks yourself! *I* don't want to sell them. Maybe once, when I was young and stupid, but not anymore. I want to read them. They're mine. I want to run my hand over the ink and feel the words he set down in his own hand. Thinking about that was all that kept me sane for thirty-six years!"

He takes another step forward.

"Yes, and what about the money in the trunk? Did you take that, too? Of course you did! You're the thief, not me! *You!*"

In that moment Pete is too furious to think about escape, because this last accusation, unfair though it may be, is all too true. He simply grabs one of the liquor decanters and fires it at his tormentor as hard as he can. Red Lips isn't expecting it. He flinches, turning slightly to the right as he does so, and the bottle strikes him in the shoulder. The glass stopper comes out when it hits the carpet. The sharp and stinging odor of whiskey joins the smell of old blood. The flies buzz in an agitated cloud, their meal interrupted.

Pete grabs another decanter and lunges at Red Lips with it raised like a cudgel, the gun forgotten. He trips over Halliday's sprawled legs, goes to one knee, and when Red Lips shoots—the sound in the closed room is like a flat handclap—the bullet goes over his head almost close enough to part his hair. Pete hears it: zzzzz. He throws the second decanter and this one strikes Red Lips just below the mouth, drawing blood. He cries out, staggers backward, hits the wall.

The last two decanters are behind him now, and there is no time to turn and grab another. Pete pushes to his feet and snatches the hatchet from the desk, not by the rubberized handle but by the head. He feels the sting as the blade cuts into his palm, but it's distant, pain felt by somebody living in another country. Red Lips has held on to the gun, and is bringing it around for another shot. Pete can't exactly think, but a deeper part of his mind, perhaps never called upon until today, understands that if he were closer, he could grapple with Red Lips and get the gun away from him. Easily. He's younger, stronger. But the desk is between them, so he throws the hatchet, instead. It whirls at Red Lips end over end, like a tomahawk.

Red Lips screams and cringes away from it, raising the hand holding the gun to protect his face. The blunt side of the hatchet's head strikes his forearm. The gun flies up, strikes one of the bookcases, and clatters to the floor. There's another handclap as it discharges. Pete doesn't know where this second bullet goes, but it's not into him, and that's all he cares about.

Red Lips crawls for the gun with his fine white hair hanging in his eyes and blood dripping from his chin. He's eerily fast, somehow lizardlike. Pete calculates, still without thinking, and sees that if he races Red Lips to the gun, he'll lose. It will be close, but he will. There's a chance he might be able to grab the man's arm before he can turn the gun to fire, but not a good one.

He bolts for the door instead.

"Come back, you shit!" Red Lips shouts. "We're not done!"

Coherent thought makes a brief reappearance. Oh yes we are, Pete thinks.

He rakes the door open and goes through hunched over. He slams it shut behind him with a hard fling of his left hand and sprints for the front of the shop, toward Lacemaker Lane and the blessed lives of other people. There's another gunshot—muffled—and Pete hunches further, but there's no impact and no pain.

He pulls at the front door. It doesn't open. He casts a wild glance back over his shoulder and sees Red Lips shamble out of Halliday's office, his chin wreathed in a blood goatee. He's got the gun and he's trying to aim it. Pete paws at the thumb-lock with fingers that have no feeling, manages to grasp it, and twists. A moment later he's on the sunny sidewalk. No one looks at him; no one is even in the immediate vicinity. On this hot weekday afternoon, the Lacemaker Lane walking mall is as close to deserted as it ever gets.

Pete runs blindly, with no idea of where he's going.

30

It's Hodges behind the wheel of Holly's Mercedes. He obeys the traffic signals and doesn't weave wildly from lane to lane, but he makes the best time he can. He isn't a bit surprised that this run from the North Side to the Halliday bookshop on Lacemaker Lane brings back memories of a much wilder ride in this same car. It had been Jerome at the wheel that night.

"How sure are you that Tina's brother went to this Halliday guy?" Jerome asks. He's in the back this afternoon.

"He did," Holly says without looking up from her iPad, which she has taken from the Benz's capacious glove compartment. "I know he did, and I think I know why. It wasn't any signed book, either." She taps at the screen and mutters, "Come on come on come on. *Load*, you bugger!"

"What are you looking for, Hollyberry?" Jerome asks, leaning forward between the seats.

She turns to glare at him. "Don't call me that, you know I hate that."

"Sorry, sorry." Jerome rolls his eyes.

"Tell you in a minute," she says. "I've almost got it. I just wish I had some WiFi instead of this buggery cell connection. It's so *slow* and *poopy*."

Hodges laughs. He can't help it. This time Holly turns her glare on him, punching away at the screen even as she does so.

Hodges climbs a ramp and merges onto the Crosstown Connector. "It's starting to fit together," he tells Jerome. "Assuming the book Pete talked about to Ricker was actually a writer's notebook—the one Tina saw. The one Pete was so anxious to hide under his pillow."

"Oh, it was," Holly says without looking up from her iPad. "Holly Gibney says that's a big ten-four." She punches something else in, swipes the screen, and gives a cry of frustration that makes both of her companions jump. "Oooh, these goddam pop-up ads make me *so fracking crazy*!"

"Calm down," Hodges tells her.

She ignores him. "You wait. You wait and see."

"The money and the notebook were a package deal," Jerome says. "The Saubers kid found them together. That's what you think, right?"

"Yeah," Hodges says.

"And whatever was in the notebook was worth more money. Except a reputable rare book dealer wouldn't touch it with a ten-foot po—"

"*GOT IT!*" Holly screams, making them both jump. The Mercedes swerves. The guy in the next lane honks irritably and makes an unmistakable hand gesture.

"Got what?" Jerome asks.

"Not *what*, Jerome, *who*! *John Fracking Rothstein!* Murdered in 1978! At least three men broke into his farmhouse—in New Hampshire, this was—and killed him. They also broke into his safe. Listen to this. It's from the Manchester *Union Leader*, three days after he was killed."

As she reads, Hodges exits the Crosstown onto Lower Main.

" 'There is growing certainty that the robbers were after more than money. "They may also have taken a number of notebooks containing various writings Mr. Rothstein did after retiring from public life," a source close to the investigation said. The source went on to speculate that the notebooks, whose existence was confirmed late yesterday by John Rothstein's housekeeper, might be worth a great deal on the black market.' "

Holly's eyes are blazing. She is having one of those divine passages where she has forgotten herself entirely.

"The robbers hid it," she says.

"Hid the money," Jerome says. "The twenty thousand."

"*And* the notebooks. Pete found at least some of them, maybe even all of them. He used the money to help his folks. He didn't get in trouble until he tried selling the notebooks to help his sister. Halliday knows. By now he may even have them. Hurry up, Bill. Hurry up hurry up hurry *up*!"

31

Morris lurches to the front of the store, heart pounding, temples thudding. He drops Andy's gun into his sportcoat pocket, snatches up a book from one of the display tables, opens it, and slams it against his chin to stanch the blood. He could have wiped it with the sleeve of his coat, almost did, but he's thinking again now and knows better. He'll have to go out in public, and he doesn't want to do that smeared with blood. The boy had some on his pants, though, and that's good. That's fine, in fact.

I'm thinking again, and the boy better be thinking, too. If he is, I can still rescue this situation.

He opens the shop door and looks both ways. No sign of Saubers. He expected nothing else. Teenagers are fast. They're like cockroaches that way.

Morris scrabbles in his pocket for the scrap of paper with Pete's cell phone number on it, and suffers a moment of raw panic when he can't find it. At last his fingers touch something scrunched far down in one corner and he breathes a sigh of relief. His heart is pounding, pounding, and he slams one hand against his bony chest.

Don't you give up on me now, he thinks. *Don't you dare.*

He uses the shop's landline to call Saubers, because that also fits the story he's constructing in his mind. Morris thinks it's a good story. He doubts if John Rothstein could have told a better one.

32

When Pete comes fully back to himself, he's in a place Morris Bellamy knows well: Government Square, across from the Happy Cup Café. He sits on a bench to catch his breath, looking anxiously back the way he's come. He sees no sign of Red Lips, and this doesn't surprise him. Pete is also thinking again, and knows the man who tried to kill him would attract attention on the street. *I got him pretty good,* Pete thinks grimly. *Red Lips is now Bloody Chin.*

Good so far, but what now?

As if in answer, his cell phone vibrates. Pete pulls it out of his pocket and looks at the number displayed. He recognizes the last four digits, 8877, from when he called Halliday and left a message about the weekend trip to River Bend Resort. It has to be Red Lips; it sure can't be Mr. Halliday. This thought is so awful it makes him laugh, although the sound that comes out sounds more like a sob.

His first impulse is to not answer. What changes his mind is something Red Lips said: *Your house used to be my house. Isn't that an interesting co-inky-dink?*

His mother's text instructed him to come home right after school. Tina's text said their mother knew about the money. So they're together at the house, waiting for him. Pete doesn't want to alarm them unnecessarily—especially when *he's* the cause for alarm—but he needs to know what this incoming call is about, especially since Dad isn't around to protect the two of them if the crazy guy should turn up on Sycamore Street. Dad's in Victor County, doing one of his show-and-tells.

I'll call the police, Pete thinks. *When I tell him that, he'll head for the hills. He'll have to.* This thought brings some marginal comfort, and he pushes ACCEPT.

"Hello, Peter," Red Lips says.

"I don't need to talk to you," Peter says. "You better run, because I'm calling the cops."

"I'm glad I reached you before you did something so foolish. You won't believe this, but I'm telling you as a friend."

"You're right," Pete says. "I don't believe it. You tried to kill me."

"Here's something else you won't believe: I'm glad I didn't. Because then I'd never find out where you hid the Rothstein notebooks."

"You never will," Pete says, and adds, "I'm telling you as a friend." He's feeling a little steadier now. Red Lips isn't chasing him, and he isn't on his way to Sycamore Street, either. He's hiding in the bookshop and talking on the landline.

"That's what you think now, because you haven't considered the long view. I have. Here's the situation: You went to Andy to sell the notebooks. He tried to blackmail you instead, so you killed him."

Pete says nothing. He can't. He's flabbergasted.

"Peter? Are you there? If you don't want to spend a year in the Riverview Youth Detention Center followed by twenty or so in Waynesville, you better be. I've been in both, and I can tell you they're no place for young men with virgin bottoms. College would be much better, don't you think?"

"I wasn't even in the city last weekend," Pete says. "I was at a school retreat. I can prove it."

Red Lips doesn't hesitate. "Then you did it before you left. Or possibly on Sunday night, after you got back. The police are going to find your voicemail—I was sure to save it. There's also DVD security footage of you arguing with him. I took the discs, but I'll be sure the police get them if we can't come to an agreement. Then there's the fingerprints. They'll find yours on the doorknob of his inner office. Better still, they'll find them on the murder weapon. I think you're in a box, even if you can account for every minute of your time this past weekend."

Pete realizes with dismay that he can't even do that. He missed *everything* on Sunday. He remembers Ms. Bran—alias Bran Stoker—standing by the door of the bus just twenty-four hours ago, cell phone in hand, ready to call 911 and report a missing student.

I'm sorry, he told her. *I was sick to my stomach. I thought the fresh air would help me. I was vomiting.*

He can see her in court, all too clearly, saying that yes, Peter *did* look sick that afternoon. And he can hear the prosecuting attorney telling the jury that any teenage boy probably *would* look sick after chopping an elderly book dealer into kindling with a hatchet.

Ladies and gentlemen of the jury, I submit to you that Pete Saubers hitchhiked back to the city that Sunday morning because he had an appointment with Mr. Halliday, who thought Mr. Saubers had finally decided to give in to his blackmail demands. Only Mr. Saubers had no intention of giving in.

It's a nightmare, Pete thinks. Like dealing with Halliday all over again, only a thousand times worse.

"Peter? Are you there?"

"No one would believe it. Not for a second. Not once they find out about you."

"And who am I, exactly?"

The wolf, Pete thinks. You're the big bad wolf.

People must have seen him that Sunday, wandering around the resort acreage. *Plenty* of people, because he'd mostly stuck to the paths. Some would surely remember him and come forward. But, as Red Lips said, that left before the trip and after. Especially Sunday night, when he'd gone straight to his room and closed the door. On *CSI* and *Criminal Minds*, police scientists were always able to figure out the exact time of a murdered person's death, but in real life, who knew? Not Pete. And if the police had a good suspect, one whose prints were on the murder weapon, the time of death might become negotiable.

But I *had* to throw the hatchet at him! he thinks. It was all I had!

Believing that things can get no worse, Pete looks down and sees a bloodstain on his knee.

Mr. Halliday's blood.

"I can fix this," Red Lips says smoothly, "and if we come to terms, I will. I can wipe your fingerprints. I can erase the voicemail. I can destroy the security DVDs. All you have to do is tell me where the notebooks are."

"Like I should trust you!"

"You should." Low. Coaxing and reasonable. "Think about it, Peter. With you out of the picture, Andy's murder looks like an attempted robbery gone wrong. The work of some random crackhead or meth freak. That's good for both of us. With you *in* the picture, the existence of the notebooks comes out. Why would I want that?"

You won't care, Pete thinks. You won't have to, because you won't be anywhere near here when Halliday is discovered dead in his office. You said you were in Waynesville, and that makes you an ex-con, and you knew Mr. Halliday. Put those together, and you'd be a suspect, too. Your fingerprints are in there as well as mine, and I don't think you can wipe them all up. What you can do—if I let you—is take the notebooks and go. And once you're gone, what's to keep you from sending the police those security DVDs, just for spite? To get back at me for hitting you with that liquor bottle and then getting away? If I agree to what you're saying . . .

He finishes the thought aloud. "I'll only look worse. No matter what you say."

"I assure you that's not true."

He sounds like a lawyer, one of the sleazy ones with fancy hair who advertise on the cable channels late at night. Pete's outrage returns and straightens him on the bench like an electric shock.

"Fuck you. You're *never* getting those notebooks."

He ends the call. The phone buzzes in his hand almost immediately, same number, Red Lips calling back. Pete hits DECLINE and turns the phone off. Right now he needs to think harder and smarter than ever in his life.

Mom and Tina, they're the most important thing. He has to talk to Mom, tell her that she and Teens have to get out of the house right away. Go to a motel, or something. They have to—

No, not Mom. It's his sister he has to talk to, at least to begin with.

He didn't take that Mr. Hodges's card, but Tina must know how to get in touch with him. If that doesn't work, he'll have to call the police and take his chances. He will not put his family at risk, no matter what.

Pete speed-dials his sister.

33

"Hello? Peter? Hello? *Hello?*"

Nothing. The thieving sonofabitch has hung up. Morris's first impulse is to rip the desk phone out of the wall and throw it at one of the bookcases, but he restrains himself at the last moment. This is no time to lose himself in a rage.

So what now? What next? Is Saubers going to call the police despite all the evidence stacked against him?

Morris can't allow himself to believe that, because if he does, the notebooks will be lost to him. And consider this: Would the boy take such an irrevocable step without talking to his parents first? Without asking their advice? Without warning them?

I have to move fast, Morris thinks, and aloud, as he wipes his fingerprints off the phone: "If 'twere to be done, best it be done quickly."

And 'twere best he wash his face and leave by the back door. He doesn't believe the gunshots were heard on the street—the inner office must be damned near soundproof, lined with books as it is—but he doesn't want to take the risk.

He scrubs away the blood goatee in Halliday's bathroom, careful to leave the red-stained washcloth in the sink where the police will find it when they eventually turn up. With that done, he follows a narrow aisle to a door with an EXIT sign above it and boxes of books stacked in front of it. He moves them, thinking how stupid to block the fire exit that way. Stupid and shortsighted.

That could be my old pal's epitaph, Morris thinks. Here lies Andrew Halliday, a fat, stupid, shortsighted homo. He will not be missed.

The heat of late afternoon whacks him like a hammer, and he staggers. His head is thumping from being hit with that goddam decanter, but the brains inside are in high gear. He gets in the Subaru, where it's even hotter, and turns the air-conditioning to max as soon as he starts the engine. He examines himself in the rearview mirror. There's an ugly purple bruise surrounding a crescent-shaped cut on his chin, but the bleeding has stopped, and on the whole he doesn't look too bad. He wishes he had some aspirin, but that can wait.

He backs out of Andy's space and threads his way down the alley leading to Grant Street. Grant is more downmarket than Lacemaker Lane with its fancy shops, but at least cars are allowed there.

As Morris stops at the mouth of the alley, Hodges and his two partners arrive on the other side of the building and stand looking at the CLOSED sign hanging in the door of Andrew Halliday Rare Editions. A break in the Grant Street traffic comes just as Hodges is trying the bookshop door and finding it unlocked. Morris makes a quick left and heads toward the Crosstown Connector. With rush hour only getting started, he can be on the North Side in fifteen minutes. Maybe twelve. He needs to keep Saubers from going to the police, assuming he hasn't already, and there's one sure way to do that.

All he has to do is beat the notebook thief to his little sister.

34

Behind the Saubers house, near the fence that separates the family's backyard from the undeveloped land, there's a rusty old swing set that Tom Saubers keeps meaning to take down, now that both of his children are too old for it. This afternoon Tina is sitting on the glider, rocking slowly back and forth. *Divergent* is open in her lap, but she hasn't turned a page in the last five minutes. Mom has promised to watch the movie with her as soon as she's finished the book, but today Tina doesn't want to read about teenagers in the ruins of Chicago. Today that seems awful instead of romantic. Still moving slowly back and forth, she closes both the book and her eyes.

God, she prays, please don't let Pete be in really bad trouble. And don't let him hate me. I'll die if he hates me, so please let him understand why I told. *Please.*

God gets right back to her. God says Pete won't blame her because Mom figured it out on her own, but Tina's not sure she believes Him. She opens the book again but still can't read. The day seems to hang suspended, waiting for something awful to happen.

The cell phone she got for her eleventh birthday is upstairs in her bedroom. It's just a cheapie, not the iPhone with all the bells and whistles she desired, but it's her most prized possession and she's rarely without it. Only this afternoon she is. She left it in her room and went out to the backyard as soon as she texted Pete. She *had* to send that text, she couldn't just let him walk in unprepared, but she can't bear the thought of an angry, accusatory callback. She'll have to face him in a little while, that can't be avoided, but Mom will be with her then. Mom will tell him it wasn't Tina's fault, and he'll believe her.

Probably.

Now the cell begins to vibrate and jiggle on her desk. She's got a cool Snow Patrol ringtone, but—sick to her stomach and worried about Pete—Tina never thought to switch it from the mandated school setting when she and her mother got home, so Linda Saubers doesn't hear it downstairs. The screen lights up with her brother's picture. Eventually, the phone falls silent. After thirty seconds or so, it starts vibrating again. And a third time. Then it quits for good.

Pete's picture disappears from the screen.

35

In Government Square, Pete stares at his phone incredulously. For the first time in his memory, Teens has failed to answer her cell while school is not in session.

Mom, then . . . or maybe not. Not quite yet. She'll want to ask a billion questions, and time is tight.

Also (although he won't quite admit this to himself), he doesn't want to talk to her until he absolutely has to.

He uses Google to troll for Mr. Hodges's number. He finds nine William Hodgeses here in the city, but the one he wants has got to be K. William, who has a company called Finders Keepers. Pete calls and gets an answering machine. At the end of the message—which seems to last at least an hour—Holly says, "If you need immediate assistance, you may dial 555-1890."

Pete once more debates calling his mother, then decides to go with the number the recording has given him first. What convinces him are two words: *immediate assistance*.

36

"Oough," Holly says as they approach the empty service desk in the middle of Andrew Halliday's narrow shop. "What's that smell?"

"Blood," Hodges replies. It's also decaying meat, but he doesn't want to say that. "You stay here, both of you."

"Are you carrying a weapon?" Jerome asks.

"I've got the Slapper."

"That's all?"

Hodges shrugs.

"Then I'm coming with you."

"Me too," Holly says, and grabs a substantial book called *Wild Plants and Flowering Herbs of North America*. She holds it as if she means to swat a stinging bug.

"No," Hodges says patiently, "you're going to stay right here. Both of you. And race to see which one can dial nine-one-one first, if I yell for you to do so."

"Bill—" Jerome begins.

"Don't argue with me, Jerome, and don't waste time. I've got an idea time might be rather short."

"A hunch?" Holly asks.

"Maybe a little more."

Hodges takes the Happy Slapper from his coat pocket (these days he's rarely without it, although he seldom carries his old service weapon), and grasps it above the knot. He advances quickly and quietly to the door of what he assumes is Andrew Halliday's private office. It's standing slightly ajar. The Slapper's loaded end swings from his right hand. He stands slightly to one side of the door and knocks with his left. Because this seems to be one of those moments when the strict truth is dispensable, he calls, "It's the police, Mr. Halliday."

There's no answer. He knocks again, louder, and when there's still no answer, he pushes the door open. The smell is instantly stronger: blood, decay, and spilled booze. Something else, too. Spent gunpowder, an aroma he knows well. Flies are buzzing somnolently. The lights are on, seeming to spotlight the body on the floor.

"Oh Christ, his head's half off!" Jerome cries. He's so close that Hodges jerks in surprise, bringing the Slapper up and then lowering it again. My pacemaker just went into over-drive, he thinks. He turns and both of them are crowding up right behind him. Jerome has a hand over his mouth. His eyes are bulging.

Holly, on the other hand, looks calm. She's got *Wild Plants and Flowering Herbs of North America* clasped against her chest and appears to be assessing the bleeding mess on the rug. To Jerome she says, "Don't hurl. This is a crime scene."

"I'm not going to hurl." The words are muffled, thanks to the hand clutching his lower face.

"Neither one of you minds worth a tinker's dam," Hodges says. "If I were your teacher, I'd send you both to the office. I'm going in. You two stand right where you are."

He takes two steps in. Jerome and Holly immediately follow, side by side. The fucking Bobbsey Twins, Hodges thinks.

"Did Tina's brother do this?" Jerome asks. "Jesus Christ, Bill, did he?"

"If he did, it wasn't today. That blood's almost dry. And there's the flies. I don't see any maggots yet, but—"

Jerome makes a gagging noise.

"Jerome, *don't*," Holly says in a forbidding voice. Then, to Hodges: "I see a little ax. Hatchet. Whatever you call it. That's what did it."

Hodges doesn't reply. He's assessing the scene. He thinks that Halliday—if it *is* Halliday—has been dead at least twenty-four hours, maybe longer. *Probably* longer. But something has happened in here since, because the smell of spilled liquor and gunpowder is fresh and strong.

"Is that a bullet hole, Bill?" Jerome asks. He's pointing at a bookshelf to the left of the door, near a small cherry-wood table. There's a small round hole in a copy of *Catch-22*. Hodges goes to it, looks more closely, and thinks, That's *got* to hurt the resale price. Then he looks at the table. There are two crystal decanters on it, probably Waterford. The table is slightly dusty, and he can see the shapes where two others stood. He looks across the room, beyond the desk, and yep, there they are, lying on the floor.

"Sure it's a bullet hole," Holly says. "I can smell the gunpowder."

"There was a fight," Jerome says, then points to the corpse without looking at it. "But *he* sure wasn't part of it."

"No," Hodges says, "not him. And the combatants have since departed."

"Was one of them Peter Saubers?"

Hodges sighs heavily. "Almost for sure. I think he came here after he ditched us at the drugstore."

"Somebody took Mr. Halliday's computer," Holly says. "His DVD hookup is still there beside the cash register, and the wireless mouse—also a little box with a few thumb drives in it—but the computer is gone. I saw a big empty space on the desk out there. It was probably a laptop."

"What now?" Jerome asks.

"We call the police." Hodges doesn't want to do it, senses that Pete Saubers is in bad trouble and calling the cops may only make it worse, at least to begin with, but he played the Lone Ranger in the Mercedes Killer case, and almost got a few thousand kids killed.

He takes out his cell, but before he can turn it on, it lights up and rings in his hand.

"Peter," Holly says. Her eyes are shining and she speaks with utter certainty. "Bet you six thousand dollars. *Now* he wants to talk. Don't just stand there, Bill, answer your fracking phone."

He does.

"I need help," Pete Saubers says rapidly. "Please, Mr. Hodges, I really need help."

"Just a sec. I'm going to put you on speaker so my associates can hear."

"Associates?" Pete sounds more alarmed than ever. "What associates?"

"Holly Gibney. Your sister knows her. And Jerome Robinson. He's Barbara Robinson's older brother."

"Oh. I guess . . . I guess that's okay." And, as if to himself: "How much worse can it get?"

"Peter, we're in Andrew Halliday's shop. There's a dead man in his office. I assume it's Halliday, and I assume you know about it. Would those assumptions be correct?"

There's a moment of silence. If not for the faint sound of traffic wherever Pete is, Hodges might have thought he'd broken the connection. Then the boy starts talking again, the words spilling out in a waterfall.

"He was there when I got there. The man with the red lips. He told me Mr. Halliday was in the back, so I went into his office, and he followed me and he had a gun and he tried to kill me when I wouldn't tell him where the notebooks were. I wouldn't because . . . because he doesn't deserve to have them and besides he was going to kill me *anyway*, I could tell just by looking in his eyes. He . . . I . . . ."

"You threw the decanters at him, didn't you?"

"Yes! The bottles! And he shot at me! He missed, but it was so close I heard it go by. I ran and got away, but then he called me and said they'd blame me, the police would, because I threw a hatchet at him, too . . . did you see the hatchet?"

"Yes," Hodges says. "I'm looking at it right now."

"And . . . and my fingerprints, see . . . they're on it because I threw it at him . . . and he has some video discs of me and Mr. Halliday arguing . . . because he was trying to blackmail me! Halliday, I mean, not the man with the red lips, only now *he's* trying to blackmail me, too!"

"This red-lips man has the store security video?" Holly asks, bending toward the phone. "Is that what you mean?"

"*Yes!* He said the police will arrest me and they will because I didn't go to any of the Sunday meetings at River Bend, and he also has a voicemail *and I don't know what to do!*"

"Where are you, Peter?" Hodges asks. "Where are you right now?"

There's another pause, and Hodges knows exactly what Pete's doing: checking for landmarks. He may have lived in the city his whole life, but right now he's so freaked he doesn't know east from west.

"Government Square," he says at last. "Across from this restaurant, the Happy Cup?"

"Do you see the man who shot at you?"

"N-No. I ran, and I don't think he could chase me very far on foot. He's kind of old, and you can't drive a car on Lacemaker Lane."

"Stay there," Hodges says. "We'll come and get you."

"Please don't call the police," Peter says. "It'll kill my folks, after everything else that's happened to them. I'll give you the notebooks. I never should have kept them, and I never should have tried to sell any of them. I should have stopped with the money." His voice is blurring now as he breaks down. "My parents . . . they were in such trouble. About *everything*. I only wanted to help!"

"I'm sure that's true, but I *have* to call the police. If you didn't kill Halliday, the evidence will show that. You'll be fine. I'll pick you up and we'll go to your house. Will your parents be there?"

"Dad's on a business thing, but my mom and sister will be."

Pete has to hitch in a breath before going on. "I'll go to jail, won't I? They'll never believe me about the man with the red lips. They'll think I made him up."

"All you have to do is tell the truth," Holly says. "Bill won't let anything bad happen to you." She grabs his hand and squeezes it fiercely. "Will you?"

Hodges repeats, "If you didn't kill him, you'll be fine."

"I didn't! Swear to God!"

"This other man did. The one with the red lips."

"Yes. He killed John Rothstein, too. He said Rothstein sold out."

Hodges has a million questions, but this isn't the time.

"Listen to me, Pete. Very carefully. Stay where you are. We'll be at Government Square in fifteen minutes."

"If you let me drive," Jerome says, "we can be there in ten."

Hodges ignores this. "The four of us will go to your house. You'll tell the whole story to me, my associates, and your mother. She may want to call your father and discuss getting you legal representation. *Then* we're going to call the police. It's the best I can do."

And better than I *should* do, he thinks, eyeing the mangled corpse and thinking about how close he came to going to jail himself four years ago. For the same kind of thing, too: Lone Ranger shit. But surely another half hour or forty-five minutes can't hurt. And what the boy said about his parents hit home. Hodges was at City Center that day. He saw the aftermath.

"A-All right. Come as fast as you can."

"Yes." He breaks the connection.

"What do we do about *our* fingerprints?" Holly asks.

"Leave them," Hodges says. "Let's go get that kid. I can't wait to hear his story." He tosses Jerome the Mercedes key.

"Thanks, Massa Hodges!" Tyrone Feelgood screeches. "Dis here black boy is one *safe drivuh*! I is goan get'chall safe to yo destin—"

"Shut up, Jerome."

Hodges and Holly say it together.

37

Pete takes a deep, trembling breath and closes his cell phone. Everything is going around in his head like some nightmare amusement park ride, and he's sure he sounded like an idiot. Or a murderer scared of getting caught and making up any wild tale. He forgot to tell Mr. Hodges that Red Lips once lived in Pete's own house, and he should have done that. He thinks about calling Hodges back, but why bother when he and those other two are coming to pick him up?

The guy won't go to the house, anyway, Pete tells himself. He can't. He has to stay invisible.

But he might, just the same. If he thinks I was lying about moving the notebooks somewhere else, he really might. Because he's crazy. A total whack-job.

He tries Tina's phone again and gets nothing but her message: "Hey, it's Teens, sorry I missed you, do your thing." *Beeep.*

All right, then.

Mom.

But before he can call her, he sees a bus coming, and in the destination window, like a gift from heaven, are the words NORTH SIDE. Pete suddenly decides he's not going to sit here and wait for Mr. Hodges. The bus will get him there sooner, and he wants to go home *now*. He'll call Mr. Hodges once he's on board and tell him to meet him at the house, but first he'll call his mother and tell her to lock all the doors.

The bus is almost empty, but he makes his way to the back, just the same. And he doesn't have to call his mother, after all; his phone rings in his hand as he sits down. **MOM**, the screen says. He takes a deep breath and pushes ACCEPT. She's talking before he can even say hello.

"Where are you, Peter?" Peter instead of Pete. Not a good start. "I expected you home an hour ago."

"I'm coming," he says. "I'm on the bus."

"Let's stick to the truth, shall we? The bus has come and gone. I saw it."

"Not the schoolbus, the North Side bus. I had to . . ." What? Run an errand? That's so ludicrous he could laugh. Except this is no laughing matter. Far from it. "There was something I had to do. Is Tina there? She didn't go down to Ellen's, or something?"

"She's in the backyard, reading her book."

The bus is picking its way past some road construction, moving with agonizing slowness.

"Mom, listen to me. You—"

"No, you listen to *me*. Did you send that money?"

He closes his eyes.

"Did you? A simple yes or no will suffice. We can go into the details later."

Eyes still closed, he says: "Yes. It was me. But—"

"Where did it come from?"

"That's a long story, and right now it doesn't matter. The *money* doesn't matter. There's a guy—"

"What do you *mean*, it doesn't matter? That was over *twenty thousand dollars*!"

He stifles an urge to say *Did you just figure that out?*

The bus continues lumbering its laborious way through the construction. Sweat is rolling down Pete's face. He can see the smear of blood on his knee, dark brown instead of red, but still as loud as a shout. *Guilty!* it yells. *Guilty, guilty!*

"Mom, please shut up and listen to me."

Shocked silence on the other end of the line. Not since the days of his toddler tantrums has he told his mother to shut up.

"There's a guy, and he's dangerous." He could tell her just *how* dangerous, but he wants her on alert, not in hysterics. "I don't think he'll come to the house, but he might. You should get Tina inside and lock the doors. Just for a few minutes, then I'll be there. Some other people, too. People who can help."

At least I hope so, he thinks.

God, I hope so.

38

Morris Bellamy turns onto Sycamore Street. He's aware that his life is rapidly narrowing to a point. All he has is a few hundred stolen dollars, a stolen car, and the need to get his hands on Rothstein's notebooks. Oh, he has one other thing, too: a short-term hideout where he can go, and read, and find out what happened to Jimmy Gold after the Duzzy-Doo campaign put him at the top of the advertising dungheap with a double fistful of those Golden Bucks. Morris understands this is a crazy goal, so he must be a crazy person, but it's all he has, and it's enough.

There's his old house, which is now the notebook thief's house. With a little red car in the driveway.

"Crazy don't mean shit," Morris Bellamy says. "Crazy don't mean shit. *Nothing* means shit."

Words to live by.

39

"Bill," Jerome says. "I hate to say it, but I think our bird has flown."

Hodges looks up from his thoughts as Jerome guides the Mercedes through Government Square. There are quite a few people sitting on the benches—reading newspapers, chatting and drinking coffee, feeding the pigeons—but there are no teenagers of either sex.

"I don't see him at any of the tables on the café side, either," Holly reports. "Maybe he went inside for a cup of coffee?"

"Right now, coffee would be the last thing on his mind," Hodges says. He pounds a fist on his thigh.

"North Side and South Side buses run through here every fifteen minutes," Jerome says. "If I were in his shoes, sitting and waiting around for someone to come and pick me up would be torture. I'd want to be doing something."

That's when Hodges's phone rings.

"A bus came along and I decided not to wait," Pete says. He sounds calmer now. "I'll be home when you get there. I just got off the phone with my mother. She and Tina are okay."

Hodges doesn't like the sound of this. "Why wouldn't they be, Peter?"

"Because the guy with the red lips knows where we live. He said *he* used to live there. I forgot to tell you."

Hodges checks where they are. "How long to Sycamore Street, Jerome?"

"Be there in twenty. Maybe less. If I'd known the kid was going to grab a bus, I would've taken the Crosstown."

"Mr. Hodges?" Pete.

"I'm here."

"He'd be stupid to go to my house, anyway. If he does that, I won't be framed anymore."

He's got a point. "Did you tell them to lock up and stay inside?"

"Yes."

"And did you give your mom his description?"

"Yes."

Hodges knows that if he calls the cops, Mr. Red Lips will be gone with the wind, leaving Pete to depend on the forensic evidence to get him off the hook. And they can probably beat the cops, anyway.

"Tell him to call the guy," Holly says. She leans toward Hodges and bellows, *"Call and say you changed your mind and will give him the notebooks!"*

"Pete, did you hear that?"

"Yeah, but I can't. I don't even know if he has a phone. He called me from the one in the bookshop. We didn't, you know, exactly have time to exchange info."

"How poopy is that?" Holly asks no one in particular.

"All right. Call me the minute you get home and verify that everything's okay. If I don't hear from you, I'll have to call for the police."

"I'm sure they're f—"

But this is where they came in. Hodges closes his phone and leans forward. "Punch it, Jerome."

"As soon as I can." He gestures at the traffic, three lanes going each way, chrome twinkling in the sunshine. "Once we get past the rotary up there, we'll be gone like Enron."

Twenty minutes, Hodges thinks. Twenty minutes at most. What can happen in twenty minutes?

The answer, he knows from bitter experience, is quite a lot. Life and death. Right now all he can do is hope those twenty minutes don't come back to haunt him.

40

Linda Saubers came into her husband's little home office to wait for Pete, because her husband's laptop is on the desk and she can play computer solitaire. She is far too upset to read.

After talking to Pete, she's more upset than ever. Afraid, too, but not of some sinister villain lurking on Sycamore Street. She's afraid for her son, because it's clear *he* believes in the sinister villain. Things are finally starting to come together. His pallor and weight loss . . . the crazy moustache he tried to grow . . . the return of his acne and his long silences . . . they all make sense now. If he's not having a nervous breakdown, he's on the verge of one.

She gets up and looks out the window at her daughter. Tina's got her best blouse on, the billowy yellow one, and no way should she be wearing it on a dirty old glider that should have been taken down years ago. She has a book, and it's open, but she doesn't seem to be reading. She looks drawn and sad.

What a nightmare, Linda thinks. First Tom hurt so badly he'll walk with a limp for the rest of his life, and now our son seeing monsters in the shadows. That money wasn't manna from heaven, it was acid rain. Maybe he just has to come clean. Tell us the whole story about where the money came from. Once he does that, the healing process can begin.

In the meantime, she'll do as he asked: call Tina inside and lock the house. It can't hurt.

A board creaks behind her. She turns, expecting to see her son, but it's not Pete. It's a man with pale skin, thinning white hair, and red lips. It's the man her son described, the sinister villain, and her first feeling isn't terror but an absurdly powerful sense of relief. Her son isn't having a nervous breakdown, after all.

Then she sees the gun in the man's hand, and the terror comes, bright and hot.

"You must be Mom," the intruder says. "Strong family resemblance."

"Who are you?" Linda Saubers asks. "What are you doing here?"

The intruder—in the doorway of her husband's study instead of in her son's mind—glances out the window, and Linda has to suppress an urge to say *Don't look at her*.

"Is that your daughter?" Morris asks. "Hey, she's pretty. I always liked a girl in yellow."

"What do you want?" Linda asks.

"What's mine," Morris says, and shoots her in the head. Blood flies up and spatters red droplets against the glass. It sounds like rain.

41

Tina hears an alarming bang from the house and runs for the kitchen door. It's the pressure cooker, she thinks. Mom forgot the damn pressure cooker again. This has happened once before, while her mother was making preserves. It's an old cooker, the kind that sits on the stove, and Pete spent most of one Saturday afternoon on a stepladder, scraping dried strawberry goo off the ceiling. Mom was vacuuming the living room when it happened, which was lucky. Tina hopes to God she wasn't in the kitchen this time, either.

"Mom?" She runs inside. There's nothing on the stove. "Mo—"

An arm grabs her around the middle, hard. Tina loses her breath in an explosive whoosh. Her feet rise from the floor, kicking. She can feel whiskers against her cheek. She can smell sweat, sour and hot.

"Don't scream and I won't have to hurt you," the man says into her ear, making her skin prickle. "Do you understand?"

Tina manages to nod, but her heart is hammering and the world is going dark. "Let me—breathe," she gasps, and the hold loosens. Her feet go back to the floor. She turns and sees a man with a pale face and red lips. There's a cut on his chin, it looks like a bad one. The skin around it is swollen and blue-black.

"Don't scream," he repeats, and raises an admonitory finger. "Do *not* do that." He smiles, and if it's supposed to make her feel better, it doesn't work. His teeth are yellow. They look more like fangs than teeth.

"What did you do to my mother?"

"She's fine," the man with the red lips says. "Where's your cell phone? A pretty little girl like you must have a cell phone. Lots of friends to chatter and text with. Is it in your pocket?"

"N-N-No. Upstairs. In my room."

"Let's go get it," Morris says. "You're going to make a call."

42

Pete's stop is Elm Street, two blocks over from the house, and the bus is almost there. He's making his way to the front when his cell buzzes. His relief at seeing his sister's smiling face in the little window is so great that his knees loosen and he has to grab one of the straphandles.

"Tina! I'll be there in a—"

"There's a man here!" Tina is crying so hard he can barely understand her. "He was in the house! He—"

Then she's gone, and he knows the voice that replaces hers. He wishes to God he didn't.

"Hello, Peter," Red Lips says. "Are you on your way?"

He can't say anything. His tongue is stuck to the roof of his mouth. The bus pulls over at the corner of Elm and Breckenridge Terrace, his stop, but Pete only stands there.

"Don't bother answering that, and don't bother coming home, because no one will be here if you do."

"He's lying!" Tina yells. "Mom is—"

Then she howls.

"Don't you hurt her," Pete says. The few other riders don't look around from their papers or handhelds, because he can't speak above a whisper. "Don't you hurt my sister."

"I won't if she shuts up. She needs to be quiet. You need to be quiet, too, and listen to me. But first you need to answer two questions. Have you called the police?"

"No."

"Have you called *anyone*?"

"No." Pete lies without hesitation.

"Good. Excellent. Now comes the listening part. Are you listening?"

A large lady with a shopping bag is clambering onto the bus, wheezing. Pete gets off as soon as she's out of the way, walking like a boy in a dream, the phone plastered to his ear.

"I'm taking your sister with me to a safe place. A place where we can meet, once you have the notebooks."

Pete starts to tell him they don't have to do it that way, he'll just tell Red Lips where the notebooks are, then realizes doing that would be a huge mistake. Once Red Lips knows they're in the basement at the Rec, he'll have no reason to keep Tina alive.

"Are you there, Peter?"

"Y-Yes."

"You better be. You just better be. Get the notebooks. When you have them—and not before—call your sister's cell again. If you call for any other reason, I'll hurt her."

"Is my mother all right?"

"She's fine, just tied up. Don't worry about her, and don't bother going home. Just get the notebooks and call me."

With that, Red Lips is gone. Pete doesn't have time to tell him he *has* to go home, because he'll need Tina's wagon again to haul the cartons. He also needs to get his father's key to the Rec. He returned it to the board in his father's office, and he needs it to get in.

43

Morris slips Tina's pink phone into his pocket and yanks a cord from her desktop computer. "Turn around. Hands behind you."

"Did you shoot her?" Tears are running down Tina's cheeks. "Was that the sound I heard? Did you shoot my moth—"

Morris slaps her, and hard. Blood flies from Tina's nose and the corner of her mouth. Her eyes widen in shock.

"You need to shut your quack and turn around. Hands behind you."

Tina does it, sobbing. Morris ties her wrists together at the small of her back, cinching the knots viciously.

"Ow! *Ow*, mister! That's too tight!"

"Deal with it." He wonders vaguely how many shots might be left in his old pal's gun. Two will be enough; one for the thief and one for the thief's sister. "Walk. Downstairs. Out the kitchen door. Let's go. Hup-two-three-four."

She looks back at him, her eyes huge and bloodshot and swimming with tears. "Are you going to rape me?"

"No," Morris says, then adds something that is all the more terrifying because she doesn't understand it: "I won't make that mistake again."

44

Linda comes to staring at the ceiling. She knows where she is, Tom's office, but not what has happened to her. The right side of her head is on fire, and when she raises a hand to her face, it comes away wet with blood. The last thing she can remember is Peggy Moran telling her that Tina had gotten sick at school.

Go get her and take her home, Peggy had said. *I'll cover this.*

No, she remembers something else. Something about the mystery money.

I was going to talk to Pete about it, she thinks. Get some answers. I was playing solitaire on Tom's computer, just killing time while I waited for him to come home, and then—

Then, black.

Now, this terrible pain in her head, like a constantly slamming door. It's even worse than the migraines she sometimes gets. Worse even than childbirth. She tries to raise her head and manages to do it, but the world starts going in and out with her heartbeat, first *sucking*, then *blooming*, each oscillation accompanied by such godawful agony . . .

She looks down and sees the front of her gray dress has changed to a muddy purple. She thinks, Oh God, that's a lot of blood. Have I had a stroke? Some kind of brain hemorrhage?

Surely not, surely those only bleed on the inside, but whatever it is, she needs help. She needs an ambulance, but she can't make her hand go to the phone. It lifts, trembles, and drops back to the floor.

She hears a yelp of pain from somewhere close, then crying she'd recognize anywhere, even while dying (which, she suspects, she may be). It's Tina.

She manages to prop herself up on one bloody hand, enough to look out the window. She sees a man hustling Tina down the back steps into the yard. Tina's hands are tied behind her.

Linda forgets about her pain, forgets about needing an ambulance. A man has broken in, and he's now abducting her daughter. She needs to stop him. She needs the police. She tries to get into the swivel chair behind the desk, but at first she can only paw at the seat. She does a lunging sit-up and for a moment the pain is so intense the world turns white, but she holds on to consciousness and grabs the arms of the chair. When her vision clears, she sees the man opening the back gate and shoving Tina through. *Herding* her, like an animal on its way to the slaughterhouse.

Bring her back! Linda screams. *Don't you hurt my baby!*

But only in her head. When she tries to get up, the chair turns and she loses her grip on the arms. The world darkens. She hears a terrible gagging sound before she blacks out, and has time to think, Can that be me?

45

Things are *not* golden after the rotary. Instead of open street, they see backed-up traffic and two orange signs. One says FLAGGER AHEAD. The other says ROAD CONSTRUC- TION. There's a line of cars waiting while the flagger lets downtown traffic go through. After three minutes of sitting, each one feeling an hour long, Hodges tells Jerome to use the side streets.

"I wish I could, but we're blocked in." He jerks a thumb over his shoulder, where the line of cars behind them is now backed up almost to the rotary.

Holly has been bent over her iPad, whacking away. Now she looks up. "Use the sidewalk," she says, then goes back to her magic tablet.

"There are mailboxes, Hollyberry," Jerome says. "Also a chainlink fence up ahead. I don't think there's room."

She takes another brief look. "Yeah there is. You may scrape a little, but it won't be the first time for this car. Go on."

"Who pays the fine if I get arrested on a charge of driving while black? You?"

Holly rolls her eyes. Jerome turns to Hodges, who sighs and nods. "She's right. There's room. I'll pay your fucking fine."

Jerome swings right. The Mercedes clips the fender of the car stopped ahead of them, then bumps up onto the sidewalk. Here comes the first mailbox. Jerome swings even farther to the right, now entirely off the street. There's a thud as the driver's side knocks the mailbox off its post, then a drawn- out squall as the passenger side caresses the chainlink fence. A woman in shorts and a halter top is mowing her lawn. She shouts at them as the passenger side of Holly's German U-boat peels away a sign reading NO TRESPASSING NO SOLICIT- ING NO DOOR TO DOOR SALESMEN. She rushes for her driveway, still shouting. Then she just peers, shading her eyes and squinting. Hodges can see her lips moving.

"Oh, goody," Jerome says. "She's getting your plate number."

"Just drive," Holly says. "Drive drive drive." And with no pause: "Red Lips is Morris Bellamy. That's his name."

It's the flagger yelling at them now. The construction workers, who have been uncovering a sewer pipe running beneath the street, are staring. Some are laughing. One of them winks at Jerome and makes a bottle-tipping gesture. Then they are past. The Mercedes thumps back down to the street. With traffic bound for the North Side bottlenecked behind them, the street ahead is blessedly empty.

"I checked the city tax records," Holly says. "At the time John Rothstein was murdered in 1978, the taxes on 23 Sycamore Street were being paid by Anita Elaine Bellamy. I did a Google search for her name and came up with over fifty hits, she's sort of a famous academic, but only one hit that matters. Her son was tried and convicted of aggravated rape late that same year. Right here in the city. He got a life sentence. There's a picture of him in one of the news stories. Look." She hands the iPad to Hodges.

Morris Bellamy has been snapped coming down the steps of a courthouse Hodges remembers well, although it was replaced by the concrete monstrosity in Government Square fifteen years ago. Bellamy is flanked by a pair of detectives. Hodges recalls one of them, Paul Emerson. Good police, long retired. He's wearing a suit. So is the other detective, but that one has draped his coat over Bellamy's hands to hide the handcuffs he's wearing. Bellamy is also in a suit, which means the picture was taken either while the trial was ongoing, or just after the verdict was rendered. It's a black-and-white photo, which only makes the contrast between Bellamy's pale complexion and dark mouth more striking. He almost looks like he's wearing lipstick.

"That's got to be him," Holly says. "If you call the state prison, I'll bet you six thousand bucks that he's out."

"No bet," Hodges says. "How long to Sycamore Street, Jerome?"

"Ten minutes."

"Firm or optimistic?"

Reluctantly, Jerome replies, "Well . . . maybe a tad optimistic."

"Just do the best you can and try not to run anybody ov—"

Hodges's cell rings. It's Pete. He sounds out of breath.

"Have you called the police, Mr. Hodges?"

"No." Although they'll probably have the license plate of Holly's car by now, but he sees no reason to tell Pete that. The boy sounds more upset than ever. Almost crazed.

"You can't. No matter what. He's got my sister. He says if he doesn't get the notebooks, he'll kill her. I'm going to give them to him."

"Pete, don't—"

But he's talking to no one. Pete has broken the connection.

46

Morris hustles Tina along the path. At one point a jutting branch rips her filmy blouse and scratches her arm, bringing blood.

"Don't make me go so fast, mister! I'll fall down!"

Morris whacks the back of her head above her ponytail. "Save your breath, bitch. Just be grateful I'm not making you run."

He holds on to her shoulders as they cross the stream, balancing her so she won't fall in, and when they reach the point where the scrub brush and stunted trees give way to the Rec property, he tells her to stop.

The baseball field is deserted, but a few boys are on the cracked asphalt of the basketball court. They're stripped to the waist, their shoulders gleaming. The day is really too hot for outside games, which is why Morris supposes there are only a few of them.

He unties Tina's hands. She gives a little whimper of relief and starts rubbing her wrists, which are crisscrossed with deep red grooves.

"We're going to walk along the edge of the trees," he tells her. "The only time those boys will be able to get a good look at us is when we get near the building and come out of the shade. If they say hello, or if there's someone you know, just wave and smile and keep walking. Do you understand?"

"Y-Yes."

"If you scream or yell for help, I'll put a bullet in your head. Do you understand *that*?"

"*Yes*. Did you shoot my mother? You did, didn't you?"

"Of course not, just fired one into the ceiling to settle her down. She's fine and you will be, too, if you do as you're told. Get moving."

They walk in the shade, the uncut grass of right field whickering against Morris's trousers and Tina's jeans. The boys are totally absorbed in their game and don't even look around, although if they had, Tina's bright yellow blouse would have stood out against the green trees like a warning flag.

When they reach the back of the Rec, Morris guides her past his old pal's Subaru, keeping a close eye on the boys as he does so. Once the brick flank of the building hides the two of them from the basketball court, he ties Tina's hands behind her again. No sense taking chances with Birch Street so close. Lots of houses on Birch Street.

He sees Tina draw in a deep breath and grabs her shoulder. "Don't yell, girlfriend. Open your mouth and I'll beat it off you."

"Please don't hurt me," Tina whispers. "I'll do whatever you want."

Morris nods, satisfied. It's a wise-con response if he ever heard one.

"See that basement window? The one that's open? Lie down, turn over on your belly, and drop through."

Tina squats and peers into the shadows. Then she turns her bloody swollen face up to him. "It's too far! I'll fall!"

Exasperated, Morris kicks her in the shoulder. She cries out. He bends over and places the muzzle of the automatic against her temple.

"You said you'd do whatever I wanted, and that's what I want. Get through that window right now, or I'll put a bullet in your tiny brat brain."

Morris wonders if he means it. He decides he does. Little girls also don't mean shit.

Weeping, Tina squirms through the window. She hesitates, half in and half out, looking at Morris with pleading eyes. He draws his foot back to kick her in the face and help her along. She drops, then yells in spite of Morris's explicit instructions not to.

"My ankle! I think I broke my ankle!"

Morris doesn't give a fuck about her ankle. He takes a quick look around to make sure he's still unobserved, then slides through the window and into the basement of the Birch Street Rec, landing on the closed carton he used for a step last time. The thief's sister must have landed on it wrong and tumbled to the floor. Her foot is twisted sideways and already beginning to swell. To Morris Bellamy, that doesn't mean shit, either.

47

Mr. Hodges has a thousand questions, but Pete has no time to answer any of them. He ends the call and sprints down Sycamore Street to his house. He has decided getting Tina's old wagon will take too long; he'll figure out some other way to transport the notebooks when he gets to the Rec. All he really needs is the key to the building.

He runs into his father's office to grab it and stops cold. His mother is on the floor beside the desk, her blue eyes shining from a mask of blood. There's more blood on his dad's open laptop, on the front of her dress, spattered on the desk chair and the window behind her. Music is tinkling from the computer, and even in his distress, he recognizes the tune. She was playing solitaire. Just playing solitaire and waiting for her kid to come home and bothering no one.

"*Mom!*" He runs to her, crying.

"My head," she says. "Look at my head."

He bends over her, parts bloody clumps of hair, trying to be gentle, and sees a trench running from her temple to the back of her head. At one point, halfway along the trench, he can see bleary gray-white. It's her skull, he thinks. That's bad, but at least it's not her brains, please God no, brains are soft, brains would be leaking. It's just her skull.

"A man came," she says, speaking with great effort. "He . . . took . . . Tina. I heard her cry out. You have to . . . oh Jesus Christ, how my head *rings*."

Pete hesitates for one endless second, wavering between his need to help his mother and his need to protect his sister, to get her back. If only this *was* a nightmare, he thinks. If only I could wake up.

Mom first. Mom right now.

He grabs the phone off his father's desk. "Be quiet, Mom. Don't say anything else, and don't move."

She closes her eyes wearily. "Did he come for the money? Did that man come for the money you found?"

"No, for what was with it," Pete says, and punches in three numbers he learned in grade school.

"Nine-one-one," a woman says. "What is your emergency?"

"My mom's been shot," Pete says. "Twenty-three Sycamore Street. Send an ambulance, right now. She's bleeding like crazy."

"What is your name, si—"

Pete hangs up. "Mom, I have to go. I have to get Tina back."

"Don't . . . be hurt." She's slurring now. Her eyes are still shut and he sees with horror that there's even blood in her eyelashes. This is his fault, all his fault. "Don't let . . . Tina be . . . hur . . ."

She falls silent, but she's breathing. Oh God, please let her keep breathing.

Pete takes the key to the Birch Street Rec's front door from his father's real estate properties board.

"You'll be okay, Mom. The ambulance will come. Some friends will come, too."

He starts for the door, then an idea strikes him and he turns back. "Mom?"

"Whaa . . ."

"Does Dad still smoke?"

Without opening her eyes, she says, "He thinks . . . I don't . . . know."

Quickly—he has to be gone before Hodges gets here and tries to stop him from doing what he has to do—Pete begins to search the drawers of his father's desk.

Just in case, he thinks.

Just in case.

48

The back gate is ajar. Pete doesn't notice. He pelts down the path. As he nears the stream, he passes a scrap of filmy yellow cloth hanging from a branch jutting out into the path. He reaches the stream and turns to look, almost without realizing it, at the spot where the trunk is buried. The trunk that caused all this horror.

When he reaches the stepping-stones at the bottom of the bank, Pete suddenly stops. His eyes widen. His legs go rubbery and loose. He sits down hard, staring at the foaming, shallow water that he has crossed so many times, often with his little sister babbling away about whatever interested her at the time. Mrs. Beasley. SpongeBob. Her friend Ellen. Her favorite lunchbox.

Her favorite clothes.

The filmy yellow blouse with the billowing sleeves, for instance. Mom tells her she shouldn't wear it so often, because it has to be dry-cleaned. Was Teens wearing it this morning when she left for school? That seems like a century ago, but he thinks . . .

He thinks she was.

I'm taking her to a safe place, Red Lips had said. *A place where we can meet, once you have the notebooks.*

Can it be?

Of course it can. If Red Lips grew up in Pete's house, he would have spent time at the Rec. All the kids in the neighborhood spent time there, until it closed. And he must have known about the path, because the trunk was buried less than twenty paces from where it crossed the stream.

But he doesn't know about the notebooks, Pete thinks. Not yet.

Unless he found out since the last call, that is. If so, he will have taken them already. He'll be gone. That would be okay if he's left Tina alive. And why wouldn't he? What reason would he have to kill her once he has what he wants?

For revenge, Pete thinks coldly. To get back at me. I'm the thief who took the notebooks, I hit him with a bottle and got away at the bookstore, and I deserve to be punished.

He gets up and staggers as a wave of lightheadedness rushes through him. When it passes, he crosses the creek. On the other side, he begins to run again.

49

The front door of 23 Sycamore is standing open. Hodges is out of the Mercedes before Jerome has brought it fully to a stop. He runs inside, one hand in his pocket, gripping the Happy Slapper. He hears tinkly music he knows well from hours spent playing computer solitaire.

He follows the sound and finds a woman sitting—*sprawling*—beside a desk in an alcove that has been set up as an office. One side of her face is swollen and drenched in blood. She looks at him, trying to focus.

"Pete," she says, and then, "He took Tina."

Hodges kneels and carefully parts the woman's hair. What he sees is bad, but nowhere near as bad as it could be; this woman has won the only lottery that really matters. The bullet put a groove six inches long in her scalp, has actually exposed her skull in one place, but a scalp wound isn't going to kill her. She's lost a lot of blood, though, and is suffering from both shock and concussion. This is no time to question her, but he has to. Morris Bellamy is laying down a trail of violence, and Hodges is still at the wrong end of it.

"Holly. Call an ambulance."

"Pete . . . already did," Linda says, and as if her weak voice has conjured it, they hear a siren. It's still distant but approaching fast. "Before . . . he left."

"Mrs. Saubers, did Pete take Tina? Is that what you're saying?"

"No. *He*. The man."

"Did he have red lips, Mrs. Saubers?" Holly asks. "Did the man who took Tina have red lips?"

"Irish . . . lips," she says. "But not . . . a redhead. White. He was old. Am I going to die?"

"No," Hodges says. "Help is on the way. But you have to help us. Do you know where Peter went?"

"Out . . . back. Through the gate. Saw him."

Jerome looks out the window and sees the gate standing ajar. "What's back there?"

"A path," she says wearily. "The kids used it . . . to go to the Rec. Before it closed. He took . . . I think he took the key."

"Pete did?"

"Yes . . ." Her eyes move to a board with a great many keys hung on it. One hook is empty. The DymoTape beneath it reads BIRCH ST. REC.

Hodges comes to a decision. "Jerome, you're with me. Holly, stay with Mrs. Saubers. Get a cold cloth to put on the side of her head." He draws in breath. "But before you do that, call the police. Ask for my old partner. Huntley."

He expects an argument, but Holly just nods and picks up the phone.

"He took his father's lighter, too," Linda says. She seems a little more with it now. "I don't know why he would do that. And the can of Ronson's."

Jerome looks a question at Hodges, who says: "It's lighter fluid."

50

Pete keeps to the shade of the trees, just as Morris and Tina did, although the boys who were playing basketball have gone home to dinner and left the court deserted except for a few crows scavenging spilled potato chips. He sees a small car nestled in the loading dock. Hidden there, actually, and the vanity license plate is enough to cause any doubts Pete might have had to disappear. Red Lips is here, all right, and he can't have taken Tina in by the front. That door faces the street, which is apt to be fairly busy at this time of day, and besides, he has no key.

Pete passes the car, and at the corner of the building, he drops to his knees and peers around. One of the basement windows is open. The grass and weeds that were growing in front of it have been beaten down. He hears a man's voice. They're down there, all right. So are the notebooks. The only question is whether or not Red Lips has found them yet.

Pete withdraws and leans against the sunwarmed brick, wondering what to do next. Think, he tells himself. You got Tina into this and you need to get her out of it, so *think*, goddam you!

Only he can't. His mind is full of white noise.

In one of his few interviews, the ever-irritable John Rothstein expressed his disgust with the where-do-you-get-your-ideas question. Story ideas came from nowhere, he proclaimed. They arrived without the polluting influence of the author's intellect. The idea that comes to Pete now also seems to arrive from nowhere. It's both horrible and horribly attractive. It won't work if Red Lips has already discovered the notebooks, but if that is the case, *nothing* will work.

Pete gets up and circles the big brick cube the other way, once more passing the green car with its tattletale license plate. He stops at the front right corner of the abandoned brick box, looking at the going-home traffic on Birch Street. It's like peering through a window and into a different world, one where things are normal. He takes a quick inventory: cell phone, cigarette lighter, can of lighter fluid. The can was in the bottom desk drawer with his father's Zippo. The can is only half full, based on the slosh when he shakes it, but half full will be more than enough.

He goes around the corner, now in full view of Birch Street, trying to walk normally and hoping that no one—Mr. Evans, his old Little League coach, for instance—will hail him.

No one does. This time he knows which of the two keys to use, and this time it turns easily in the lock. He opens the door slowly, steps into the foyer, and eases the door closed. It's musty and brutally hot in here. For Tina's sake, he hopes it's cooler in the basement. How scared she must be, he thinks.

If she's still alive to feel anything, an evil voice whispers back. Red Lips could have been standing over her dead body and talking to himself. He's crazy, and that's what crazy people do.

On Pete's left, a flight of stairs leads up to the second floor, which consists of a single large space running the length of the building. The official name was The North Side Community Room, but the kids had a different name for it, one Red Lips probably remembers.

As Pete sits on the stairs to take off his shoes (he can't be heard clacking and echoing across the floor), he thinks again, I got her into this, it's my job to get her out. Nobody else's.

He calls his sister's cell. From below him, muffled but unmistakable, he hears Tina's Snow Patrol ringtone.

Red Lips answers immediately. "Hello, Peter." He sounds calmer now. In control. That could be good or bad for his plan. Pete can't tell which. "Have you got the notebooks?"

"Yes. Is my sister okay?"

"She's fine. Where are you?"

"That's pretty funny," Pete says . . . and when you think about it, it actually is. "Jimmy Gold would like it, I bet."

"I'm in no mood for cryptic humor. Let us do our business and be done with each other, shall we? Where are you?"

"Do you remember the Saturday Movie Palace?"

"What are you—"

Red Lips stops. Thinks.

"Are you talking about the Community Room, where they

used to show all those corny . . ." He pauses again as the penny drops. "You're *here*?"

"Yes. And you're in the basement. I saw the car out back. You were maybe ninety feet from the notebooks all along." Even closer than that, Pete thinks. "Come and get them."

He ends the call before Red Lips can try to set the terms more to his liking. Pete runs for the kitchen on tiptoe, shoes in hand. He has to get out of sight before Red Lips can climb the stairs from the basement. If he does that, all may be well. If he doesn't, he and his sister will probably die together.

From downstairs, louder than her ringtone—*much* louder— he hears Tina cry out in pain.

Still alive, Pete thinks, and then, The bastard hurt her. Only that's not the truth.

I did it. This is all my fault. Mine, mine, mine.

51

Morris, sitting on a box marked **KITCHEN SUPPLIES**, closes Tina's phone and at first only looks at it. There's but one question on the floor, really; just one that needs to be answered. Is the boy telling the truth, or is he lying?

Morris thinks he's telling the truth. They both grew up on Sycamore Street, after all, and they both attended Saturday movie-shows upstairs, sitting on folding chairs and eating popcorn sold by the local Girl Scout troop. It's logical to think they would both choose this nearby abandoned building as a place to hide, one close to both the house they had shared and the buried trunk. The clincher is the sign Morris saw out front, on his first reconnaissance: CALL THOMAS SAUBERS REAL ESTATE. If Peter's father is the selling agent, the boy could easily have filched a key.

He seizes Tina by the arm and drags her across to the furnace, a huge and dusty relic crouched in the corner. She lets out another of those annoying cries as she tries to put weight on her swollen ankle and it buckles under her. He slaps her again.

"Shut up," he says. "Stop being such a whiny bitch."

There isn't enough computer cord to make sure she stays in one place, but there's a cage-light hanging on the wall with several yards of orange electrical cord looped around it. Morris doesn't need the light, but the cord is a gift from God. He didn't think he could be any angrier with the thief, but he was wrong. *Jimmy Gold would like it, I bet,* the thief had said, and what right did he have to reference John Rothstein's work? Rothstein's work was *his*.

"Turn around."

Tina doesn't move quickly enough to suit Morris, who is still furious with her brother. He grabs her shoulders and whirls her. Tina doesn't cry out this time, but a groan escapes her tightly compressed lips. Her beloved yellow blouse is now smeared with basement dirt.

He secures the orange electrical cord to the computer cord binding her wrists, then throws the cage-light over one of the furnace pipes. He pulls the cord taut, eliciting another groan from the girl as her bound hands are jerked up almost to her shoulder blades.

Morris ties off the new cord with a double knot, thinking, *They were here all along,* and he thinks that's *funny*? If he wants funny, I'll give him all the funny he can stand. He can die laughing.

He bends down, hands on knees, so he's eye to eye with the thief's sister. "I'm going upstairs to get my property, girlfriend. Also to kill your pain-in-the-ass brother. Then I'm going to come back down and kill you." He kisses the tip of her nose. "Your life is over. I want you to think about that while I'm gone."

He trots toward the stairs.

52

Pete is in the pantry. The door is only open a crack, but that's enough to see Red Lips as he goes hustling by, the little red and black gun in one hand, Tina's phone in the other. Pete listens to the echo of his footfalls as they cross the empty downstairs rooms, and as soon as they become the *thud-thud-thud* of feet climbing the stairs to what was once known as the Saturday Movie Palace, he pelts for the stairs to the basement. He drops his shoes on the way. He wants his hands free. He also wants Red Lips to know exactly where he went. Maybe it will slow him down.

Tina's eyes widen when she sees him. "Pete! *Get me out of here!*"

He goes to her and looks at the tangle of knots—white cord, orange cord—that binds her hands behind her and also to the furnace. The knots are tight, and he feels a wave of despair as he looks at them. He loosens one of the orange knots, allowing her hands to drop a little and taking some of the pressure off her shoulders. As he starts work on the second, his cell phone vibrates. The wolf has found nothing upstairs and is calling back. Instead of answering, Pete hurries to the box below the window. His printing is on the side: **KITCHEN SUPPLIES**. He can see footprints on top, and knows to whom they belong.

"What are you *doing*?" Tina says. "Untie me!"

But getting her free is only part of the problem. Getting her out is the rest of it, and Pete doesn't think there's enough time to do both before Red Lips comes back. He has seen his sister's ankle, now so swollen it hardly looks like an ankle at all.

Red Lips is no longer bothering with Tina's phone. He yells from upstairs. *Screams* from upstairs. "*Where are you, you fucking son of a whore?*"

Two little piggies in the basement and the big bad wolf upstairs, Pete thinks. And us without a house made of straw, let alone one made of bricks.

He carries the carton Red Lips used as a step to the middle of the room and pulls the folded flaps apart as footfalls race across the kitchen floor above them, pounding hard enough to make the old strips of insulation hanging between the beams sway a little. Tina's face is a mask of horror. Pete upends the carton, pouring out a flood of Moleskine notebooks.

"Pete! What are you doing? He's *coming*!"

Don't I know it, Pete thinks, and opens the second carton. As he adds the rest of the notebooks to the pile on the basement floor, the footfalls above stop. He's seen the shoes. Red Lips opens the door to the basement. Being cautious now. Trying to think it through.

"Peter? Are you visiting with your sister?"

"Yes," Peter calls back. "I'm visiting her with a gun in my hand."

"You know what?" the wolf says. "I don't believe that."

Pete unscrews the cap on the can of lighter fluid and upends it over the notebooks, dousing the jackstraw heap of stories, poems, and angry, half-drunk rants that often end in mid-thought. Also the two novels that complete the story of a fucked-up American named Jimmy Gold, stumbling through the sixties and looking for some kind of redemption. Looking for—in his own words—some kind of shit that means shit. Pete fumbles for the lighter, and at first it slips through his fingers. God, he can see the man's shadow up there now. Also the shadow of the gun.

Tina is saucer-eyed with terror, hogtied with her nose and lips slathered in blood. The bastard beat her, Pete thinks. Why did he do that? She's only a little kid.

But he knows. The sister was a semi-acceptable substitute for the one Red Lips *really* wants to beat.

"You *better* believe it," Pete says. "It's a forty-five, lots bigger than yours. It was in my father's desk. You better just go away. That would be the smart thing."

Please, God, *please*.

But Pete's voice wavers on the last words, rising to the uncertain treble of the thirteen-year-old boy who found these notebooks in the first place. Red Lips hears it, laughs, and starts down the stairs. Pete grabs the lighter again—tight, this time—and thumbs up the top as Red Lips comes fully into view. Pete flicks the spark wheel, realizing that he never checked to see if the lighter had fuel, an oversight that could end his life and that of his sister in the next ten seconds. But the spark produces a robust yellow flame.

Peter holds the lighter a foot above the pile of notebooks. "You're right," he says. "No gun. But I did find this in his desk."

53

Hodges and Jerome run across the baseball field. Jerome is pulling ahead, but Hodges isn't too far behind. Jerome stops at the edge of the sorry little basketball court and points to a green Subaru parked near the loading dock. Hodges reads the vanity license plate—BOOKS4U—and nods.

They have just started moving again when they hear a furious yell from inside: *"Where are you, you fucking son of a whore?"*

That's got to be Bellamy. The fucking son of a whore is undoubtedly Peter Saubers. The boy let himself in with his father's key, which means the front door is open. Hodges points to himself, then to the Rec. Jerome nods, but says in a low voice, "You have no gun."

"True enough, but my thoughts are pure and my strength is that of ten."

"Huh?"

"Stay here, Jerome. I mean it."

"You sure?"

"Yes. You don't happen to have a knife, do you? Even a pocketknife?"

"No. Sorry."

"All right, then look around. Find a bottle. There must be some, kids probably come back here to drink beer after dark. Break it and then slash you some tires. If this goes sideways, he's not using Halliday's car to get away."

Jerome's face says he doesn't much care for the possible implications of this order. He grips Hodges's arm. "No kamikaze runs, Bill, you hear me? Because you have nothing to make up for."

"I know."

The truth is he knows nothing of the kind. Four years ago, a woman he loved died in an explosion that was meant for him. There's not a day that goes by when he doesn't think of Janey, not a night when he doesn't lie in bed thinking, *If only I had been a little quicker. A little smarter.*

He hasn't been quick enough or smart enough this time, either, and telling himself that the situation developed too quickly isn't going to get those kids out of the potentially lethal jam they're in. All he knows for sure is that neither Tina nor her brother can die on his watch today. He'll do whatever he needs to in order to prevent that from happening.

He pats the side of Jerome's face. "Trust me, kiddo. I'll do my part. You just take care of those tires. You might yank some plug wires while you're at it."

Hodges starts away, looking back just once when he reaches the corner of the building. Jerome is watching him unhappily, but this time he's staying put. Which is good. The only thing worse than Bellamy killing Peter and Tina would be if he killed Jerome.

He goes around the corner and runs to the front of the building.

This door, like the one at 23 Sycamore Street, is standing open.

54

Red Lips is staring at the heap of Moleskine notebooks as if hypnotized. At last he raises his eyes to Pete. He also raises the gun.

"Go ahead," Pete says. "Do it and see what happens to the notebooks when I drop the lighter. I only got a chance to really douse the ones on top, but by now it'll be trickling down. And they're old. They'll go up fast. Then maybe the rest of the shit down here."

"So it's a Mexican standoff," Red Lips says. "The only problem with that, Peter—I'm speaking from your perspective now—is that my gun will last longer than your lighter. What are you going to do when it burns out?" He's trying to sound calm and in charge, but his eyes keep ping-ponging between the Zippo and the notebooks. The covers of the ones on top gleam wetly, like sealskin.

"I'll know when that's going to happen," Pete says. "The second the flame starts to go lower, and turns blue instead of yellow, I'll drop it. Then, *poof*."

"You won't." The wolf's upper lip rises, exposing those yellow teeth. Those fangs.

"Why not? They're just words. Compared to my sister, they don't mean shit."

"Really?" Red Lips turns the gun on Tina. "Then douse the lighter or I'll kill her right in front of you."

Painful hands squeeze Pete's heart at the sight of the gun pointing at his sister's midsection, but he doesn't close the

Zippo's cap. He bends over, very slowly lowering it toward the pile of notebooks. "There are two more Jimmy Gold novels in here. Did you know that?"

"You're lying." Red Lips is still pointing the gun at Tina, but his eyes have been drawn—helplessly, it seems—back toward the Moleskines again. "There's one. It's about him going west."

"Two," Pete says again. "*The Runner Goes West* is good, but *The Runner Raises the Flag* is the best thing he ever wrote. It's long, too. An epic. What a shame if you never get to read it."

A flush is climbing up the man's pale cheeks. "How dare you? How dare you *bait* me? I gave my *life* for those books! I *killed* for those books!"

"I know," Pete says. "And since you're such a fan, here's a little treat for you. In the last book, Jimmy meets Andrea Stone again. How about that?"

The wolf's eyes widen. "Andrea? He does? How? What happens?"

Under such circumstances the question is beyond bizarre, but it's also sincere. Honest. Pete realizes that the fictional Andrea, Jimmy's first love, is real to this man in a way Pete's sister is not. *No* human being is as real to Red Lips as Jimmy Gold, Andrea Stone, Mr. Meeker, Pierre Retonne (also known as The Car Salesman of Doom), and all the rest. This is surely a marker of true, deep insanity, but that must make Pete crazy, too, because he knows how this lunatic feels. Exactly how. He lit up with the same excitement, the same *amazement*, when Jimmy glimpsed Andrea in Grant Park, during the Chicago riots of 1968. Tears actually came to his eyes. Such tears, Pete realizes—yes, even now, *especially* now, because their lives hang upon it—mark the core power of make-believe. It's what caused thousands to weep when they learned that Charles Dickens had died of a stroke. It's why, for years, a stranger put a rose on Edgar Allan Poe's grave every January 19th, Poe's birthday. It's also what would make Pete hate this man even if he wasn't pointing a gun at his sister's trembling, vulnerable midsection. Red Lips took the life of a great writer, and why? Because Rothstein dared to follow a character who went in a direction Red Lips didn't like? Yes, that was it. He did it out of his own core belief: that the writing was somehow more important than the writer.

Slowly and deliberately, Pete shakes his head. "It's all in the notebooks. *The Runner Raises the Flag* fills sixteen of them. You could read it there, but you'll never hear any of it from me."

Pete actually smiles.

"No spoilers."

"The notebooks are mine, you bastard! *Mine!*"

"They're going to be ashes, if you don't let my sister go."

"Petie, I can't even *walk*!" Tina wails.

Pete can't afford to look at her, only at Red Lips. Only at the wolf. "What's your name? I think I deserve to know your name."

Red Lips shrugs, as if it no longer matters. "Morris Bellamy."

"Throw the gun away, Mr. Bellamy. Kick it along the floor and under the furnace. Once you do that, I'll close the lighter. I'll untie my sister and we'll go. I'll give you plenty of time to get away with the notebooks. All I want to do is take Tina home and get help for my mom."

"I'm supposed to trust you?" Red Lips sneers it.

Pete lowers the lighter farther. "Trust me or watch the notebooks burn. Make up your mind fast. I don't know the last time my dad filled this thing."

Something catches the corner of Pete's eye. Something moving on the stairs. He doesn't dare look. If he does, Red Lips will, too. *And I've almost got him,* Pete thinks.

This seems to be so. Red Lips starts to lower the gun. For a moment he looks every year of his age, and more. Then he raises the gun and points it at Tina again.

"I won't kill her." He speaks in the decisive tone of a general who has just made a crucial battlefield decision. "Not at first. I'll just shoot her in the leg. You can listen to her scream. If you light the notebooks on fire after that, I'll shoot her in the other leg. Then in the stomach. She'll die, but she'll have plenty of time to hate you first, if she doesn't alre—"

There's a flat double clap from Morris's left. It's Pete's shoes, landing at the foot of the stairs. Morris, on a hair trigger, wheels in that direction and fires. The gun is small, but in the enclosed space of the basement, the report is loud. Pete gives an involuntary jerk, and the lighter falls from his hand. There's an explosive *whump*, and notebooks on top of the pile suddenly grow a corona of fire.

"*No!*" Morris screams, wheeling away from Hodges even as Hodges comes pelting down the stairs so fast he can barely keep his balance. Morris has a clear shot at Pete. He raises the gun to take it, but before he can fire, Tina swings forward on her bonds and kicks him in the back of the leg with her good foot. The bullet goes between Pete's neck and shoulder.

The notebooks, meanwhile, are burning briskly.

Hodges closes with Morris before he can fire again, grabbing at Morris's gun hand. Hodges is the heavier of the two, and in better shape, but Morris Bellamy possesses the strength of insanity. They waltz drunkenly across the basement, Hodges holding Morris's right wrist so the little automatic points at the ceiling, Morris using his left hand to rip at Hodges's face, trying to claw out his eyes.

Peter races around the notebooks—they are blazing now, the lighter fluid that has trickled deep into the pile igniting—and grapples with Morris from behind. Morris turns his head, bares his teeth, and snaps at him. His eyes are rolling in their sockets.

"*His hand! Get his hand!*" Hodges shouts. They have stumbled under the stairs. Hodges's face is striped with blood, several pieces of his cheek hanging in strips. "Get it before he skins me alive!"

Pete grabs Bellamy's left hand. Behind them, Tina is screaming. Hodges pounds a fist into Bellamy's face twice: hard, pistoning blows. That seems to finish him; his face goes slack and his knees buckle. Tina is still screaming, and the basement is growing brighter.

"The roof, Petie! The roof is catching!"

Morris is on his knees, his head hanging, blood gushing from his chin, lips, and broken nose. Hodges grabs his right wrist and twists. There's a crack as Morris's wrist breaks, and the little automatic clatters to the floor. Hodges has a moment to think it's over before the bastard rams his free hand forward and upward, punching Hodges squarely in the balls and filling his belly with liquid pain. Morris scuttles between his spread legs. Hodges gasps, hands pressed to his throbbing crotch.

"Petie, Petie, the ceiling!"

Pete thinks Bellamy is going after the gun, but the man ignores it entirely. His goal is the notebooks. They are now a bonfire, the covers curling back, the pages browning and sending up sparks that have ignited several strips of hanging insulation. The fire begins spreading above them, dropping burning streamers. One of these lands on Tina's head, and there's a stench of frying hair to go with the smell of the burning paper and insulation. She shakes it away with a cry of pain.

Pete runs to her, punting the little automatic deep into the basement as he goes. He beats at her smoldering hair and then begins struggling with the knots.

"No!" Morris screams, but not at Pete. He goes to his knees in front of the notebooks like a religious zealot in front of a blazing altar. He reaches into the flames, trying to push the pile apart. This sends fresh clouds of sparks spiraling upward. *"No no no no!"*

Hodges wants to run to Peter and his sister, but the best he can manage is a drunken shamble. The pain in his groin is spreading down his legs, loosening the muscles he has worked so hard to build up. Nevertheless, he gets to work on one of the knots in the orange electrical cord. He again wishes for a knife, but it would take a cleaver to cut this stuff. The shit is *thick*.

More blazing strips of insulation fall around them. Hodges bats them away from the girl, terrified that her gauzy blouse will catch fire. The knot is letting go, finally letting go, but the girl is struggling—

"Stop, Teens," Pete says. Sweat is pouring down his face. The basement is getting hot. "They're slipknots, you're pulling them tight again, you have to stop."

Morris's screams are changing into howls of pain. Hodges has no time to look at him. The loop he's pulling on abruptly loosens. He pulls Tina away from the furnace, her hands still tied behind her.

There's going to be no exit by way of the stairs; the lower ones are burning and the upper ones are catching. The tables, the chairs, the boxes of stored paperwork: all on fire. Morris Bellamy is also on fire. Both his sportcoat and the shirt beneath are blazing. Yet he continues to root his way into the bonfire, trying to get at any unburned notebooks still left at the bottom. His fingers are turning black. Although the pain must be excruciating, he keeps going. Hodges has time to think of the fairy tale where the wolf came down the chimney and landed in a pot of boiling water. His daughter, Alison, didn't want to hear that one. She said it was too sca—

"Bill! Bill! Over here!"

Hodges sees Jerome at one of the basement windows. Hodges remembers saying *Neither one of you minds worth a tinker's dam*, and now he's delighted that they don't. Jerome is on his belly, sticking his arms through and down.

"Lift her! Lift her up! Quick, before you all cook!"

It's mostly Pete who carries Tina across to the basement window, through the falling sparks and burning scarves of insulation. One lands on the kid's back, and Hodges swipes it away. Pete lifts her. Jerome grabs her under the arms and hauls her out, the plug of the computer cord Morris used to tie her hands trailing and bumping behind.

"Now you," Hodges gasps.

Pete shakes his head. "You first." He looks up at Jerome. "You pull. I'll push."

"Okay," Jerome says. "Lift your arms, Bill."

There's no time to argue. Hodges lifts his arms and feels them grabbed. He has time to think, Feels like wearing hand-cuffs, and then he's being hoisted. It's slow at first—he's a lot heavier than the girl—but then two hands plant themselves firmly on his ass and shove. He rises into clear, clean air—hot, but cooler than the basement—and lands next to Tina Saubers. Jerome reaches through again. "Come on, kid! Move it!"

Pete lifts his arms, and Jerome seizes his wrists. The basement is filling with smoke and Pete begins coughing, almost retching, as he uses his feet to pedal his way up the wall. He slides through the window, turns over, and peers back into the basement.

A charred scarecrow kneels in there, digging into the burning notebooks with arms made of fire. Morris's face is melting. He shrieks and begins hugging the blazing, dissolving remnants of Rothstein's work to his burning chest.

"Don't look at that, kid," Hodges says, putting a hand on his shoulder. "Don't."

But Pete wants to look. Needs to look.

He thinks, That could have been me on fire.

He thinks, No. Because I know the difference. I know what matters.

He thinks, Please God, if you're there . . . let that be true.

55

Pete lets Jerome carry Tina as far as the baseball field, then says, "Give her to me, please."

Jerome surveys him—Pete's pale, shocked face, the one blistered ear, the holes charred in his shirt. "You sure?"

"Yeah."

Tina is already holding out her arms. She has been quiet since being hauled from the burning basement, but when Pete takes her, she puts her arms around his neck, her face against his shoulder, and begins to cry loudly.

Holly comes running down the path. "Thank God!" she says. "There you are! Where's Bellamy?"

"Back there, in the basement," Hodges says. "And if he isn't dead yet, he wishes he was. Have you got your cell phone? Call the fire department."

"Is our mother okay?" Pete asks.

"I think she's going to be fine," Holly says, pulling her phone off her belt. "The ambulance is taking her to Kiner Memorial. She was alert and talking. The paramedics said her vital signs are good."

"Thank God," Pete says. Now he also starts to cry, the tears cutting clean tracks through the smears of soot on his cheeks. "If she died, I'd kill myself. Because this is all my fault."

"No," Hodges says.

Pete looks at him. Tina is looking, too, her arms still linked around her brother's neck.

"You found the notebooks and the money, didn't you?"

"Yes. By accident. They were buried in a trunk by the stream."

"Anyone would have done what you did," Jerome says. "Isn't that right, Bill?"

"Yes," Bill says. "For your family, you do all that you can. The way you went after Bellamy when he took Tina."

"I wish I'd never found that trunk," Pete says. What he doesn't say, will never say, is how much it hurts to know that the notebooks are gone. Knowing that burns like fire. He does understand how Morris felt, and that burns like fire, too. "I wish it had stayed buried."

"Wish in one hand," Hodges says, "spit in the other. Let's go. I need to use an icepack before the swelling gets too bad."

"Swelling where?" Holly asks. "You look okay to me."

Hodges puts an arm around her shoulders. Sometimes Holly stiffens when he does this, but not today, so he kisses her cheek, too. It raises a doubtful smile.

"Did he get you where it hurts boys?"

"Yes. Now hush."

They walk slowly, partly for Hodges's benefit, partly for Pete's. His sister is getting heavy, but he doesn't want to put her down. He wants to carry her all the way home.

AFTER

PICNIC

On the Friday that kicks off the Labor Day weekend, a Jeep Wrangler—getting on in years but loved by its owner—pulls into the parking lot above the McGinnis Park Little League fields and stops next to a blue Mercedes that is also getting on in years. Jerome Robinson makes his way down the grassy slope toward a picnic table where food has already been set out: A paper bag swings from one of his hands.

"Yo, Hollyberry!"

She turns. "How many times have I told you not to call me that? A hundred? A thousand?" But she's smiling as she says it, and when he hugs her, she hugs back. Jerome doesn't press his luck; he gives one good squeeze, then asks what's for lunch.

"There's chicken salad, tuna salad, and coleslaw. I also brought a roast beef sandwich. That's for you, if you want it. I'm off red meat. It upsets my circadian rhythms."

"I'll make sure you're not tempted, then."

They sit down. Holly pours Snapple into Dixie cups. They toast the end of summer and then munch away, gabbing about movies and TV shows, temporarily avoiding the reason they're here—this is goodbye, at least for awhile.

"Too bad Bill couldn't come," Jerome says as Holly hands him a piece of chocolate cream pie. "Remember when we all got together here for a picnic after his hearing? To celebrate that judge deciding not to put him in jail?"

"I remember perfectly well," Holly says. "You wanted to ride the bus."

"Because de bus be fo' free!" Tyrone Feelgood exclaims. "I takes all the fo' free I kin git, Miss Holly!"

"You've worn that out, Jerome."

He sighs. "I sort of have, I guess."

"Bill got a call from Peter Saubers," Holly said. "That's why he didn't come. He said I was to give you his best, and that he'd see you before you went back to Cambridge. Wipe your nose. There's a dab of chocolate on it."

Jerome resists the urge to say *Chocolate be mah favorite cullah!* "Is Pete all right?"

"Yes. He had some good news that he wanted to share with Bill in person. I can't finish my pie. Do you want the rest? Unless you don't want to eat after me. I'm okay with that, but I don't have a cold, or anything."

"I'd even use your toothbrush," Jerome says, "but I'm full."

"Oough," Holly says. "I'd never use another person's toothbrush." She collects their paper cups and plates and takes them to a nearby litter barrel.

"What time are you leaving tomorrow?" Jerome asks.

"The sun rises at six fifty-five AM. I expect to be on the road by seven thirty, at the latest."

Holly is driving to Cincinnati to see her mother. By herself. Jerome can hardly believe it. He's glad for her, but he's also afraid for her. What if something goes wrong and she freaks out?

"Stop worrying," she says, coming back and sitting down. "I'll be fine. All turnpikes, no night driving, and the forecast is for clear weather. Also, I have my three favorite movie soundtracks on CD: *Road to Perdition*, *The Shawshank Redemption*, and *Godfather II*. Which is the best, in my opinion, although Thomas Newman is, on the whole, much better than Nino Rota. Thomas Newman's music is *mysterious*."

"John Williams, *Schindler's List*," Jerome says. "Nothing tops it."

"Jerome, I don't want to say you're full of shit, but . . . actually, you are."

He laughs, delighted.

"I have my cell phone and iPad, both fully charged. The Mercedes just had its full maintenance check. And really, it's only four hundred miles."

"Cool. But call me if you need to. Me or Bill."

"Of course. When are you leaving for Cambridge?"

"Next week."

"Done on the docks?"

"All done, and glad of it. Physical labor may be good for the body, but I don't feel that it ennobles the soul."

Holly still has trouble meeting the eyes of even her close friends, but she makes an effort and meets Jerome's. "Pete's all right, Tina's all right, and their mother is back on her feet. That's all good, but is *Bill* all right? Tell me the truth."

"I don't know what you mean." Now it's Jerome who finds it difficult to maintain eye contact.

"He's too thin, for one thing. He's taken the exercise-and-salads regimen too far. But that's not what I'm really worried about."

"What is?" But Jerome knows, and isn't surprised *she* knows, although Bill thinks he's kept it from her. Holly has her ways.

She lowers her voice as if afraid of being overheard, although there's no one within a hundred yards in any direction. "How often does he visit him?"

Jerome doesn't have to ask who she's talking about. "I don't really know."

"More than once a month?"

"I think so, yes."

"Once a week?"

"Probably not that often." Although who can say?

"*Why?* He's . . ." Holly's lips are trembling. "Brady Harts-field is next door to a *vegetable*!"

"You can't blame yourself for that, Holly. You absolutely can't. You hit him because he was going to blow up a couple of thousand kids."

He tries to touch her hand, but she snatches it away.

"I *don't*! I'd do it again! Again again again! But I hate to think of Bill obsessing about him. I know from obsession, and it's *not nice*!"

She crosses her arms over her bosom, an old self-comforting gesture that she has largely given up.

"I don't think it's obsession, exactly." Jerome speaks cautiously, feeling his way. "I don't think it's about the past."

"What else can it be? Because that monster has no future!"

Bill's not so sure, Jerome thinks, but would never say. Holly is better, but she's still fragile. And, as she herself said, she knows from obsession. Besides, he has no idea what Bill's continuing interest in Brady means. All he has is a feeling. A hunch.

"Let it rest," he says. This time when he puts his hand over hers she allows it to stay, and they talk of other things for awhile. Then he looks at his watch. "I have to go. I promised to pick up Barbara and Tina at the roller rink."

"Tina's in love with you," Holly says matter-of-factly as they walk up the slope to their cars.

"If she is, it'll pass," he says. "I'm heading east, and pretty soon some cute boy will appear in her life. She'll write his name on her book covers."

"I suppose," Holly says. "That's usually how it works, isn't it? I just don't want you to make fun of her. She'd think you were being mean, and feel sad."

"I won't," Jerome says.

They have reached the cars, and once more Holly forces herself to look him full in the face. "*I'm* not in love with you, not the way she is, but I love you quite a lot, just the same. So take care of yourself, Jerome. Some college boys do foolish things. Don't be one of them."

This time it's she who embraces him.

"Oh, hey, I almost forgot," Jerome says. "I brought you a little present. It's a shirt, although I don't think you'll want to wear it when you visit your mom."

He hands her his bag. She takes out the bright red tee and unfolds it. Printed on the front, in black, it shouts:

SHIT DON'T MEAN SHIT
Jimmy Gold

"They sell them at the City College bookstore. I got it in an XL, in case you want to wear it as a nightshirt." He studies her face as she considers the words on the front of the tee. "Of course, you can also return it for something else, if you don't like it."

"I like it very much," she says, and breaks into a smile. It's the one Hodges loves, the one that makes her beautiful. "And I *will* wear it when I visit my mother. Just to piss her off."

Jerome looks so surprised that she laughs.

"Don't you ever want to piss your mother off?"

"From time to time. And Holly . . . I love you, too. You know that, right?"

"I do," she says, holding the shirt to her chest. "And I'm glad. That shit means a lot."

TRUNK

Hodges walks the path through the undeveloped land from the Birch Street end, and finds Pete sitting on the bank of the stream with his knees hugged to his chest. Nearby, a scrubby tree juts over the water, which is down to a trickle after a long, hot summer. Below the tree, the hole where the trunk was buried has been reexcavated. The trunk itself is sitting aslant on the bank nearby. It looks old and tired and rather ominous, a time traveler from a year when disco was still in bloom. A photographer's tripod stands nearby. There are also a couple of bags that look like the kind pros carry when they travel.

"The famous trunk," Hodges says, sitting down next to Pete.

Pete nods. "Yeah. The famous trunk. The picture guy and his assistant have gone to lunch, but I think they'll be back pretty soon. Didn't seem crazy about any of the local restaurant choices. They're from New York." He shrugs, as if that explains everything. "At first the guy wanted me sitting on it, with my chin on my fist. You know, like that famous statue. I talked him out of it, but it wasn't easy."

"This is for the local paper?"

Pete shakes his head, starting to smile. "That's my good news, Mr. Hodges. It's for *The New Yorker*. They want an article about what happened. Not a little one, either. They want it for what they call 'the well,' which means the middle of the magazine. A really big piece, maybe the biggest they've ever done."

"That's great!"

"It will be if I don't fuck it up."

Hodges studies him for a moment. "Wait. *You're* going to write it?"

"Yeah. At first they wanted to send out one of their writers—George Packer, he's a really good one—to interview me and write the story. It's a big deal because John Rothstein was one of their fiction stars in the old days, right up there with John Updike, Shirley Jackson . . . you know the ones I mean."

Hodges doesn't, but he nods.

"Rothstein was sort of the go-to guy for teenage angst, and then middle-class angst. Sort of like John Cheever. I'm reading Cheever now. Do you know his story 'The Swimmer'?"

Hodges shakes his head.

"You should. It's awesome. Anyhow, they want the story of the notebooks. The whole thing, from beginning to end. This was after they had three or four handwriting analysts check out the photocopies I made, and the fragments."

Hodges *does* know about the fragments. There were enough charred scraps in the burned-out basement to validate Pete's claim that the lost notebooks really had been Rothstein's work. Police backtrailing Morris Bellamy had further buttressed Pete's story. Which Hodges never doubted in the first place.

"You said no to Packer, I take it."

"I said no to *anyone*. If the story's going to get written, I have to be the one to do it. Not just because I was there, but because reading John Rothstein changed my . . ."

He stops and shakes his head.

"No. I was going to say his work changed my life, but that's not right. I don't think a teenager has much of a life to change. I just turned eighteen last month. I guess what I mean is his work changed my *heart*."

Hodges smiles. "I get that."

"The editor in charge of the story said I was too young—better than saying I had no talent, right?—so I sent him writing samples. That helped. Also, I stood up to him. It wasn't all that hard. Negotiating with a magazine guy from New York didn't seem like such a big deal after facing Bellamy. *That* was a negotiation."

Pete shrugs.

"They'll edit it the way they want, of course, I've read enough to know the process, and I'm okay with that. But if they want to publish it, it'll be my name over my story."

"Tough stance, Pete."

He stares at the trunk, for a moment looking much older than eighteen. "It's a tough world. I found that out after my dad got run down at City Center."

No reply seems adequate, so Hodges keeps silent.

"You know what they want most at *The New Yorker*, right?"

Hodges didn't spend almost thirty years as a detective for nothing. "A summary of the last two books would be my guess. Jimmy Gold and his sister and all his friends. Who did what to who, and how, and when, and how it all came out in the wash."

"Yeah. And I'm the only one who knows those things. Which brings me to the apology part." He looks at Hodges solemnly.

"Pete, no apology's necessary. There are no legal charges against you, and I'm not bearing even a teensy grudge about anything. Holly and Jerome aren't, either. We're just glad your mom and sis are okay."

"They almost weren't. If I hadn't stonewalled you that day in the car, then ducked out through the drugstore, I bet Bellamy never would have come to the house. Tina still has nightmares."

"Does she blame you for them?"

"Actually . . . no."

"Well, there you are," Hodges says. "You were under the gun. Literally as well as figuratively. Halliday scared the hell out of you, and you had no way of knowing he was dead when you went to his shop that day. As for Bellamy, you didn't even know he was still alive, let alone out of prison."

"That's all true, but Halliday threatening me wasn't the only reason I wouldn't talk to you. I still thought I had a chance to keep the notebooks, see? *That's* why I wouldn't talk to you. And why I ran away. I wanted to keep them. It wasn't the top thing on my mind, but it was there underneath, all right. Those notebooks . . . well . . . and I have to say this in the piece I write for *The New Yorker* . . . they cast a spell over me. I need to apologize because I really wasn't so different from Morris Bellamy."

Hodges takes Pete by the shoulders and looks directly into his eyes. "If that were true, you never would have gone to the Rec prepared to burn them."

"I dropped the lighter by accident," Pete says quietly. "The gunshot startled me. I *think* I would have done it anyway—if he'd shot Tina—but I'll never know for sure."

"*I* know," Hodges says. "And I'm sure enough for both of us."

"Yeah?"

"Yeah. So how much are they paying you for this?"

"Fifteen thousand dollars."

Hodges whistles.

"It's on acceptance, but they'll accept it, all right. Mr. Ricker is helping me, and it's turning out pretty well. I've already got the first half done in rough draft. I'm not much at fiction, but I'm okay at stuff like this. I could make a career of it someday, maybe."

"What are you going to do with the money? Put it in a college fund?"

He shakes his head. "I'll get to college, one way or another.

I'm not worried about that. The money is for Chapel Ridge. Tina's going this year. You can't believe how excited she is."

"That's good," Hodges says. "That's really good."

They sit in silence for a little while, looking at the trunk. There are footfalls on the path, and men's voices. The two guys who appear are wearing almost identical plaid shirts and jeans that still show the store creases. Hodges has an idea they think this is how everybody dresses in flyover country. One has a camera around his neck; the other is toting a second light.

"How was your lunch?" Pete calls as they teeter across the creek on the stepping-stones.

"Fine," the one with the camera says. "Denny's. Moons Over My Hammy. The hash browns alone were a culinary dream. Come on over, Pete. We'll start with a few of you kneeling by the trunk. I also want to get a few of you looking inside."

"It's empty," Pete objects.

The photographer taps himself between the eyes. "People will *imagine*. They'll think, 'What must it have been like when he opened that trunk for the first time and saw all those literary treasures?' You know?"

Pete stands up, brushing the seat of jeans that are much more faded and more natural-looking. "Want to stick around for the shoot, Mr. Hodges? Not every eighteen-year-old gets a full-page portrait in *The New Yorker* next to an article he wrote himself."

"I'd love to, Pete, but I have an errand to run."

"All right. Thanks for coming out and listening to me."

"Will you put one other thing in your story?"

"What?"

"That this didn't start with you finding the trunk." Hodges looks at it, black and scuffed, a relic with scratched fittings and a moldy top. "It started with the man who put it there. And when you feel like blaming yourself for how it went down, you might want to remember that thing Jimmy Gold keeps saying. Shit don't mean shit."

Pete laughs and holds out his hand. "You're a good guy, Mr. Hodges."

Hodges shakes. "Make it Bill. Now go smile for the camera."

He pauses on the other side of the creek and looks back. At the photographer's direction, Pete is kneeling with one hand resting on the trunk's scuffed top. It is the classic pose of ownership, reminding Hodges of a photo he once saw of Ernest Hemingway kneeling next to a lion he bagged. But Pete's face holds none of Hemingway's complacent, smiling, stupid confidence. Pete's face says *I never owned this*.

Hold that thought, kiddo, Hodges thinks as he starts back to his car.

Hold that thought.

CLACK

He told Pete he had an errand to run. That wasn't precisely true. He could have said he had a case to work, but that isn't precisely true, either. Although it would have been closer.

Shortly before leaving for his meeting with Pete, he received a call from Becky Helmington at the Traumatic Brain Injury Clinic. He pays her a small amount each month to keep him updated on Brady Hartsfield, the patient Hodges calls "my boy." She also updates him on any strange occurrences on the ward, and feeds him the latest rumors. Hodges's rational mind insists there's nothing to these rumors, and certain strange occurrences have rational explanations, but there's more to his mind than the rational part on top. Deep below that rational part is an underground ocean—there's one inside every head, he believes—where strange creatures swim.

"How's your son?" he asked Becky. "Hasn't fallen out of any trees lately, I hope."

"No, Robby's fine and dandy. Read today's paper yet, Mr. Hodges?"

"Haven't even taken it out of the bag yet." In this new era, where everything is at one's fingertips on the Internet, some days he never takes it out of the bag at all. It just sits there beside his La-Z-Boy like an abandoned child.

"Check the Metro section. Page two. Call me back."

Five minutes later he did. "Jesus, Becky."

"Exactly what I thought. She was a nice girl."

"Will you be on the floor today?"

"No. I'm upstate, at my sister's. We're spending the week-end." Becky paused. "Actually, I've been thinking about trans-ferring to ICU in the main hospital when I get back. There's an opening, and I'm tired of Dr. Babineau. It's true what they say—sometimes the neuros are crazier than the patients." She paused, then added: "I'd say I'm tired of Hartsfield, too, but that wouldn't be exactly right. The truth is, I'm a little scared of him. The way I used to be scared of the local haunted house when I was a girl."

"Yeah?"

"Uh-huh. I knew there were no ghosts in there, but on the other hand, what if there were?"

Hodges arrives at the hospital shortly after two PM, and on this pre-holiday afternoon, the Brain Injury Clinic is as close to deserted as it ever gets. In the daytime, at least.

The nurse on duty—Norma Wilmer, according to her badge—gives him a visitor's pass. As he clips it to his shirt, Hodges says, just passing the time, "I understand you had a tragedy on the ward yesterday."

"I can't talk about that," Nurse Wilmer says.

"Were you on duty?"

"No." She goes back to her paperwork and her monitors.

That's okay; he may learn more from Becky, once she gets back and has time to tap her sources. If she goes through with her plan to transfer (in Hodges's mind, that's the best sign yet that something real may be going on here), he will find someone else to help him out a little. Some of the nurses are dedicated smokers, in spite of all they know about the habit, and these are always happy to earn butt-money.

Hodges ambles down to Room 217, aware that his heart is

beating harder and faster than normal. Another sign that he has begun to take this seriously. The news story in the morning paper shook him up more than a little.

He meets Library Al on the way, pushing his little trolley, and gives his usual greeting: "Hi, guy. How you doin?"

Al doesn't reply at first. Doesn't even seem to see him. The bruised-looking circles under his eyes are more prominent than ever, and his hair—usually neatly combed—is in disarray. Also, his damn badge is on upside-down. Hodges wonders again if Al is starting to lose the plot.

"Everything all right, Al?"

"Sure," Al says emptily. "Never so good as what you don't see, right?"

Hodges has no idea how to reply to this non sequitur, and Al has continued on his way before he can think of one. Hodges looks after him, puzzled, then moves on.

Brady is sitting in his usual place by the window, wearing his usual outfit: jeans and a checked shirt. Someone has given him a haircut. It's a bad one, a real butch job. Hodges doubts if his boy cares. It's not like he's going out boot scootin' anytime soon.

"Hello, Brady. Long time no see, as the ship's chaplain said to the Mother Superior."

Brady just looks out the window, and the same old questions join hands and play ring-a-rosie in Hodges's head. Is Brady seeing anything out there? Does he know he has company? If so, does he know it's Hodges? Is he thinking at all? *Sometimes* he thinks—enough to speak a few simple sentences, anyway—and in the physio center he's able to shamble along the seventy feet or so the patients call Torture Avenue, but what does that really mean? Fish swim in an aquarium, but that doesn't mean they think.

Hodges thinks, Never so good as what you don't see.

Whatever *that* means.

He picks up the silver-framed photo of Brady and his mother with their arms around each other, smiling to beat the band. If the bastard ever loved anyone, it was dear old mommy. Hodges looks to see if there's any reaction to his visitor having Deborah Ann's picture in his hands. There doesn't seem to be.

"She looks hot, Brady. Was she hot? Was she a real hoochie-mama?"

No response.

"I only ask because when we broke into your computer, we found some cheesecake pix of her. You know, negligees, nylons, bras and panties, that kind of thing. She looked hot to me, dressed like that. To the other cops, too, when I passed them around."

Although he tells this lie with his usual panache, there's still no reaction. Nada.

"Did you fuck her, Brady? I bet you wanted to."

Was that the barest twitch of an eyebrow? The slightest downward jerk of a lip?

Maybe, but Hodges knows it could just be his imagination, because he *wants* Brady to hear him. Nobody in America deserves to have more salt rubbed in more wounds than this murderous motherfucker.

"Maybe you killed her and *then* fucked her. No need to be polite then, right?"

Nothing.

Hodges sits in the visitor's chair and puts the picture back on the table next to one of the Zappit e-readers Al hands out to patients who want them. He folds his hands and looks at Brady, who should never have awakened from his coma but did.

Well.

Sort of.

"Are you faking, Brady?"

He always asks this question, and there has never been any reply. There's none today, either.

"A nurse killed herself on the floor last night. In one of the bathrooms. Did you know that? Her name has been withheld for the time being, but the paper says she died of excessive bleeding. I'm guessing that means she cut her wrists, but I'm not sure. If you knew, I bet it made you happy. You always enjoyed a good suicide, didn't you?"

He waits. Nothing.

Hodges leans forward, staring into Brady's blank face and speaking earnestly. "The thing is—what I don't understand— is how she did that. The mirrors in these bathrooms aren't glass, they're polished metal. I suppose she could have used the mirror in her compact, or something, but that seems like pretty small shit for a job like that. Kind of like bringing a knife to a gunfight." He sits back. "Hey, maybe she *had* a knife. One of those Swiss Army jobs, you know? In her purse. Did you ever have one of those?"

Nothing.

Or is there? He has a sense, very strong, that behind that blank stare, Brady is watching him.

"Brady, some of the nurses believe you can turn the water on and off in your bathroom from here. They think you do it just to scare them. Is that true?"

Nothing. But that sense of being watched is strong. Brady *did* enjoy suicide, that's the thing. You could even say suicide was his signature. Before Holly tuned him up with the Happy Slapper, Brady tried to get Hodges to kill himself. He didn't succeed . . . but he *did* succeed with Olivia Trelawney, the woman whose Mercedes Holly Gibney now owns and plans to drive to Cincinnati.

"If you can, do it now. Come on. Show off a little. Strut your stuff. What do you say?"

Nothing.

Some of the nurses believe that being whopped repeatedly in the head on the night he tried to blow up Mingo Auditorium has somehow rearranged Hartsfield's brains. That being whopped repeatedly gave him . . . powers. Dr. Babineau says that's ridiculous, the hospital equivalent of an urban legend. Hodges is sure he's right, but that sense of being watched is undeniable.

So is the feeling that, somewhere deep inside, Brady Hartsfield is laughing at him.

He picks up the e-reader, this one bright blue. On his last visit to the clinic, Library Al said Brady enjoyed the demos. *He stares at it for hours,* Al said.

"Like this thing, do you?"

Nothing.

"Not that you can do much with it, right?"

Zero. Zippo. Zilch.

Hodges puts it down beside the picture and stands. "Let me see what I can find out about the nurse, okay? What I can't dig up, my assistant can. We have our sources. Are you glad that nurse is dead? Was she mean to you? Did she pinch your nose or twist your tiny useless peepee, maybe because you ran down a friend or relative of hers at City Center?"

Nothing.

Nothing.

Noth—

Brady's eyes roll in their sockets. He looks at Hodges, and Hodges feels a moment of stark, unreasoning terror. Those eyes are dead on top, but he sees something beneath that looks not quite human. It makes him think of that movie about the little girl who was possessed by Pazuzu. Then the eyes return to the window and Hodges tells himself not to be an idiot. Babineau says Brady's come back as far as he's ever going to, and that's not very far. He's your basic blank slate, and nothing is written on it but Hodges's own feelings for this man, the most despicable creature he has encountered in all his years of law enforcement.

I want him to be in there so I can hurt him, Hodges thinks. That's all it is. It'll turn out the nurse's husband ran off on her, or she had a drug habit and was going to be fired, or both.

"All right, Brady," he says. "Gonna put an egg in my shoe and beat it. Make like a bee and buzz. But I have to say, as one friend to another, that's a really *shitty* haircut."

No response.

"Seeya later, alligator. After awhile, crocodile."

He leaves, closing the door gently behind him. If Brady *is* in there, slamming it might give him the pleasure of knowing he's gotten under Hodges's skin.

Which, of course, he has.

When Hodges is gone, Brady raises his head. Beside the picture of his mother, the blue e-reader abruptly comes to life. Animated fish rush hither and yon while cheery, bubbly music plays. The screen switches to the Angry Birds demo, then to Barbie Fashion Walk, then to Galactic Warrior. After that, the screen goes dark again.

In the bathroom, the water in the sink gushes, then stops.

Brady looks at the picture of him and his mother, smiling with their cheeks pressed together. Stares at it. Stares at it.

The picture falls over.

Clack.

July 26, 2014